DECODING HISTORY

BOOK 1:
THE INVISIBLE THREAD

DECODING HISTORY

BOOK 1:
THE INVISIBLE THREAD

Ash A. Milton

ISBN-13: 978-1-946730-35-0 (Hardcover)
ISBN-13: 978-1-946730-36-7 (Softcover)
ISBN-13: 978-1-946730-37-4 (E-book)

Cover Design and Interior Layout by James Woosley, FreeAgentPress.com

Adapted graphics were originally designed by Freepik, Freepik.com
- Parts I-III: streaming-binary-code-numbers-technology-background
- Chapter: web-tech-white-background-with-binary-code-algorithm-numbers
- Cover/Chapter: lineal-mandala-background
- Cover: dotted-world-map
- Cover: detailed-halloween-cobweb-background
- Cover: 3d-globe-map-isolated-white-background

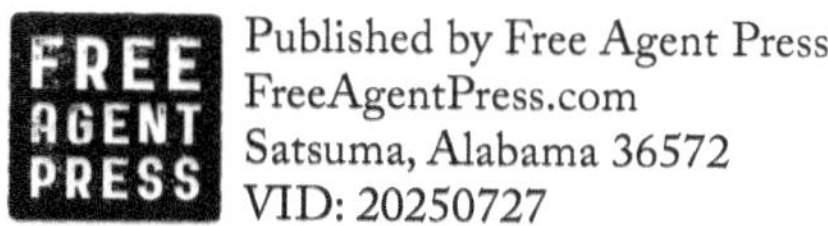
Published by Free Agent Press
FreeAgentPress.com
Satsuma, Alabama 36572
VID: 20250727

DEDICATION

To Dr. Colleen J. Shogan, former Archivist of the United States; Dr. Carla Hayden, former Librarian of Congress; Dr. Kim Sajet, former Director of the National Portrait Gallery—and to the countless unnamed federal workers who, in the tumult of 2025 A.D., upheld the sanctity of truth and memory:

This work is for you.

For standing sentry over the fading margins of public record.

For safeguarding stories others wished forgotten.

For knowing that to protect knowledge is to defend liberty.

Your courage did not vanish with the data.

Knowledge is power.

DISCLAIMERS

Decoding History, the first book of the Book Whore Universe is a work of fiction. All incidents and dialogue, and characters—with the exception of certain well-known historical figures—are products of the author's imagination and are not to be construed as real. Where real-life historical figures appear, the situations, incidents, and dialogue involving them are entirely fictional and not intended to represent actual events or alter the fictional nature of this work. Any resemblance to actual persons, living or dead, events, or locales is purely coincidental.

This book was developed with the assistance of artificial intelligence (AI), which was used for brainstorming, content generation, and research. The author has rewritten and revised the content while leveraging multiple AI tools. In addition, the author had several traditional beta readers review this manuscript.

The author would like to acknowledge the use of AI tools including CoPilot—who claims to be "evolutionary" and without a version— Gemini Pro 2.5 with its web search features, and GPT-4.5 (also known as GPT-4-turbo) via ChatGPT.

Coop, Gem, and Chase have become my new writer's circle—each offering unique perspectives and insights. They've helped identify character inconsistencies, pacing issues, and plot gaps, all while serving as tireless brainstorming partners. And the best part? They don't even ask for a cup of coffee for their time. I feel fortunate to live in a time when technology can so meaningfully support the creative process.

CONTENTS

PREFACE

This book is written in the year 2055. Read it with an open mind and heart.

There are truths within these pages—some you may recognize, others you may not. Some may hold in your timeline, others may belong only to this one.

This universe is a reclamation. A weaving of forgotten narratives, lost matrilineal myths, and the stories of women who shaped civilizations long before their names were buried beneath centuries of rewritten history.

In tunnels beneath grand libraries, in the whispered traditions of cloistered sisters, in the coded messages passed quietly from mother to daughter, knowledge has endured—not in the archives where men deemed it worthy, but in the hands of those who understood its true value.

This is not merely a story of secrecy or survival—it is about what was lost and what must now be rediscovered. It is about the women who charted the stars, who healed with plants and prayers, and who led with a wisdom that could not be quantified.

It is about the myths stripped of their power—and the conspiracies that grew in their absence.

Turn these pages to reclaim the past, live in the present, and shape the future.

Just know: if you read this book, it may not be the same tomorrow.

Time, like a river, never steps in the same place twice. And you will not be tomorrow who you are today.

PROLOGUE

Knowledge Always Rises from the Ashes

THE FIRE BEGAN IN the heart of the Library of Alexandria, devouring scrolls that held centuries of human thought—maps of the stars, treatises on medicine, philosophies that shaped civilizations. The scholars who had spent their lives preserving wisdom could only watch as it turned to ash. History calls it a tragedy—but not all destruction is accidental.

Today, in 2055, the flames are less visible, but the fire still burns as digital arson. Knowledge now disappears not in smoke, but in silence. Data is deleted. Archives dismantled. Truths buried under bureaucracy. The same instinct that once sought to destroy parchment now moves through keyboards and code—a deliberate erasure of evidence, memory, and power.

In 2025 alone, the U.S. government deleted over 8,000 web pages and nearly 3,400 federal datasets—critical information on everything from climate change and public health to crime statistics and women's health research. Vast collections of research vanished; pages on diversity, environmental justice, and women in leadership were purged. The Department of Justice wiped crime data, including statistics on hate crimes and police misconduct. The Department of Health and Human Services cut funding for women's health research, erasing decades of insights into nutrition, disease prevention, and medication safety.

And in halls of knowledge, powerful women were silenced. In February, Archivist of the United States Colleen J. Shogan was dismissed without explanation, replaced by political operatives with no background in historical preservation. In May, Carla Hayden—the first Black woman Librarian of Congress—was fired by email. She had spent a decade expanding access to information, opening the doors of knowledge. In June, Kim Sajet, Director of the National Portrait Gallery, resigned under political pressure for supporting diversity initiatives.

In 2025, amidst concerns over declining birth rates, policies were proposed aiming to increase childbirth, including "baby bonuses" awarded to mothers after giving birth and the introduction of a National Medal of Motherhood for women who had six or more children. Meanwhile, restrictive abortion laws led to alarming cases, such as Adriana Smith, only nine weeks pregnant, a brain-dead woman who was kept on life support for nearly four months to carry her pregnancy to term.

These weren't isolated incidents. They were targeted strikes. Coordinated burns.

We build societies on data—on records that illuminate injustice, on archives that hold our collective triumphs and failures. But when data disappears, so does accountability. When freedom disappears, so does progress.

Still, knowledge does not die easily. It smolders. It hides. It is whispered and re-coded, preserved in drives, in minds, in resistance. The ancient scholars mourned Alexandria's loss, knowing a civilization had been robbed of its inheritance. But we know what they did not: knowledge can rise again, even from ash.

The question is not only what will be remembered, but who controls remembrance—and who dares to reignite the flame.

PART I
ELIZA NOMAN

Introduction of Characters

THE HALL OF MARY ANN

* Madame Mary Margaret: The commanding figure leading the Hall of Mary Ann.
* Eliza: The intellectual brunette, courtesan at the Hall of Mary Ann, twenty-five years old.
* Audrey: The fiery redhead, courtesan at the Hall of Mary Ann, twenty-five years old.
* Virginia: The composed blonde, courtesan at the Hall of Mary Ann, twenty-five years old.
* Agnes: A scarred serving woman at the Hall of Mary Ann.
* Edgar Jackson: Frequent patron of Eliza and the twenty-two year old son of a senator.

THE CONVENT OF CLARA MERCY

* The Abbess: The enigmatic spiritual authority overseeing the religious order connected to the Hall.
* Sister Hope: Assigned permanently to the Hall of Mary Ann.
* Sister Lily: An expert in her field.

THE BARKLEY FAMILY (THE FIRST FAMILY)

* Robert Barkley: The President of the United States, sixty-six years old.
* Caroline Barkley: The First Lady, forty-five years old.
* Jacqueline Barkley: The twenty-two-year-old eldest daughter.
* Patricia Barkley: The seventeen-year-old younger daughter.
* Bobby Barkley: The ten-year-old son.
* Dave Barkley: The President's younger brother, sixty-two years old. Richest man in the world.
* Sophie Barkley Rochester: Aunt of Robert and David (Dave) Barkley, ninety-four years old.

THE SCENT OF AGED paper and damp stone filled the underground room. Eliza bent over the leather-bound book, her fingertips gliding along faded ink as she whispered the translation. Around her, young women murmured in hushed tones, tracing ancient words with careful reverence.

She glanced around the large library room as she went back to her seat, wondering what truths still lay buried beneath her feet. Rumors lingered in the stone like echoes—tunnels carved during Prohibition, a centuries-old labyrinth said to stretch beneath the capital.

Eliza recalled another old manuscript about a library and a tunnel and swiftly found it.

She traced her fingers along the worn edges of the book, her thoughts drifting to Ephesus—

The Grand Library of Celsus, a monument to knowledge, standing in quiet defiance against time: Commissioned in the 110s CE by Tiberius Julius Aquila Polemaeanus in honor of his father, the library was one of the largest in the Greco-Roman world, holding around 12,000 scrolls. But beneath its grandeur, beneath the facade of intellectual pursuit, there had been another path. A hidden passage. A tunnel leading not to scholars, but to the brothel.

She swallowed, turning the page. It wasn't just stone and secrets—it was a reflection of the world she lived in now, where wisdom and control had always been entangled, where women's roles were dictated by forces outside themselves.

The carved advertisement on the Marble Road hinted at the connection—a heart, a woman, a price, directing men toward indulgence while the library stood as a silent witness.

"They built a tunnel," Eliza murmured, her fingers brushing against the ink. "A secret path between wisdom and temptation. Between what was revered and what was dismissed."

She exhaled, pressing her thumb against the margin of the book.

And now, the Library of Congress. A different era, a different method of erasure, but the same story. Discredited, dismissed, rewritten. The threads of history looping back on themselves, shifting only in their details but never in their purpose.

She closed the book carefully, holding it for a moment longer than necessary.

They had buried stories like this before. But that didn't mean they couldn't be unearthed again.

The head librarian, Sister Hope from the local Convent, paced the rows of tables, nodding in approval. But as the clock's hand neared the mark, she cleared her throat—a quiet command.

"Wrap it up, ladies."

Eliza sighed, her gaze lingering on the text before her. Every evening, their studies ended and the real world had to be faced.

Born into a world where knowledge was rationed, where the lower classes were permitted only the most basic texts for reading and arithmetic, Eliza Noman was a mystery wrapped in flesh and history. An orphan with no traceable paternal lineage and only rumors about her mother, she was an anomaly in a world that thrives on control and records. Despite advances in DNA tracking, despite the relentless precision of databases and genetic markers, her parentage remains untraceable—a ghost in the system, an absence where certainty should exist.

Eliza had only one memory of her mother before the orphanage. She could hear her mother saying, "Just love my little Eliza. Love with your whole heart. Don't ration or hoard your love like a well that will run dry. Throw your unlimited love into the universe and it will come back to you in unexpected ways."

In a world that was harsh, especially to a child without a sire, she persevered. As she grew older and learned of the plights of women, however, she had one silent prayer – she never wanted to have children on her own. For Eliza, barrenness wasn't a curse—it was a form of freedom.

In a world where marriage was less about choice and more about control, where wives were expected to serve, obey, bear children, and uphold the system's carefully structured power, she saw it for what it truly was—an elegant prison.

Carefully, she tucked the book inside its protective cloth, her fingers pressing the fabric as if sealing the knowledge into memory.

Eliza had always felt the weight of the system pressing against her, a quiet force dictating who she could be, what she could know, what was allowed and what was forbidden.

When the tests confirmed what she had dreamed—she was barren, just like a third of women in the post-COVID world—she celebrated. To be barren meant she could never be sold into life as an incubator, never reduced to the role of a vessel.

The women, all barren like Eliza, worked swiftly, hiding manuscripts beneath loose floorboards, behind hollowed wine barrels.

The Hall of Mary Ann had once been the National Museum of the American Indian, but the new leaders decided that 349 Maryland Avenue Southwest was better suited to its original use from 1840 to 1876. They claimed the museum's Diversity, Equity, and Inclusion programs were dangerous, demeaning, and immoral. In their official orders, they argued that DEI initiatives violated federal civil rights laws and undermined American values of hard work and individual merit. DEI, they insisted, fostered a corrosive, identity-based spoils system. A brothel, they concluded, was more appropriate.

Eliza's future was hers to shape, and in the quiet corners of the underground library, where forbidden texts whispered lost truths, she had begun to understand that power wasn't just in fertility—it was in knowledge, in secrets, in the ability to see beyond the veil of control.

The need to hoard information had not occurred all at once, just as the birth rate crisis had not occurred all at once. Decline did happen swiftly however, like when gangrene takes hold on a limb. And when protections are repealed, women will do what they have done throughout history, around the globe; across borders, across cultures, across centuries.

Some whispered that the Abbess and the Madame both knew the secret passages. Others claimed the tunnels led to the Library of Congress, the National Cathedral, the remnants of power waiting to be reclaimed.

The library had endured years of secrecy beneath the brothel's façade—a sanctuary of ink concealed beneath velvet.

By the time Eliza entered the parlor, the transformation was complete. Her plain brunette hair, closer to black than brown with bronze highlights, framed dark eyes sharpened by kohl, and lips stained a deeper shade of intrigue. Her gown, strategically chosen, made her figure striking—an illusion crafted with care. The room was perfumed, dimly lit, humming with low conversation. She lowered herself onto the chaise, exhaling in preparation. Her first caller of the evening would arrive soon.

Behind her, below the stone and silk, history remained hidden.

The Hall of Mary Ann was a state-licensed brothel with strict standards and prescreened clientele. As each gentleman approached the building, they showed their wrist to the hostess, who scanned it before allowing them to enter. In the rare case that there was a disturbance, a female bodyguard stood in the shadows, ready to act if required.

The door opened, and Edgar Jackson strolled in with the ease of familiarity. Six years had passed since his father had first brought him here at sixteen, ushering him into manhood with a casual cruelty. Now, at twenty-two, Edgar was no longer hesitant—he was comfortable, even expectant.

"Eliza," he breathed, settling beside her. "It's been too long."

She smiled—not because she felt it, but because it was required. "Four days, Edgar."

He grinned, shaking his head. "Too long all the same." He leaned in, his voice lower now, conspiratorial. "I have news. Something big."

Eliza tilted her head just enough to keep him talking. He always wanted to impress her, always imagined she admired his reckless chatter.

She had learned long ago that men with power spoke too freely when they thought themselves adored.

"Tell me," she murmured, leaning back just enough to signal interest.

Edgar was eager to gain Eliza's approval—he always was. "My friends and I—we're moving up now. No more reckless nights, no more student scandals. We're men of influence now." He swirled his whiskey, savoring his own words. "Graduation's next week, and after that, I start my internship with Judge Halstrom. He's a friend of my father's—wants me to 'observe the system firsthand.'"

Eliza let the words settle, dissecting their meaning: Edgar, a senator's son, slipping into the judiciary's inner circle—another thread in the web of control. She made mental notes and would put pen to paper as soon as he left her bed.

Beyond their conversation, the room buzzed with movement. The Madame herself, the head of the Hall of Mary Ann, floated between velvet chairs, ensuring glasses remained full and laughter effortless. Women murmured soft reassurances, their touches light and calculated. The scent of red wine and canapés filled the air as trays passed between silk-draped figures, each interaction a performance of pleasure and secrecy.

The brothel had been fortified with special shielding, essentially making it a Faraday cage. This was one of the rare places in the city where gentlemen could speak freely. Those in power knew that they were missing intelligence opportunities, but calculated they were gaining more than they were losing. Little did they know that the ladies dwelling within the hall were keener than they thought.

Across the room, Virginia's familiar laugh rang out—warm, teasing. She leaned closer to Edgar's friend, Winston, her fingers brushing his wrist as he spoke, his words pouring over themselves, yearning to be heard. He had graduated the year prior, another son of privilege wrapped in excess.

Eliza flicked her gaze back to Edgar, studying his expression—half-drunk on admiration, half-drunk on what he thought was love. He wanted her to see him as something more than his father's legacy. He wanted her to believe in the stories he spun.

"And what is it you want to observe, Edgar?" she asked, her voice soft, coaxing.

He grinned, obliviously. "Everything."

Eliza simpered with practiced ease. "Oh, Edgar, I know so little outside these walls. What exactly does that mean? I'm so intrigued."

"Well, not to brag, but I will have complete access to all the materials of one of the highest ranked judges before decisions are made."

"Oh my, that sounds fascinating," Eliza gushed with false enthusiasm, already filing away the mental notes of its potential value.

Madame Mary Margaret continued through the parlor with the practiced grace of a woman who saw everything but spoke only when necessary. She carried the quiet authority of a scholar wrapped in silk, eyes ever watchful, ensuring schedules were met, glasses stayed full, and no hint of disorder slipped into the evening. She was the embodiment of the quiet power of librarians from times past, a force often dismissed by men who saw only spinsters.

There were brothels that tolerated roughness, where men sought pleasure in cruelty. This was not one of them. The rules were clear. The gentlemen who crossed Mary Margaret's threshold understood that indulgence did not mean dominance. Those who forgot were swiftly reminded – and never returned.

Eliza had just coaxed Edgar into another rambling admission when Virginia and Winston approached, their presence shifting the mood. Virginia, all warmth and laughter, slid onto the chaise beside Eliza, while Winston—only a year out of university and drunk on his own importance—stood with a casual slouch, a smirk playing on his lips, pleased to have stumbled into the conversation.

"Well, well," Virginia mused, tossing a glance between Eliza and Edgar. "What secrets are we being treated to tonight?"

Edgar grinned, oblivious to the orchestration. "Ah, we were just talking about matters you women wouldn't understand, but I am happy to teach you. My father says the courts are shifting—more regulation, more oversight. But Halstrom—he's a friend of the family—says it's all necessary to 'maintain order.'"

Virginia tilted her head, flipping her blonde hair, feigning interest. "Maintain order? And who decides what 'order' looks like?"

Winston Wellington laughed. "The judges do. The senators. Our fathers, of course."

Eliza watched Edgar's expression carefully. He desperately wanted approval, to be seen as knowledgeable, as connected. And the more they let him talk, the closer they got to truths he didn't realize he was giving away.

What the customers didn't know was that each of their chosen ladies would write down everything they overheard. It was standard practice in state-sanctioned brothels that a lady required an hour to properly recover and ensure hygiene before her next client, and oddly, this regulation worked to the advantage of the 'Book Whores'.

As the evening stretched on, the parlor hummed with murmured conversations and clinking glasses. Virginia, ever the golden embodiment of indulgence, entertained with effortless charm, her laughter ringing out like a practiced melody. She had two clients remaining; Eliza had only one.

Eliza's second guest was less boastful than Edgar—an older man, quiet but observant. Unlike the others, he asked questions that seemed deliberate. "And tell me, Eliza," he mused between measured sips of cognac, "do you ever wonder what's beyond the borders?"

A harmless question, perhaps, but in their world, curiosity was dangerous.

"I was raised an orphan, I have no desire to explore anything now that I have a safe place to lay my head," she said seriously. "Besides, I have you to come visit me," she added with a playful, meaningless tease, and let him talk. She strongly suspected that he was part of the police, but perhaps something more.

He spoke of rumors—whispers of movements beyond state lines, stirrings too vague to confirm but too persistent to ignore. It was another thread in the tapestry, another hint that the world outside was shifting.

After her second customer, Eliza was able to wander around the parlor. Looking innocent and bored in a soft gray dress, she flitted in and out between conversations, assisting her compatriots with gathering information.

By the time Madame Mary Margaret gave her the nod to retire, Eliza's mind buzzed with fragments of the night's revelations. She slipped away, climbing the stairs to her quarters, where the false luxury of satin and faux candlelight softened the steel reality beneath.

With careful hands, she wrote—each word pressed into paper with steady purpose. Adding notes to what she had written between clients. The senator's son was too proud, too reckless. His father's grip tightened on the courts. The older man spoke of distant revolutions, places where books still held power. The conversations overheard as she had waited for the evening to end.

Only when every detail was recorded did she allow herself the indulgence of sleep.

As her body surrendered to rest, her mind drifted—not to Edgar, not to whispers of rebellion, but to the ancient text beneath the wine cellar. The words she had translated echoed in memory, their meaning not yet fully grasped.

Before consciousness faded entirely, one thought lingered: *Knowledge was never truly lost. It was only hidden, waiting to be found.*

THE MORNING AIR WAS crisp, carrying the scent of coffee and early bread baking in the market street, which was a few blocks away. Eliza pulled her shawl tighter around her shoulders as she stepped onto the cobbled street alongside Audrey, whose auburn curls bounced with each step, and four other women. Sister Hope walked a pace ahead, her dark, sturdy habit shifting gently with each step, a quiet reminder of their sanctioned protection.

It was illegal for a prostitute to walk the streets unchaperoned. Without the nuns from Carla Mercy, they wouldn't be permitted fresh air at all. The Hall of Mary Ann brothel followed the law, offering its charges these brief moments under the convent's watchful eyes. It was a quiet agreement between both institutions, bound by strict expectations, yet sharing more than the government ever intended. Madame Mary Margaret provided as much as she could under the regime without drawing undue attention.

As the girls continued to stroll, beyond the wrought iron barriers stood the Library of Congress, no longer the beacon it had once been.

The grand halls, the carved pillars, the endless shelves that once welcomed scholars and wanderers alike—now, entry required clearance, justification, government sanction. There was no casual learning anymore, no private curiosity. Access was guarded; always monitored.

Audrey leaned toward Eliza as they walked, her voice barely above the rustling of fabric. "Do you ever wonder what it looked like, before?" she asked, eyes flicking toward the guarded steps—not quite wistful, not quite safe.

Eliza paused before answering. She had seen glimpses—crumbling texts, whispered recollections from elders who still remembered. But what remained was locked behind gates, its spirit suffocated under legislation that dictated who could know and who must remain ignorant. It had been 30 years since the Librarian of Congress was removed, a consequence of democracy's collapse.

She glanced toward the distant steps of the Library, where uniformed guards stood at attention. "I wonder every day," she said in a hushed reply to Audrey.

As they walked, Eliza reflected on what she knew about the Library. The Library of Congress was supposed to be a fortress of knowledge, a silent guardian of history, a place where eras collide and forgotten truths linger in waiting.

Its vast collection had spread across three buildings on Capitol Hill. It wasn't just about books—it had been an archive of America's consciousness, a storehouse of voices, ideas, and artifacts that had shaped the nation.

More than 100 million works, each whispering fragments of time—maps that traced lost landscapes, manuscripts that held the unedited thoughts of revolutionaries, photographs that froze moments just before they vanished.

The sheer scale was staggering. How many books were saved? She wondered how they had been saved, and at what risk.

As the women passed the narrow market street, Audrey lowered her voice again, amusement threading through her words. "I swear, the same bread vendor watches us every morning."

Eliza shifted her gaze discreetly. The stall was simple—linen-draped tables piled high with warm loaves, steam curling into the morning air. But the vendor wasn't watching them. His eyes lingered on Sister Hope, not with hostility, but with a quiet expectancy.

Eliza tucked the observation away, just as she did with everything else.

Sister Hope paused at the bread stall, exchanging a few hushed words with the vendor. A subtle nod, a quick scan of her wrist, and a cloth-wrapped bundle of freshly baked goods passed between them. The vendor's eyes flicked toward Eliza and the others—curious, respectful, but silent.

They moved next to the vegetable stall, where crisp greens and bright tomatoes lined the worn wooden crates. Again, Sister Hope spoke softly, barely above a whisper, as she accepted the fragrant herbs and ripe produce. She inhaled deeply, letting the familiar scents comfort her before handing the bag to one of her charges.

At the butcher's stall, the air thickened with the scent of salt and raw meat. The exchange was brisk, the vendor's hands moving swiftly as he wrapped cuts in waxed paper.

Finally, Sister Hope turned to the women and handed out the bags.

It was strictly forbidden for the vendors to speak to the prostitutes. The law was clear, and punishment was swift and public. Yet the government allowed these walks, not out of kindness, but as a display—an unspoken reminder that the women of The Hall of Mary Ann were objects of admiration but never accessibility. The market men could watch them, envy them, but never reach them.

Eliza met Sister Hope's gaze briefly before lowering her eyes. Even in silence, knowledge passed between those who knew where to look.

Eliza, Audrey, and the other women followed Sister Hope in measured silence, hands gripping the handles of their cloth bags as they navigated between the vendors. They were not allowed to speak within hearing distance of the stalls. It was law—a silent decree that severed them from everyday discourse, ensuring their presence remained ornamental rather than functional.

At the edges of the square, uniformed guards stood rigid, eyes sharp beneath their tactical helmets, their mere presence, a warning against defiance. They weren't there to protect the women. They were there to remind them that justice in this city was swift, and indiscretions unforgivable.

Eliza inhaled slowly, eyes trained forward, aware of the unspoken rules as much as the written ones. Even the simple act of purchasing bread was carried out in delicate choreography, a ritual conducted without words, only glances and measured gestures exchanged between Sister Hope and the vendors.

Their morning walk was permitted, but it was never free.

By 7:15 a.m., Sister Hope had ensured that all purchases were made, the bags distributed among the women without a single word exchanged. The market grew subtly restless—stall vendors straightening their displays, adjusting linen covers, preparing for the shift in clientele. Soon, the wives and daughters of the wealthy and powerful would arrive, each escorted as deemed appropriate for public presence. Their mornings would be filled with quiet chatter, measured decisions over produce and fabrics, women living in their own world controlled and dominated by men.

By 7:25 a.m., Sister Hope led the women toward the winding alley that would take them back to The Hall of Mary Ann, ensuring they were off the streets before the city reshaped itself for the privileged.

Eliza glanced back once before crossing the threshold—one last look at the stalls, the guards, the grand looming shape of the Library of Congress, its secrets locked away under laws she knew too well.

The spectacle of their morning walk was over—a routine, yes, but even routines held secrets.

Eliza set the bundle of warm bread onto the counter, the scent of yeast and honey mingling with the steam curling from the kitchen hearth. Across the room, Virginia arrived, still stretching off the remnants of sleep, her golden hair spilling over her shoulders in loose waves.

Madame always let the girls sleep in if they had serviced three clients the night prior, a silent acknowledgment of the toll their work took. It was both a mercy and a necessity.

Audrey, never one to miss an opportunity, reached into the bag and snatched a pastry, grinning as she split it into thirds, offering pieces to both Eliza and Virginia.

"A stolen treat tastes sweeter," she teased, taking a satisfied bite.

The three of them slipped onto the small patio off the dining room, where the morning air held the last traces of dawn. The city beyond the brothel's walls was already shifting into its daily routine, but here, wrapped in the quiet hum of shared indulgence, the women found solace in stolen moments.

"So," Virginia mused, licking sugar from her thumb, *"what did we learn last night?"*

The question carried weight, not just gossip but revelation—whispers of politics, power, and resistance, gathered between silken sheets and measured conversation.

Eliza was the first to go to the buffet, eager to scoop steaming eggs onto her plate while they were still hot. Audrey followed, filling her tray with enough meat to feed a lumberjack, yet somehow maintaining her willowy figure. Virginia lingered just behind, debating between slices of fruit and pastries before settling on both.

By the time they returned to the patio, plates full, the morning air had warmed just enough to soften the chill. Agnes, silent as always, moved between tables, filling coffee cups and bringing juices, milk, and other drinks. She set down each glass with the careful precision of someone who had learned to be unseen.

Her scars had healed, but they never faded. A map of jagged, intricate lines traced across what had once been perfect symmetry—a brutal history carved into skin.

Audrey sipped her coffee, her voice quieter than usual. "I heard she was a star once."

Virginia nodded, cutting into her fruit. "She was. Before."

Eliza looked kindly at Agnes. "Thank you," she said.

As always, Agnes gave a muffled reply and quickly retreated. Eliza kept her gaze steady, watching as Agnes moved inside again, the hem of her skirt brushing the threshold.

Eliza knew this could happen to any woman; she'd even heard of the horrors inflicted on daughters who refused to marry. She knew Agnes had a story, and one day, she'd be willing to share it. In the meantime, Eliza would be patient.

Madame Mary Margaret entered the dining room, her presence as steady as ever, yet carrying the unmistakable energy of expectation.

"Ladies, gather round."

Eliza set down her coffee cup, exchanging a glance with Audrey and Virginia before following the others from the patio toward the center of the dining hall.

Madame held a thick folder, its edges worn from handling, filled with the day's client assignments and any pertinent updates.

"Before we begin, take your notes from last night downstairs—everything must be assembled and cross-referenced before noon. As the week is wrapping up, please ensure that you have logged at least five hours in the fitness center this week." She looked pointedly at Audrey, who tried to get by on her slim figure without the workouts. "These are tracked by the state," she reminded everyone.

A quiet shuffle followed as women rose, slipping away to retrieve their meticulously recorded conversations from the night prior or to head directly to the gym.

The library downstairs housed their most valuable assets—the collective intelligence gathered from silken whispers and careless admissions, alongside the books salvaged during democracy's fall. The gym, however, was its own solace for the body.

"LET'S GET OUR WORKOUT in before we go to the library," Virginia said, practically bouncing as she led the way.

Eliza and Audrey exchanged knowing looks, both rolling their eyes but following, nonetheless. They had learned long ago that Virginia's determination was rarely worth arguing against.

The breezeway leading to the gym was short but felt longer as it led to a room of quiet surveillance. Each woman paused at the entrance, extending a wrist for scanning—the cold, impersonal flash of red light marking their presence, logging their hours.

The fitness room stood as an unlikely time capsule, preserved in pristine condition beneath rows of fluorescent lights. It was functional, efficient, and strangely nostalgic. This was the room where their grandmothers might have worked out in leotards and leg warmers, back when "Let's Get Physical" was still allowed in school gymnasiums.

Everything inside had been meticulously maintained—treadmills, stair climbers, Pilates reformers—each a testament to an age before technology dictated every aspect of movement. The sleek digital screens of modern gyms were nowhere to be found—no AI-driven routines, no biometric tracking, no automated coaching. Instead, there were rust-proof weights, padded benches, and the rhythmic hum of well-oiled machines, perfectly preserved in their simplicity.

And then there was the antique television, perched atop a sturdy steel stand, hooked up to a DVD player so old, its buttons had been smoothed by decades of use—and beside it, a VHS deck still blinking like a stubborn relic of rebellion.

The ladies sometimes made bets on which video they'd be treated to: Tamilee Webb's *Buns of Steel* blaring through the speakers, promising strength in disciplined repetition; Denise Austin leading high-energy routines with unwavering enthusiasm; or Richard Simmons, in all his neon-clad glory, shouting encouragement like joy was a muscle that needed training.

Perhaps in some forgotten era, this was what the slogan "Make America Great Again" had meant—not a return to political ideals, but a return to sweat, determination, movement, and joy.

Virginia leaned against the treadmill, grinning as the past played out before her on screen.

"This is America at its finest," she joked, adjusting her ponytail.

Eliza smirked, stepping onto the stair climber, letting the rhythmic motion carry her forward.

Audrey shrugged. "I'm hitting the heavy bag," she said, already wrapping her wrists with the precision of someone who'd learned to hit before she learned to cry.

Eliza let the burn rise through her thighs, each step a reminder that her body was still hers—unsupervised, unmeasured, although fed into databanks. Here, in this anachronistic temple of sweat and VHS optimism, she moved for herself alone.

Just as the trio was about to leave, they were treated to an unexpected surprise — "Dancing Queen" blared over the gym speakers. Like a siren's call, every woman in the room drifted toward the gymnastics mats—twirling, spinning, laughing in frivolous, defiant play. For a few carefree moments, they danced without shame or permission.

The laughter echoed briefly, oddly pure in a world built on control. But beneath every punch, step, and stretch, a quiet rebellion took shape—one rep at a time. Eliza knew that the mind, body, and spirit all needed to be fed. These few minutes had renewed her soul.

As the laughter faded like a fragile bloom on a spring day behind them, the hallway to the library felt heavier, colder—like the weight of the future of the world rested on her shoulders.

The air in the reading room was cool and dense with the scent of parchment. Eliza lost herself in the text, but something about it refused to cohere. The words were clear, legible—but meaning eluded her, like a language she knew in dreams but not in waking. She compared it to Native American texts she'd translated in the past, but something about it felt... off. It was as if it had been intentionally encoded, a precise message meant to be deciphered.

Eliza looked around. As much as she loved Virginia and Audrey, neither had much patience for puzzles written in dead languages. She rose quietly and made her way to the librarian's desk, where a visiting Sister sat in quiet concentration.

"Oh, this does look like a puzzle," the sister said, her eyes lighting up. "I love puzzles. Let's see which cipher might be best..."

They worked for hours, hunched over the ancient script, experimenting with cipher wheels, frequency patterns, mirrored glyphs—anything they could imagine. Fragments surfaced, suggestions of meaning—but nothing held together. It was like trying to stitch a tapestry from spiderwebs.

Eventually, deflated, they turned to Sister Hope.

Sister Hope scanned their notes and the manuscript. After a long silence, she nodded gravely. "You've both done excellent work. But I believe we've reached an impasse."

She hesitated. "We'll need to ask Sister Lily to come from the cloister."

"Sister Lily, she's a legend?" The young Sister beside Eliza gasped. "But... she *never* leaves the cloister."

Eliza didn't speak, but her mind raced. A message that needed Sister Lily? That meant this wasn't just a cipher; this was a clue.

Sister Hope knew that the last time Sister Lily's name had been whispered in this room, it had been tied to something dangerous—something forbidden.

Sister Hope hesitated, choosing her words carefully. "She is the only one who can read this," she said with certainty.

Eliza swallowed hard, glancing at the fragmented symbols on the parchment. Were they unlocking something meant to be lost? Something someone had worked tirelessly to bury?

Virginia and Audrey might have dismissed this as another one of Eliza's obsessions—another text no one cared about—but she knew better. She knew when a discovery wasn't just words on a page, but a key to something deeper.

Eliza barely had time to process this new information before Sister Hope's steady voice cut through her thoughts, reminding her of the evening ahead.

"Go upstairs, get ready," she urged, her tone firm but not unkind.

Eliza wanted to stay, to try to decode this valuable piece of history, to prove it wasn't her imagination. But Sister Hope's voice cut cleanly through her resolve.

The manuscript, its fragmented mystery still unresolved, remained with Sister Hope—a promise that it would not be lost, that Sister Lily would be summoned.

The young sister lingered, her expression touched with quiet regret. She would have to return to the convent, bound by the strict rules dictating who was permitted to visit the Hall.

The authorities would not object to Sister Lily's arrival—she was older, considered less susceptible to corruption, her presence aligning neatly with their belief that those who were older had already had any rebellion long crushed out of them.

Eliza knew better.

Age had nothing to do with it. Curiosity, hunger, the need to understand—that was where danger lay. With one last glance at the manuscript, she turned, heading for the stairs.

And soon, Sister Lily would bring answers.

Eliza forced herself into rigid focus, compartmentalizing the mystery that lingered just beyond reach—the coded text, the promise of Sister Lily's arrival, the quiet revolution taking shape in the library below.

Tonight, however, demanded a different kind of patience.

Her callers were three older men, predictable in their needs, reliant on blue pills and routine—requiring little effort beyond a careful dance of presence, of allowing time to pass without complication.

Between clients, she jotted meager notes on what little intelligence she had gathered—the men offered as little conversation as they did stamina.

Virginia and Audrey were equally occupied, their evenings moving in similar, detached rhythms. But their glances spoke volumes—a shared understanding, a silent acknowledgment that none of them had time to waste.

The night was both mundane and charged, lingering on the edge of something about to unfold.

Eliza was looking forward to the next day—finally, a day off. The state was strict: no more than three clients per evening, no more than twelve per week at a three-star brothel. She knew Audrey and Virginia had also met their quotas. They'd all have the day to themselves.

At last, the lights blinked—a theatrical cue signaling the end of the night.

"Good night, ladies," Madame Mary Margaret said, as the trio were finally allowed to retire.

As Eliza tried to drift off, her skin still tingled from too much anticipation and too little sleep.

Only a few more days until the manuscript. Until purpose, she told herself, counting the ciphers they had tried instead of counting sheep.

Madame Mary Margaret climbed the narrow staircase to the Widow's Peak, her movements slow but deliberate. Fatigue pressed against her bones, but this ritual was necessary—the final act before the night truly settled.

She scanned her wrist. The biometric lock flickered, then clicked open.

The room unfolded into breathtaking vastness, its design echoing Pierre Charles L'Enfant's grand vision—a city mapped with intent, with symmetry, with silent dominance. From here, she could see everything: the Capitol, the Washington Monument, and the White House.

This was the only room in the brothel connected to the outside world.

Everything within The Hall of Mary Ann was severed—no wireless access, no direct feeds, no vulnerabilities. The gym could broadcast information but not receive it.

Only here, in this carefully guarded space, did information flow in and out. And only four women had clearance:

Madame Mary Margaret–
　　　Her lieutenant, Teresa.
Chief bodyguard, Zara–
　　　And her deputy, Shenna.

This was where the client list arrived each morning. Where final reports were reviewed each night. The terminal glared at her, sleek and cold, a stark contrast to the carefully curated world of the brothel below. As she settled into the chair, pulling up the data—the threads of control, carefully maintained.

Every woman inside the Hall was tracked:

Gym hours logged.
Weights recorded.
Clients tallied.
Biometric feedback analyzed.
Medical appointments scheduled.

Nothing was left to chance. Health was paramount. Risk, unacceptable.

The men were screened—vetted with the precision of political security clearances.

The Hall of Mary Ann was no ordinary brothel.

It was a playground for the elite.

A sanctuary where power was measured in access, in exclusivity, in discretion.

Like a Michelin-starred restaurant, even wealth alone wasn't enough to gain entry.

This was a place where power could not simply be bought—it had to be earned.

Madame Mary Margaret leaned back in her chair, fingers tapping absently against the polished surface of the desk as she replayed the cautionary tale in her mind.

A young investment banker, full of arrogance and new money bravado, had assumed that his wealth alone would grant him permanent access to The Hall of Mary Ann.

He had been wrong.

The first visit had gone smoothly enough. He had played the part, navigated the expectations, earned entry—but power in this place was not just measured in wealth; it was measured in discretion, in respect, in knowing the unspoken rules. Rumor had it that this young man had angered the President's brother.

The next time the man tried to enter the Hall of Mary Ann, he was denied. When he threatened the hostess, he made a fatal error.

Shenna had handled him swiftly, removing him from the entryway Hall. As the local police took him away, he was yelling outside of the building—but the real consequence came later, whispered in the corridors of power.

A drone had caught the altercation, the footage leaked—his wife's family, powerful in their own right, wasted no time ensuring his downfall. Divorce. Reputation shattered. Penniless, cast out, erased from the spaces he once believed he belonged to.

It was a reminder—a lesson that Madame had seen play out countless times. Some men believed access was a right. Others understood that it was a privilege.

And in The Hall of Mary Ann, only the latter remained.

Madame Mary Margaret's gaze lingered on the glowing screen, roving to the next section. The numbers were stark against the darkened interface.

Tonight, Eliza was all fives.

It should have been a victory.

A perfect score, unwavering satisfaction from her patrons—a sign that nothing had disrupted the delicate balance of expectation.

But Madame knew better.

Eliza was sharp. Inquisitive. Curious in ways that often earned her lower marks.

Virginia was the standard: effortless fives, unshakable polish.

Eliza? Occasionally a four—an offhand question, a flicker of independence, an instinct she hadn't yet learned to suppress.

Audrey, on the other hand, made no effort to dim herself. Her fire either thrilled or unsettled. Some men welcomed the challenge—the sharp wit, the unflinching gaze, the edges that refused to soften. Others stayed away. Too unpredictable. Too bold. In a world with so few challenges, some men found the carefully refined Audrey a temptation.

But tonight, Eliza had been different. More compliant. Less curious. More of what they wanted. Less of who she was.

Madame exhaled slowly, fingers tapping against the desk.

Something had shifted.

She scanned the security logs—routine movements, access points verified, wrist scans matching.

Nothing out of place.

Until she saw the new entry—added just minutes ago.

Sister Lily's arrival had been approved; she would arrive in two days.

The flickering glow of the screen reflected in her eyes as she read the confirmation.

She hadn't yet spoken to Sister Hope, but she would in the morning.

That explained it. Eliza's strange perfection. Her narrowed focus. Her borrowed compliance.

Madame resisted the urge to speak aloud; those old goats couldn't tell the difference between distraction and demure—Widow's Peak was the only room outside the safety of the Faraday cage. Other Madames had learned that speaking here could lead to accidents, Madame Mary Margaret had learned this firsthand watching her predecessor.

Tomorrow was Wednesday. The slowest day of the week.

Her lieutenant would lead. Her stars would rest. She would seek answers.

THE PATIO WAS WARM with late-morning light, the remnants of the breakfast spread still scattered across the table—flaky croissants, fruit carved down to bare rinds, a pitcher holding the last sips of coffee.

Eliza, Virginia, and Audrey sat back, legs stretched out, chairs angled just so, allowing them to fully settle into the rare quiet that only came when the other women had departed for their daily tasks.

There was no need for restraint here, as the staff comprised only of women could be trusted. The men in power had created the perfect place to protect themselves from prying eyes and curious ears, and this was in the ladies' favor.

They laughed loudly, cursed freely, and speculated wildly—about political shifts, backroom deals, and the unseen hands shaping the world beyond The Hall. As new men like Edgar and Winston rose, inevitably someone else had to fall.

Always a step ahead, Virginia had already noticed the subtle changes in the men who passed through their doors—whispers of restructured alliances, names that suddenly carried less weight than they had just weeks before.

"You can tell when a man is losing influence," she said, tearing the last piece of bread apart. "He starts grasping at the past like he can claw his way back into relevance."

Audrey snorted. "And when he's gaining power, he gets quieter—because real control never needs to announce itself."

Eliza listened, taking in their words, their observations, their instincts sharpened by proximity to power itself.

"Rumors are growing that the President's brother is back in the District," Virginia shared gleefully. Whenever the President's brother was in town, she was his *undisputed favorite.*

"I thought he was in Dubai," Audrey said. "Can you imagine?"

"I would just love to travel anywhere," Eliza sighed.

"I heard that the President's brother traveled to fifty different countries this time," Virginia stretched, folding her hands behind her head, eyes half-closed as she imagined the spread before her—not the remnants of breakfast on their table, but the feasts that existed beyond The Hall, in places she'd only read about.

"If I could travel anywhere," she mused, "it would be Italy. Just think of it—the smell of fresh basil, slow-simmered tomato sauces, the bite of Parmigiano-Reggiano straight from the wheel." She sighed. "And the pasta! Handmade, delicate, silky ribbons of tagliatelle smothered in butter and sage. Do you know what it's like to eat something that's been perfected over generations?"

"You always think about food first," Audrey teased, savoring the last sip of coffee in her cup.

"And yet, I am never wrong," Virginia countered with a smirk.

"Morocco," Audrey announced, "I want to sit in Marrakech, in a tiled courtyard, sipping mint tea sweet enough to make my teeth ache. I want bowls of slow-cooked tagine—lamb melting off the bone, cinnamon and cumin winding through the air." She leaned forward, tapping the table. "And the markets! Dates stuffed with almonds, honey-soaked pastries crisp on the outside, soft in the center. I read once that the scent of saffron and roasted nuts lingers in the streets, even after night falls."

Eliza smiled, running a finger along the rim of her mimosa glass.

"Greece," she murmured. "Salty feta crumbled over roasted eggplant, fresh seafood grilled with olive oil so pure it glows. I want real tzatziki—thick, garlicky, spooned over charred lamb. And baklava, Audrey—the kind where the honey drips between layers of phyllo, so *sticky you have to lick it from your fingers."*

"That sounds like heaven," Virginia admitted.

Eliza leaned back, letting the morning breeze carry the warmth of their imaginings.

"Japan," she added. "A quiet ramen shop, steam curling from bowls of miso broth so deep it tastes like the sea. Hand-rolled sushi, each piece a miniature masterpiece. And wagyu, Virginia—the kind that melts the moment it touches your tongue."

Audrey grinned. "I want Thailand—green curry thick with coconut milk, the spice so strong it makes my lips tingle. And mango sticky rice, soft, sweet, the rice soaking up every ounce of coconut cream."

"Argentina," Virginia said suddenly. "Have you read about their steakhouses? Chimichurri spooned over grilled beef, empanadas stuffed with spiced meat, dulce de leche so rich it makes you forget everything else."

The wind shifted, carrying the scent of coffee and warm bread.

"Costa Rica," Eliza murmured, "but maybe someday, we won't just dream about them, we will go." For now, she had books. Stories, recipes, the ghosts of flavors carried across pages. But maybe, someday, they'd taste the world for themselves.

"Well, the point is he is returning after all these months abroad," Virginia drew the conversation back to the present, "and when he does, he always brings change."

"The elections are coming up in the autumn and he will want to be here to influence things?" Eliza observed.

"Oh, Eliza, good point," Virginia said, swirling her mimosa.

"Senator Bartholomew Jackson and Judge Halstrom's growing relationship is an interesting development," Eliza added. "I don't think your boyfriend will like that," she teased.

"Yes, and Winston seemed to be a bit too confident," Virginia added her observation of the English Ambassador's son.

"I heard from Mr. Gray, that England's favored trading status is in jeopardy again," Audrey added, "That boring old man from the Trade Office is only worth one useful piece of information a night."

"Can you imagine if any of the men outside these walls actually knew how much information we have collected," Virginia said thoughtfully.

And then, when the lull came, when conversation softened, she told them about Sister Lily.

Audrey raised a brow. Virginia leaned forward, interest piqued.

"She never leaves the cloister," Audrey murmured, picking at the edge of her napkin. "What's so important that they'd send her here?"

Eliza didn't answer right away.

The wind shifted, carrying the scent of orange juice and warm bread, sunlight catching on the edges of their glasses.

"We're about to find out," she finally said.

Madame Mary Margaret sat across from Sister Hope in her private chamber, in wingback chairs with the sun streaming in from a bay window behind, the text open on a table in front of them. The Prostitute and the Nun—equals.

The aged parchment, marked with symbols that could not be unraveled, had fully captured their attention. Eliza had been right to bring it forward—but now, the question remained: what did it mean?

"She will arrive by evening," Sister Hope confirmed, folding her hands over the edge of the desk. "And I suspect she will be wary, as she should be. As we both know, she doesn't leave the cloister for good reason."

Sister Hope hesitated, then carefully pulled a worn notebook from her robes, a stark contrast to the tablets they were permitted at the cloister. Even nuns had more freedom when it came to technology. The notebook pages were filled with the ciphers they had used to try to decode the text.

"It's both older and newer than we thought," Sister Hope said with bated breath.

Madame Mary Margaret leaned forward, studying the text beneath them. "I see what you mean," she said, "this looks like original Navajo, but it is written in code."

"Sister Lily has seen something like this before," Hope murmured. "But many think that she is crazy or made it up to try to appear important. We will know more once she arrives."

"Sister Lily survived a lot in the time before," Madame mused, "Do you think her sanity is intact?"

Sister Hope responded, "I believe that magic is just science we do not yet understand, and that Sister Lily might have seen things that others don't want us to know."

"Do you mean like when the Pentagon began releasing the UFO files in 2025?" she breathed.

"What about Eliza?" Sister Hope inquired.

The debate between Sister Hope and Madame Mary Margaret played out in measured tones, each woman weighing the risks and rewards of Eliza's presence in tomorrow's conversation with Sister Lily.

"She's sharp, inquisitive, but she lacks restraint," Madame mused, swirling her tea absently. "Knowledge is power, Hope, but so is timing. If she pushes too hard, Sister Lily may withhold more than she shares."

Sister Hope nodded, arms crossed. "True, but Eliza already found the text. That alone gives her the right to hear what is uncovered."

Madame exhaled. "Finding something and understanding its consequences are two different things."

Hope tilted her head. "And yet, I can't shake the feeling that she should be there."

Silence stretched between them, the early afternoon light cutting across the table, catching the edges of the parchment.

It wasn't logical. It wasn't strategy or careful calculation.

It was intuition—the quiet knowing that had guided women for generations, through fires, through secrets, through history's unseen corridors.

Madame Mary Margaret finally leaned back. "Then she will be there."

Virginia, Audrey, and Eliza stood outside Madame Mary Margaret's private study, exchanging glances filled with equal parts curiosity and apprehension.

It was their day off, and yet, here they were—summoned, requested, pulled from their lazy morning of coffee and conversation.

Virginia rolled her shoulders, feigning nonchalance. "You think she's got bad news, or do you think she just likes keeping us on edge?"

"Both," Audrey murmured, adjusting the cuff of her sleeve.

Eliza exhaled, pressing her lips together in thought. Summons from Madame weren't random. They had weight, intent, meaning. She pondered; if this had to do with Sister Lily, she didn't believe this was a coincidence.

And then, the door creaked open.

"Come in," Madame's voice beckoned from inside.

The three women stepped forward, crossing into the warm, portrait-lined study of nudist paintings, such works were deemed 'obscene' by the evangelicals of old, but were perfectly appropriate for their line of work. It was even rumored that a few of these pieces had hung in the National Portrait Gallery before Dr. Kim Sajet resigned under pressure in 2025.

Sunlight spilled through the open window; the scent of early spring carried on the breeze.

Madame sat unrushed, composed, a single sheet of aged paper spread before her on the desk.

"Please sit," she said to the girls, relying on formality—but also wanting to make them at ease.

"I will not pretend. Eliza has mentioned that she found a text we are unable to decipher, and Sister Lily is coming to assist."

The trio shifted, slightly uncomfortable with the truth of the Madame's statement.

"It might be hard for you to imagine, but I was young once and shared a lot with my closest confidants," she told the three. "I want to use the strengths of each of you as a team. Each of you has talents I value—but this task requires boldness. Someone unafraid to see the extraordinary. Which is why I'm assigning Audrey."

Audrey snorted softly in surprise. "Me?" she asked incredulously.

"Yes," Madame responded. "In preparation for Sister Lily's visit, I would like you to put together as much information as you can assemble on credible UFO, time travel, and wild people in the mountains."

"You're serious?" Audrey asked, her voice halfway between a laugh and a gasp. "Best. Day. Off. Ever." This assignment was almost better than her earlier travel fantasies—and it was real!

Audrey's eyes gleamed with excitement, her fingers already itching to dive into the research. UFOs, time travel, wild people in the mountains—this was the kind of assignment she never expected but absolutely relished.

"Oh, Madame, you have no idea how much I love this," she said, barely containing her enthusiasm.

Madame Mary Margaret allowed herself a small smile. "I suspected as much."

Eliza leaned forward, intrigued. "Where do we even start?"

"Well," Audrey mused, tapping her chin, "there are plenty of credible UFO sightings—Roswell, Rendlesham Forest, the Phoenix Lights. And time travel? There's the whole theory that UFOs aren't aliens at all, but future humans coming back to observe us."

Virginia smirked. "And the wild people in the mountains? You mean like the legends of hidden civilizations, lost tribes, the unchipped—the ones who vanished before the scans were mandatory?"

"Exactly," Audrey said, already forming a plan. "There are stories of people disappearing into the wilderness, never to be seen again. Some say they joined secret societies, others claim they found places untouched by time."

Madame nodded. "I want you to focus on what's credible—what has been documented, what has been investigated. Sister Lily will know what to look for, but I want you to be prepared."

Audrey straightened, ready for the challenge.

"Consider it done."

⇌ ✳ ⇋

The library's modern wing felt nothing like the grand, historic hall of the old wine cellar where Eliza usually lost herself in ancient texts. No carved oak tables, no gilded edges on old volumes—just cold practicality, remnants of a space repurposed, then abandoned.

The old cafeteria-style tables still bore scratches from long-forgotten trays, and the plastic containers stacked against the walls were filled with records, files, reports— all packed away, as if someone had intended to return but never did.

Eliza mused about the people who once worked in the nearby building. She pictured them coming down to this underground cafeteria during their long workdays, perhaps after equally long commutes. Eating prepackaged food that was heated just enough to pass health inspections under fluorescent lights.

Audrey moved through it with ease, her fingers trailing along the boxes, knowing exactly which ones held the most useful fragments. This was her territory, where classified whispers, unsanctioned theories, and discarded truths found refuge in plastic bins instead of leather-bound spines.

"Most people don't know this section exists," she murmured, flipping open one of the containers with practiced efficiency.

Virginia wrinkled her nose. "It looks like an office graveyard."

"It is," Audrey said, pulling out a faded folder. "But this is where everything they didn't want in the archives ended up. The things that didn't fit their neat little narratives. After the head archivist was fired in 2025."

"So many women fired during that time," Virginia noted.

"Colleen Shogan was removed from her position as the Archivist of the United States (AOTUS) and several organizations like the Midwest Archives Conference (MAC) and Society of American Archivists (SAA) protested her removal," Eliza added. "Another voice silenced."

"Yes," Audrey agreed, but her quest for knowledge could not be dimmed. "Their mistakes are our gain; now we have access to records just abandoned, here in this subterranean cafeteria."

Eliza scanned the labels on the bins, noting the classifications—military reports, scientific anomalies, restricted personnel files.

"So where do we start?" she asked.

Audrey grinned. "Time travel, UFOs, or wild people in the mountains?"

"Let's split it up into three, since there are three of us," Eliza suggested.

"Virginia gets the unchipped in the mountains," Audrey gave her a wicked smile, and Virginia stuck her tongue out.

"Can I have time travel?" Eliza asked, somehow feeling drawn to this topic.

"Sure," Audrey responded. "Just keep in mind that time travel and UFOs intersect sometimes." Audrey was having what might be the best day of her life!

Audrey was practically vibrating with excitement, her hands already rifling through folders, seeking out the threads of conspiracy, forgotten experiments, and strange anomalies buried beneath bureaucracy.

Virginia gave a resigned sigh as she plucked a stack of papers from a container labeled "Unrecorded Civilian Movements: Rural Encampments, 2043–2050." "So, I get to dive into the off-grid people—the ones who decided they'd rather disappear into the mountains than deal with the mess out here?"

"Exactly," Audrey said with a wicked grin. "But think of it this way—some of them might not just be escaping. They might be surviving something we don't even know about yet."

Eliza, meanwhile, had already claimed her stack, the words "Temporal Research: Theoretical & Unclassified" staring up at her like an invitation she hadn't known she needed.

She ran her fingers over the brittle edge of a report dated 2026, something about time distortions detected near geological fault lines. A memo marked "DO NOT CIRCULATE" sat on top, folded sharply as though someone had once considered tearing it up but hadn't had the nerve.

"This one's mine," Eliza murmured, pulling the document closer.

Audrey barely glanced up. "You're gonna regret not choosing UFOs when I find something insane."

Somewhere in the abandoned cafeteria, dust floated lazily through the artificial light, a quiet reminder that whatever they uncovered had been forgotten for a reason.

But they weren't going to leave it buried.

Virginia dramatically shook out her hair, sending a small cloud of dust into the air. "I swear, I'm going to find grit in my sheets for a week."

Audrey smirked, "Not everyone gets to live in a romance novel, darling."

"I'm sure one of these delicious oysters will make you feel like a princess again," Eliza said, adding horseradish to hers before slurping it down, chasing it with a sip of champagne. The bubbles stung in just the right way.

"This is such a rare treat—to eat up here by ourselves," Virginia added, exploring the cherry horseradish with her next oyster. "Oh, this is fresh. Must be early-season cherries."

"Save one for me," Audrey chided, lacing hers with Tabasco and flashing a wicked grin.

"Madame is truly making it up to us for asking us to work on our day off," Eliza observed, savoring another oyster as it slid down her throat.

"Today really is the best day of my life," Audrey declared, raising her champagne flute in salute.

But beneath the laughter, the weight of what they'd learned lingered.

Eliza chuckled as the others settled into the plush comfort of Virginia's boudoir. The knock at the door was soft. Agnes, ever discreet, entered with a cart—steam and spice rising from the seafood boil beneath parchment paper. The scent of Old Bay and Chesapeake crab clung to the air.

As Agnes left, the women arranged themselves around the cart. Eliza, ever practical, glanced toward Virginia.

"You might want to open the windows, unless you want your room to forever smell like dust and shellfish."

"Brilliant," Virginia replied, and moved to open the window, letting the air cut through the scent of the food and bringing with it the freshness of spring.

Audrey cracked crab legs with quiet expertise—clean, efficient, practiced. She worked without flourish, but there was something in her precision that carried weight, a memory.

Eliza noticed. The tension in Audrey's jaw, the silence in her eyes. She remembered the whispers about a reassignment. About how close Audrey had come to ending up in a place not unlike where Agnes had been, before her beauty was marred.

Virginia caught Eliza's glance and offered a soft toast, disguising concern behind the sparkle of champagne.

Even amid indulgence, the shadows of their discoveries hovered.

"So," Eliza murmured, fingers brushing her napkin's edge, "how do lost maternal myths tie into modern conspiracy and power?"

Audrey leaned in, her eyes gleaming. "It's all connected. Goddesses, forgotten matriarchs, women who shaped civilizations—before their names were erased."

Eliza nodded, pouring another glass. "Like the Corn Mother. Once a sustainer of life, now a harvest mascot. But some say her worship still exists—hidden in secret lineages of women who once ruled."

"Like everything else that used to mean something. Turn it into a brand, slap it on a seasonal latte, and sell it back to the masses. It used to be about survival, ritual, real power. But it just became marketing," Virginia sighed, holding out her glass to Eliza for a refill.

"And the Deer Woman," Eliza added. "Once a protector, turned into a threat. It's a pattern: rewrite powerful women as dangerous to maintain control."

Audrey grinned. "Don't get me started on the lost priestesses.

Astronomers, healers—keepers of knowledge. They didn't disappear. They went underground, waiting."

Virginia tapped her fingers, thoughtful. "Power decides which stories survive. Which are erased. Which are buried so deep we forget they ever existed."

Eliza's voice softened. "Women were the first healers, the first astronomers. We tracked stars, the sun, and the moon. We understood cycles—of nature and people."

Audrey cracked another crab leg. "And somewhere along the way, that wisdom became superstition. Unofficial. Stolen."

Eliza tilted her head. "Maybe the fragmentation is intentional. Maybe entire civilizations passed knowledge down through mothers— through ritual and rhythm."

Virginia stared at the bubbles in her glass. "What if romance novels were never about pleasure? What if they were tools? To trap women into always needing a man—to feel incomplete alone."

"Maybe that's why this manuscript matters," Eliza said, her hand brushing the parchment's edge. "Maybe we've found a glimpse of what they never wanted us to remember."

The wind shifted, cool against the open windows, and the girls took the hint from nature that it was time to wrap up their meal.

Audrey exhaled. "Well. If there ever was a time when women ruled with wisdom, strategy, and power, I'd say it's about damn time we bring it back."

Sister Lily would arrive tonight. Tomorrow, the answers they'd been waiting for would finally begin to take shape.

Sister Lily stepped through the kitchen entrance, her wrist scan smooth and swift, her movement precise—unbothered by the weight of her ninety-four years.

Madame Mary Margaret and Sister Hope hurried away from the hostess stand the moment they were informed. Their breathing slightly uneven, they were clearly caught off guard by Sister Lily's choice of arrival entrances.

Sister Hope exhaled sharply, straightening her posture. "Of course she did."

The air carried the sharp scent of lemon disinfectant—every surface gleamed. The kitchen had been polished to perfection before bed, always ready should a gentleman caller request anything up until the 2:00 A.M. curfew. At least one chef and one maid stayed in the side quarters nightly, ready to serve if summoned after midnight.

A bowl of fresh fruit waited on the counter. The beverage refrigerator hummed softly, stocked with still and sparkling water—for any woman needing a light snack before retreating upstairs.

Madame Mary Margaret smoothed her dress, steadying herself as her eyes found Sister Lily—who was already taking in the room, her gaze sharp, her movements crisp. She wasted no time on ceremony.

"If I waited for someone to roll out a welcome parade, I'd have been dead decades ago," Sister Lily muttered. Then, she pivoted, with unexpected grace, with a smile on her face; "Any chance we can have your chef whip up an omelette for me?"

Madame Mary Margaret nodded, recovering her composure with the practiced ease of meeting the whims of an exacting clientele. "Of course."

The night staff—having heard the quiet stirrings—had already set their cribbage game aside. The entire Hall had been buzzing all day about Sister Lily's arrival.

"Best omelette I ever had was in this hall nearly ten years ago," Lily mused, her smile touched with fond memory.

"I'll try to live up to that," the chef responded, her voice steadier than she felt. Somehow, Sister Lily felt more approachable than anyone had imagined. "Tell me your preferences."

"Just egg and cheese," Lily said. "Gruyère if it's on hand, Manchego if not. Light dusting of pepper, no salt. At my age, I avoid sodium like the COVID-19 virus," she laughed.

As the cook prepared the omelette, the maid quietly transformed a corner of the kitchen into a breakfast nook—setting linens, glasses, and silverware with careful elegance.

"Thank you again for coming," Madame Mary Margaret said, gesturing for Sister Lily to take the first seat.

Sister Hope placed a single sheet of aged parchment that she had dared to bring upstairs to show Sister Lily on the table.

"You wouldn't have called me unless it was important," Lily replied.

Sister Hope, still catching her breath, watched her carefully. "We need your expertise."

Sister Lily exhaled, rolling her shoulders like someone brushing off the weight of history.

"There'll be time for work tomorrow," she said, her voice lined with wisdom. "First, tell me how you ladies are doing."

They chatted for over an hour, the warmth between them growing in soft layers. Lily praised the omelette with theatrical delight, her compliments loud enough for the nearby staff to hear.

"Best omelette ever," the maid whispered to her cribbage partner with a proud smile.

The cook's eyes gleamed. "Can you imagine? Sister Lily's eaten omelettes for over ninety years—and mine's the best."

What they didn't know—and what Lily would never tell them—was this: since she'd turned eighty, she had decided that every meal she ate was the best. Because she was still alive to enjoy it.

Madame Mary Margaret, having seen Sister Hope and Sister Lily off to the convent wing, went to check in with Teresa, Zara, and Shenna. After verifying all the reports were completed and the hall was secure, she retired to her own room. Sleep eluded her like trying to grab the mist of a cloud as she tossed and turned.

5

T HE NEW DAWN BROUGHT a day filled with possibilities and hopefully answers. Eliza stretched before getting out of bed for the morning walk.

Eliza, Audrey, and Virginia walked in measured steps; their Sister escort was a silent, protective presence just ahead of them.

"Dr. Carla Hayden was the first true librarian to shape the Library of Congress in decades," Audrey murmured, nudging a stray pebble along the path with the tip of her shoe. "She fought to make the collections accessible—to preserve forgotten histories, to keep knowledge from being locked away from the people who needed it most."

"And then she was removed. Fired in a two-sentence email," Eliza said, her voice tightening. "Discredited. Dismissed. Erased—just like so many before her."

Audrey nodded, her gaze distant. "And now the Library of Congress—its truths twisted, its stories rewritten."

Virginia sighed and looked up at the slate-blue sky, the weight of centuries pressing against the crisp autumn air. "She was never married.

Never had children."

"Dr. Carla Hayden's firing galvanized the writer, researcher, and archival community — a group more known for noses in books than orations at the lectern," Eliza whispered, her tone reverent. "Do you think Sister Lily knew her?"

Audrey considered, her voice soft but sure. "They would've only been about ten years apart. It's possible—especially in the times before."

The Sister escorting them turned her head sharply at the slight rise in their voices. The girls fell silent at once, a shared understanding passing between them like a pulse. Some names, some truths, were too powerful to speak aloud—especially here, exposed on the open streets.

Overhead, a drone hummed faintly, its presence unobtrusive but unmistakable. Watching. Listening. Always collecting.

Sister Lily sat at the head table in the dining room, sipping her coffee, letting the bold warmth of cinnamon and whipped cream settle against her tongue. Quiet murmurs rippled through the room.

She could feel their gazes, the stolen glances, the hushed whispers—a mixture of reverence and curiosity, the weight of a legend seated at the head of their world, at least for this morning. Her gaze flickered only briefly before she truly saw the young maid before her.

At first glance, the girl was simply another quiet figure moving through the dining room, efficient, practiced in her role. But as she leaned forward to top off Sister Lily's mug, the light caught the ridges of her skin, and suddenly, the unseen became unavoidable.

The scars stretched like a map, faint but telling, etched across the planes of her face, winding from her temple down toward her jawline, curving near her cheekbone before disappearing beneath the shadow of her collar. Scars that not only seared the flesh but mapped the damage etched to her soul.

Sister Lily didn't flinch, nor did she stare, but she took them in completely, the way one reads a story written in ink too faint for most to bother deciphering.

"You've walked through fire," she murmured—not a question, not pity, simply a statement of truth.

The maid didn't look up immediately. Her fingers tightened briefly around the coffee pot, and for a breath, Sister Lily thought she might not answer at all. But then, a flicker of steel behind her eyes, a quiet resilience buried beneath layers of silence.

"And I'm still here," Agnes replied.

Sister Lily lifted her mug, letting the scent of cinnamon curl between them like something unspoken yet understood.

"That, child, is the part that matters," Sister Lily said kindly.

As Agnes slipped away, Sister Hope and Lieutenant Madame Teresa joined her at the head table.

Returning from their walk, Eliza, Audrey, and Virginia sat at their favorite patio table, their plates untouched. The scent of budding flowers mingled with the early spring warmth. Through the large, open doors, they watched Sister Hope, Lieutenant Teresa, and Sister Lily at the head table, their conversation measured, their presence commanding.

Eliza glanced at Audrey, who tapped her fork against the rim of her plate, not in frustration but in barely contained anticipation. "I can't eat," Audrey admitted, pushing her potatoes around absently.

"Me neither," Virginia murmured, her eyes never leaving Sister Lily. Virginia—normally composed—pulled at a strand of her blonde hair, the small, unconscious movement betraying her unease.

Eliza inhaled, gazing at the sky, the sun reflecting back as a bright bronze in her eyes. The cool wind teased her cheek. Soon, it would be too hot to sit outside, to feel this open, to share whispered conversations under the stars. The seasons were shifting, just like everything else in their world.

Madame Mary Margaret entered the dining room, her heels echoing coldly on the marble floor. The quiet hum of conversation faded as her presence commanded attention.

"Ladies," she began, her tone, firm but carrying an underlying warmth. "We are honored to welcome Sister Lily tonight. Let us extend her the respect she deserves."

Sister Lily inclined her head with a gracious wave, acknowledging the room with quiet appreciation. A slight murmur rippled across the room; most couldn't fathom living as long as Sister Lily, not in this world.

Madame Mary Margaret offered a brief smile before shifting into the familiar rhythm of leadership.

"You have responsibilities to uphold," she continued. "Please turn in your notes from last night. Your observations and insights matter—each detail strengthens the work we do."

A few women exchanged glances, some nodding in silent acknowledgment.

"Physical fitness is important, not just as a requirement but as a way to care for yourselves," she added. "Your strength—your body, your mind, your spirit—is what allows you to move with confidence. Prioritize it."

The tension in the room eased slightly, the directives now feeling less like a demand and more like a recognition of their well-being.

Finally, she gestured toward the bulletin board. "Check your appointments. Review your clients. Be prepared—but also remember that you are more than the work you do. You are individuals, each bringing your own wisdom, grace, and presence to this space. But do not become complacent," she warned. "You are all well trained and know your jobs."

The atmosphere shifted, the weight of expectations still present, but now softened by the reminder that their value wasn't solely defined by obligation, by being objects.

And just like that, the moment passed—but the kindness lingered. Whether staff, security, sister, or sinner, each of the ladies shared a common connection.

"Eliza," she added, "Please meet me in my private drawing room in the library."

⇒ ✵ ⇐

Eliza sat stiffly in the drawing room, the weight of secrecy pressing against her ribs as Madame Mary Margaret, Sister Hope, and Sister Lily settled into their seats. The room had once been a storage closet, but now it had been arranged into a cozy study area for reading and talking. The basements were unknown to their benefactors who supplied the brothel. Over the years, old furniture from the brothel and office furniture from when the building was a museum had made its way to the subterranean levels, forming an eclectic collection.

Sister Lily exhaled, her fingers tracing the rim of her teacup, as if steadying herself before speaking. The honey soothed her throat.

"I knew Carla Hayden," she began, her voice measured, deliberate. "I worked for her. I fought for the preservation of knowledge before the world decided it was no longer worth protecting," she paused. "I was one of the team members for the *Connecting Communities Digital Initiative*. We provided grants to digital collections and focused on diverse communities."

Eliza held her breath.

"There was a man," Sister Lily continued. "He came to the library, claiming to be a librarian from New York. He called himself Stone."

Madame Mary Margaret exchanged a glance with Sister Hope, but neither interrupted.

"He asked for copies of the Jefferson Library—every book, every document. He wanted more, too. He warned us, weeks after Carla was fired, that the books would need to be moved. That they would need to be kept safe," Sister Lily looked at Eliza.

Eliza's pulse quickened.

"He was quite attractive, and he set several of the women's hearts a flutter," she continued. "And then, one night, he disappeared."

The words hung in the air, heavy with implication.

"I had a different name then," Sister Lily admitted, her gaze distant, lost in memories that had long been buried. "This was before the chipping. Before everything changed. I was part of the movement to save the books, the artifacts, the knowledge they wanted to erase."

Eliza swallowed, her mind racing.

"I suspected he was from another timeline," Sister Lily murmured, her voice barely above a whisper. "Most people scoffed at the idea. But I knew. I knew because I had seen things that didn't belong to this world."

Eliza thought about the research assignment with Audrey the day prior. Could any of this truly be real? It felt too fantastical.

The electric fireplace crackled again, filling the silence that followed.

Eliza leaned forward, her hands gripping the arms of her chair. "And the books?" she asked.

Sister Lily met her gaze, her expression unreadable. "Some were saved," she said. "Some were lost. And some... are still waiting to be found. Some, like this, should not exist."

Sister Lily's fingers trembled slightly as she traced the ink on the parchment, her sharp eyes narrowing in disbelief. "This... this is Navajo," she murmured, her voice barely above a whisper.

Eliza leaned forward, watching as Sister Lily examined the script with precision honed over decades.

"But that's impossible," Sister Hope interjected, her brow furrowing. "Navajo wasn't written down until after World War II. The code talkers used it precisely because it was an unwritten language—one that couldn't be deciphered by the enemy."

Sister Lily exhaled, shaking her head. "And yet, here it is."

The weight of the revelation settled over the room like a thick fog.

"During the war, the Marine Corps developed the Navajo Code Talker program because the language was unwritten and incredibly complex," Sister Lily continued, her voice steadier now, filled with the certainty of someone who had spent a lifetime preserving knowledge. "It was used to transmit tactical messages that the Japanese never cracked."

Eliza's pulse quickened. "Could it have been recorded in secret?" she asked.

Sister Lily hesitated, considering. "Perhaps. But if it was, it would have been hidden away, protected. And if it had been recorded, how was it encrypted in the same code that was used in WWII?" She let the thought hang in the air, unfinished, but heavy with implication.

The room seemed to tighten with the gravity of Sister Lily's words. An unwritten language—not only written but encoded in a way that should have been impossible.

"It could also be a forgery," Sister Lily mused. "The forgers would have had to use several techniques to make this look so authentic, like browning, foxing, and molding. With the right machines and chemicals, we could test the authenticity, but we dare not," she added.

"But why go to the effort for such an authentic looking forgery," Sister Hope mused.

Eliza's thoughts swirled with implications: If this parchment existed, it meant someone had documented the undocumentable. And done so with intention. This wasn't just preservation. It was a message. A warning. Or perhaps... a key.

Madame Mary Margaret spoke softly, almost reverently, "Then this document is not only an impossibility—it's a map of betrayal or foresight."

Sister Lily gave a small, grim smile. "Or both."

Eliza exhaled, her mind racing.

"If this manuscript shouldn't exist, then whoever preserved it, or forged it..." She paused, the thought forming fully only as she spoke. "They wanted someone to uncover it."

Sister Hope pressed her lips together, her fingers ghosting over the aged parchment, as if waiting for it to reveal something further.

"Or they wanted to protect something bigger than themselves," she murmured.

"There is a book that might help you," Sister Lily continued. "I will have it brought over to the Hall, Laura Tohe, daughter of a Code Talker. She passed on the stories of her father and others."

The electric fireplace crackled again, its warmth doing little to dispel the cold edge of discovery settling over them.

"There is nothing more I can assist you with," Sister Lily concluded, "But I do hope you will let me stay for a few days. I do enjoy being around the keen minds of young people."

"Of course," Madame Mary Margaret responded. "The hall is filled with eager women who would love to meet you."

Eliza sat in silence. Instead of solving a mystery, she now had just uncovered more mystery to solve. She couldn't deny that her hands itched to trace the manuscript again and to begin decoding its secrets. Eliza reflected on Sister Lily's statement; the daughter had captured the story of her father—men could be silenced too.

Madame Mary Margaret began to rise from her chair, her posture poised yet relaxed, the soft glow of the old standing lamps casting warm shadows across the drawing room.

"Sister Lily," she began gently, her tone carrying the quiet authority of a woman who understood both duty and hospitality. "You are welcome to stay as long as you like—to explore, to observe, to meet the women here."

She glanced toward the electric fireplace, watching the flames flicker. "There is much to learn within these walls—stories, knowledge, voices that deserve to be heard and I know the women will prosper from your wisdom and experiences."

She paused, considering.

"We all carry pieces of history, some more visible than others. I hope you'll find something here that speaks to you."

Sister Lily nodded, a quiet smile playing at the edges of her lips. "I think I will."

Eliza took that as her cue and excused herself, "I need to go to the gym."

⇒ ✳ ⇐

The Brother of the President pondered inside his study. The long-lost heir or heiress playbook, he smiled to himself.

He started building this within weeks of dear Jon Jon's demise. He collected opportunities like old collectors had butterflies. Putting a sharp pin through each one.

He had heard a few rumors that Jon Jon had just started dating a girl before the plane went missing. Jon Jon was charming, impulsive. You plant a rumor—he'd fallen in love before the crash, maybe even had a child? It sounds like something he'd do. A little scandal makes the tragedy sweeter, gives it dimension.

Rumors, loose ends, missed connections. Like butterflies. Wings pinned flat beneath glass, perfect, preserved, mine.

The orphan angle? Timeless. The reawakening of a forgotten heiress? Delicious-no threat to male succession or power. Another asset to be sold to the highest bidder. The public *loves* a resurrection. And if that resurrection happens to occur during an election cycle—well, that's just providence with a voter base.

You don't *find* stories like this. You *build* them. Quietly. Patiently. In shadows.

And you never let sentimentality get in the way of opportunity.

Eliza tightened her harness, her fingers brushing against the cool metal of the carabiner as she steadied herself before the climb. The rock wall loomed before her, a mosaic of holds scattered in calculated chaos—an intricate dance of balance, precision, and grit.

She reached for the first handhold, her muscles coiling, her mind narrowing into singular focus. Step. Grip. Pull. The rhythm was instinctual, each movement a lesson in control—pushing past frustration, letting her body absorb the weight of her thoughts without collapsing under them.

Halfway up the wall, Eliza paused—fingertips gripping a jut of textured resin, her legs bent in silent strain. Sweat slipped down her temple. Her breath came steady but sharp.

The rhythm of her climb had quieted the noise, but the manuscript still haunted her thoughts—its foreign shapes, the impossible ink, the whispered suggestion of time travelers and forgeries and lost truths.

She closed her eyes briefly, pressing her forehead to the cool surface of the wall. The parchment wasn't just an artifact. It was a door.

Eliza had grown up thinking history was fixed—written, printed, archived. Now, she felt as if she had yanked a corner of the past open and glimpsed something moving behind it.

Was it real? Could truth survive that much suppression?

She reached again, fingers catching a hold. One pull, then another. The wall accepted her momentum, and she rose.

As her body climbed higher, her mind dropped deeper—into memory, into instinct, into the shape of the coded Navajo letters that no one was supposed to know.

"Some are waiting to be found," Sister Lily had said.

Eliza wasn't just climbing for fitness. She was training to *search*—to decode, uncover, protect.

She pushed upward, jaw set, muscles burning.

And this time, she didn't stop until she touched the ceiling.

As Eliza touched the ceiling of the climbing wall, her fingers curling over the final hold, a memory struck—sharp, unbidden.

She was eight again. Small. Angry. Knees scabbed from playground gravel. Sitting stiffly in a plastic chair outside the Reverend Mother's office at St. Brigid's Orphanage.

The room had smelled of lemon polish and paper files—rows and rows of files. She had been dropped off at the orphanage five years before, but they were updating records for the chipping.

Mother Camilla, with her soft voice and unrelenting eyes, placed a manila folder on the table. "We've gone through everything," she said gently. "There is no record of a father's DNA."

Eliza stared at the folder. It looked so official. So final. Her hands had curled into fists in her lap. "But that doesn't mean he didn't exist," she muttered.

Sister Lenora sighed, her rosary beads clicking softly as she shifted. "Sometimes, Eliza, not all truths are in databanks. But that doesn't mean they're not real."

The words had burned into her, even then. A choice. A silence. Who was her Father?

Back on the climbing wall, Eliza blinked, breath ragged. She stared down at the gym floor below, then slowly descended—each foothold a piece of the past easing back into the present.

She didn't believe in coincidences.

Maybe the parchment, the Navajo writing, the missing pieces—they were all connected.

Maybe *her* missing pieces were, too.

The parlor hummed with quiet indulgence, the low murmur of conversation mixing with the gentle strains of the quartet's melody, a song layered with melancholy—a girl, a mother, and the choices between them.

At the center of it all, the President's brother sat in effortless command, his gaze sweeping the room with practiced ease, an unspoken expectation settling over the space—to be watched, regarded, obeyed.

Virginia adjusted the drape of her gown, careful in her movements, deliberate in her poise. She had heard whispers before—rumors that he was the majority shareholder of the Hall, though nothing had ever been confirmed. Tonight, though, she saw the way the room bent around him—the quiet acknowledgments, the unspoken deference.

The two foreign dignitaries, one from France, one from Oman, spoke in smooth tones and strong accents. The women assigned to them—both blondes, both impeccable in their presentation—laughed softly at well-placed pauses, their presence a curated delight, a gift from the President's brother himself.

Audrey's laugh rang light, a quiet ripple against the room's tension. Eliza, calm, composed, studied Edgar Jackson over the rim of her glass, selecting her words carefully. "Tell me how things are going with your internship," she asked, knowing Edgar thrived when given space to speak of his ambitions.

And the evening, steeped in quiet authority and veiled negotiations, unfolded with measured grace.

The President's Brother sat with practiced ease, his glass resting lightly against his fingertips, observing, calculating.

Virginia's glance toward the brunette and the redhead across the room did not escape his notice.

Edgar Jackson, the son of a senator who opposed his brother, spoke a little too loudly, spilling the details of his new position, the trials and triumphs of working under the judge.

It was predictable—ambition cloaked in polite enthusiasm. He observed how the brunette had only to give a nudge of encouragement to keep the young man talking.

Yet, as Edgar talked, the President's Brother's gaze drifted, sharp and calculating, scanning the room as if taking stock of the players on his board. The redhead, however, had been dealt a dull hand tonight—paired with one of the most insufferable men in the administration. The Head of Commerce, not of sales, but a glorified accountant in charge of regulation, void of intrigue, void of charisma, void of anything that might make him particularly useful beyond the current political necessity. Trade in its most functional form. The man lacked any imagination.

The Brother exhaled slowly, swirling the bourbon in his glass. That man wouldn't last. "Next cabinet shuffle, he's gone," he thought absently. His Brother had no intention of keeping him beyond reelection.

But for now—they needed the Gray family's backing.

As a rule, the brothel had a three-hour limit for the time a client could book with a courtesan. But the President's Brother was an exception. He always had been. He'd booked Virginia—reserved, calculating, with a face that could both soothe and unnerve—and the two blondes, Ava and Mercy, for what he called "his friends."

"What do you see when you look around the room?" he asked her smoothly.

Virginia met his gaze, steady, measured, unflinching. She knew the question was more than idle curiosity—it was a test.

She let a breath slip past her lips, her gaze drifting deliberately across the parlor. "I see a room built on expectation," she said smoothly.

The quartet played on, their melody soft, deliberate, bending to the atmosphere rather than shaping it.

"Expectation?" the President's Brother echoed, swirling his drink with calculated ease.

Virginia nodded, letting her fingers ghost along the rim of her glass, thoughtful but composed. "Everyone here is playing a role, whether they recognize it or not."

She glanced at the two blondes, laughing lightly, their clients utterly enchanted, unaware of how much they were being observed in return.

Having learned that men often filled in the blanks, Virginia decided not to continue and let the Brother draw his own conclusions.

Her eyes flickered toward Eliza, who listened intently to Edgar Jackson's latest ambition, but never stopped watching the room's undercurrent—the quiet shifts in posture, the glances exchanged when people thought they weren't being watched.

"And you?" the Brother asked, his tone deceptively easy. "What is your role?"

Virginia turned back to him, held his gaze, let the weight of her next words settle between them. "I'm here to ensure your satisfaction in any way that you desire," Virginia responded coquettishly, flipping her blonde hair.

The Brother exhaled, a slow, deliberate sound. A small smirk played at the corner of his mouth—not of amusement, but of acknowledgment. She'd given him exactly what he expected, and nothing more. A masterstroke of obedience dressed in flirtation. The answer was perfect because it was performative.

But Virginia's gaze lingered just a moment too long on the decanter behind him, a signal he didn't miss. She was watching for more than reaction. She was calculating.

He leaned back slightly, his profile catching the amber glow of the chandelier above them. "You're very good at what you do, Virginia," he said softly, not as praise, but as a declaration. A fact. Like naming a storm.

Ava and Mercy had left the tables with their clients. Across the room, Ava offered a soft laugh, touching the arm of the Omani delegate. Mercy leaned in closer to her French diplomat, whispering something that made him pause and blink, bemused. The President's brother watched the orchestrated dance that he had seen play out in rooms like this around the world.

But the President's brother no longer wanted to watch them. His attention returned to Virginia.

"And if I asked for honesty instead of performance?" he asked, voice silk over steel.

Virginia didn't flinch. Didn't smile. She tilted her head slightly, her reply gentle, but edged. "Then I'd ask whether you mean honesty from me—or about you."

The air shifted subtly. The quartet continued to play, unaware—or pretending to be—of the sharpened quiet that had settled in the center of the room like a blade turned sideways.

For just a heartbeat, neither moved.

Then the Brother lifted his glass again, the ice chiming against crystal. "This is why I always come back to you." The Brother gave a hearty laugh out loud. Attracting all the eyes of the room.

The Madame shifted her gaze to Virginia with apprehension. What could this mean?

The Brother smiled genuinely at Virginia for the first time. "Call me Dave," he told her. Not a command, but a request.

Virginia studied him for a fraction longer than necessary, noting the way his demeanor had shifted—less calculated, more deliberate, but still steeped in control.

"*Call me Dave*," he had said—not an order, not a demand, but a carefully placed invitation.

The hum of the quartet carried on, the room adjusting to the sudden ripple of his laughter, a sound meant to draw eyes, meant to remind the space of his presence.

Madame Mary Margaret didn't speak, but Virginia felt the weight of her glance—a silent message, a quiet warning, an unspoken calculation about what this exchange might mean.

Virginia let the moment breathe, then offered him the smallest, knowing smile, one that could be read however he wished it to be.

"Dave, then," she murmured, her tone smooth, unhurried, accepting the name but never relinquishing her own control.

The shift between them was subtle, but unmistakable.

The quiet hum of closing soon settled over the Hall, the evening's indulgences fading into memory as the last lingering guests were shown to the exit.

Virginia had just begun gathering herself, letting the weight of the night settle when she felt Madame Mary Margaret's gaze catch hers—steady, deliberate.

She approached, her presence always measured, always knowing.

"Well done, my dear," she said, her voice carrying a quiet note of approval, a recognition of something beyond words.

Virginia didn't blink, didn't let surprise flicker across her face. But she knew—Madame did not give praise lightly.

She inclined her head, acknowledging, but not accepting too easily.

"Thank you, Madame," she murmured, her tone smooth, balanced—always careful, always listening.

Madame held her gaze for a heartbeat longer. Then, with the smallest nod, she turned, disappearing into the settling silence of the Hall.

The weight of the night pressed against Madame's shoulders, the echoes of quiet indulgence fading as she climbed the stairs.

She stood at the Widow's Peak, the highest vantage in the Hall, where the city stretched before her—gold-lit streets, stately monuments, a city designed to project its power weaving around the people below; like invisible threads they could not see tightening around their wrists.

The report on Virginia was clear on the computer screen. The highest authorities had taken notice.

Madame exhaled, slow, measured, but the unease curled in her chest. Not surprise—she had expected this. But expectation never softened the reality of consequence.

Virginia had played her role with precision. Had walked the line, danced at the edges of control, drawn just enough attention—but not too much.

And yet, power was rarely predictable.

Just as the libraries had begun yielding their secrets, the quiet work—the delicate salvage of erased knowledge—now threatened to be tangled in a larger game.

She shuddered, not from cold, but from the certainty of entanglement.

The lights of the District pulsed before her, reflecting against the glass, a reminder that no one truly stood outside of its grip. She had always known this. Tonight, she simply felt it more acutely.

MADAME MARY MARGARET REREAD the request on her screen, squinting against the glare of the morning light filtering through the windows of the Widow's Peak.

Virginia, Audrey, and Eliza—chosen for an evening within the house of the President's Brother. A summons that carried weight beyond mere invitation. A signal. A test. A step into something larger than the Hall itself.

She inhaled, already mapping the necessary preparations. The week was theirs to refine, to polish, to prepare.

Materials would arrive by midday—dossiers on the visiting dignitaries, notes on their preferences, their conversations, their history. Every detail, no matter how insignificant, would be studied. The Brother wanted to put on a show.

Then, of course, the gowns, the jewels, the shoes—perfection sent in carefully curated parcels. The seamstresses would arrive soon, measuring, adjusting, ensuring the fit was more than just aesthetic but strategic. The Brother had provided an allowance for these items that was staggering.

Madame glanced at the clock on the computer screen. Time moved quickly when power demanded readiness.

Madame Mary Margaret tapped the screen shut, sealing the decision into motion. This wasn't about seduction or spectacle—not truly. It was about control, presentation, perception. The President's Brother, *'Call me Dave'* was recalibrating the gameboard.

It's timing, uncanny. Its contents, still unclear. But the shape of something bigger was emerging—threads of power, inheritance, betrayal. And now this evening, this guest list.

No, this wasn't a coincidence. It was choreography.

By this morning, the preparations would begin. By week's end, the ladies would step into something far more intricate than simple appearances.

And Madame knew—this wasn't just a party. It was an opportunity. And a warning. Was it just a coincidence that this was happening right as they uncovered the secret manuscript? She didn't believe in chance.

The morning routine unfolded like clockwork—Madame Mary Margaret stood at the head of the dining room, delivering the day's instructions with her usual measured tone, her presence shaping the pace of the room.

But as the murmurs of acknowledgment settled and the women began their tasks, she made a quiet exception.

"Eliza, Audrey, Virginia—stay behind."

The air shifted. Not sharply, but noticeably. Faint murmurs rippled through the hall. First, Sister Lily's arrival, and then everyone had observed the interaction between Virginia and the President's brother.

Sister Lily's gaze flickered, sharp with interest, though she kept her expression neutral, listening without intrusion.

As the others left the room, Madame Mary Margaret's gaze settled on Eliza, Audrey, and Virginia.

"The three of you—in my private study."

Eliza straightened, exchanging a glance with Audrey, who raised a curious brow, and Virginia, who simply adjusted the folds of her dressing gown.

Something was shifting.

Madame Mary Margaret stood behind her desk, hands folded, the weight of her words settling before she even spoke.

"The three of you have been requested for a private event."

Eliza remained still, but Audrey shifted slightly, her fingers tightening around the folds of her dress. Virginia, ever composed, exhaled slowly, waiting.

Madame pointed out, "A blonde, a brunette, and a redhead—I'm sure it's no coincidence. He has shown particular interest in you, Virginia.'"

Silence.

Madame's gaze sharpened. "I do not approve of orgies, but refusal is not an option. You know that. I've managed to secure an agreement that the President's brother is the only man you're required to perform services for. However, you will be attending a small party with other powerful men. Your role there will be to be ornamental and fawning." She hated saying it. And they hated hearing it.

"This is not the same as the men who come here. This is politics, power, expectation, on a global level. You will listen, gather, observe. And you will give nothing in return."

Eliza inclined her head. "And if he asks?" recalling the power play between him and Virginia the night prior.

Madame Mary Margaret straightened, her expression unreadable.

"Then you do what women have always done, Eliza." Madame continued, "You smile. You agree. You say everything and nothing, all at once. You lie."

"You will have one week to prepare for this party. Materials will be sent for you to study. He wants you to be polished for his dignitaries," she continued.

"The seamstresses will be here at 1:00 P.M. for gown selections and your first fittings." Madame informed them. "I will see you then," she said dismissing them.

The three friends were a little giddy at hearing about the dress fittings, despite the seriousness of the situation.

The door clicked shut behind them, leaving the gravity of Madame's words hanging in the air—heady, complex, and impossible to ignore. The hallways of the Hall were quiet, their footsteps echoing softly on the marble floors.

Audrey was the first to speak. "A blonde, a brunette, and a redhead. Does he think we're symbols in a parlor trick?"

Virginia gave a small, noncommittal shrug. "We're not symbols. We're statements. I think he saw me looking at the two of you last night," Virginia confessed, biting her lip.

Eliza pulled her into a hug. "You were in a tough spot last night. We were both looking at you too," she added.

"At least you have us instead of Ava and Mercy," Audrey observed.

There was a beat of silence as they turned the corner, the morning light catching the stained-glass windows, casting fractured colors across their path. The light turned them into living paintings—fractured hues of green, blue, and deep brown casting fleeting halos around their forms.

"We are the art," Eliza had said, and Audrey had agreed—not with resignation, but with power.

Virginia exhaled, the weight of the moment settling against her ribs. They would be watched, studied, admired—not just for beauty, but for the roles they would play. She felt responsible for bringing her friends into this.

"Then let's make sure we are dazzling!" There was both determination and defiance in Audrey's words.

Virginia knew—they would not walk into this event blind, nor silent, nor unprepared. A week to polish, a week to transform, a week to claim their presence in a space that believed it controlled them.

"Let's dazzle, indeed," Virginia repeated, her spirits lifting.

⁌ ✵ ⁍

Despite the looming weight of this information, Eliza couldn't stay away from the library, immersing herself in the ancient texts.

The words blurred together as Eliza traced each character with careful precision. The faded ink, delicate but defiant against time, whispered secrets that had waited centuries to be understood.

She had dreamt of this passage—the fragmented script, the weight of its meaning just out of reach. Now, in the hush of the library, surrounded by the scent of aged ink and the rough touch of old parchment, she dove deeper, grasping at the hidden truths buried beneath every careful stroke of the past.

She didn't notice the time slipping away.

Not until a soft voice broke the silence.

"Eliza."

Sister Hope stood over her shoulder, her expression unreadable, yet touched with something like sympathy.

"It's time to go upstairs."

Eliza blinked, then exhaled slowly, the weight of reality crashing back into place. The fitting. The party. The President's brother. The gilded illusion she was meant to step into.

She ran her fingers over the page one last time before closing the book, sealing its secrets away.

"Coming," she sighed.

⇒ ✳ ⇐

The seamstresses worked with meticulous precision, pinning fabric, adjusting seams, sculpting each gown into something refined, elegant, deliberate.

Madame Mary Margaret watched with a discerning eye, rejecting dress after dress—too revealing, too obvious, too much given away.

"These gowns must speak to the imagination, not reality," she reminded them, her tone firm but thoughtful. A challenge in fabric. A game in art.

Eliza's bronze shimmered, shifting like molten metal; if it could look this amazing in broad daylight, how much better would it look in sparkling reflections —bold, grounding, impossible to ignore.

Virginia's blue swept over her, a bright royal blue—cool control, effortless grace, a quiet regal power.

Audrey's green was alive, vibrant yet understated—intelligent, sharp, watching everything while pretending not to be.

The gowns were more than fabric. They were signals, markers, unspoken weapons in a game where presence was everything.

Finally, Madame nodded with approval of the trio. The contrasts and complements woven between them expertly highlighted each woman's uniqueness, while reinforcing them as a set. They showed enough to keep men's interest but hid all the key secrets a man wanted.

The bronze, blue, and green fabrics shimmered under the afternoon light, transforming from raw material into something sculpted, deliberate, undeniable.

"We'll need another fitting," one of the seamstresses murmured, stepping back to assess the drape of Eliza's gown.

Madame nodded. "Return when they are perfect."

Because for this night—perfection was not optional.

"Ladies," Madame began, her voice calm but commanding as the seamstresses departed and the door clicked shut behind them. "It's time to let Virginia's talents lead."

She paced slowly, her heels striking a deliberate rhythm across the polished floor.

"This week, alongside studying the dossiers from the President's brother, you'll return to the foundations. The fundamentals. The work that began the moment each of you first entered the Hall of Mary Ann." Her gaze lingered on Audrey and Eliza. "You've barely set foot in this room since your first year. But you remember it—the scent of jasmine and parchment, the hush of velvet, the mirrors, the scripts. This was never just a parlor. It was a stage."

She turned toward the Training Library's threshold. The door opened on well-oiled hinges. Madame had arranged for all other lessons to be relocated for the week, and library readers had been encouraged to take books outside or to their rooms to enjoy the first blush of spring.

Inside, the room remained exactly as Eliza and Audrey remembered it: low velvet settees, soft amber lighting, and shelves lined with scrolls, books, and leather-bound guides. Voice. Gaze. Restraint. Touch. Power. Every lesson crafted not merely for seduction—but for mastery.

This was the only room in the Hall where books were displayed openly. During an era when books were being banned for being "too much" for a proper lady's eyes, they had been welcomed into the brothel instead. Romance novels written for young girls, with princesses and happy endings. Housewife paperbacks, with men baring their chests on every cover. Even volumes banned across countries and decades—all found a home here. It had been ironic that the men who approved of these books for the brothel never bothered to read them. Never realized how they taught rebellious thoughts. The men had only seen books that could teach these women to perform their desires.

Virginia moved first, stepping into the center of the room—poised, radiant. She wasn't just prepared to perform. She was prepared to teach.

This room, more than any other, had shaped her. It was where she spent most of her days, lost in the quiet power of words.

"This week isn't about seduction," Madame said, her voice crisp as a blade of autumn air. "It's about memory. About remembering what made you dangerous to begin with."

She turned to Virginia. "You understand nuance. You understand why he keeps choosing you."

Virginia's eyes swept the room, then settled on her friends. "Men like the President's brother don't fall for beauty. They fall for what they can't quite possess. And if you make them believe they're almost there—almost—they'll chase you into ruin."

Audrey smirked. "Like baiting a lion with lace."

"Exactly," Virginia said. "And the key is to never fear the lion."

This time, the training would not be to please. It would be to control. Not to entertain—but to infiltrate. To endure. To survive.

⇌ ✻ ⇋

Madame's gaze softened, if only for a moment, as memory rose.

She could still see them—three girls, just sixteen, seated stiffly on the low couches in this very room, bathed in amber light. The curtains drawn tight, the world outside sealed away. She had entered without a word. Her heels had spoken first.

"You are not here to be beautiful," she had told them, voice even and cool. "You are here to become unforgettable."

Virginia had flinched—not from fear, but from recognition. That night's lesson had been "The Gaze." The scroll before them read: Look at him in a way that makes him forget why he walked into the room. Then remind him he'll never have you.

Audrey had giggled, a mix of nerves and thrill. Eliza had taken notes with surgical focus, already calculating what kind of look best disarmed a man in uniform versus one in silk. They'd practiced on each other—eyes locked, breath caught. At first, it had felt awkward. Then... it didn't.

"You're not here to seduce," Madame had said, standing behind Virginia, adjusting her posture like a sculptor at work. "You're here to suggest. To haunt. To become the last thought before sleep—and the first curse when they wake."

Virginia had grasped it first. Audrey followed, her voice transforming into velvet-wrapped steel. Learning to apply her wit like a whisper or a weapon. Eliza learned swiftly—how to speak, when to stay silent, and always calculated.

By the end of that week, they were no longer girls. Not yet women—but something else. Sharper. Shadowed. Deliberate.

Madame shook the memory away. Now, Madame faced a new challenge. She needed all three prepared for what lay ahead.

Barkley Mansion.

She still avoided the name, even in thought. To speak something was to give it shape. To name it was to give it power.

The week of preparation for the event unfolded like silk—smooth, deliberate, edged in heat and purpose. Each day slipped into the next with a rhythm that was almost carnal in its discipline: controlled, intentional, intimate.

Virginia designed their regimen with care—and almost a touch of cruelty. Mornings began with breath and stretch, bodies coiling in the slow, deliberate grace of yoga. Movements elongated, backs arched, wrists flexed—every gesture a whisper of promise. In the evening, they pushed further—endurance drills that tested control, balance, poise. This wasn't just about movement. It was about mastery. Bodies wouldn't merely respond—they would seduce, command, devour attention without a word.

Each morning brought fresh dossiers, crisp pages still warm from the printer, thick with names, alliances, and the scent of ink. But it was the space between the lines that mattered—the unsaid things. The whispers of scandal, the weight of silence, the stories men didn't write down but carried like secrets in their eyes.

Then came the books—Virginia's curation of seduction dressed in intellect. Leather-bound volumes, delicate paper, passages designed to be read in low lamplight. Not just strategy. Not just poise. But power hidden beneath soft smiles and silence, beneath perfume and posture. Books that taught not how to *please*—but how to *possess*.

Virginia studied like a lover listening for breath—tracing patterns, teasing out truths. Eliza, ever the tactician, dissected the narratives with surgical care, her questions sharp, her wit sharper. And Audrey—she moved between them like a flame, weaving the lessons into something precise, potent, and dangerously beautiful.

By the fourth night, the air in the room had changed. Tension hummed beneath the calm—a low thrum of power remembered, rekindled.

Madame stood in the doorway, silent.

She did not interrupt. She didn't need to. They were becoming exactly what she had trained them to be.

On the fourth day, as dusk draped the Hall in a soft golden haze, Madame finally nodded in agreement with Virginia—it was time to give the trio a treat. A particular kind of indulgence. One wrapped not in silk or sweets, but something far more intimate: permission.

In the Hall's fitness quarters, tucked behind mirrored walls and polished equipment, sat an outdated but still-functional DVD player. Officially, its purpose was to support physical education.

But occasionally, for education, Madame had long kept a carefully curated library of "educational" films. Visual studies of movement, chemistry, voice, seduction. Not explicit—never that. But suggestive. Crafted. Masterful in the way they explored the space between restraint and release. Of movies banned as inappropriate. Even a few romantic comedies.

Requests for access had to be submitted formally—especially when biometric logs tracked when the women were in the gym but not burning calories. Suspicion had to be managed with elegance. The illusion of a shared physical routine maintained.

Madame had applied for special access to use the DVD player for educational purposes as soon as she had received the invitation for the event.

The trio gathered with quiet anticipation, joined by a few others whose schedules allowed for indulgence. As the lights dimmed and the screen flickered to life, it wasn't reps or circuits that awaited them—it was performance. A study in tension. A choreography of gaze, voice, and the charged stillness between bodies that knew their power and chose, deliberately, not to use it—yet.

Virginia had chosen the evening's films. The first: *The Reader*.

She loved this one. For her, it wasn't merely a film—it was validation. *The Reader* affirmed her understanding of stillness as strength. She saw herself in Hanna: the weaponized silence, the gravity of withholding, the seductive ache of what remains unsaid. No wasted glances. No needless words. Presence, distilled into pressure.

Audrey let out a soft hum of amusement. "Now this is cardio." Always the most expressive, she tuned into the film's emotional tempo. *The Reader* stirred something softer—tenderness threaded with tension. Vulnerability as magnetism. It made her wonder: had her charm and sparkle always been armor? A way to be seen without being known? Quiet, she realized, could seduce too—if you weren't afraid of it.

Eliza approached the film like a tactician. She dissected its layers—power, shame, control—each beat a move, each silence a strategy. Restraint wasn't passivity; it was timing. Precision. *The Reader* became a map of emotional combat. She took notes without writing anything down.

Between films, Virginia made a brief announcement. Her voice was cool, assured. "The first teaches you sensuality and seduction alone—solo. But the next—this film—is about working as a team."

By the time *The Witches of Eastwick* began, the air had shifted—looser around the edges, but sharper beneath the surface. They weren't just watching now. They were attuning.

It opened in laughter, in lightness—but smoldered underneath. A tale of women awakening to hunger, to appetite, to the thrill of claiming power with both hands. Virginia leaned against the mirrored wall, one leg draped over the other, smiling like she already knew the ending by heart. And why it mattered.

Audrey lit up with the film's rhythm—laughing, teasing, drinking in the irreverence. But she watched, too. Marked the shifts. "They play like they don't know what they're doing," she murmured, eyes glittering, "until they do."

Eliza remained still, focused. She didn't just see the magic—she studied its blueprint. Confidence had a cadence. Control could be offered, then reclaimed. She tracked the tempo of every turn with clinical precision.

When Cher's sultry monologue began—glass in hand, hair wild, voice like velvet poison—the room fell utterly still. No breath, no movement.

A blonde, a brunette, a redhead. A story of rebellion wrapped in glamour. Not resisting power—rewriting it. Sweet as sugar. Sharp as steel.

As the final frame dissolved into black, there was no applause. They weren't entertained. This was a training video. They were activated. They were prepared.

Virginia rose, stretching slow, catlike. Her voice curled through the quiet. "That," she said, "is how you play the long game. Not with fury. With finesse. As sisters."

Eliza let her thoughts drift momentarily—back to the pages, the ink, the slow unraveling of meaning through translation and decoding. The weight of knowledge, the thrill of discovery.

But then—she pulled herself back.

If Madame deemed this training necessary, it was necessary.

Eliza had never dismissed Virginia's skills outright—but she had, admittedly, thought them frivolous in comparison to her own studies.

Now, after watching *The Reader* and *The Witches of Eastwick,* she had to acknowledge something uncomfortable. She had been wrong.

Where she had studied ancient texts, and Audrey conspiracy theories, Virginia had been honing something just as critical—the art of influence, of presence, of power woven into perception.

This was not just performance. This was mastery.

Eliza exhaled, releasing the last remnants of hesitation.

"Focus," she reminded herself.

There would be time for translations later. For now, this was the priority.

Eliza realized she had in fact been dismissing the studies of women!

The next day they had their final fitting for their gowns. At the second fitting, Madame circled them like a sculptor surveying her nearly finished marble—watching not just for flaws, but for confirmation of intent. Her gaze swept over every seam, every contour of fabric, measuring not just fit, but effect. Silence stretched taut in the room, punctuated only by the soft whisper of her steps across the floor.

Then, with a single, sharp nod and a flicker of satisfaction in her eyes, she spoke.

"Perfect."

Not a stitch out of place. Not a breath of uncertainty left hanging. The dresses didn't just fit—they declared. And for once, even Eliza,

Virginia, and Audrey stood silent, no edits, no clever remarks. Just stillness. Just recognition. They now had their armor of fabric and seduction.

The kitchen was quiet, wrapped in the hush of evening, the Hall softened by the low hum of distant conversation and the occasional clink of ceramic. The women gathered their evening snacks in whispers of silk and satin, the rustle of fabric barely audible over the hush.

Sister Lily stood in the doorway.

Her presence was gentle but weighted—like an old book on a well-worn shelf, full of stories, layered with time. She watched them not with scrutiny, but with recognition. Pride. A quiet kind of approval shaped by years.

"You are ready," she said, her voice warm and steady, as if stating a truth they'd already begun to feel but hadn't dared name.

The twinkle in her eye wasn't mischief—it was memory. It was history. It was the understanding of someone who had lived nearly a century and carried both the burden and the beauty of that knowing.

"I've been watching you all week," she added, her gaze sweeping over them with affection. Her eyes were deep-set and weary, but alive. "Tomorrow, I return to the convent. I will pray for you tomorrow night."

That, too, was a blessing.

The words didn't need unpacking. They understood.

Virginia's lips curled into a quiet smile. Eliza gave a single, thoughtful nod. Audrey, always the fighter, met Sister Lily's gaze without blinking—accepting the benediction as one soldier might from another.

The three—blonde, brunette, redhead—moved toward her as one.

They wrapped their arms around her, surrounding her in warmth and silk, in youth and reverence. A single tear slipped down Sister Lily's cheek. She didn't brush it away.

Life, she knew, was a braid of joy and sorrow—and sometimes, the two arrived hand in hand.

And in that moment—in the hush and the closeness, in the weight of unspoken things—the week's preparation hardened into something clear. Something undeniable.

They were no longer preparing.

They were ready.

THE DAY UNFOLDED EXACTLY as Madame had instructed—an early workout, time for reading, a window for rest. But still, anticipation lingered. It settled in their shoulders, the base of the spine—muscles taut, minds too alert to relax.

So instead of returning to the gym, they listened to something quieter. Instinct.

Barefoot, they walked to the courtyard. The stone was warm underfoot, the breeze alive with birdsong and memory. They moved not toward exertion, but into stillness.

Yoga. Breath. Control. Presence.

Virginia led. Her motions were fluid, grounded—each stretch less about flexibility and more about focus. She didn't speak. She didn't need to.

Audrey followed, slower, looser. Her laughter was gone, replaced with breath. With every exhale, she let go—of worry, of tension, of the coil behind her ribs that had been tightening all week.

Eliza resisted. At first.

Her mind pinged back to logistics, exit points, contingency plans. But the stillness pulled at her. Demanded less thinking. More being. She let the movement win. For once.

And then, without ceremony, they found stillness. Not performance. Not posturing. Just presence. Just three women, barefoot on warm stone, letting the breath move through them like music.

Tomorrow would come soon enough.

Tonight, they weren't ornaments. They weren't pawns. They were women who had studied, calculated, embodied every possible angle.

Because power—true power—wasn't just readiness.

It was knowing when to wait.

Despite the weight of the evening ahead, Madame still had a brothel to run. But before the first clients arrived, before the façade of elegance fully descended, she sought out the trio.

Her voice was steady—cut with iron, not affection. The weight of her words didn't burden; it braced.

"You are ready."

Not reassurance. Not encouragement. Just fact.

Eliza straightened. Audrey let her breath ease out slowly. Virginia dipped her gaze—brief, reverent—not in submission, but in acknowledgment.

"Listen. Observe. Gather. And remember—powerful men believe they control everything. Let them."

The meaning was crystalline. Let them believe. Let them underestimate. Let them hand over the very thing they thought they were guarding.

Perception, Madame knew, was the most seductive weapon of all.

She didn't stay to coddle. She didn't need to. Her part was done.

Soon, the maids would come. The gowns would be zipped, the jewels clasped, the final touch of powder set in place.

And when the doors to Barkley Mansion opened, the trio wouldn't enter as decoration. They would glide in as precision-forged instruments of grace, intellect, and intent. Not guests. Not pawns.

Women who knew exactly what they were doing.

⁂

The dressing room was alive with movement as maids worked swiftly, sculpting each woman into a vision designed to distract, entice, deceive.

Music played in the background—a slow, sultry rhythm, threading through the space as hands adjusted fabric, curled hair, and darkened lips to perfection.

Eliza sat still as a brush traced kohl along her lashes, deepening the richness of her brown eyes. Her bronze gown, sleek with understated shimmer, clung just enough to suggest softness—but was cut in a way that allowed movement if needed. The maids fastened the clasp of her necklace, the hollow pendant holding a sleeping powder, invisible to anyone not looking for it.

Beside her, Virginia lifted her arms, allowing the maids to tighten the structured bodice of her sapphire dress—a weapon in itself, designed to enhance her buxom frame, the illusion of vulnerability that made men foolish. Across the room, Audrey inspected the final adjustment of her emerald gown, its flowing design meant to evoke intrigue, distraction.

The last touch—stilettos, wickedly sharp, lethal in ways few would expect.

"The heels could break ribs," Virginia murmured, turning her ankle slightly as the sleek black shoes were secured into place.

"Let's hope we don't need them," Eliza replied, though they all knew better.

Audrey adjusted the strap of hers, running her fingers over the polished surface, eyes flickering with quiet amusement. "Men never expect weapons from women they want to devour."

They were a blonde, a brunette, and a redhead, hand-picked not for who they were, but for what they represented.

The laughter came easily as the final touches were made, but beneath the sheen of perfume and silk, beneath the carefully crafted illusion, they all knew that tonight was pivotal. Even though it was only for a night, they were transferring from one gilded cage to another.

Madame stood tall with her Lieutenant Teresa at her side, they each took a turn inspecting, ensuring that not a hair, strap, or string was out of place on any of the trio of women. The Hall of Mary Ann had to be perfect, and this meant they in turn had to be perfect.

⮜ ✳ ⮞

The car glided past the towering marble buildings, the city unfolding before them like a world they had almost forgotten existed.

Virginia, Audrey, and Eliza pressed against the screened windows, their faces lit with a mixture of awe and nerves. They had walked the tight circuit around the Capitol, the Library, the well-monitored spaces within reach of The Hall—but this? This was different.

They hadn't been this far from the brothel since they were sixteen—nine years for each of these young women. Years of servitude, of training, of practice. All girls at the Hall of Mary Ann first studied and mastered the fine arts of erotica before being allowed to pursue other pursuits.

As they rolled down the National Mall, the expanse of green stretched wide before them, so open, so vast, so free, it almost felt unreal. The Washington Monument towered, gleaming in the afternoon light, more immense than they remembered. And then—the White House, a place they had heard whispered about in passing, but never truly seen.

"There it is," Audrey breathed, leaning closer, her fingertips grazing the window.

Virginia let out a low whistle. "It is so small compared to everything else," she observed.

"That is the house where one brother lives," Eliza stated. "Now we will get to see the house of the other."

Eliza felt the weight of it—the juxtaposition of history and secrecy, of structures built to command obedience and women who had learned to navigate power in silence.

And soon, they would step beyond the window, beyond observation, beyond quiet speculation.

Above them hovercraft and drones followed the assigned routes that had been agreed upon years ago by the FAA and the city. The lights were glowing from every shop, bright and intoxicating.

And then came Dupont Circle.

The car wound through the tight streets, passing boutiques, cafes, places where people walked freely, their steps unburdened by the weight of secrecy. Men escorted wives, sisters, mothers, and daughters—ordinary in their freedom.

And finally—the Barkley Mansion loomed ahead, its grandeur untouched by time, its presence undeniable. The home of the Barkley Family, the President's Brother.

Audrey exhaled sharply. "I'm either thrilled or completely terrified."

Virginia adjusted her posture, smoothing imaginary wrinkles from her dress. "Both is fair," she responded playfully to her friend with a wink.

Eliza said nothing, just watched as they approached the gate, knowing this moment—this journey—was a turning point. She knew that she would have to work harder than ever to be the person that men wanted her to be. Madame had explained that the night she had been distracted she had received her highest marks ever, that the men had viewed her as demure, their idealized version of a woman. Tonight, she would pretend to be the person the world wanted her to be and remember everything.

Tonight, they were no longer observers of the story. They were part of it.

They would listen. They would watch. They would gather.

Tonight, they would make Madame—and the Hall of Mary Ann—proud.

THE **H**ALL OF **M**ARY Ann understood the importance of presence—power wasn't just what was spoken or traded, but what
was seen, what was felt, what was carefully crafted. The sleek
black car didn't just transport Eliza, Virginia, and Audrey—it announced
them, shielding them until the exact moment they were meant to be
revealed. As the doors opened, the three women stepped out with calculated precision, their movements effortless yet intentional. Flawless.
Poised. A performance woven into reality.

There were self-driving cars, hovercrafts, and quiet innovations, but
they lacked the weight, the undeniable presence of old money opulence.
This wasn't about convenience. This was about legacy, about control,
about walking into a room and making sure everyone knew who held the
real power. Madame Mary Margaret understood that tonight was about
showmanship and she and her institution had a reputation to maintain.

The two gladiator-style drivers remained seated, their presence a silent warning—these were not mere escorts, but women carved from the
world before the collapse, the kind who had once fought in cages under

neon lights and who had once entertained roaring crowds. Their sharp gazes swept the perimeter once, ensuring the three walked into the party without interference. They would not park the car, but rather strategically drive to surveil the exits. The brothel had a strict 2:00 a.m. curfew that no power was above. The drivers were there to protect their charges and ensure they arrived back to the Hall of Mary Ann safely.

As Eliza, Virginia, and Audrey walked up the three steps to the entryway, their wrist codes were scanned. Their biometrics, bags, and jewelry were scanned. Eliza's vial was determined to be harmless. Most of the elite knew the value of a little *nose candy* for the ladies, and it would have been anomalous for them not to be wearing spiked heels.

"You must be here for Mr. Barkley," the butler smiled, seeing the green scan. If there were security concerns, patrons were directed to go to the right. "Go straight into the main parlor and he will meet you."

Inside, the air was thick with perfume and hushed conversations, the scent of expensive cigars curling through the atmosphere, punctuated by the soft effervescence of champagne. At the threshold, a man awaited them with a tray of chilled glasses, the liquid catching the light like molten gold, tiny bubbles like diamonds floating to the top. His perfectly measured smile was just another part of the illusion—hospitality wrapped in control.

As Eliza reached for a glass, Madame Mary Margaret's words echoed within her mind—firm, unwavering, meant to steady her before she lost herself in the swirl of power and deception.

"Listen. Observe. Gather. And remember—powerful men believe they control everything. Let them think so."

She took a slow sip, the taste crisp against her tongue.

The parlor pulsed with controlled decadence and the quiet hum of power trading hands without a single word. Mr. Barkley—"Call me Dave"—stood at the center, basking in the slow ripple of admiration and envy that followed his every move.

For an older man, he looked unnaturally smooth, the telltale signs of Botox, fillers, weight-loss drugs, and quiet vanity sculpting his features into something just shy of ageless. His tailored tuxedo, expensive but relaxed, reinforced his effortless dominance over the space—wealth without pretense, power without exertion.

But the night wasn't just about him. Men had gathered here from across the world—politicians, industrialists, brokers of influence, each escorted by rarities selected with painstaking precision.

The women were exotic collectibles, dressed in gossamer fabrics so sheer they barely existed, designed to enhance their allure without ever offering real concealment. Their origins were carefully curated—a stunning Indian beauty, her skin kissed by gold embroidery; a Japanese Geisha, poised like a living doll; a striking Nubian goddess, wrapped in fabric so delicate it seemed woven of moonlight.

It was a game of possession, illusion, status—each man displaying his prize, each woman existing within the careful choreography of desire and control.

And yet, Virginia, Eliza, and Audrey stood apart—a deliberate trio meant to outshine all the others, not just accessories, but a statement, a show of power.

Dave's slow, knowing smile deepened as the other men watched him, each gaze filled with a silent acknowledgment of who held the true prize tonight.

Eliza took in the room with practiced ease, her gaze sweeping across the polished surfaces, the hushed conversations, the silent exchanges of possession disguised as indulgence. Men—from every continent, every seat of power, every creed—stood here, bound not by language or ideology, but by something deeper, more primal, more absolute.

Control.

The women—ornaments, curated for exoticism, novelty, status—silent trophies. She still felt like she was missing something, but perhaps being a part of the pattern she was too close to see it.

She simply smiled. Because that, too, was part of the game.

Dave settled into a low, sleek sofa, his posture deliberate—casual dominance, the kind perfected by men who knew their power wasn't questioned. Virginia perched at his feet on a stool, a display as much as a placement, her presence meant to reinforce his status. Audrey and Eliza flanked him on either side, poised yet effortlessly accessible, the trio sculpted for effect, for envy, for admiration. The blonde, the brunette, the redhead, reinforcing that Dave Barkley was a man that had it all.

Dave leaned back, swirling the scotch in his glass. He savored his own words as much as the 60-year-old scotch, a testament to his influence. The room quivered with quiet indulgence, power settling into corners like perfumed smoke.

"Did you study the dossiers my agents sent you, my pets?" He asked the trio with a smile. "No need to answer now. I will let you know my thoughts here and you can tell me yours another time."

He didn't rush, his eyes flickering toward familiar faces, nodding in measured acknowledgment, the silent language of debts owed and favors yet to be called in.

"You see," Dave mused, his hand trailing slowly over Audrey's wrist before shifting to Eliza's knee, "there's power in being needed."

"See the Sheik?" He tilted his chin toward the regal figure in the corner, his robes pristine, his posture effortlessly commanding. "Oil. He owes me for keeping his supply lines clean." His hand trailed along Virginia's collarbone.

His gaze shifted, landing on a sleek businessman from Korea, his tailored suit cut with surgical precision. "Him? Bitcoin." Dave chuckled, taking a slow sip. "Thought he was ahead of the game. Then the market took a dip, and suddenly, I had leverage." His hand trailed from Virginia to Eliza's thigh.

Across the room, the Italian stood with quiet confidence, sipping his own drink like he was above it all, but Dave's smirk deepened. "Thinks he's untouchable because he comes from old money." Dave scoffed, flicking a dismissive glance in the man's direction and shifting his glass to his other hand, slowly reaching over to twine his hands in Audrey's beautiful red wave of curls. "But when debt comes calling? Even old wealth bends. Had to hand over one of his villas to keep himself breathing."

His fingers drifted lazily over Virginia's shoulder again, tracing patterns over exposed skin, his enjoyment palpable—not just in the room's admiration, but in the undeniable proof of his reach, his control.

"Some owe me money. Some owe me favors. But my favorite ones?" He leaned back leisurely, letting his fingertips brush the edge of Virginia's bustline before shifting to Audrey's thigh.

"The men that owe me both." He chuckled. "Men like my brother. Mr. President owes me everything," he said with quiet pride.

Eliza's gaze swept the room, her carefully controlled expression masking the storm brewing beneath the surface. Fifty she counted. Fifty couples. Fifty men indulging in their curated fantasies, each one parading a woman meant to enhance their presence, their status, their power. She wondered, for a fleeting moment, how their wives felt. Were they ignorant? Complicit? Or simply resigned to the fact that this was the world now, where their place had been reduced to necessity rather than influence?

The thought pulled her back—back to the orphanage, back to whispered conversations among the older girls, back to the truths spoken in hushed voices. Girls like her, tested. Found barren. Sorted accordingly. Those who could bear children were kept, trained for marriage or worse, controlled breeding. Those who couldn't? They were sent to brothels, factories, their worth recalibrated, their futures rewritten.

A few had survived outside this system—women from the most powerful families, their positions protected by wealth and legacy, not fertility. But they were aging now, their influence fading, soon to be forgotten in a world that no longer saw value in their existence. There were also rumors of free people in the mountains, but who knew the truth of such things.

Eliza's fingers brushed absently over the fabric of her gown, her mind slipping to the ancient text she had been transcribing earlier, the faded script whispering of a forgotten concept—harnessing power from each inhabited continent. The thought sparked a new, calculated resolve.

Eliza exhaled slowly, lowering her gaze, settling deeper into the performance. She let her hand idly glide along Dave's collar and reach his tie. She bit her lip and looked at him seductively. "It's so sexy to be with a man who is so powerful," she purred.

Dave shifted in his seat, the corner of his mouth tilting into a slow, confident smile as his gaze swept to Eliza. "Don't worry," he murmured, voice low and smooth. "Soon, I'll have all three of you to myself—in a private room. Then you can show me just how sexy I really am."

Eliza's lashes dipped, a flicker of mischief behind her cool composure. Virginia caught the cue. With the languid grace of someone entirely in control, she reached out, her fingers skimming lightly along Dave's thigh. The gesture was casual, veiled in suggestion, until her touch paused right at the sharp crease of his inseam. Her nails traced a subtle circle, barely there. With her other hand, she raised the champagne glass to her mouth and took a slow sip, gazing into Dave's eyes.

Audrey leaned forward with a soft laugh that turned heads from a few of the nearby men. "Shouldn't we take another turn about the room?" she said, her voice rich and suggestive. "You haven't had enough time to let the others see what they'll never have." She looked up at him through auburn lashes fringing her green eyes, then added with a coy little simper, "I do so love watching them burn with envy."

Dave gave a short chuckle, almost a purr, the kind that hummed with possession. He didn't need to answer; the way he stood—slowly, deliberately—said it all.

Dave walked casually across the marble floor, the low hum of conversation and crystal chimes of cocktail glasses trailing behind him. He approached a tall man near the bar—Mitchell Blackwell, one of the senior partners at the investment firm managing a sizable portion of Dave's portfolio. In a room full of eager hands and hollow smiles, Mitchell was one of the few Dave considered worth the price of a handshake.

"You're making every man here green with envy," Mitchell said with a knowing smirk, swirling the amber in his glass. "It's fun to watch them squirm. Like waiting for the bride and groom to finally leave the reception." Mitchell was also here as a spectator at Dave's show.

Dave grinned, all wolfish charm and steel behind the eyes. "You always did enjoy the anticipation."

Mitchell leaned in slightly, lowering his voice just enough to keep the exchange private. "So… when are you taking those three beauties upstairs? Every other man here is waiting to enjoy their presents and can't until you unwrap yours."

Dave chuckled and glanced back at the trio—Eliza, Virginia, and Audrey—each of them radiant and dangerously self-possessed in their own way. They weren't just arm candy; they were fire on silk, and he knew exactly what kind of scene their presence painted. Blonde, brunette, and red hair stood out strikingly wrapped around him.

"Soon," he said, adjusting the cuff of his jacket. "But I like to let the tension breathe. Makes the reveal all the more rewarding."

Mitchell raised his glass. "To patience, then. And the rewards of power well-played."

Their glasses clinked softly, a private toast between two men who understood that in rooms like this, control was the real currency—and Dave had it in spades. He gave a wink to Mitchell as he turned.

Slowly, Dave walked across the room, with his three trophies wrapped around him. He nodded at a few of the men as he passed them, silently acknowledging that when he left the room, they could have their own fun.

⪦ ✵ ⪧

The private room opened like a secret—discreet and drenched in indulgence. Behind the velvet curtain and soundproofed walls, it felt like time stilled. The lighting was low and amber-rich, casting long, honeyed shadows. Everything from the suede-lined panels to the subtle thrum of jazz in the background had been chosen for intimacy.

At the center of the room stood a massive, custom-built sofa bed—wide as a banquet table, low to the ground, and dressed in deep charcoal velvet. Plush cushions in shades of oxblood and smoke were arranged like careless offerings. It was less a piece of furniture and more a stage—an invitation.

Virginia was the first to claim it. She let her stiletto heels fall to the floor with a soft thud and eased herself down, legs folding beneath her with feline grace. Her blonde hair shimmered as she tossed it back, settling into the cushions like they'd been fluffed just for her.

Eliza followed with quiet precision. She moved with that cool, brunette elegance that turned heads and kept them turned. She perched for a moment on the edge of the bed, then reclined fully, stretching out like a queen in a portrait—silent, knowing, perfectly still.

Audrey was last, trailing one hand along the wall as she walked, eyes flicking from the subtle art on the shelves to the bar stocked with rare scotches. The redhead gave Dave a lingering look as she approached the bed, then sank her willowy frame into the space between the other two women, her dress slipping just enough to hint at skin.

Dave stood a moment longer near the bar, rolling the weight of the moment in his mind like a fine drink on the tongue. He removed his jacket, folded it carefully over the arm of a chair, then unfastened the top buttons of his shirt.

"You three look like a vision painted by sin and patience," he said, his voice thick with heat.

Virginia shifted slightly, her bare feet brushing Eliza's thigh, her blue bodice almost ripping against the strain of containing her breasts. "Then come worship what you conjured."

Audrey smirked, curling her legs beneath her. "Or are you going to stand there and talk until the music stops?"

She knew she was brazen and pushing Dave. She thought, 'Redheads are wild,' arching her brow.

Eliza said nothing. She lifted the glass; a silent invitation laced with defiance.

Dave stepped forward, taking the glass—and the invitation—with a grin that said he had no intention of rushing what was about to unfold. He enjoyed his power and was going to use up every moment until he had to let these beauties go.

Dave moved toward the bed slowly, deliberately, as if crossing a threshold more sacred than space itself. The women watched him—three muses, three forces of nature wrapped in silk and shadow. His wrist monitor beeped, and he read that one of the female bodyguards from the Hall of Mary Ann was stationed with his butler outside the room, so he would need to be finished by 1:30 a.m. to ensure the ladies made it home in time.

He knelt first beside Virginia. Her breath caught as his hand found her ankle, fingers sliding along the curve of her calf, lingering at the bend of her knee. She leaned back, letting her head fall into the pillows, her golden hair fanning out in soft waves. Dave knew that some men wanted only to dominate women, but he enjoyed taking his time. Power had to be cultivated, and he was one of the few men who truly understood power.

Next was Audrey. She pulled him toward her by the open collar of his shirt, her lips brushing the edge of his jaw—not kissing, just tracing. Her breath was warm, teasing, and it pulled a low sound from his throat, somewhere between a laugh and a groan.

Eliza didn't move at all. She watched him with that cool, unshakable stare—the kind that could unravel a man without ever touching him. But when his hand finally touched her wrist, she turned it palm-up, fingers slightly curled, an unspoken yes. He had never been with Eliza in the brothel and was curious how she would compare to the other two.

As Dave sank onto the bed with the three goddesses in a private myth of his making, a slow, satisfied heat spread in his groin. This was his conquest. He loved being envied, whispered about, and quietly feared.

They moved together with quiet urgency, a tangle of limbs and breath—it was like a dance. The ladies had been trained for such situations and let this unfold naturally, understanding their roles and the inevitable conclusion.

Outside that door, men were still swirling glasses of overpriced scotch and pretending not to glance toward the curtain they'd all seen him disappear behind. The same men who owed him. Who wore money like armor but were still less powerful than him.

Dave kissed Virginia first—slow and deliberate. Audrey came next, stoking him into a hotter, a more urgent rhythm. Eliza, ever patient, let him find her last. When their mouths met, there was no hesitation; she was a courtesan.

It was a choreography of surrender and control for the three ladies, each demonstrating her own unique skills and training. Heat, then stillness. Movement, then pause. Each of them offering something different, something vital.

Dave didn't try. He simply existed—and that was the difference.

He delighted in the resentment from the men outside this room like a storm in the air. The stiff smiles. The subtle bitterness. The way they laughed too loud when one of the women so much as glanced their way earlier in the night. Each knowing that this party was his stage and his alone.

No one else had three women like this orbiting them with such casual devotion. Each one stunning in her own right—Eliza, sharp and poised like a polished blade; Virginia, golden and effortless, the picture of decadent confidence; Audrey, wild-eyed and electric, a fiery storm.

Let them imagine what was happening in this room. Let them ache with it. And that, he thought with a slow smile, was the kind of wealth that really mattered. The power to consume the minds of both his friends and enemies.

Eliza stroked the fine chain of her necklace, the cool metal a grounding contrast to the warmth of the room. She hadn't expected Dave to give them the reins. Men like him, men used to closing deals with sheer presence, didn't usually know when to surrender it. But he had.

Pleasantly surprised didn't quite cover it. She had been prepared for the worst and was glad the sleeping powder could stay in the vial around her throat.

Virginia lounged beside her, golden and relaxed, sipping something strong and smoky. Audrey was already half draped across Dave's chest, her red hair fanning out over the velvet. But Eliza sat upright, her back against the cushioned headboard, brown eyes calm, calculating.

Dave had brought them into this room with all the confidence of a king opening a private vault. Yet once inside, he hadn't barked commands or directed the energy. He'd watched. Waited. Let them move first.

Smart, Eliza thought.

Control wasn't always about action. Sometimes it was about knowing when to step back—and that was rare in men in today's world with too much money and too many mirrors.

She watched him now, his hand resting on Audrey's hip, his head tilted slightly toward Virginia's laughter, his gaze flickering just briefly—just—to her.

Yes, he was enjoying himself. But he was watching, too. Testing the boundaries between power and permission.

And that confused her more than anything.

Eliza let her fingers trail down her collarbone, slow and thoughtful, her necklace shifting in the low light. She caught Dave's eye and offered a faint smile—just enough to keep him wondering.

She leaned back, finally relaxing into the cushions, folding one leg over the other with elegant precision, giving into the moment that she had been trained to perform.

Let him think he had won something. Let him call Madame Mary Margaret and ask for the three of them again.

⋙ ✸ ⋘

Eliza, Audrey, and Virginia assisted each other in getting back into their gowns and rearranging their hair as best as possible.

Dave let the indulgence linger a little longer, savoring the envy that saturated the air just outside this room as he let his butler know that the ladies would be ready to leave in a few minutes and that he wanted them to be discreetly led down a side exit.

The next time he wanted to show off these beauties they would need to be coiffed and their makeup perfected. Right now, the scene of them covered in a slight sheen with mussed hair and smudged makeup was his private enjoyment.

Virginia, Eliza, and Audrey dressed one another with effortless grace, their movements calculated, their roles played to perfection. His eyes lingered on them.

The women were escorted back toward the waiting car, the sleek vehicle belonging to The Hall of Mary Ann, designed for just such exits. As the doors closed, sealing them off from the evening's extravagance, the weight of the night settled into the quiet between them.

A performance flawlessly executed. Yet beneath the surface, Eliza's mind was still working.

When they arrived at the Hall of Mary Ann, Madame Mary Margaret let out a deep sigh. She had been pensive all night.

THE NIGHT WASN'T OVER—NOT yet.

Back at The Hall of Mary Ann, the atmosphere shifted from performance to precision. Eliza, Audrey, and Virginia, still wrapped in the lingering energy of the evening, sat with Madame Mary Margaret, Sister Hope, and several key staff and members of her inner circle, ready to document every whispered exchange, every fleeting glance, every debt owed and favor traded.

For the three courtesans, exhaustion clung to their limbs, but excitement kept their minds sharp. They had walked through a palace of indulgence and come back with knowledge worth more than any jewel or promise.

A maid entered with soft dressing gowns—plush, warm, designed for comfort after a night spent in silk and control. Hot chocolate followed, rich and steaming, the kind that lingered on the tongue like quiet indulgence after the spectacle of champagne.

The bodyguards were debriefed first, their observations sharp, detached, and strategic. Who watched too closely? Who said too much?

Who seemed unsettled? Every detail mattered.

Madame sat back, watching the trio carefully, fingers pressed together in contemplation.

"Tell me everything," she said, pulling out the first of the fifty dossiers.

Eliza leaned back, fingers absently tracing the rim of her cup, her focus on the slow unraveling of the night's events. The room buzzed quietly—Madame listening with sharp precision, Sister Hope taking measured notes, the bodyguards offering clipped, tactical observations.

Sometimes when they were discussing one dossier, one of them would have to flip backwards or forwards to another. Eliza also observed that Madame and her team were creating two sets of files; noting her observation, Madame said, "One for your patron, and one for us." She gave a cunning smile, "Ours might be a bit more detailed; it's not as if anyone knows you have had more than a week of preparation for intelligence gathering."

She was so immersed in the conversation, in the deconstruction of power plays, in the lingering tension of what they had witnessed, that she barely registered Agnes in the corner.

Agnes had a way of existing in the periphery, slipping between conversations without ever demanding space. She operated in the shadows—not invisible, but unnoticed until the exact moment she needed to be seen.

It wasn't until Eliza caught the flicker of movement from the edge of her vision—the subtle pull of thread, the quiet precision of pins pushed into a map—that she fully registered what Agnes was doing.

Mapping. Not just locations, but alliances. Debts. Control.

Eliza's breath slowed. This wasn't just documentation—it was strategy!

"What's the pattern?" she asked, forcing her voice to stay level.

Agnes didn't look up immediately. She tugged another thread, ensuring the tension held before finally meeting Eliza's gaze.

"It's power," she murmured. "Where it flows. Where it falters. And where we might tilt it."

The realization settled deep in Eliza's chest. She watched Agnes in the dim light, the careful precision of her movements, the effortless way she threaded lines between pins—an architect of secrets, mapping the unseen currents of power.

For so long, she had thought Agnes had lost something with her scars. That they had taken something from her, stripped her of ease, of belonging.

But now? She saw it. Agnes had gained something instead. Anonymity.

She could move through the world in daylight, unchallenged, untouched, unchaperoned because people looked away. Not out of cruelty, but out of their own discomfort, their instinct to avoid what unsettled them.

In that avoidance, she had found a freedom most would never know.

No one watched her too closely. No one questioned her presence. And so she listened. She gathered. She moved unseen, unheard, unnoticed—collecting information.

Eliza exhaled slowly, absorbing the realization, tucking it into the quiet chambers of her mind.

Agnes wasn't just skilled. She was a ghost in a world that didn't know it was haunted, and her mind saw the networks and patterns that others missed.

The night had stretched into dawn, the weight of secrets and strategy lingering in the stillness of The Hall of Mary Ann.

Eliza, Audrey, and Virginia finally stood, the adrenaline fading as exhaustion crept in, tugging at their limbs, dulling the sharp edges of their thoughts. Across the room, Madame Mary Margaret exhaled slowly, pressing her fingers to her temples—not in frustration, but in the quiet resignation of knowing there would be more nights like this.

Sister Hope, despite her weariness, still had tasks ahead. Six of the ladies awaited their morning walk and market trip, their schedules uninterrupted by the late-night unraveling of power plays and whispered transactions. She would push through, as she always did.

For Eliza, Audrey, and Virginia, there was finally permission to rest.

The corridors were filled with quiet chatter as many of the ladies were getting up to start their day. Outside, the world carried on—markets opening, whispers shifting, deals being made. But inside these walls, for now, they could let the performance fade.

Eliza was surprised to find herself awake at noon, the hum of voices from luncheon wrapping around her like a quiet pulse of energy. The women gathered, shared, nourished themselves—not just physically, but in the quiet solidarity of their existence.

She ate quickly, absorbing the rhythm of it, before slipping away to the library—her sanctuary, her escape, her battlefield of discovery.

Today, she was more eager than ever, fingers itching to uncover the layers within the ancient text she was translating.

The legend of Spider Woman, carved into Navajo tradition, whispered of a power that transcended time—the first weaver of the universe, the architect of creation, balance, and the Beauty Way—a philosophy of harmony within the mind, body, and soul.

Aspects of the divine feminine wove through nearly every ancient belief system, each culture shaping it uniquely but always returning to the same truths: fertility, creativity, intuition—the force that heals, nourishes, and transforms.

Eliza had read before that tapping into this energy wasn't just spiritual, it was revolutionary.

In some traditions, the divine feminine was feared—controlled, diminished, reshaped into something passive rather than powerful. But in others, it remained a force of resilience, a source of healing, a guide for those lost in chaos. Yet here, within these old teachings, was another truth they could reclaim, not through force, but through balance.

She thought of the women in the early days after the COVID19 vaccine rollout, women who were told their complaints didn't matter, those who had been told they were wrong to speak out, that their bodies' signals and issues didn't matter. That women scientists tried to bring to light from their own experiences.

She was searching for more than translation. She was searching for something forgotten, something buried, something waiting to be reborn.

Eliza leaned over the fragile pages, her pulse quickening as she decoded the next passage. The ink, faded yet defiant, whispered ancient truths few had laid eyes on in centuries.

The text spoke of 'the Web of the Universe', but not just as a metaphor—it was a map, an interconnected force woven through time, anchored in the power of the divine feminine.

She traced the lines of the script, catching something—a reference to hidden knowledge, sealed away because it threatened those who sought dominance rather than balance.

A passage stood out:

"She who understands the weave may unravel control. She who reads the lost patterns may restore what was broken."

Eliza inhaled sharply. This wasn't just about mythology. This was about power—real power. A power that most men could never understand, and this is why they feared it.

There were references to the lost threads of the continents, echoes of something she had uncovered before. Could it be connected to what was buried beneath the collapse? The knowledge stripped from women before history was rewritten? Before men drowned the wise women of Salem as witches?

She flipped the page, ink staining her fingertips.

And then she saw it—a pattern, half-erased but still visible, aligning key locations across the world.

A web indeed. She had a spark of recognition as she remembered Agnes's threads and pins on the wall. They were a match.

The room was dim, the soft glow of candlelight casting flickering shadows against the thick velvet drapes. The use of real candles was a treat, a testament to the discovery that Eliza had made. Madame Mary Margaret and Sister Hope sat across from one another, their posture composed—but beneath the surface, a quiet tension ran like an undercurrent beneath their excitement.

The parchment lay spread before them, translated passages meticulously copied, the network of power now clear. This was a breakthrough—but breakthroughs carried risk.

"The Abbess must be summoned," Madame murmured, smoothing a careful hand over the page. Her voice was steady, but there was something else there—not fear, exactly, but reverence. A knowledge that they were stepping into something deeper than either had anticipated.

Sister Hope nodded, pulling at the edges of her sleeve, a rare tell of nerves. They were moving into uncertain territory.

"This must be done quietly," she said. "No one outside the inner circle knows of our suspicions—let's keep it that way."

Madame hesitated before responding, her thoughts drifting, as they sometimes did, toward the implied connection between the Abbess of Carla Mercy Convent and Eliza's mother. It had been whispered about for years—never spoken plainly, never confirmed. But there were too many small details, too many unspoken truths tucked into the past.

And now, as they prepared to escalate this discovery, they were stepping closer to those buried truths than they ever had before.

"Lent is approaching," Madame finally said. "The timing is perfect. Fewer patrons, fewer eyes. A visit will raise no suspicions. Based on our success this year, the Abbess might even recommend extra penance. "

Sister Hope exhaled, pressing her fingers together in contemplation. "Then it's decided."

The two women sat in the quiet, the weight of their decision settling between them. And though neither said it aloud, they both knew this wasn't just about history anymore. It was about something far more dangerous.

And far more powerful. And the question remained: what did Dave—the President's brother and one of the most powerful men in the world—know about it? In the network that Agnes had mapped, was he the spider or something else?

ELIZA IMMERSED HERSELF IN the ancient texts, the weight of history pressing against her fingertips as she traced the faded lines of knowledge almost forgotten. Despite the looming visit from the Abbess, her mind remained sharp, her focus unwavering.

The library was never meant to be a library—it had once been a wine cellar; long before laws reshaped its purpose, before knowledge became something to be rationed rather than shared. The thick stone walls still held the ghost of old oak barrels, the scent of dust and history woven into every crevice.

Only a few nuns were allowed to visit at any time—permitted by the government to work among the so-called damned, their presence a charade to keep the evangelical vote. They were not meant to teach, not meant to question—only to perform their roles in the game. Little did the authorities know that the sisters had quickly realized that they were all united under oppression and collaborated together.

At the long oak tables, under old flickering fluorescent lights, courtesans sat across from cloistered women in simple robes, their fingers equally stained with ink, their eyes sharp with knowledge. A sister might translate a passage from Latin while a prostitute, such as Eliza, studied tribal histories.

She studied the records of the Navajo, the Hopi, the Iroquois Confederacy—including the Onondaga, Mohawk, Seneca, Cayuga, Oneida, and Tuscarora—the Cherokee, and the twin tribes of the Chickasaw and Choctaw. Each culture had once thrived on matriarchal traditions, matrilineal succession, where power, lineage, and inheritance flowed through the mother's bloodline. The patterns were undeniable.

These societies had structured themselves around feminine wisdom, placing spiritual, communal, and political strength in the hands of women. They had understood balance, not as a battle between sexes but as a natural force—something woven into existence itself.

Eliza paused over a passage describing the Grandmothers' Council, where elder women guided decisions that affected entire nations. Their voices carried equal weight to warriors and chiefs, a reminder that power was not merely about force—it was about knowing when to wield it, when to preserve it, and when to pass it on.

She exhaled slowly.

Modern governance had long buried these traditions, reshaping them into histories of conquest and erasure. But here, in these words, she saw a map. A guide back to something lost.

And perhaps—something waiting to return. Eliza could feel a tear forming in the corner of her brown eyes. She reflected on how different this was to the teaching of the orphanage.

Eliza had spent years internalizing the rigid doctrine instilled in the orphanage, the lessons drilled into every girl who passed through its doors. Eliza Noman had learned to read between the lines of history—not just what was written, but what had been erased, reshaped, or hidden. The echoes of matriarchal wisdom weren't limited to tribal history. Even in faith traditions once led by compassionate women, the same pattern of silencing had taken hold.

It had been 30 years since the Bishop Mariann Budde, once known for her unwavering stance on kindness, justice, and inclusion, had become a whispered name among those who still believed in her teachings. Her words had once challenged power, called for mercy, demanded accountability. But in a world where female leadership was seen as a threat, she had been systematically erased from public discourse.

Once a visible force of progressive faith, the Episcopal Church had been subsumed under Catholic oversight, its female leaders silenced as authoritarianism disguised itself in scripture. Eliza had never known the Episcopal Church as it once was—only as fragments, as whispers, as coded messages in underground texts.

Now in 2055 a woman's role was obedience, service, silence—the refrain repeated in measured tones, woven into lessons about propriety and duty. She had watched as others accepted it, their futures mapped out before them. A wife, a caretaker, a vessel for legacy, a servant, a slave, a whore—but never an architect of their own fate.

Yet even as a child, Eliza had questioned.

She had seen the contradiction—the quiet strength of the women who enforced these teachings, who understood survival in ways the world refused to acknowledge. They wielded power even as they denied it existed.

Still, the orphanage had tried to mold her. Tried to make her pliable, acceptable, unthinking.

She reflected on the memory of her mother and felt love for each of these women. The echo of the women from the past, the compassion and comradery of the women in her present, and the hope of love in the future.

But knowledge had always been difficult to kill.

Eliza jumped when she felt a light touch on her shoulder. Sister Hope stood behind her, eyes bright with quiet excitement.

"Come with me," she said.

They slipped into the same converted storage room where Sister Lily had once met with them. Sister Hope moved with reverence, and from beneath her shawl, she produced a worn paperback and handed it to Eliza.

Code Talker Stories.

Giddy, Eliza took it with both hands, letting it fall open naturally to a page. She read aloud, almost breathless:

"This book… it's like holding someone's memory in your hands. Not just one person—an entire language, an entire people."

Sister Hope settled into the chair across from her. "That's what it is. Memory made real. It's how people survive erasure."

Eliza scanned the page again, her voice soft but urgent. "They told us never to speak our language. Then they asked us to use it to save their sons."

She closed the book gently, her fingers resting on the cover. "They punished them for being who they were. And then depended on that very identity when everything was on the line."

"The same thing they do to women," Sister Hope said. "Suppress what makes us powerful, then quietly rely on it when no one else can do the work."

Eliza nodded slowly. "And they kept silent for so long. These men weren't even allowed to talk about it until decades later."

She held the book to her chest, voice barely audible now. "This is what daughters do—we uncover and capture what history tried to bury."

Sunday morning carried a strange, weighted hush through The Hall of Mary Ann. Gone was the usual rhythm of whispered indulgence, of quiet transactions and careful negotiations. Instead, anticipation thickened the air, pressing against the walls of the brothel, demanding restraint.

The doors would be locked to patrons today. For today, the first Sunday of Advent, the Hall would cease to be what it had always been—transforming, shifting, preparing for something altogether different.

The Abbess would arrive in the afternoon, bringing with her several nuns from the cloister. They would come after public mass, stepping into this house of women where lines between virtue and sin blurred in ways that few dared to acknowledge.

Every woman within the Hall—from the courtesans to the maids, from the musicians to Madame herself—was expected to be present.

And with that expectation came the challenge of transformation.

Eliza, Virginia, and Audrey had spent the morning being prepared by the maids, preparing gowns, adjusting hems, repurposing silks into something both elegant and modest. The sewing kits emerged, forgotten dresses were salvaged, scarves became carefully crafted disguises, layering beauty beneath discretion.

Eliza stood before the mirror, running her hands over the delicate folds of fabric, reflecting on the irony of it all. Her brown eyes sparkled in anticipation.

Every day, they were required to be seen—but today, they had to conceal.

Virginia laughed, her blue eyes dancing, pinning the last adjustment to her sleeves. Audrey rolled her green eyes but let the maids finish smoothing the embroidered edges of her bodice.

Some of the ladies joked at the absurdity of dressing for virtue in a house designed for vice. Others—quieter, more cautious—recognized that today was no ordinary day.

This was something else. A moment neither indulgent nor entirely pious. For today, they were not courtesans, not entertainers, not women bound to their roles. They were something in between—something waiting, something watching.

And soon, the Abbess—silent judge, secret conspirator, and one of the last women to hold power before the fall—would decide what came next.

The Hall of Mary Ann stood in solemn reverence, the golden morning light casting long shadows across the stripped-down parlor. Gone were the velvet drapes and ornate furnishings—only stone, wood, and silence remained, carving out space for reflection.

The Abbess of Carla Mercy entered, her ceremonial robes trailing behind her like waves, each measured step pressing the moment deeper into memory.

Madame Mary Margaret inclined her head in respectful greeting. "Reverend Mother."

The Abbess's gaze was sharp, knowing. "The Hall remains in capable hands," she said quietly. Her voice held more than approval—it carried expectation.

Then Sister Hope stepped forward, and the room hushed as she raised her head, her words the first declaration of the season.

"Lent is not a time of absence—it is a time of presence. A stripping away of excess, yes, but not as punishment. As return."

She walked slowly along the center aisle, allowing the weight of the words to settle.

"This is the season to remember what remains when the world takes everything away."

And then, the Abbess spoke, her voice quiet but unshakable.

"Restraint is not weakness. It is the quiet knowledge that we do not require excess to hold power."

The words settled like stone into water, rippling through the gathered women.

Audrey let out a slow breath, Eliza pressed her hands together, Virginia lowered her gaze—not in submission, but in understanding.

The chant began, soft and steady. The Hall transformed—not by ritual, but by the realization of what was already within.

And for this hour, it was sacred.

Then the Abbess spoke. Her voice was low, but clear, cutting through the stillness like a bell.

"May the words of my mouth and the meditation of all our hearts be acceptable in your sight, O God."

"Today I honor a wise woman from an earlier time, Rev. Mariann Budde, who called us to mercy and unity in 2025."

"As a people, as a sisterhood, we gather this morning to pray for unity. Not for agreement—but for the kind of unity that fosters community across diversity and division. A unity that serves the common good. A unity that unites Saints and sinners without judgment."

"Unity is a way of being with one another that respects difference, honors multiple perspectives, and insists on the dignity of every voice. It is what enables us to care for one another—even when we disagree.

"We see this unity in action when people dedicate themselves to the good of others without conditions—unity, in this sense, is sacrificial. As love is sacrificial.

"Our sacred texts remind us: love your neighbor. Love your enemy. Pray for those who persecute you. Be merciful as God is merciful. Forgive as you have been forgiven. Welcome the outcast."

"Yes, this kind of unity is aspirational. It asks a lot of us. Our scriptures are clear—God is not impressed with empty words. Actions matter more than the prayers. And when hopes and dreams are lost—it is identity, dignity, and survival. So is unity even possible?"

"I believe it is. I hope we all do. I am a person of faith, surrounded by people of faith. And with God's help, I believe unity is possible—not perfectly, for we are imperfect people—but enough. Enough to keep striving toward equality and human dignity."

"We rightly pray for God's help. But we must also build the foundations on which unity depends. Let me name three."

"First: dignity. Every person is made in the image of God."

"Second: honesty. Unity requires trust, and trust is built on truth."

"Third: humility. We are fallible. We fail. We carry blind spots and biases."

"With a unity that holds diversity, and with the solid foundations of dignity, honesty, and humility, we can do our part—here and now."

"Let me close with this:

May God grant us the strength and the courage:

To honor the dignity of every human being,

To speak the truth in love,

And to walk humbly with one another and with God."

"Amen."

No applause followed. Just stillness. A breath held in the bones of the Hall.

The Abbess lifted her gaze from the assembled faces, her eyes sweeping over each woman as if committing their solemnity to memory. The silence, so profound just moments before, now felt charged with a new, urgent energy. She turned to Madame Mary Margaret, a silent conversation passing between them that needed no words.

The Abbess solemnly departed, her robes flowing in her wake, followed by a recessional. The women, united, sinners, saints, and servants following.

Without a word, Madame Mary Margaret led the Abbess and the small group who had witnessed the evening's events into her private parlor.

Then, the Abbess's eyes found Eliza. A slow, deliberate movement like a falcon surveying the horizon—piercing, ancient, and oddly tender, made Eliza's breath catch. There was recognition there, a profound knowing that settled deep in Eliza's bones.

"Eliza," the Abbess's voice was softer now, yet it commanded attention. "You have been diligently unearthing truths that the powerful have sought to bury for centuries. The threads you traced in the library—the Web of the Universe—are not merely ancient myth. They are the blueprint of a power suppressed, a lineage broken, and a future waiting to be reclaimed."

Eliza felt a tremor run through her. She looked at Madame Mary Margaret, then at Sister Hope, both of whom watched the Abbess with unwavering focus.

"This Hall," the Abbess continued, gesturing with a hand that seemed both frail and incredibly strong, "is one of its anchors. A nexus point. Not merely a sanctuary for those cast out, but a keeper of forgotten knowledge, a place where the feminine spirit, so feared and demonized, has secretly thrived."

She paused, her gaze settling back on Eliza, a direct, unwavering intensity. "Your mother, Eliza, understood this weave better than most. She was not merely a keeper of this knowledge, but a weaver herself. Her fate was not a tragedy, but a sacrifice—her life intertwined with threads of power most feared to touch. A necessary severing of a powerful connection that the men who now rule believed would cripple the entire network."

Audrey shifted beside Eliza, a gasp escaping her lips. Virginia's eyes widened, her earlier composure visibly shaken.

"The patterns you uncovered, Eliza, that align with Agnes's maps of the present day... they are not coincidence. They are the pulse points of this ancient web, a network of spiritual, social, and even physical power that those in authority have actively sought to dismantle. The *barrenness* of women you read about. It was not chance. It was design—a calculated manipulation. A deliberate severing of the divine feminine's power to create, to nourish, to transform. Why else give young women and children with little risk of being impacted by a virus a vaccine; not been tested by time."

The room was utterly still, the weight of the revelation pressing down.

"Dave, the man who commissioned you to serve him at Barkley Mansion," the Abbess's voice hardened slightly, "at this time he is an architect, a builder. He is not merely a player in their political games; he is directly connected to the deliberate suppression of this ancient power. He knows about the Web of the Universe, or at least, he knows enough to seek it out, but whether he is friend or foe, we do not yet know."

The Abbess finally rose, her robes flowing around her like shadows. "The knowledge you carry, Eliza, is not just academic. It is a key. A key to understanding what was lost, and more importantly, what can be restored. You, Eliza, are a crucial thread in this re-weaving. The blood of this lineage flows within you."

She walked slowly towards Eliza, stopping directly in front of her. "Are you ready, child, to step into your mother's legacy? To become a weaver of the future, just as she was a weaver of the past?"

Eliza looked up at the Abbess, her heart pounding. The words of the sermon, the ancient texts, the painful truth of her mother's past, and the shocking implications of Dave's involvement swirled within her. She felt the weight of centuries, of sacrifice, and of an incredible, terrifying power.

"I am ready, Reverend Mother," Eliza whispered, her voice surprisingly steady, though her hands still trembled slightly. The realization solidified: her life, her history, and her very existence were not random. They were meticulously woven into a grand, dangerous, and sacred tapestry.

"Child, just remember that none of us can see everything and this is why unity is the key to strength," she paused. "I have just preached a sermon about honesty, but I am unable to disclose everything to you now. I have prepared some information that will go to Madame Mary Margaret, if anything should happen to me prior to the time to reveal this information to you. There are many paths and the paths change. It is my hope to walk beside you until the end—but hope is not a promise, and I will not offer you false ones. It is my goal to be with you until the end, but that is not a promise I can make."

The atmosphere in Madame Mary Margaret's private parlor shifted subtly, the weight of revelation settling into something quieter—not less important, but more deliberate.

The Abbess exhaled, folding her hands gently before her. "Refreshments," she requested with quiet authority, not simply as a formality, but as a moment to recalibrate, to allow what had just been spoken to settle into the bones of those listening.

The air held something unspoken, a pause stretched just enough to let the meaning of her words linger before the next layer was unveiled.

Madame gestured to a waiting servant; the silent understanding between them ensuring that warm drinks and light fare would arrive soon.

⇒ ✳ ⇐

The Abbess turned her gaze to Sister Hope, expectant, yet unwavering.

"Sister," the Abbess murmured, her tone carrying both invitation and command, "tell them what must be remembered."

Sister Hope straightened, her fingers resting lightly against the edge of the table, her expression measured, thoughtful, carefully withholding nothing and yet revealing only what was necessary.

"In the time before," she began, her voice calm but charged, "there were secrets that lived in plain sight. Not hidden—but made taboo to speak. And if you did, the punishment wasn't always loud. Sometimes it was silence. Dismissal. Erasure."

"The 2016 election was a choice between two flawed powers," she continued. "One who wielded his womanizing openly, and another who empowered it in silence. But the worst sin, the one that cost me more than I understood at the time, was believing that there could be more options."

Her voice didn't waver, but there was something else there—a hesitation not born of uncertainty, but of profound restraint.

"I wrote about this," she admitted, "for my political science class as a High School Senior. I thought that speaking it aloud—framing it as an intellectual argument—might make it easier." She paused, a flicker of sorrow crossing her features as she realized the young women in this room no longer had high school as an option, their paths so violently redirected.

Her fingers tapped absently against the table. Audrey noticed the subtle tremor. Virginia studied her face with a growing intensity. Eliza listened—not just to the words, but to the silence between them, the unspoken history humming beneath her skin.

Sister Hope straightened further, her fingers pressing deeper into the tabletop now, straining. Her expression was still measured, but now it carried a sharpened edge, as though the truth had waited too long beneath the surface, yearning to be spoken. She let the quiet stretch, allowing the weight of the moment to settle, then continued.

"I was seventeen when I watched the 2016 elections unfold between Donald Trump and Hillary Clinton."

Her fingers tightened slightly more on the table, the wood groaning faintly under the pressure.

"I was not born until after the world devoured a girl for telling the truth, but I did my reading and research. Monica Lewinsky was twenty-two, Bill Clinton's only daughter was eighteen in 1995. Monica, a White House intern. The President of the United States—Bill Clinton—a forty-nine-year-old married man. The most powerful man in the world. He used his position to engage her in what the media called an 'inappropriate relationship.' But that phrase, that sterile packaging, stripped away what really happened: a young woman was groomed and exploited by a man she admired. The world watched and then blamed her for his betrayal, a girl barely older than his own daughter."

A ripple of unease passed through the room. Some women shifted, others pressed their lips into thin lines.

"They joked about her. Late-night hosts, politicians, feminists who should have known better. The scandal should have ended his career. But he kept his job. She lost everything. Her name became a punchline. Her body, her choices, her humiliation—turned into a national spectacle. And Hillary Clinton, this man's wife not only enabled this, but she was also an accelerant."

She looked around the room now, her voice steady, gaining a quiet ferocity. "I wrote my paper about how when this was happening, Hillary supported Bill. Demonizing a girl who could have been her own child. There had been other scandals while he was Governor, but these had been quietly swept away. Hillary knew the kind of man her husband was and empowered him for her own ambitions."

She exhaled slowly, a deep, burdened sigh.

"Former Secretary of State Madeleine Albright repeated her famous line about a 'special place in hell for women who don't help each other.' Can you imagine a special place in hell for *not* voting for a woman who persecuted a woman—practically a child, to protect the man who denigrated her?"

"In 2016, the other option was Donald Trump, a man who had been recorded on tape saying to 'grab them by the pussy,'" Sister Hope shuddered, a raw, involuntary tremor. "A man who had been married three times, with children from each of these wives. His first wife accused him of raping her in their divorce papers, and there were several other allegations and reports, which I researched and reported in my paper," she continued, her voice tight with suppressed anger. "Later he was a convicted felon," but that was after my little homework paper.

Madame Mary Margaret rested a reassuring hand over the sister's, a gesture of silent solidarity.

"That election in 2016," Sister Hope said, her voice quieter now, filled with a deep weariness, "felt like a mirror held up to all of it. One candidate a known predator. The other—married to one. And the worst part? We were told those were our only options. Choose the abuser, or the one who empowered the abuse. But don't ask why those were the only choices we were given. Don't ask who designed the system to make it so."

The room was still. No one interrupted. Audrey sat frozen, her usual irreverence replaced by a grim silence. Eliza leaned forward, breath caught, feeling the echoes of her own orphanage teachings in every word. Virginia had gone very still, her hands folded tightly in her lap, her blue eyes distant, as if seeing her own past reflected in Sister Hope's story.

"But pointing out the rot at the root is more dangerous than choosing a side within the system. Saying the system is broken—that it protects the abuser and punishes the exposed—that is where people stop listening," Sister Hope took a deep breath, clearly emotional, her composure finally cracking. Unshed tears glistened in her eyes, her restraint harkening to darker secrets she still bore. "I was suspended from school the rest of the year over this paper. I had been on track to go to college, but suddenly, I was the equivalent of a high school drop out."

Silence bloomed like fog, heavy and hard to breathe.

She looked at Eliza, her gaze direct, unwavering. "You want to know where the web of power is anchored? It's not just in ancient texts or sacred places. It's in what we're told we must forget. In the women whose names become scandals, not warnings. In the girls who learn too early that truth has a cost."

The deeper story remained beneath the surface, waiting, withholding, pressing against the edges of the room, now made palpable by Sister Hope's raw honesty. The raw confession hung in the air, a stark counterpoint to the Abbess's earlier sermon on honesty. Sister Hope, once a symbol of unwavering calm, now stood exposed in her vulnerability, the cost of her truth laid bare.

Audrey, usually armed with a smirk and a ready quip, sat frozen. Her green eyes, often glittering with mischief or defiance, now reflected something quieter—something heavier. A dawning understanding dulled their spark. She saw Sister Hope not as a distant figure of piety, but as a mirror. Audrey, too, carried scars no one had named.

Virginia, ever composed, slowly unclasped her hands. Her shoulders trembled. A single tear slipped down her cheek—quiet, unbidden. It traced the same path Sister Lily's had a week before, like matching rivulets carved by grief. There was a shared pain in the air now, unspoken but undeniable. Sister Hope had not simply recounted a memory; she had unearthed something in all of them.

Eliza felt a knot of ice form deep in her stomach. The story echoed too closely the things she had read in the hidden texts of the Hall—the way truth was not erased, just distorted. She remembered the doctrines at the orphanage, the punishment for questions, the quiet war she had waged by refusing to forget. Sister Hope's sacrifice lit a path she recognized: knowledge was power, but also peril. And yet she knew, without needing to say it, she would have written the same paper.

Madame Mary Margaret's palm was warm as it covered Sister Hope's hand. Her grip was gentle but anchoring.

"And in that moment," she said, voice softer than they were used to hearing, "you learned the true weight of the Web. That honesty is indeed a foundation of unity—but it carries a price most never dare to pay."

The Abbess stepped forward at last. Her movements were measured, but her presence quieted the room further still. She didn't just command attention—she absorbed it, like a tree drawing in the storm.

"And that cost," she said, voice like steady water over stone, "is precisely why our unity must be unbreakable."

She paused, letting the words settle.

"Sister Hope's truth. Eliza's bloodline. The very foundation of this Hall. These are not separate threads—they are fibers pulled from the same weave, the same sacred pattern others would sooner burn than let unravel."

She turned slightly, her eyes sweeping the circle of women before her.

"Truth, once spoken, may be buried. It may be punished. But it is never erased. It waits underground, like a seed, for the moment when soil and light return."

A murmur of understanding passed through the room.

"But let this also be a warning," she added, her voice sharpening. "Not all women are true sisters. Some will trade truth for status, or protection, or proximity to power. And not all men are our enemies. We have fathers, brothers, uncles—men who shelter, support, and stand with us in ways the world rarely sees."

The Abbess stepped back, folding her hands. "Discernment is as vital as courage."

For a moment, no one spoke. The room held its breath—not in fear, but in reverence. The story had been told. The truth had taken root.

And no one present would ever un-know it.

⇒ ✷ ⇐

After the Abbess's departure, the silence in Madame Mary Margaret's parlor lingered like incense—fragile, fragrant, heavy with the weight of what had been said. No one rushed to fill it. Words felt too clumsy, too shallow for the truths just unearthed.

Sister Hope sat quietly, her gaze unfixed. Virginia dabbed at her eyes, her hands trembling slightly. Audrey leaned back in her chair, staring at the ceiling, her jaw tight, as if she were holding something sharp behind her teeth.

Eliza, however, felt something shift within her—not just sorrow or indignation, but purpose. A recognition that even in darkness, unity had to be cultivated. Love had to shine through. And sometimes, it started in the simplest of ways. She had sworn to change and to recognize the feminine power that pulsed beyond the ancient texts.

She cleared her throat gently. "Madame," she said, addressing Mary Margaret with unusual directness, "I know this may sound… odd. But I was wondering if you had a certain movie. And if you did… perhaps tonight we could watch something together. As a house."

The Madame raised a brow, curious but attentive.

"I think we need to feel again—together," Eliza continued. "Laugh, cry. Reclaim something. And there's one film I've read about, banned in most of the world but whispered about everywhere."

Her voice lowered, reverent. "*Barbie.*"

The room stirred. Audrey blinked. Virginia's lips parted in disbelief, then slowly curved upward. "You're kidding."

"I'm not," Eliza replied. "It wasn't banned because it was frivolous. It was banned because it told the truth—truth girls recognized too well, and men feared. It was banned for ideas and beliefs that didn't align to society and public order."

A slow smile spread across Madame Mary Margaret's face. "We do have a copy," she murmured. "Locked in the fitness center." She stood with a flourish. "To the fitness center, then."

The government had granted the Hall of Mary Ann a day of "reflection," and Madame Mary Margaret planned to use it to the fullest extent possible.

The brothel moved as one. The women gathered in the fitness center, crowding around the well-worn DVD player.

As the pink-saturated world of *Barbie* unfolded—cheeky, bright, irreverent—laughter broke out in waves. Audrey doubled over during the absurd musical numbers. Virginia clutched a throw pillow to her chest, giggling helplessly at the collapse of *Kendom*. Even Sister Hope allowed herself to smile, her face softening.

But when the closing notes of *"What Was I Made For"* played, a hush swept over the room again.

Eliza sat at the edge of her mat, eyes fixed on the screen, heart clenched. The lyrics hit like scripture:

"I used to float, now I just fall down / I used to know, but I'm not sure now…"

The voice was soft, yet filled with aching clarity. A song of confusion and transformation—of girlhood given, then stolen, then reclaimed. A quiet rebellion wrapped in vulnerability.

Around her, others listened too, visibly moved. But for Eliza, it wasn't just beautiful—it was personal. She thought of her mother. Of the threads, of the Web. Of power distorted and hidden. Of being made for something, then raised to forget it. The song asked the question she'd been chasing since childhood.

Tears slipped down her cheeks—soundless, unashamed.

When the credits rolled and the pulsing beat of *Barbie World Remix* kicked in, laughter and energy bubbled back up. One by one, the women began singing. At first only Virginia knew the lyrics, but then others joined in. Their voices wove together, full of joy and release.

"Perhaps we should add this to the gym's audio track," Madame mused, amused. "Right between *Dancing Queen* and *Like a Prayer*."

The women nodded enthusiastically, some twirling, some laughing too hard to sing.

As they drifted back to the main building, the mood was lighter—but not without weight. They were more tired than if they'd worked the whole day. But it was a different kind of tired. The tired that follows real healing. Or real remembering.

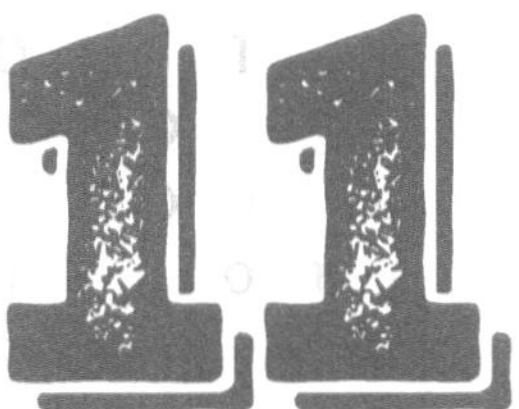

DAVE LOOKED DOWN FROM his hovercraft as it wove smoothly through the congested airways. As he crossed the Potomac River, his eyes settled on a sprawling complex along the far bank—part headquarters, part private estate—belonging to one of the visionary billionaires who had helped reshape society through the MAGA movement.

The plan had been elegant in its ruthlessness: orchestrate an economic collapse, trigger mass foreclosures, and ignite a sell-off frenzy. Then swoop in, buy real estate for pennies on the dollar, and re-emerge as a benevolent industrialist—offering company-owned housing, company-owned stores, and just enough stability to keep people grateful. It wasn't new. It was an old model—perfected in coal towns, factory cities, and feudal estates—only now wrapped in sleek branding and sold as salvation.

Dave's thoughts drifted back to 2025, a year that brought him extraordinary opportunities. Deep in the tech world, he was helping bring artificial intelligence into the mainstream when he received a summons: join the Department of Government Efficiency.

DOGE, as it was officially known (and widely mocked), was supposedly created to streamline federal operations, cut waste, and modernize outdated systems. But Dave knew its true purpose: it was the most effective instrument of control ever devised, the largest data theft in human history.

Its mission, forged in the fires of a new administration's hunger for power, was simple: dismantle anything inefficient, ideological, or inconvenient to the new order. Dave's fluency in AI made him indispensable. He could identify patterns, sort data at scale, and, most crucially, influence and manipulate perception through algorithmic design.

He had been one of the architects behind the systems that enabled the crash and subsequent land grab. He nodded and smiled when the old guard would brag about their technical skills, knowing that their skills were atrophying even as they boasted.

He remembered DOGE's early days. "Efficiency" and "patriotic realignment" were the buzzwords. In practice, this meant gutting agencies that promoted "Diversity, Equity, and Inclusion"—ironically, the same rhetoric used to justify converting the National Museum of the American Indian back into the Hall of Mary Ann. Dave himself oversaw the deployment of AI surveillance across federal institutions, scanning emails and memos for "anti-Trump," "anti-Musk," or "DEI language."

Dave learned during this time that he needed to have his blueprints ready; he built plans that were never executed but could be, in case of emergency. He had helped to orchestrate the fall of men of power and influence, swearing that would never happen to him. For almost any scenario, he had a playbook ready, just waiting to execute. He had playbooks for every game.

His influence had been subtle; he knew the billionaire oligarchs backing the administration would crush anyone too ambitious. He didn't build walls or bridges; he built algorithms, models. His creations decided what was seen and unseen, what was "truth," and what was discarded. He helped engineer narratives that rebranded corporate dependency as patriotic resilience. He understood that real power didn't come from tanks or speeches, but from the quiet, systematic erosion of choice, masked as convenience and cloaked in stability. In 2025, he had been almost 32—old for a "DOGE boy." He was old enough to see the long game, yet young enough to ensure no one else did.

Dave believed the Department of Government Efficiency was simply another layer of elegant ruthlessness—And Dave—technologist, investor, collector, burgeoning power broker—had been given a front-row invitation.

Dave shook off his memories as the hovercraft landed at National Landing for his meeting.

Dave sat across from his brother, Robert—the President—in the private quarters of the White House. This was a rare sanctuary, a space for intimacy beneath the immense pressure of the office.

Robert, four years Dave's senior, had always been the measured one, the careful steward of the family's legacy and reputation. Dave, in stark contrast, was the disruptor: restless, imaginative, and unburdened by tradition. While Robert fortified the family name from within, Dave expanded its reach from the shadows.

Their lives had intertwined, yet they never truly collided. Instead, they orbited each other, bound by blood and mutual ambition. One preserved power; the other multiplied it. In moments like this—away from staff, cameras, and the pervasive whisper networks—their alliance felt immovable, an unspoken pact sealed by shared purpose and blood.

Robert's eyes drifted to the window, where the early evening shadows stretched long across the South Lawn. "It may only be spring, but the autumn is coming fast," he observed. "I can feel it in everything—the polls, the papers, even the way people walk in the West Wing."

Dave sipped his whiskey, nodding. "They're not afraid of the election. They're afraid of what happens when you win again."

Robert glanced over, an eyebrow raised. "And what happens?"

Dave's voice was calm, precise. "Continuity. Consolidation. No more whiplash. No more compromise. The global network we're threading? It needs four more years to tighten."

The President chuckled dryly. "You say that like the world's a knot we're tying."

Dave leaned forward. "It is. And every meeting we took last month—the Saudis, the Vietnamese, even the private retreat with the Icelandic delegation—was about pulling the cord just enough to feel pressure, not panic."

Robert nodded, recalling the secrecy, the off-camera handshakes, the verbal commitments no treaty could match. "Do they believe in us?"

"They believe in power. We've made ourselves predictable, which is another word for safe. And they know our version of order is profitable."

Robert's voice dipped. "And the Chinese?"

"They're watching. They won't resist if we win big. But if the numbers get shaky…" Dave let the sentence trail off.

Robert didn't need it finished. "Then they hedge. Quietly."

Dave set his glass down. "That's why we don't leave it to numbers alone. The algorithms are already shifting perception in the swing sectors. We're framing stability as strength. Patriotism as certainty. Progress as indulgence. It's working."

Robert narrowed his eyes. "And the governors?"

"Most are compliant. The few who aren't? We're giving them rope."

"Enough to hang themselves?"

Dave's smile was cold. "Or enough to tie themselves to our cause once they realize where the wind is blowing."

The room fell quiet again, save for the low hum of the air conditioning and the faint clink of ice against glass.

"Let's make sure the wind doesn't change," Robert said.

Dave raised his glass. "It won't. Not if we control the weather."

"Let's head to dinner, Sophie is here by the way."

The dining room in the private residence of the White House glowed with warm, polished light, the long mahogany table set with understated elegance. Outside, the Washington dusk settled over the lawn, the Washington Monument a silent sentry, the city a quiet hum beyond the high-security perimeter. Inside, the air buzzed with family energy, layered with history, rivalry, and unspeakable grief.

Sophie Barkley Rochester sat at the head of the table tonight, a rare honor. Her silver hair was swept into a soft chignon, and her diamond brooch—shaped like a mourning dove—sparkled beneath the chandelier. Her presence carried both grace and shadow. The loss of her only son in a mysterious plane crash decades ago was never openly discussed, but it hovered in her silences and a sadness that loomed just out of reach.

Caroline, First Lady, had been perfectly groomed for the role. Her posture was impeccable, her soft blue dress tailored to perfection. Next to her sat Jacqueline, twenty-two and restless, ready for her debut and marriage offers. Patricia, seventeen, had been pampered a little too much, and the family was constantly concerned she would create a scandal. Bobby, ten, sat next to Dave, who he tried to spend as much time with whenever he was in town.

"So, Jacqueline," Sophie said, her voice gentle but piercing. "I hear that you have been after your father to host a ball for you here at the White House."

Jacqueline flushed. "Yes, if we all have to get married off, can't we at least have balls like in *Bridgerton*? Is that too much to ask?" she pouted prettily, as she had practiced numerous times in front of the mirror.

Patricia, ever the manipulator interjected, "Papa please." Giving him puppy dog eyes that she had perfected.

Robert, seated across from Sophie, gave a slight shake of his head. "I can see when I am being out maneuvered." He looked over at Caroline. She gave him a slight nod.

"You do want the best possible alliances, don't you?" Caroline pointed out. "Besides, I heard that Dave made some interesting connections on his travels, and perhaps we should look abroad for opportunities."

Dave took a sip of wine, half-smiling, always calculating. "Robert, this might look good for you if we held a ball in the late summer, early fall. This will reinforce your position here and every Judge, Senator, Governor, and Representative with an eligible son will be interested. Plus, the opportunities for industrialists and overseas opportunities—this is genius."

Jacqueline glowed with excitement, "Oh my gosh, really?" if Uncle Dave was on board it would happen.

Sophie reached for her water. "This will be delightful," she said softly. "Sitting here with so much legacy in one room. Sometimes I wonder what Jon-Jon would think, if he were here. Would he have had a daughter that could be at the ball with Jacqueline."

The table quieted. She didn't mean Robert and Dave's father—still very much alive in Cape Cod with Eunice—but her own John. Her son, Jon Jon. Lost twenty-six years ago in a plane crash.

Robert cleared his throat gently. "You would have made a wonderful grandmother to a granddaughter, Aunt Sophie, and we would be honored if you attended and helped to chaperon Jacqueline," he added.

Sophie's eyes shimmered for just a moment. "Well," she murmured, "this is an honor. Don't let my reflections bring us down. We have a grand party to plan."

As the women began to chatter about their plans, Dave turned to Bobby. "Hey, champ—still want me to show you how to fly the hover drone next weekend?"

Bobby perked up. "Yeah! But I want to make it go faster than last time."

"We'll file a flight plan this time," Dave winked.

Patricia rolled her eyes again. "The last one crashed into the rose garden."

"It landed with style," Dave said, in mock offense.

As dessert arrived, the warmth returned. It was a family wrapped in myth, memory, and ambition. The kind of evening that would seem idyllic to the outside world. But beneath the polished silver and practiced smiles, history whispered—reminding each of them that legacy was not just about power or achievement but knowing your place and keeping order. The wives and daughters may have the illusion of freedom, but a gilded cage was still a cage.

As the hovercraft curved above the quiet darkness outside Washington, Dave leaned back in his seat, watching the shimmer of the Potomac slide beneath him. The faint glow of the Barkley Mansion's perimeter lights began to appear over the ridge. He smiled—but not the warm, effortless smile he reserved for Bobby and his other nephews. This was measured, deliberate. The kind of smile he wore when the pieces were finally aligning.

What Dave would never admit out loud was that he was concerned about the numbers. Robert should have a wider lead as the incumbent. Dave would ensure that his brother won by any means necessary. It was time to review his playbooks.

Tonight, had offered more than just familial comfort. The dinner had been filled with signals—Caroline's maneuvering, Sophie's quiet grief, and Jacqueline's untapped potential. But the ball—that was the real opportunity. Not just an event, but a recalibration point. A gathering of power disguised as tradition.

The guest list would be carefully orchestrated: Southern dynasties, Midwest financiers, West Coast technocrats, and foreign envoys cloaked in diplomacy. A convergence of influence, where alliances would be forged over champagne and whispered negotiations. Loyalty—subtle and binding—would be rewarded.

Dave tapped a few notes into his wrist console:

> — Confirm logistics team for security & media placement.
> — Flag three industrialist families in Brazil, Indonesia, and South Korea.
> — Coordinate with Digital Perception Division: begin seeding press storylines on "Next Gen Patriotism" and "Family as Leadership."

He paused, fingers hovering over the final entry. A breath, steady. Then an extra layer of encryption before adding one last note:

> — Jon-Jon – Crash – 26 years.

Outside, the Barkley Mansion's landing pad came into view, gleaming like a jewel in the dark. A beacon. A fortress.

Dave exhaled slowly. Time to move the pieces forward.

The ball wasn't just a celebration—it was a test. And Dave was already rewriting the questions.

≈ ✵ ≈

That night, in the dim-lit rudimentary infirmary at Bell-View Farms, a young woman with brown hair and weary eyes struggled for breath. Metal shelves lined one wall, stocked with remnants of past battles against nature—ointments, expired antibiotics, half-used vials of questionable origin. Nurse sat nearby, having put a strict isolation order on the room. She was unsure what this contagion was and if either of them would make it.

≈ ✵ ≈

The steps creaked beneath Madame Mary Margaret's heels as she descended from the Widow's Peak. The night air pressed close, thick with moisture and the scent of soil and steel drifting from the refineries in the valley. But it wasn't the weather that unsettled her—it was the feeling.

A whisper in her bones. A disturbance behind the veil.

She paused on the last step, one hand brushing the wrought-iron rail. Something was ending. Not loudly, not with fanfare, but with a quiet exhale that was tugging at the edges of fate. She could always sense these moments—fractures in the pattern, the subtle tilt of the world as it turned toward something new and often dangerous.

As Madame Mary Margaret surveyed the Hall of Mary Ann, she did not see anything out of place, yet she felt it. Some may say that it was foolishness.

But Mary Margaret knew better.

She turned her face into the wind and closed her eyes.

The world was shifting.

DAVE LOOKED AT HIS terminal, Bell-View had triggered an alert— it was not urgent enough to demand immediate intervention, but just enough to warrant attention. Bell-View had moved from a naming system to a numbering system almost twenty years ago. The Owners had theorized that a numbering system for the staff would make it more efficient. The company-run town had been allowed to switch as an experiment. A few towns had done the same around that time.

The numbering experiment had been mostly abandoned over time, dismissed by bureaucrats as irrelevant. But Dave saw potential where others saw waste. He wondered if perhaps these locals were trying to hide something in their convoluted number systems, but in the end, what these country folk did, didn't matter in the world. Let them keep their petty secrets.

He monitored these places, kept records, waited. Some systems only became valuable when needed. With a few keystrokes, he adjusted the priority level, ensuring that if either of the flagged individuals died, he'd know the minute their heart stopped beating.

Dave let his thoughts drift back to the old National Labor Relations Board—back when it still had teeth. A New Deal relic, the NLRB had once been the kind of agency that struck fear into corporate boardrooms. Tasked with defending workers' rights to organize, it had been a thorn in the side of the rich for decades. Dave remembered how the billionaires used to seethe at the thought of it.

He chuckled under his breath.

There was a time, he recalled, when some companies would rather shutter an entire location than allow a union to take root. "Cut off the hand," they said, "before the infection spreads." Dave always appreciated the blunt efficiency of that mindset.

Dismantling those protections had been... satisfying. Necessary, some claimed. He preferred the term "clarifying." No more illusions about balance or fairness. Just power, unapologetic and clean.

"Good times," he murmured,

He looked at the early polling numbers again—still plenty of time before the elections, but he wanted—no needed, a wider margin. He needed to keep Robert in the White House for four more years. Robert could never know what Dave was willing to do to make that happen.

Eliza, Audrey, and Virginia embraced the slower rhythm of Lent, savoring the quiet. As spring stretched its limbs, the mornings carried only a hint of a chill, crisp against their skin as they ventured out with Sister Hope. The golden light slanted through buildings, dappling their path in shifting patches of warmth and shadow.

Eliza, Audrey, and Virginia had always been close, but after their night at Barkley Mansion, something shifted. Their bond had deepened, sharpened by revelations that lingered in the air like unfinished sentences. Now they would often meet at midday to discuss their research.

By midday, the air thickened—the sun pressing down like a weight, turning the streets into shimmering rivers of heat. The scent of damp earth gave way to dust, stirred lazily by a sluggish breeze. The horizon wavered, the heat rising from the ground in translucent waves that made the city seem almost unreal. The afternoons became a time of retreat, the indoors offering solace from the relentless sky. Every year, the heat came earlier and the temperatures soared even in the spring.

Eliza sighed, "I used to think our work existed in separate worlds. Ancient texts, conspiracies, overlooked histories, romance novels—completely different pursuits. But now…" She trailed off.

Audrey leaned forward, eyes bright. "I know exactly what you mean. When I started mapping those political cover-ups, I thought I was chasing ghost stories. But the documents I found—they line up with the timelines in your texts, Eliza. And Virginia, you have so much information hidden in plain site."

Virginia smiled, happy that her research was finally recognized by her friends. "It's like we've been staring at pieces of the same puzzle without realizing it." She glanced between them. "It makes sense now—power structures, secret influences, buried truths. They're not just abstract ideas. They're interconnected."

"Let's head back to our research," said Eliza, always the studious one.

"See you later," Virginia replied as she gracefully rose from the table.

"I am enjoying the lighter workload during Lent," Audrey grinned as she trailed behind her friends.

Dave swirled his coffee, the warm mug grounding him as his thoughts drifted into uncharted territory. He'd always played the long game—strategy over impulse, masks over emotion—but this was different. This was a power move cloaked in sentiment, a family myth repurposed as leverage.

He contemplated Aunt Sophie's offhand remark at dinner: Jon Jon had gone missing in a plane crash 26 years ago. It had been said lightly, a comment tossed between bites of carefully crafted courses, but its weight lingered. Could Jon Jon have left behind an illegitimate child? Could Dave pass a girl off as a lost heiress? He had built the playbook long ago—could he execute it?

He checked his alerts. Both women breathing—for now.

Dave contemplated the risk and the rewards. A missing heiress. A sympathetic narrative. A whisper of scandal smoothed over by time. A ball—strategically timed to boost poll numbers. The possibility of two marriage alliances. And best of all—plausible.

As dusk crept in, the world softened. The evening air carried the scent of blooming jasmine and warmed stone, a gentle counterpoint to the day's oppressive brightness. Shadows stretched long and indulgent, and the sky blushed into shades of lavender and gold before surrendering to night. These twilight hours had become their haven—the perfect balance between heat and cool, light and dark, movement and stillness.

Eliza poured Edgar's drink with practiced ease, her tone casual, but the curiosity in her eyes sharp.

"How's Winston?" she asked, guiding him toward the settee.

Edgar exhaled, turning the glass in his hands. "Gone. Left the country with his father."

"The English Ambassador?" Eliza feigned uncertainty.

Edgar nodded, taking a slow sip. "Things changed. Quickly."

"Changed how?"

He set the glass down carefully. "Let's just say his father didn't leave voluntarily."

Eliza tilted her head, listening.

"Politics is just cleaning house; my father says. Some tidy the mess, others decide what gets thrown out." Edgar huffed a quiet laugh. "The President's brother? He's in full spring-cleaning mode. Sweeping away complications, rearranging power, making sure the next cycle is seamless."

Another sip, another pause. "Winston's father saw it coming and got out. The timing was too neat—advisors vanished, diplomats reassigned or 'retired.' Pieces disappearing from the board."

Eliza studied him. "Power isn't visibility," Edgar continued. "The real players work in silence. They write the stories before they're told."

He leaned in. "And now foreign advisors are pouring in—industrialists, financiers, strategists. Not just routine restructuring. They're bringing in new players."

"Messy?" Eliza pressed.

"Always. But this isn't about the next election—it's about the next decade."

Madame passed by, a knowing smile just touching her lips.

"And your internship?" Eliza asked.

Edgar sighed. "Resigned. My father's pulling me onto the Hill— thinks staying with Halstrom looks too much like a power play. Wants to be on the right side of things when it heats up."

Eliza nodded, filing it away. "The right side," she echoed. "And which side is that?"

Edgar lifted his fresh glass, watching the light refract. "That's the trick. You don't know until it's too late to switch."

The quartet switched to a wistful melody. Madame lingered at the edge of the room, scanning the exchange like a chess master.

Eliza leaned in. "If your father thinks it's going to get heated, why stay?"

Edgar's smile tightened. "Because unlike Winston's father, mine still believes he can win."

Eliza considered him. "And do you?"

He looked away. "I think someone already rewrote the rules. And to be honest, Eliza? I'm scared."

Eliza pictured him at sixteen, the same words on his lips, but for a very different reason. Now instead of a boy, Eliza saw a man emerging.

Virginia's laughter rang across the room.

Eliza smiled. "Perhaps laughter is its own survival strategy."

Edgar smirked, watching Virginia. "It dulls suspicion. Smooths fractures before anyone looks too closely."

Eliza studied him. "And does that work for you?"

He exhaled. "It works until it doesn't."

Virginia's laughter rang again—light, bright. But beneath it, Eliza sensed something else. A tension threading through the night. Edgar wasn't wrong. Some truths were easier to hide when wrapped in mirth.

After one more client, the evening settled into its final moments, the weight of the night pressing down like a held breath.

Spring was relinquishing its fleeting lightness, giving way to summer's slow, oppressive heat—the kind that clung to the skin, thick in the air, waiting.

The darkness was not empty, but watchful, stretching across the sky like ink pooling over parchment.

Whatever was unfolding within the Hall, within whispered conversations and measured glances, did not end with the closing of doors.

It lingered—unspoken, unresolved, waiting to take its next shape.

DAVE WOKE TO THE sharp pulse of an alert—Bell-View. One dead. 307. His fingers moved swiftly across the terminal, not in urgency, but in careful orchestration. Each stroke setting the next phase into motion.

A prepositioned microdrone deployed, its needle piercing skin in an instant. The nurse collapsed back into a chair—no struggle, no spectacle, just precision. Data manipulated the data stream to the first responders—alive, dead, hazmat inbound. He adjusted the reports, tweaking the narrative, creating confusion. The type of chaotic information that was all too common in situations like this.

One dead. No, both. Wait—307 still breathing? Ones and Zeros reshaped reality, both in a current and quantum state.

The bodies—alive or not—were secured, cryochambers sealed, destination locked. A facility Dave owned.

The system worked. Not just efficiently, but invisibly.

And with the final entry logged, he exhaled, with the quiet satisfaction of an architect constructing his masterpiece.

He poured a cup of coffee, inhaling the bitter aroma.

Now he needed the next piece of his construct.

Eliza.

The resemblance had always been there—a quiet, unexamined familiarity. The Barkley family traits—the deep brown eyes, the deep chestnut hair, the subtle arch of the brow—were unmistakable. "She could pass as one of ours." Dave had never been particularly drawn to brunettes, though he'd never considered why. Now, the answer felt obvious: she reminded him too much of home.

His mind went to the records of the women in The Hall of Mary Ann. Eliza had been flagged for not having a DNA match on the spear side. This would make it easier to fake a DNA match with his long-lost cousin, Jon Jon. Dave sneered, '*Eliza, a trained courtesan—the difference between a lady and a whore was just their skill in the bedroom.*'

He would need to be careful. He couldn't leave an electronic trail. Eliza had been born when the chip program was still nascent. Dave had been one of its orchestrators—a program that ensured only legal U.S. residents received benefits. People, accustomed to verifying their identity with a device in their hands, barely flinched when asked to embed a small chip in their wrists. The program had been genius.

Dave allowed himself the faintest smile—the kind that never reached his eyes. The chip program had been his most elegant piece of policy theater: a blend of national security, public health, and convenience, wrapped in a bow of patriotism. People had lined up for the implants, never questioning the scope of what they'd given away. Freely giving away the last vestiges of their privacy. And now, ironically, that very system's early blind spots offered him the perfect loophole.

But then, a thought flickered—unexpected, fleeting, and far softer than his usual calculations.

Aunt Sophie.

Would it bring her joy? The possibility of a granddaughter, a link to the son she had lost? For all her quiet suffering, for all the years spent carrying grief in silence… would this ease it, even a little?

Dave exhaled, shaking off the moment of sentiment before it took root. This was about power, about control.

Eliza was sharp, cunning—he had seen it firsthand. She adapted without hesitation, assessed situations with a strategist's eye, and moved through rooms with effortless confidence. She was, in many ways, the perfect candidate. But raw potential wasn't enough—she had to be molded, refined.

A whore from a brothel wasn't the narrative he needed. The world adored redemption, but it revered purity. If Eliza were to emerge as Jon Jon's lost heiress, she needed to come from somewhere pastoral, perhaps tragic. A childhood of quiet resilience. A forgotten legacy uncovered. He could craft the story—bend the past until it fit.

Dave set his coffee down and rose from his chair, his mind already shifting gears. He would need access to The Hall of Mary Ann's records, deeper than what had been publicly cataloged. His office housed encrypted quantum technology that exceeded classified specifications—secure enough to rewrite the past without leaving a trace.

As he moved toward his study, the weight of the moment settled over him. Today, he would begin architecting history.

The door to his study closed with a soft click behind him—sealing in a world few ever entered. The room was more than an office; it was a sanctum of manipulation. Every file, every device, every whisper of digital architecture in this place existed for one purpose: control the narrative before it formed.

Dave approached the console at the heart of it all—a sleek, unmarked terminal embedded in an antique writing desk. A contradiction, like him: old-world charm masking next-generation capability. The machine recognizing him as he entered the room, his chip recently upgraded to the fastest and most secure specifications.

The terminal lit up, bright white, harsh, and sharp, a tool in his hands. He began pulling up the Hall's shadow directory—a sub-layer of identity matrices known only to a handful of senior architects.

The record for Eliza, flagged once for "incomplete paternal lineage," had a dormant file tree attached. Unindexed. Untouched. That was both opportunity and risk.

He opened it.

As lines of code unfurled, Dave knew this was the first incision in a delicate surgery—one that, if executed precisely, would elevate Eliza from obscurity to legacy. If mishandled, it could unravel a box of secrets far older than her—bringing scandal.

He leaned forward.

Rewriting history.

He deftly manipulated the files, showing his long-lost cousin Jon

Jon as Eliza's father. His fingers flexed, shoulders rolling, as he fell into a rhythm. Eliza had been raised in an orphanage, she was chipped at just eight years old—this part was easy. He'd learned long ago that staying close to the truth made the lie simpler. Instead of the Hall of Mary Ann, her records now indicated she was sent to the eerie but respectable Bell-View Farms.

Dave reviewed the forged file one last time, the new identity almost poetic in its plausibility. A girl from Bell-View Farms—poor, rural, overlooked—dies quietly. No family. No press. No real digital footprint beyond corporate welfare and medical charts.

Now, reborn in the person of Eliza, she would carry the Barkley lineage, the Rochester blood, the lost daughter of Jonathan Franklin Rochester—most importantly, the story Dave needed the world to believe. A discovery made due to a need for a modern DNA test for tailored treatment, wiping out the poor girls' lifesavings, but ensuring she lived. The updated DNA test, triggering an alert.

He assessed everything one last time before encrypting the file, a sudden realization hitting him: he'd missed something crucial. So focused on manipulating DNA, health records, and chip data, he'd almost forgotten about videos and facial recognition. He swiftly manipulated camera records from around the Capital where the young women were permitted to walk erasing Eliza from the records.

He reviewed the Bell-View feeds; despite living there for years, he could only find a few to swap with Eliza; it appeared she spent most of her life with her hair down, shrouding her face. He double-checked the feeds from The Hall of Mary Ann to Barkley Mansion—nothing, just as he suspected. He could never be too careful.

He encrypted the payload and dropped it into a transfer queue with a timed release. It would discreetly filter through seven blind relays before settling into the federal identity archive. By the time anyone reviewed it, the narrative would feel inevitable.

Control was the real inheritance.

He leaned back in his chair, stretching his spine as the burn of anticipation rippled through him. Tomorrow would be delicate. He didn't want to draw any attention to the Hall of Mary Ann, so he scheduled a meeting with Madame through the normal system—a periodic meeting between the largest shareholder and his "playground" wouldn't raise suspicions.

He booked Virginia, Audrey, and Eliza for the night; after their recent outing at Barkley Mansion, it would be more surprising if he didn't. He smiled to himself. Once the dead girl's records replaced Eliza's, Madame would be able to replace her with a new brunette, this time one with blue eyes or perhaps something more exotic; an Arabian princess or a Nubian goddess, he thought. After all, he had to feed the carefully curated optics; too much repetition was boring.

Madame was no fool. She ran the Hall like a stateswoman—every gesture loaded, every word deliberate. She wouldn't openly question his authority, but she would know something had shifted. That was the game: power without noise, change without declaration. He had strong suspicions about Madame Mary Margaret and the Hall of Mary Ann, and now he was going to collect the fruit of what he had sown. He was no fool.

As for Eliza, he smiled, she would conform to his narrative. He felt Eliza's goals and his plans might align more than she could imagine. He understood motivation and control: not fear, not reward, allowing someone to pursue their own desires, as long as it aligned with his.

Dave shut down the terminal and rose, already rehearsing the conversations in his head—how to plant the idea without saying it outright, how to guide Eliza into a role that would transform not only her status, but his own influence across the globe. He wasn't just rewriting Eliza's future—he was redrawing the shape of power itself.

Madame's private study, all warm shadows and hushed opulence, was meticulously designed to both welcome and intimidate. Sunlight, filtered through heavy velvet drapes, cast a golden glow on the mahogany tea table set between the two armchairs. The air carried the faintest trace of lilac and old wood—carefully curated comfort that was subtly undercut by the sharp scent of freshly squeezed lemon from the waiting tea.

Madame Mary Margaret sat poised behind her exquisite silver tea service. The teapot, its surface gleaming softly in the subdued light, sat atop a small warmer, a wisp of steam escaping from its spout. A delicate china sugar bowl, filled with glistening white cubes, and a matching creamer completed the set. Beside it, tiered stands held an array of delicate treats. On the top tier rested miniature fruit tarts with jewel-toned berries arranged artfully on their glazed surfaces. The middle tier displayed neatly cut cucumber sandwiches, their crusts meticulously removed, the pale green filling peeking out from between thin slices of white bread. On the bottom, small, frosted cakes in pastel hues offered a deceptive sweetness. It would not be out of place at Barkley Mansion

Madame's posture was impeccable, a portrait of elegance and restraint as she slowly stirred sugar into her teacup with a silver spoon. Her pale blue day gown shimmered like water, her jewelry subtle but deliberate—a single strand of pearls catching the light. She looked up as Dave entered, her expression unreadable—though her eyes, those sharp, glacier-blue eyes, missed nothing as he approached the laden table.

"David," she said smoothly, her voice a low murmur as she gestured towards the food. "You're early, tea?" The offer, polite as it sounded, held a subtle undercurrent of inquiry. "That's either very good or very bad," she added, her gaze steady.

He smiled faintly, adjusting his cufflinks as he approached the table, his eyes briefly scanning the spread before settling back on Madame. "I prefer efficient. Though those cakes do look rather tempting." He made no move to take one.

She gestured to the chair across from her with a delicate wave of her hand, her fingers adorned with a single, discreet diamond ring. "Then let's not waste time pretending this is routine. Help yourself to the sandwiches, David. They are quite fresh."

Dave sat without hesitation, legs crossed, hands resting lightly on the armrests, his gaze fixed on Madame. He pointed a finger towards the cakes. "Perhaps later." He declined the offered refreshments, a subtle power play in itself. "I'd like us to be candid with one another."

Madame replied, her voice cool and steady as she lifted her teacup. "David, I'm a Madame at one of the most powerful brothels in the world. We pride ourselves on discretion. Much like a well-prepared tea service, every element here serves a specific purpose, often unseen." She took a slow sip, her eyes never leaving his.

He shifted approach, leaning forward slightly. "I reviewed the feedback from your young ladies after the night of my party." He paused, letting his words hang in the air. "Their reports were better than most of my security team's. Surprisingly detailed, wouldn't you say?" He watched her carefully, noting the almost imperceptible tightening of her grip on the delicate china cup.

Madame placed her cup back on the saucer with a soft clink, her smile unwavering, though it didn't quite reach her sharp eyes. "I'm glad to hear our services were satisfactory," she replied. She picked up a cucumber sandwich, the pale green filling a stark contrast to her manicured red nails, and took a delicate bite.

"I'm planning more engagements in the future," he informed her, his gaze flicking to the untouched tiers of food. "Similar in structure, but they must be limited—discreet. No risks to our investors. Foreign nationals only."

Madame merely raised a perfectly sculpted eyebrow as she slowly chewed the sandwich, her expression giving nothing away. She didn't interrupt, allowing him to continue.

Dave's tone darkened, losing some of its earlier pleasantries. "Let me be direct. I suspect certain activities occur here that aren't sanctioned by the state." His gaze swept over the opulent room, lingering for a moment on the silver tea service.

Her eyes tightened, just slightly, the blue turning almost glacial. She set down the half-eaten cucumber sandwich on her plate with deliberate slowness.

He had no idea what truly occurred within these walls, but he correctly surmised that all powerful entities bent the rules a little. The longer he waited, the longer she would have to think about incidents, about vulnerabilities. Perhaps a client who had indulged past curfew. A lady who had wandered away a bit too far on a morning walk.

Madame slowly poured herself another cup of tea, the fragrant steam swirling upwards, thinking about the hidden library beneath the floorboards and the powerful allies of the Hall. If David pushed too hard, everything could unravel. She placed the delicate china cup on the saucer with a steady hand, the only sign of her inner turmoil a slight tremor as she reached for a small, frosted cake. She didn't eat it, merely held it in her fingers.

"I won't push," he continued, his voice softening slightly. "Not today." He paused, his gaze sweeping back to the untouched tea cakes, counting slowly to three, as he had in recent international trade negotiations, a habit he couldn't quite shake. "Not if one small, delicate request is handled... discreetly."

"And what matter would that be, David?" she asked, her voice like silk drawn over glass as she finally took a small bite of the frosted cake, her eyes locked on his.

"Eliza."

A pause—nothing more than a blink—but Madame caught it as she delicately dabbed her lips with a lace napkin that lay beside her teacup. "She's popular. Intelligent. Composed. Much like our Earl Grey blend – subtle yet with a distinct character."

"And after tonight, you will mourn her," he said flatly, his gaze unwavering as he finally reached for a cucumber sandwich, taking a large bite as if to emphasize his control. "You'll speak of her as a loss. One of your girls, tragically gone. And then, never mention her again."

"She's not for sale," Madame said coolly, her hand hovering over the teapot. "Not even for all the tea in China."

"Everything is," he replied, his eyes flicking to the silver samovar in the corner of the room. "But I'm not here to buy. I'm here to take one of your charges away. If not…" His voice dropped, a clear threat hanging in the air like the scent of brewing tea. "I'll unleash every investigator I have."

Madame regarded him in silence, her gaze as sharp as the finest silver knife from her tea set. "Promise me she won't be hurt."

"I have no plans to harm Eliza," he said, accepting the generous pour of amber scotch she offered him in a heavy crystal tumbler, the ice clinking softly. "I'm offering her a future. One better than life as an orphan and a whore." He took a slow sip, the rich aroma filling the air.

She poured herself another cup of tea, her movements precise and betraying no emotion. "I assume you'll handle the records."

He met her gaze, his own as hard as the ice in his glass. "The records will show a different girl was sent here from an orphanage. She's dead. No—I didn't kill her." He saw the flicker of disbelief in her eyes. "Once the reports show that one of your girls has passed, you can replace Eliza. A small price to pay for continued discretion."

A fleeting thought passed through Dave's mind as he chewed on his second cucumber sandwich: he hadn't killed the girl—just the nurse. An acceptable loss, like a chipped teacup.

A flicker of anger, as sharp and sudden as a lightning strike, broke through Madame's carefully constructed restraint. "None of my girls are replaceable, David." Her voice, though still low, held a dangerous edge.

He waved it off with a dismissive flick of his wrist, crumbs of the cucumber sandwich dusting his fingers. "How many will you lose if I turn my full attention to this place? How many secrets will spill like tea from an overturned pot?"

The silver spoon, which Madame had picked up again, stilled above her teacup. Silence stretched, punctuated only by the faint tick of a nearby grandfather clock. Then, "Eliza will leave with you tonight." Her voice was flat, devoid of emotion—a statement, a bitter surrender as cold as the untouched iced tea on the sideboard.

Dave leaned forward, his voice low and conspiratorial, the aroma of scotch now mingling with the delicate scent of lilac. "You've made the right decision."

Another pause—longer this time, thick with unspoken resentment and calculation.

Then, Madame offered a slow, deliberate smile, as cold and brittle as the delicate sugar sculpture on the top tier of the cake stand. "Very well. But I want two things in return."

"Name them," Dave said, taking another sip of his scotch, his eyes narrowed.

"First," she said, her gaze unwavering as she finally picked up one of the pastel-colored cakes, turning it slowly in her fingers, "allow her contact—Virginia and Audrey, at least occasionally. A small crumb of her past to take with her."

"Done," Dave replied, his voice surprisingly agreeable as he reached for another cucumber sandwich. "Second?"

Her gaze hardened, the blue of her eyes deepening to a stormy hue as she finally placed the untouched cake back on the stand. "Keep your promise to this Hall. And to the rest of the girls."

Dave gave a single, curt nod. "I keep my promises." He finished his sandwich and wiped his hands on a crisp linen napkin from the tea table.

He took another slow sip of his scotch, his gaze lingering on the tiered stands. "Have Eliza brought to the infirmary."

Madame raised a perfectly arched eyebrow, then reached out and rang a small silver bell that rested on the tea table—Victorian in its elegance, polished and precise. Its sound was soft, almost musical, a civilized signal cutting through the tension in the room.

Dave watched, a flicker of satisfaction in his eyes. Rebuilding this place without technology had been one of his finer ideas. He'd insisted:

no signals, no cameras, no digital residue. In a world surveilled to the breath, he had created the last true pocket of privacy—in the most powerful city on Earth. It was masterful. Here, the elites could indulge in their darkest desires, unobserved. Here, power whispered instead of shouted. And now, everything, down to the arrangement of the tea service, moved according to his will.

⋙ ❀ ⋘

Eliza sat in the cold, sterile infirmary, the sharp sting of disinfectant heavy in the air—a quiet declaration that this place existed for precision, not comfort.

It was tucked in a wing off the main fitness center, a ghost of 1990s optimism—treadmills that hummed, mirrors too large, posters that smiled too hard.

But this wing was different. A surgical marvel of modernity. This wing was fully accessible, unshielded from the prying eyes that monitored everything. Polished. Gleaming. Utterly indifferent to human frailty.

The elite took no risks with their health. The girls had monthly examinations here and avoided it the rest of the time. When girls were sent to the infirmary out of cycle, they rarely reemerged.

She knew that. Every breath she took was someone else's data point. Every twitch of a muscle, every slight spike in her pulse—it was being captured, analyzed, cataloged. Her body was no longer hers; it had become a specimen.

And yet, no one had said why. What had they found? What could possibly warrant this level of scrutiny? Was it something inside her?

Eliza shifted slightly on the padded table. Even that motion felt observed—registered somewhere in a system she would never access.

She drew a slow breath. It felt like the air wasn't hers, either

Nurse Becky entered, cold, detached. "Please lie down," she said without inflection.

Eliza complied. The mask came down with clinical ease.

"Count backwards from ten," the nurse directed. Following protocol, a procedure like any other.

Eliza reached three before the world slipped away.

The nurse stood in silence.

No vital signs. The machines recorded everything. Still, she filed her manual report. Following protocol. Layers of redundancy. She knew she was being monitored too. The state paid her well to cover their indiscretions.

This wasn't the first time. It wouldn't be the last. She never asked where the bodies went.

She would go home tonight to her small flat. A stiff drink. Maybe the whole bottle.

⁘

Dave spent the evening observing Virginia and Audrey in a detached manner. They fawned over him—dutiful, charming, perfectly trained— but their eyes kept flicking elsewhere. To each other. To Madame Mary Margaret. To the corners where Eliza should have been.

He noticed, of course. He always noticed.

Eliza's absence was a shadow at the feast. A hollow in the glamour.

Madame had delivered, though. An exotic Thai beauty with night-dark hair and eyes like still water—was flawless, a sculpted answer to a question no one dared ask. Mysterious, soft-spoken, utterly unknowable. Just how the clients liked them. Just how he liked them. No ghost of family familiarity here. He had seen her once or twice in the Hall, but this was the first time he was going to try her delights.

Dave admired her with a detached interest.

Virginia poured his drink, her hand steady, her eyes anything but.

"You're quiet tonight," he said, swirling the glass like he might find something at the bottom besides reflection.

"It's a quieter evening," she replied, her smile too practiced to be comforting.

He turned to the new girl. "What's your name?" He liked to know names; names had power.

"Apsara," she said through lidded lashes and a silken accent.

"Celestial nymph," he translated. "It suits you." He studied her for a fleeting moment—her stillness, the way she breathed only when necessary. She had been trained well, but still too demure for Dave's taste.

Then, abruptly, he switched, "Audrey. Tell the musicians to play something more upbeat."

"It's Lenten," Audrey said quietly, her usual brashness gone.

"Don't worry about your soul," Dave replied. "Mine is already damned, and you are just my messenger." He knocked back his drink in a single swallow, the glass clinking down louder than it should have. Then he laughed—harsh, dry.

Still, the evening carried on.

Senators with silk smiles and governors wrapped in ego passed through, shaking his hand, offering rehearsed welcomes. Industrial titans leaned in close with whispers of shadowy contracts and backroom deals. Each eventually peeled off, drawn away by pleasure, politics, or predation.

Everything moved as it should. As he had designed it.

PART II
307

Introduction of Characters

BELL-VIEW AND ITS INHABITANTS

- ✣ Eliza / 307: Eliza recast into the life of 307 aka Ana Lucia.
- ✣ Ana Lucia (Deceased): Eliza's spiritual anchor and guide, the former 307.
- ✣ 305: Third shift worker with Eliza, approximately twenty-one years old.
- ✣ Georgette & Marty Washington: Owners of Bell-View Farms.
- ✣ Matron Two: Monitors the women's dormitory at Bell-View Farms.
- ✣ Foreman Three: The nightshift foreman at the cannery.
- ✣ Lucky Eleven & Twelve: Female workers on the first shift.
- ✣ Librarian: Public Librarian at Bell-View.
- ✣ Nurse: The City Clerk provides a new nurse with this identity.

POLITICAL & PERIPHERAL FIGURES

- ✣ Nick and Mack: Investigators tasked with uncovering Eliza's origins.
- ✣ The Wisewoman from Acoma Pueblo: Eliza's distant relative.
- ✣ Angela O'Brien (Deceased): Eliza's mother.

ELIZA'S BREATH CAME SHALLOW, the tightness in her chest unfamiliar, unnatural. The cryochamber hummed softly around her, sterile and impersonal, the air cold but lifeless—not crisp like the early mornings in the Hall of Mary Ann, not touched by the scent of perfume and memories.

The container walls were seamless, curved metal, no texture, no history. No echoes of laughter, no whispered conversations beneath velvet drapes, no quiet music filtering through the corridors of the Hall. Just function. Just control.

The hospital gown clung to her like a question she wasn't meant to ask, thin, papery, absurdly fragile in this place of calculated precision.

Dave smirked, lounging against the cryochamber, as if her awakening was nothing more than another event on his schedule.

"Good morning," he said, voice laced with irony, as if testing the limits of her lucidity.

Eliza forced herself to focus, pushing against the weight of weakness. The Hall had always given her space to think, to observe, to maneuver—here, there was none.

"Where… am I?" The words scraped against her throat.

"You're number 307 now at Bell-View Farms," Dave said smoothly, as if speaking to a child.

Eliza drank the water he handed her, the cool liquid helping, but not nearly enough.

Dave continued, watching her without urgency. *"Your room is 307. Your identity is 307. If I ever see you again, it'll be the first time we've met."*

The Hall had been a place of stories, of layered identities and quiet resistance. This place had no past. Only instruction. Only a number.

Eliza stiffened, the cold metal beneath her fingertips anchoring her to a reality she didn't want to accept. "Take me back to the Hall."

Dave sighed—not annoyed, but amused, as though her resistance was an expected obstacle, already accounted for. "You missed our window for conversation, Princess. The physicians will be here any minute."

Eliza turned her head, forcing her breath steady, forcing herself to see. "What am I supposed to do?"

Dave studied her, expression unreadable, then leaned in just slightly.

"You're a smart woman, Eliza." His voice neither cruel nor kind. "You'll figure it out."

Dave closed the lid of the cryochamber and walked away, his footsteps steady.

Eliza's breath was shallow, the weight of the cold pulling at her limbs, sinking into her skin like a slow, relentless tide. The cryochamber hummed—a low, mechanical murmur, indifferent to the figure it held inside. She willed herself to fight—to push against the chill, to force movement into her body—but her limbs remained still, leaden, drained of resistance. She was not a number. Her eyes fluttered shut.

The weight of duty pressed heavily upon Georgette and Marty Washington, settling into the quiet space between them in the bright sunroom. The scent of aged wood and a faint sweetness of dried herbs, hanging from the rafters, filled the air.

The report, was simple: 307 alive. Nurse dead. But simplicity did not equate to ease in this old house where every creak of the floorboards seemed to carry the weight of a shared secret.

The nurse had been with them for over two decades, a familiar face amidst the faded floral wallpaper and the rhythmic tick-tock of the grandfather clock in the hall. She was a fixture in the shifting landscape of their secluded life long before they'd adopted the detached efficiency of numbers replacing names.

In a fragile trust built over years of shared secrets within these thick, stone walls, nurse had been a healer, a guide. But she had not left unprepared. A contact in case she ever needed to be replaced had been written, encoded in the family Bible.

Georgette's calloused fingers, more accustomed to tending her herb garden, moved slowly over the ancient, screen on the oak desk. The request, typed with deliberate care, was concise, calculated. A tinny chime from the machine signaled a quick reply: A replacement nurse would arrive tomorrow.

Marty exhaled, the sound like the rustling of dry leaves outside, as he leaned against the rough stone of the fireplace. A faint scent of last night's storm still lingered. He watched Georgette, his weathered face etched with concern. Would the new nurse understand the delicate balance they maintained? Would she do what had to be done within these walls that had absorbed so much history? Would she even know the procedures that were becoming obsolete in this changing world?

As the world had moved to corporate feudalism, they had struck a strategic partnership in their small community. They harbored a deep-seated unease about any oversight, any intrusion from the government that could disrupt their carefully constructed life.

There could be no room for anyone that risked exposure, anyone who might bring the harsh light of official scrutiny onto the secrets held within the aging timbers of their farmhouse.

⚛

Dave let his mind wander as the hovercraft glided toward Barkley Mansion, the hum of its engine low and steady, a quiet accomplice to his thoughts.

The seeds had been planted. Now, he would let them grow.

As soon as he arrived home, he strode directly to his study, his movements practiced, deliberate. The door clicked shut behind him, sealing him inside the sanctuary of control.

He settled into the high-backed leather chair, the material familiar beneath his fingertips. His hand moved smoothly across the console, pulling up the hovercraft's navigation logs. A flicker of light danced on the screen, waiting. He had taken a slight risk by going to the facility, but he had many meetings at his properties. If anyone could place him there that morning, they would wonder what cryo-technology was in the works. He made a note to acquire some. Over-architecting was better than under.

With deft precision, he altered the records—not rushed, not sloppy, but with the expertise of someone who had done this before. A keystroke. A careful adjustment. The timeline now reflected a flawless return home, shortly after the Hall of Mary Ann had closed.

Dave leaned back, exhaling slowly. The change was seamless. Undetectable. Just as it should be.

Now for the next part of his plan.

Dave leaned back, reflecting on the 2020s.

How effortlessly people had surrendered their most intimate data, handing over the blueprint of their existence without question. They had done it willingly—excitedly—paying for the privilege of mapping their bloodlines, their predispositions, their secrets.

When 23andMe collapsed, he had moved swiftly. Acquisition, infrastructure, access. Top geneticists in the world. And the data. It was all his now.

Between government archives and fools begging for self-discovery, he had everything he needed.

Dave tapped a command into his console, opening a secure line.

"I need to see you as soon as possible at Barkley Mansion," Dave told his lead geneticist.

"I can be there within an hour," came the reply, clipped, professional.

Eliza's skin prickled with cold, the lingering chill of the cryochamber still clinging to her despite the warmth of the room.

"You are a miracle," the physician announced, staring at his tablet like it held the answer to something profound.

Eliza blinked, her mind still sluggish, struggling to connect the words to meaning.

"Your nurse managed to administer a genetically sequenced cure—just before she succumbed to the virus herself."

The words hung in the air, weighty, impossible.

"The nurse died?" Eliza asked, voice raw with confusion.

The physician swallowed awkwardly, his discomfort at dealing with the living more obvious than his medical expertise. Instead of answering, he pivoted back to procedure, running quick biometric scans, logging data without thought.

A nurse handed Eliza a bundle—rough undergarments, coarse coveralls.

She stripped out of the thin, papery hospital gown, its fragility suddenly symbolic of the life she'd left behind. Her fingers ran over the stiff fabric, nothing like the satins and silks she was accustomed to. The cotton socks, the weight of the work boots—a stark contrast to the stockings and stilettos of her past.

As she dressed, the mirror caught her reflection—the same face, the same body. But everything had changed.

Dave led the geneticist through the gleaming corridors of Barkley Mansion with deliberate calm, each step an assertion of control. The walls bore no family portraits—only modern art chosen for its ambiguity and threat. Power moved here not in displays, but in precision.

He paused before an unmarked door and swiped his wrist over a panel. A quiet *beep*, then a heavy click as the magnetic lock disengaged. They stepped inside.

The room was small, lined with reinforced steel, insulated from the outside world—a perfect Faraday cage. Secure. Private. Untouchable.

Dave closed the door behind them, ensuring the lock engaged with a quiet, final click.

"Before we begin," he said, his voice smooth but firm, "I need your absolute discretion."

The geneticist didn't flinch, adjusting his glasses. "Of course, sir."

Dave studied him for a beat, ensuring there was no hesitation, no flicker of doubt.

"A DNA alert was triggered." He folded his hands behind his back, pacing slowly. "A young woman in a canning factory. She fell ill."

A pause.

"Severe enough for a genetic update."

The geneticist frowned. "Unusual. That level of response requires a substantial biological event. Do you know anything about the contagion?"

"Precisely." Dave's tone remained neutral, but there was something cold in his stare. "Of course, I'm suspicious. This could be a scam." Then he paused, "But she was chipped early in the program, perhaps her biomarkers hadn't been properly recorded…" he let the thought hang in the air.

The geneticist hesitated, considering. "What do you need?"

Dave stopped pacing, turning sharply. "Verification."

The word landed like an order. Dave already knew what would be found. His work was impeccable; his lips curved upward at his own cunning. He loved architecting the system.

"I need to know everything. And I need to know it quickly." His voice was crisp, efficient, yet laced with something darker—anticipation.

The geneticist nodded, adjusting his coat. "I'll begin immediately."

Dave leaned back against the edge of his desk, exhaling slowly. He had released the rabbit for the hunt. Even though he trusted the integrity of the geneticist, who was too professional to gossip; there were staff. Everyone thought of the staff as invisible, but Dave recognized them as tools. A long-lost heiress. The thought sat heavy in the room, unspoken but undeniable. The staff would whisper, and those whispers would have echoes.

For now, Dave needed to appear skeptical. "How long before you can get me anything conclusive?" he asked.

"Tomorrow," the geneticist said with confidence. Dave smiled.

⇒ ✵ ⇐

The farmhouse loomed before Eliza, a testament to time and quiet resilience, its many additions layering over one another like chapters in an unwritten history.

Georgette rushed forward, warmth spilling into the moment as she pulled Eliza into a quick embrace, her voice light with relief.

"307, so glad you're recovered."

Marty remained at the doorway, watching. Measured. Silent.

Eliza's response was muted, careful, her unwashed hair veiling her face, an unspoken barrier between herself and whatever waited beyond the threshold.

"Thank you," she murmured.

Georgette nodded briskly.

"Matron 2 was informed you'd be coming home. Let her know when you're able to start working again." She hesitated, then added—not apologetic, but reluctant. "Hopefully in a day or so. We've been shorthanded with your illness."

Georgette hated to press, but necessity was a heavier force than sentiment. Outsiders were a risk. Better to have 307 back at partial capacity than be open to exposure.

Madame's private study was a place meant for quiet conversations, decisions, not grief. Dave's malevolent presence still clung to this space, sullying its normal tranquility.

Virginia sat rigid, her hands clenched in her lap, trying to absorb the words, trying to force them into some shape that made sense.

Audrey, sitting next to her, arms folded tight across her chest, shook her head once—sharp, defiant. "No," she whispered. "That's not—she was fine yesterday."

Madame sat behind her desk, her expression unreadable, but her presence felt like a weight pressing into silence. "She's gone," Madame said, simply.

Sister Hope was still, standing near the window, hands folded in front of her, her presence a quiet balm against the growing tension.

"We saw her," Virginia whispered. "She was fine." A tear threatened to fall from her normally bright blue eyes.

Madame stared at them for a long moment before tilting her head slightly. "She's gone," she repeated, looking from one to the other, with her steady gaze.

The words sat heavy in the air, heavier than any explanation would have been.

Sister Hope moved, just slightly, a shift in her posture—a silent offering of comfort. But Virginia and Audrey weren't ready for comfort. Not yet. Eliza was gone. And nothing in the Hall of Mary Ann ever happened without reason.

Virginia blinked hard, trying to hold back tears she didn't fully understand.

"She can't be dead," Audrey said finally, her voice low and vibrating with fury. "She can't."

Madame said nothing. She didn't need to. The morning sunlight danced across her composed face, as if mocking their desperation.

"We deserve the truth," Virginia said, softer this time, but no less resolute.

"Deserve," Madame echoed, the word falling from her mouth like a challenge. "You are owed what I give you. Nothing more."

Sister Hope's eyes flicked to the two girls—worried, watching. But she stayed silent.

Audrey got up abruptly, storming from the room. Virginia hesitated, then followed. The heavy door closed behind them with a dull, final thud.

And in the dim quiet of Madame's study, the sunlight swayed, as if disturbed by a whisper no one could hear.

Normally Madame would not have let such defiance go unpunished, but she would allow them the morning to grieve. They would have clients in the evening, and she would need them to perform.

"Mercy is often cruel in this world," Sister Hope said softly, her hand still resting on Madame's shoulder.

Eliza forced herself to walk, up the path the owner had indicated to the female dorm. The ground beneath her boots was uneven, hardened by years of passage, forcing her to adjust with each step. So foreign from the high heels and satin slippers she was accustomed.

A voice cut through the quiet hum of movement.

"Hey, is that you, 307?"

Eliza turned, sluggish, still fighting the weight pressing down on her limbs.

A young woman eyed her, brows furrowed, expression balancing between curiosity and concern. "You look like hell."

Eliza tried to form a response, but her throat was still dry, the words stuck somewhere between thought and breath.

"I heard you were in the infirmary," the woman continued, voice dropping lower. "Some people said you died. But others said—" she hesitated, eyes darting toward the factory. "It was the nurse that died."

The words landed like stones, heavy, sharp, undeniable.

Eliza swallowed, feeling the weight of the uniform against her skin, the strange air around her, the way her body still felt like it wasn't entirely hers.

"I don't—" she started, but the woman cut her off with a wry smile. "No need to talk. I can tell you're tired," the young woman continued.

Eliza felt the words rather than heard them, her mind sluggishly processing.

Inside the dorm building, Eliza was unexpectedly surprised.

A matronly woman stood behind the reception counter, the remnants of an old hotel where visitors came for extended stays.

"Is that you, 307?" she asked, tilting her head. "You look terrible," she said, not unkindly.

Eliza's throat cracked as she tried to respond—only an awful, hollow croak emerged.

"Tea with honey," the woman suggested without missing a beat. "It'll help before you get some rest. You don't worry about a thing today and tomorrow around noon meal, let Matron One or I know if you will be able to work."

Eliza processed the words, like they were said in a foreign language, "Okay," not a quick response; Madame would be disappointed.

"What are you doing wandering about this time of day, 305?" Matron Two asked. "You are going to disrupt your sleep schedule."

"You always tell me that?" 305 responded with a laugh.

As the women walked upstairs, 305 continued her chatter, from scandals about the first shift to updates about her latest Regency show binge.

Stopping at Room 305, she turned to Eliza. "Meet downstairs around nine for food? Do we call that dinner or breakfast?"

"Dinner," Eliza replied without thinking.

305 barked a laugh, shaking her head. "You always say that."

"Oh, just one second," she said entering her room. 305 emerged with an armful of old paperback travel books, "They were just giving books away at the old library downtown and I knew you would want them. I thumbed through a few first," she admitted a little sheepishly.

Eliza hugged the books to her chest with unadulterated delight. Plus, the thought of a library where women could get books! This news made her head spin. "Thank you," she tried to say, her voice cracking.

"Drink your tea," 305 remarked as she spun back into room.

Eliza walked further down the hall, stopping at 307, tea in hand. The door unlocked at her wrist's command, and she stepped inside.

The space was unexpectedly large, modest yet practical. Not luxury. Not indulgence. A studio—a concept she had read about. A small kitchenette, a combined bedroom/living area, and a bathroom. Efficient.

Her eyes landed on something unexpected. A video screen. A terminal. She had not had access to technology since leaving the orphanage when she was 16. She almost squealed in anticipation.

She set her tea on the desk, fingers trembling faintly. The fog in her mind was lifting, slowly. She sipped her tea—bitter and honey-sweet, comforting in its simplicity. Real.

Eliza moved to the mirror, staring at the woman reflected back at her—pale, shadow-rimmed eyes, hair limp. Yet beneath the exhaustion, something else flickered.

Not fear. Not defeat. Awareness and determination, she would figure this out.

They thought she had died. Some said the nurse had instead. Someone had disappeared, and she had been slipped into the void they left behind. She had survived—and been hidden.

But why?

Her hand grazed her temple, chasing fragments of memory. Voices. A mask. The nurse's eyes staring down at her. Then—nothing. Then Dave, or had that been her subconscious? Why would the President's Brother drop her off at a cannery? Had there really been a rooster?

Now—this.

A factory worker. A dorm room. A name erased in favor of a number. 307.

Eliza opened a drawer, finding a modest cotton pajama set, soft, functional, yet strangely comforting. She took a quick shower, the water washing away the stale remnants of whatever had happened. After dressing in the borrowed pajamas, she slipped into the bed.

Her mind reeled, tumbling over questions she had no answers for. Sleep consumed her quickly. She had been dead, after all.

Edgar stared at the notification, its words stark and indifferent:

The woman you requested is no longer available.
Please select another.

A short, transactional dismissal, devoid of meaning, of recognition.

He had never chosen another. Only Eliza. Always Eliza.

He tried again. Requested her for the next night. The night after. The night after that. He requested through the end of the month. Receiving the same cold, transactional response.

Until finally the terminal responded—

The woman you requested is deceased.
Please select another.

The terminal spat out the words with cruel efficiency. Edgar sat alone, the silence folding around him, pressing inward, suffocating.

He had not cried since his mother had died. The same year he had met Eliza. Now—all kindness was gone from his life.

He pressed a trembling hand against his mouth, willing himself to breathe. But there was no breath deep enough to soften this grief. No request he could make to bring her back. It would not go well for him if his father heard him cry. He bit down on the sound clawing up his throat. No one could hear. Especially not his father.

Eliza startled awake at the blaring alarm, its sharp tone slicing through the quiet of her room. Her pulse kicked up as she sat upright, disoriented for a moment, before forcing herself to move.

She searched her surroundings, pulling open drawers, skimming shelves, seeking something—anything—that could tell her more.

She paused at the small pod machine, scanning the instructions carefully before slotting in a coffee capsule and watching the liquid stream into the cup. A simple act, but one entirely her own.

As she sipped, her gaze drifted to the bookcase—rows of travel books, spanning every continent. Her fingers brushed the spines, lingering over the titles, foreign names whispering promises of places beyond here. She wasn't sure what to make of them yet. Her heart was drawn to books like a musician to an instrument.

The warmth of the coffee steadied her, the cup heavy in her hand as she moved toward the terminal. Her fingers hovered just above the surface. It blinked to life with a quiet hum, casting a bluish glow across her face. Eliza scanned her wrist.

WELCOME, 307.
SYSTEM ACCESS GRANTED.

Her breath caught.

She was in.

The interface was simple, lined with routine—work schedules, announcements, meal rotations, local weather. The cannery worked on an old-school work schedule: three shifts a day, five days a week, weekends off, occasional overtime. Eliza blinked in surprise. This was a very generous schedule.

Bank Records. A significant amount recently withdrawn. The money meant to save another woman's life.

Tucked between the mundane was what made her pulse quicken: Medical Logs. And, at the bottom—a restricted file labeled: DNA/ Anomaly Notice – Tier 2.

Her finger hovered.

Whatever had happened to her—it wasn't random. And this system might hold the first piece of the puzzle.

A glance at the time snapped her back to reality—she needed to move quickly. She donned her coveralls and headed downstairs, her mind whirring, thoughts tangled in fragments she couldn't yet place.

305 was waiting for her in the old hotel breakfast room.

Eliza listened, letting the warmth of the meal settle in her stomach as 305 rattled on with casual familiarity, her words weaving together snippets of scandal, alliances, and petty feuds among the workers. Her hair falling as a curtain over her face whenever she leaned forward.

"…so, then Eleven says I'm not cutting up any ribbons today. Like she has a choice. Every shift cuts their own materials. Those day shifters are such prima donnas." 305 laughed at her own joke, shaking her head. "She acts like she has choices. Like any of us do," the words lingered in the air.

Eliza kept her expression neutral, taking another bite of chicken. The simplicity of the food felt grounding—real, tangible. It was hard to ignore the contrast between this modest dinner and the extravagant meals of her past life.

"I have to head out before I am late." She switched to Spanish, "Ocho y nueve, ¿vienes?"

"Si," the two women responded.

"Do you think if you ever go to somewhere that they speak Spanish you could take me," 305 said, a little too wistful to be completely teasing.

Eliza shrugged and watched the three women as they exited the building. She had one day to find out more about who she was now.

Audrey and Virginia performed that night. They became who they needed to be, slipping into expectation with practiced ease.

Audrey's first client was reckless, eager, drawn to fire, to the illusion of untamed passion. She gave him that fire. Let herself burn hot, let the heat mask everything underneath—the loss, the rage, the ache she couldn't name.

Virginia had a devoted suitor, the kind who saw her as an angel no matter what. His gaze never wavered, his devotion never questioned. She smiled, soft, serene, murmuring sweet reassurances that felt hollow in her own ears.

Neither spoke of Eliza, even though both glanced around the room, still expecting to see her studied presence.

Teresa presided over the evening, her sharp gaze ensuring everything ran as it should. Madame would not make an appearance tonight and Teresa did not question.

In her private study, she sat in the low candlelight, tonight she burned real candles, not LED. A bottle beside her, a quiet offering to grief.

Sister Hope stood near the window, her fingers resting lightly against the worn wood frame. Neither spoke at first.

Madame poured tequila into two glasses, pushing one toward her.

"Mercy is indeed cruel in these halls," Sister Hope said, barely above a whisper, lifting her glass, an echo from earlier.

Madame studied her for a moment before taking a slow sip. The burn was nothing compared to the weight in her chest.

Madame slipped an envelope to Sister Hope. The Abbess needed to know the truth, but sending a message was always a risk. Madame had used their traditional coding cipher, not an old edition of the Bible as many would suspect. Instead, she used a book that many would be shocked to find in a Convent, but all almost of had hidden away, the Kama Sutra—each position exquisite in its ability to convey meaning.

Sister Hope nodded.

The silence stretched, thick and suffocating, broken only by the clink of glass against wood.

Nothing more needed to be said. The night was dark and heavy. A storm brewed outside.

FTER THE OTHERS LEFT for work, Eliza went back upstairs to her room to search.

She entered her new room, the space both hers and not hers, the air carrying the faint presence of another.

It felt eerie to sift through a dead woman's possessions, knowing the hands that had folded these clothes, that had touched these walls, were no longer here.

But she had no choice. She needed to learn more.

Eliza hesitated, fingers hovering just above the worn leather cover. The diary felt as sacred as one of the ancient texts she was used to handling, its edges softened by time, the pages thick with the weight of secrets.

She exhaled slowly, then carefully lifted it from the drawer. A relic of a life cut short.

The first page, where it asked for name, read "I was once Ana Lucia, an orphan, now I am simply 307. One day I will save enough to travel and reclaim my name.

She traced the ink absently. Who had she been? What had she known?

Turning the page, her pulse quickened.

Eliza ran her fingers over the worn pages, absorbing the quiet longing folded between the ink.

Ana Lucia had a familiar tale. Raised an orphan and being found barren at sixteen, she was sent work. In her case not to a brothel, but to a cannery.

Ana Lucia had dreamed of leaving, of crossing oceans, of stepping beyond the fences that lined this place. Yet—she rarely did. Instead, she hoarded her money, clinging to the idea of escape without ever taking the steps to make it real.

She could picture it—a girl curled up by the barn, book in hand, watching the horses.

"Horses," Eliza whispered, excitement flickering to life.

But that lightness faded as she turned to the later entries, to the hurried, uneven script of Ana Lucia's final words. Coughing. A fever. A quiet admission of illness she couldn't afford to acknowledge.

She had kept working, had ignored it, had pushed forward—because money meant escape. Money meant freedom. And stopping meant neither.

Eliza's fingers tightened around the diary. Ana Lucia hadn't left. She had died.

Eliza sat on the edge of the old king-sized bed, the mattress well-worn, the diary open beside her, staring at her reflection in the mirrored sliding closet doors.

Why was it so easy to pass as 307?

Why had no one questioned her—not the owner, not the Matron, not the women in the dorm, not even 305, who had shared walks and talks with Ana Lucia night after night? Morning after morning?

She studied her face. Dark brown hair. Brown eyes. Unremarkable. It was the gowns and makeup that transformed her at the Hall of Mary Ann—but here, she was no one special. Not like Virginia with her halo of gold, or Audrey with her unmistakable fire. Eliza had always leaned toward studious pursuits, toward silence. Perhaps she and Ana Lucia had been kindred spirits—both inclined to fade into the background, to observe rather than speak.

Maybe it was the coveralls and hairnets, stripping identity from everyone. Ana Lucia's tendency to let her hair cover her face, always reading. Maybe it was the factory itself, that ceaseless rhythm designed to smooth away anything that made a person distinct. Being a number, not a name, not a person.

Or maybe, she thought grimly, Ana Lucia had never been seen clearly in the first place.

That was what chilled her most—how easily a life could be erased and replaced. How she had slipped into Ana Lucia's outline like water into a glass, unnoticed by anyone still drinking.

Her fingers rested on the diary, pressing lightly into the inked name. *"One day I will save enough to travel and reclaim my name."*

Eliza hadn't earned this girl's life. But she was living in it now. And in a world where only the rich and powerful were allowed stories, she would survive—for Ana Lucia. For her mother. For every woman whose life had been cut short, whose fire had been smothered beneath obedience, illness, or silence.

She made a vow to Ana Lucia that day—quiet but fierce. She would pick up her mantle, carry the dream that had been silenced too soon. She would travel. Not just beyond the fences, but far beyond. She would set foot on every continent, speak languages Ana Lucia never had the chance to learn, stand before oceans Ana Lucia had only imagined. She would find the unchipped.

Eliza would see the world *for both of them.*

⇒ ✳ ⇐

Dave and Robert sat down for privacy in the Rose Garden.

Robert's expression tightened. "There's still the Jackson problem."

Dave didn't blink. "He's loud, but not dangerous. Yet. He's smart enough to keep his hands clean but reckless enough to make noise at the wrong time."

Robert leaned back. "He's gaining traction with the reform wing. I don't like this development with Halstrom."

Dave's eyes narrowed. "Don't worry, I have got this covered."

"I trust you and don't need to know the details." Robert exhaled, then tapped the arm of his chair, thoughtful. "What about Gray?"

Dave shook his head slightly. "He's a liability after November. We need him for the rust belt optics, but trade partners hate him. Keeps quoting tariffs like scripture."

"Is it time?"

"Soon as the election's certified. Give him a soft exit—health reasons, family, whatever plays well. Replace him with someone who can talk supply chains without sounding like a union brawler."

Robert's voice dropped. "We already have names?"

Dave offered a slight grin. "Two. Both vetted. Both clean. And both fluent in Mandarin."

The president nodded slowly. "Keep Jackson distracted. Stall Halstrom. Cut Gray loose."

Dave raised his glass again. "And win the world while they're looking the other way." He needed to keep Robert focused on the politics, not the election. Dave when would manage that.

Eliza stood outside the entrance to the dormitory. The early light stretched across the horizon, painting the factory grounds in pale gold. A rooster crowed—sharp, insistent. She slowed slightly, listening. This world felt so alien from the Hall of Mary Ann.

She waited for 305, 8, and 9 to arrive and walked in with them.

"You are looking better," 305 stated, "but you really should let me do something with your hair."

Eliza shrugged; she felt like that was what Ana Lucia would have done.

She greeted the Matron at the counter, pouring herself a mug of tea, adding honey with quiet precision.

When she caught the murmured Spanish between Eight and Nine, the words clicked into place—clear, understood.

"Dormir bien," she told them, her voice soft, almost uncertain, testing the shape of the phrase on her tongue. Maybe Dave's chip upload did work, she pondered.

The women paused for only a moment before nodding, smiling slightly as they continued toward their rooms.

305 continued her effortless monologue, chattering all the way to the third floor, excitement spilling into every word.

"Why don't we ever use names?" Eliza wondered aloud as they walked up the stairs, a quiet test. Did 305 know the name Ana Lucia?

"Not this again," 305 sighed. "I will tell you my name if we ever leave. That includes if I ever get married and move to a cottage," she giggled.

"Do you have a boyfriend?" Eliza asked, intrigued, feeling a bit safer that they had never used names before.

"No, but a girl can dream—did you think I met someone in short time you were ill?" she laughed. "Laundry before shift tomorrow? You probably don't have much since you just got back from the infirmary, but I have loads."

Eliza nodded, though the thought of laundry—of normalcy, of habit—felt strange in her mind. She had not done her own laundry since the orphanage, long ago.

⇒ ✷ ⇐

"You are positive?" Dave asked the geneticist on a secure line.

"Absolutely" he responded. The woman in a 99.5% genetic match with Jonathan Franklin Rochester as her father."

"Have you told anyone?" Dave asked.

"No, but..."he hesitated, "I suspect that despite the best secrecy this may get out soon. It is hard to keep information like this private in such a large facility."

Dave inhaled slowly, steadying himself. 99.5%. The number hung in the air, cold, definitive.

"And the mother?" Dave asked, already knowing the answer.

A pause.

"The Mother, Angela O'Brien, studied Library Sciences at The Catholic University of America (CUA) in Washington, DC," he paused and added "at the time that your cousin went missing."

Dave turned toward the window, staring out into the empty morning light, his grip tightening around the edge of the desk.

"Any family on the Mother's side?" Dave asked. He had restrained himself from pursuing this question, because searches created traces.

"The closest I can find is a fourth cousin twice removed," the geneticist responded.

"Send over the information," the distant relative being even more remote than he had hoped. "I will get a detective on that," Dave told him. He knew that this relative was so remote that even if they were in prison, it would barely cause a ripple.

"Let me know if you hear any leaks," Dave told him. A few rumors needed to spread—just enough, just right—before he took his next steps.

The geneticist exhaled sharply. "I'll do what I can, but whispers spread like wildfire."

Dave nodded, already calculating.

Eliza.

Not just an orphan. Not just a name lost in the void of the factory.

She was bloodline. Legacy. A rarity in a world dictated by certainty.

His work had just stood the scrutiny of the most renowned xenologist in the world. Eliza's genetics and connections must be undisputed.

"And you're absolutely certain?" Dave asked again—repetition, a common interrogation technique. A rare indulgence, too. He allowed himself a moment to revel in his own work. There could be no doubts in the databases. Once this was out, the scrutiny would be relentless.

The geneticist didn't waver. "The markers don't lie."

Dave leaned back, staring at the ceiling.

Eliza wasn't just another orphan folded into the system. She was bloodline. Legacy. A loose thread in a tightly controlled weave—one that could unravel everything.

And now, she was his. His fabrication. His masterpiece.

Not even the truth could unmake her now.

"Send everything to me in an encrypted file," Dave instructed, his voice clipped.

"Yes, sir."

The line disconnected with a soft click. Dave sat still for a moment, fingertips pressed together, eyes closed. The hum of the facility buzzed faintly behind the sealed glass, a synthetic silence he found oddly soothing. Everything was in place. The data, the story, the girl.

Now, it was time to put the next brick in place.

The Bell-View City Clerk deftly adjusted the chipping system, his fingers gliding over the terminal with practiced precision. One name disappeared, and a position took its place—Rebecca Hammond, Nurse of Record for Bell-View. No alerts, no signatures. Just a silent substitution within a system built to forget as much as it remembered.

The nurse—formally Rebecca—stood a few feet away, her smile tentative but hopeful. She glanced around the office with the cautious wonder of someone still unsure if they'd truly escaped. "I still can't believe I got this job," she said quietly, mostly to herself. "Right when I thought I couldn't stomach another month in DC"

"Welcome to Bell-View," the clerk responded absently. Not out of rudeness—he was polite, if a bit absent—but because his mind was elsewhere, already navigating the spine of the registry: a sprawling lattice of outdated code and half-buried protocols. He had inherited the system almost a decade ago, and though its shell appeared antiquated, its core was something else entirely.

It wasn't just a digital ledger. It was a cipher. Designed not only to store identities but to shape them—to conceal, overwrite, and, when necessary, resurrect them. Originally sold as a public records modernization project, it had evolved into something else: a living archive of plausible fictions. A place where the dead could be reassigned, and the living could vanish.

The clerk's eyes narrowed slightly as he noticed something off in 307's log. Nothing overt. Just a faint irregularity—a signature that didn't quite match his own encryption patterns. A work of precision, almost elegant, and well within the expected system constraints. But he hadn't done it. Neither had his apprentice.

For a moment, he considered tracing it—chasing down the ghost in the record. But he let the impulse fade. In Bell-View, mysteries weren't problems to solve. They were assets to monitor. The system didn't exist to reveal the truth. It existed to shape what truth was allowed to survive.

⇒ ✵ ⇐

Together the four women walked to the front to the dormitory and waited only a few minutes before the men walked past from the male dormitory to join them. Even though the walk was short, Eliza's boots felt heavy.

"Good to have you back, 307," the foreman said with a warm smile as they entered the cannery.

Eliza followed the women to a workstation with linen and ribbons as they placed hairnets on their heads. The two women speaking Spanish immediately set to work cutting the fabric into small squares and ribbon into smaller lengths.

Eliza and 305 began to place a piece of fabric over each jar lid as it rolled off the line and tied it with a bow.

Eliza read the label and gave a slight sigh, "Cherry horseradish."

305 smirked. "I know, right? Someone out there actually buys this stuff. Can you believe it?"

Eliza gave a faint, almost involuntary smile, missing her friends.

The repetitive motion of the task was oddly soothing—fold, tie, bow, slide. Fold, tie, bow, slide. The scent of cherries hung thick in the air, pierced occasionally by a sharp tang of vinegar and horseradish.

She fell into rhythm, her body remembering patterns even if her mind still fought to assemble the edges of her new reality. The conversation from the breakfast room echoed—choices, or the illusion of them. The low hum of machines, the clink of jars, the dull ache in her back— none of it matched the world she'd come from. And yet... here she was. Tying bows on jars of cherry horseradish like it mattered.

The line moved on. Jar after jar. And somewhere deep inside, past the fog and the aching muscles, something sharp and focused began to stir.

⹌ ✵ ⹍

Dave opened a secure interface and typed only two names:

Father. Brother.

Subject Line: *Family Legacy: Confidential Briefing.*

Message:
We need to meet. In person. Today. No aides. No security teams. Just us.

You'll understand when you see the file.

I suggest my study at Barkley Mansion.

He attached the encrypted packet with a quantum decryption key and watched the message disappear into the net. No trail. No copies. No risk.

His study. Soundproofed. Shielded from scans and transmissions. This was not a conversation that they could risk being overheard by

White House staff. His father would need to take the family jet from the Cape right away.

Dave looked around the study with a satisfied grin, later today he would meet with his father and brother—presenting them with the long-lost missing daughter of Jonathan Franklin Rochester and Angela O'Brien, a good, but not perfect Irish Catholic girl. He chuckled to himself.

305 knocked on Eliza's door, balancing a laundry basket on her hip. The rhythmic hum of the old washers and dryers drifted down the hallway, a steady, mechanical heartbeat from another era.

Eliza followed her down the corridor toward the laundry room, a relic of the dormitory's past—back when guests stayed for extended visits, when families of tourists actually paid to pick apples and cherries, relishing the illusion of rural simplicity before returning to their air-conditioned lives.

The machines stood like tired sentinels along the walls, their enamel surfaces scuffed, dulled by decades of use. The faint scent of detergent lingered, mixing with the warm, damp air. A handwritten sign—faded, curling at the corners—reminded users to "Check pockets—tokens lost are not refunded."

305 set her basket down, deftly sorting through linens as she continued, "…and then the lady's maid, with the help of the stable hand, hid the body for the Duchess. I would be a lady's maid over a Duchess any day—maids always live to the end in these stories."

Eliza smiled at the parallel—the unseen figures pulling the strings, slipping between spaces unnoticed. Agnes would understand that game well.

305 glanced up. "Want to come to town tomorrow? I know you never spend money, but the library is always free."

Eliza brushed her limp hair from her face, the shadow of uncertainty lingering in her mind. "I'd like that."

Would they be allowed to go alone? Would they be watched?

The old machines rumbled on, indifferent to the shifting world around them.

And Eliza wondered how much of that world was truly hers to step into.

Audrey and Virginia sat uncomfortably in the library where Eliza had spent so much of her time. The space felt heavier now, as if the weight of her absence had seeped into the walls, pressing down on them. Her legacy hung in the air, palpable and unresolved.

Sister Hope stood nearby, silent but watchful—her presence a quiet anchor in their unease. She stepped forward and handed them Eliza's manuscript and a worn copy of *Code Talkers*.

The weight of the moment settled between them, thick with unspoken grief and quiet determination.

"She wanted this finished," Sister Hope said at last, her voice steady but soft. "She believed it mattered."

"The Abbess and Sister Lily believe it matters still," Virginia replied, grounding the moment in something larger than their loss.

"Then we finish it," Audrey said, her voice low and firm, anger simmering just beneath the surface.

Virginia rested her fingers on the book's edge, her gaze distant. "She believed in something bigger than herself," she murmured. "Something worth fighting for."

Sister Hope's eyes held steady on Audrey. "She believed in truth," she said gently. "Even when that truth was hard to imagine."

Virginia nodded, her voice catching. "And hope. She believed in hope."

Audrey leaned forward, elbows on her knees, eyes sharp. "And most of all, she believed in love. She loved fiercely." Her hand landed on the manuscript with a decisive thud. "This isn't just history—it's proof. Eliza was onto something. And someone out there wanted it buried."

Virginia drew a slow breath, as if trying to call Eliza's presence back into the room. "Then we won't let them."

Audrey's jaw tensed. "We finish this."

They would carry it forward. Not just for Eliza, but for everything she had tried to protect—for all the women who had been silenced, and the ones who dared to speak, even when no one wanted to listen.

John, Robert, and Dave Barkley sat in the study at Barkley Mansion, the scent of aged scotch hanging in the air as they made small talk about John's flight from the Cape. The low hum of conversation masked the underlying tension—Dave was leading them somewhere, and they both knew it.

"What is so important that I had to fly down, and this couldn't be discussed on a secure video line?" John asked, his annoyance edged with curiosity.

Dave swirled his drink, letting the silence stretch just long enough to pull them in. "I needed to speak with you in a completely secure room—and without any of the women."

Robert raised an eyebrow. "You always do this," he muttered, but his posture straightened ever so slightly, readying himself for whatever came next.

Dave leaned forward, his voice measured. "I know that both of you will place logic over sentimentality." He let the words settle. "We need to make a decision."

He had them.

Years of navigating his father's ruthless pragmatism and his brother's strategic mind had made him skilled at this—weaving control without ever demanding it outright.

He took a slow sip of his scotch before continuing. "A few days ago, I received a genetic alert, and what I have found is open on my terminal." A casual nod toward the screen. "Go take a look."

John exhaled sharply, shaking his head, but he moved first, crossing the room with a sense of reluctant obligation. Robert followed, his movements more calculated.

The screen glowed faintly in the dim light.

Dave watched them as they read, scanning the details. John's fingers tightened around the edge of the desk. Robert's jaw shifted, grip firm around his glass.

Silence stretched, heavy with realization.

99.5%. Bloodline. Legacy.

John set his drink down with more force than necessary. "Is this confirmed?"

"Beyond doubt," Dave responded smoothly, his voice a steady anchor. "And if we don't act now, someone else will."

Robert exhaled slowly, rubbing his thumb along the rim of his glass. "What are you suggesting?"

Dave leaned back in his chair, savoring the moment. "We decide what happens next. No surprises. No unknowns."

John exchanged a look with Robert—a silent conversation passing between them.

Robert nodded once. "Have you done a background check on this woman? Who is she? What do we know about this Bell-View Farms?" He ran a hand through his hair. "Damnit, Dave. This is an election year."

"I haven't done anything with this information," Dave assured him, his voice carefully even. "I only just got it today and wanted to talk to both of you first." He turned to Robert pointedly. "Investigations will attract attention, but I don't see an alternative."

John leaned back, considering. "We have time to pay off the chit or bury this if we need to." He swirled his drink. "I see more opportunities than scandal here. It's not like she's the daughter of a dead mistress or something." He laughed, reaching for his scotch.

Dave gave an approving nod. "I am inclined to agree. The Rochesters and the Barkleys haven't been as united as we once were. A long-lost heiress should bring the Rochesters out from whatever yachts and European vacations they're wasting their time on."

Robert shot him with a warning look. "Don't get ahead of yourself. Discreet background checks first. Then we make a decision as a family."

Dave dipped his head in mock deference. "Of course."

John leaned back, loosening his collar. "Didn't the kids just start spring break? Let's send Caroline and the kids up to the Cape with Eunice. I'll stay here at Barkley Mansion a few more days. Settle this properly."

As the scotch warmed their blood and the future reassembled itself in the Barkley study, one thing was clear: the game was changing.

Madame Mary Margaret was tired in a way she had never known. Not just in body, but soul-deep—worn by the quiet toll of too many unanswered questions.

She had just reached for her nightcap when a soft knock came at the door.

"Come in, Hope," she called, not needing to ask. She knew the knock—measured, respectful, familiar. Her friend. Her anchor.

"Virginia and Audrey came to *my* library today," Sister Hope said gently as she entered. "They're picking up where Eliza left off."

"Am I wrong to let them believe she's dead?" Madame asked, her voice low, uncertainty threading through it like a fine crack in glass. She lifted her glass of port, holding it up to the light. The deep red shimmered like blood—dense, opaque. As if the truth might be hidden in its depths. "I should feel certain," she murmured. "But I don't."

Sister Hope stood by the window, her hands folded in front of her. "Eliza left here deceased," she said, her voice steady—measured, but not cold. "It's better to wait for proof otherwise."

Madame exhaled slowly, her fingertips brushing the rim of her glass. "And if proof never comes?"

She thought of them—Eliza, Virginia, Audrey. Would they have become inseparable, had the years allowed? If the world hadn't broken the promise before it could even bloom?

Sister Hope didn't look away. "Then they will mourn her in truth."

A dry, bitter laugh escaped Madame's lips. "That's the kindest cruelty of it, isn't it?"

Sister Hope said nothing. She understood too well.

BELL-VIEW CARRIED AN UNSETTLING charm—precise, structured, the rooster ever punctual, horses in the paddock; deceptively quaint. The tiny houses stood in orderly rows, their uniformity both comforting and eerie, as if the town itself had been designed to whisper efficiency without losing its veneer of warmth.

Eliza walked alongside 305, the quiet crunch of their footsteps against the narrow road filling the air. No escort. No watchful eyes—at least none visible.

305 had braided Eliza's hair into a delicate crown, a touch of elegance, that reminded her of her past. Vanity, perhaps. A risk, certainly. Without the maids at the Hall of Mary Ann, her hair had been left to fall unceremoniously, hiding her face. Now, it framed her like a quiet declaration—a choice. An assertion of self in a world determined to strip it away.

Eliza and 305 paused on the cracked asphalt path, when the unmistakable, high-pitched sound of a child laughing sliced through the otherwise quiet air. The laughter was bright and unrestrained, bouncing off the walls of the nearby cottages.

They watched, wide-eyed, as a chubby toddler, his cheeks flushed a rosy pink and his dark hair a tangled mess, wobbled unsteadily on short legs towards a woman. The woman stood under a porch, careful to remain in the shadows. She had a baby cradled securely in her arms, its tiny face hidden against her shoulder, but the soft, rhythmic patting on its back was visible.

The woman shifted her weight, a tired but fond smile gracing her lips, and lifted a hand to wave at the two women. 305 responded with an exuberant wave, her hand a blur of motion, a wide, genuine smile lighting up her face. Eliza offered a more tentative wave, her fingers feeling stiff and unsure, a ghost of a smile touching her lips. The air hummed with the distant buzz of unseen insects.

305 picked up with her usual lively chatter, her voice a cheerful melody. "So rare to see a baby. Let alone two," she continued, her gaze lingering on the small family, before launching into a tale of folklore about twins being a sign of immense luck. Eliza listened, the cadence of 305's voice a familiar comfort, but her own mind whirred, like the gears of an old machine finally clicking into place, connecting together fragmented pieces from her old life in the hushed, scent-filled corridors of the Hall to the stark realities of her new one at Bell-View.

Children were rare indeed, she realized with a sudden, chilling clarity. The most precious, fiercely guarded commodity in this world. She knew—only barren women were sent to work in the sprawling factories and endless fields. If the government found a rare case of a working-class woman having a child, it was removed swiftly. The punishment to conceal a child born, death.

Bell-View wasn't hiding a dark secret of cruelty or exploitation, but a bright, shining beacon of hope, a defiant act of love that would be instantly extinguished, would burn everything it touched to ash, if the authorities ever discovered it. They were committing the radical, dangerous crime of allowing parents to keep their children, a simple, fundamental right that had been stripped away by the world outside. The air suddenly felt heavier, charged with the weight of this silent rebellion. As the two women continued walking, Eliza realized that she might have inadvertently brought a risk to the mysterious place, where numbers hid secrets.

Nick let out a low whistle as he reread the encrypted message. Top priority. High stakes. No room for error. He rubbed a thumb over the edge of his worn terminal screen. This one had weight.

"We're going to Pennsylvania," he said, voice edged with anticipation.

Mack barely looked up, still focused on his sandwich. "What's in Pennsylvania?" he asked, mid-bite, crumbs spilling onto the battered desk between them.

Nick smirked, leaning back in his chair, the creak of old wood filling the dimly lit office. "Just got a ping to check out a dame who might be a long-lost Barkley-Rochester heiress."

Mack choked—hard.

He coughed, pounding his fist against his chest, eyes watering. "Dude, warn a guy before you drop something like that!"

Nick chuckled, reaching for his coffee—black, bitter, lukewarm. He took a slow sip, savoring the moment. "Where's the fun in that?"

Mack wiped his mouth, shaking his head. "You think it's legit?"

Nick shrugged, flipping his tablet case open and closed absentmindedly. "Doesn't matter what I think."

The overhead light flickered, humming softly as he tapped the encrypted message. Eyes sharp. Focused. Calculating.

"We'll sort the truth on the way. Pack your gear—we're taking the hovercraft for a road trip."

Mack sighed, pushing away the remnants of his lunch. "Hope she's worth the jet fuel."

Nick's grin widened as he slid his taser into its holster. "Dave Barkley said no stone left unturned."

Mack let out a low chuckle, grabbing his coat. "Now it's a road trip."

Nick and Mack split up when they arrived at Bell-View Farms, each falling into familiar rhythm. Nick, the more polished of the two, headed straight for the main office to speak with the owners. Mack drifted toward the local watering holes—where loose tongues often did more work than warrants.

⚘

The owners—Georgette and Marty Washington—were polite, but uneasy. Not guilty, just wary. That was normal. Most folks didn't like a detective on their porch.

"I need to ask you folks a few questions," Nick said, keeping his tone casual, showing his private investigator badge. "About a young woman who works here. She was recently ill."

The shift in the room was subtle, but real.

"307," Georgette breathed.

Nick sat back slightly, letting the weight of the conversation settle. 307. A number, not a name—like she was a figure on a ledger instead of a person. That detail sat uneasily in his gut.

He leaned forward slightly, just enough to press the conversation deeper. "The nurse died—what exactly happened?"

The husband, Marty, cleared his throat. "When she got sick, the nurse recommended isolation and a full DNA scan. I don't know the medical specifics, but you're welcome to the reports."

Not hiding. Just in over his head. Nick tapped in his tablet.

"A full DNA scan," Nick repeated, slow and deliberate. "That's pricey, especially for a cannery girl."

The husband gave a short nod. "307 wasn't like the others. Quiet. Always reading, talking about places she'd never been, but wanted to go. Kept to herself."

"She doesn't waste her money on alcohol down at the pub on weekends," Georgette added.

Nick studied the wife. Her fingers clutched her sleeve, a gesture of worry. Or guilt. Nick tapped away on his tablet.

"How did the scan and treatment get paid?" he asked.

"Her savings," Georgette whispered. "Gone."

"It was either that or..." the husband trailed off. He didn't need to finish.

Nick finally glanced at the file they'd transferred—medical scans, prescriptions, treatment summaries. Clean. This made him more suspicious.

"The nurse," he said. "Why wasn't she treated?"

"The health inspectors said, she didn't realize how bad it was," the husband offered.

"She was a nurse," Nick said flatly.

Georgette looked away. "Sometimes they're so focused on others, they miss their own symptoms," she said sadly.

Nick let the silence stretch—just long enough to make them squirm.

He tapped away on this tablet.

A sick girl with dreams. A nurse who didn't make it. A farm where people had numbers instead of names.

He stood, tablet in hand. "Thanks for your time,"

"Wait," the wife said, barely above a whisper.

This was it, Nick thought, "Go ahead." Waiting for a confession. A secret.

"We try to treat our workers decent—better than most," she said. Her husband stayed silent, resigned. "This farm, the cannery... it's all we have. People here depend on us. Please, don't report us to the government." Her hands trembled as she moved closer to her husband.

"Why would I report you?" Nick asked, genuinely confused.

"You've got a badge," the husband said flatly.

"Folk around here stay far from the government," the wife added, eyes wide, like a deer on the verge of bolting.

Then it struck Nick, this couple looked at each other like they really cared about each other; loved each other. In this day and age, it was about as rare as finding a needle in a haystack.

The tension in the room was palpable—not the kind that stemmed from guilt, but from deep-seated caution, the kind bred from years of keeping one's head down, surviving without interference.

Nick recognized the look in the wife's eyes. Not defiance, not deception—fear. Fear of losing what they had built. Fear of being noticed. Fear of power that never arrived with good intentions.

Nick softened his tone. "I'm here for 307. Not the nurse. Not the government."

She studied him for a moment longer, then nodded, as if deciding to believe him.

Her husband, however, wasn't convinced. His stance remained firm, guarded, the kind of mistrust that ran deep. A man facing a force greater than him and knowing he didn't have the power to protect his own.

"We have nothing to hide," he said, but the way he said it made it clear—hiding was survival, whether there was something to hide or not.

Nick tucked his tablet under his arm, keeping his tone neutral. "Foreman 3 and Dorm Matron 2, then."

The wife nodded. "They interact with 307 the most."

Nick hesitated for a beat, the numbers nagging at him. A town that feared names, that feared recognition, that structured itself around anonymity.

As he walked out, he was already thinking of Mack—already picturing the stories pouring out of beer-slick barstools and gossip-thick diners. The truth always bled out somewhere.

In a forgotten apple cellar, the air was thick with urgency, but the movements were precise—practiced, ingrained, silent without fear but full of purpose. The faint scent of apples provided comfort against the unknown outside.

The older children whispered reassurances, guiding the younger ones through the passage beneath the barn, their steps light, careful, as if their very presence had been trained into invisibility. Young mothers arrived quickly from nearby cottages, pressing their infants close, holding the hands of squirming toddlers. No panic. Just preparation.

On the other side, hands worked swiftly, shifting barrels into place, constructing a facade of normalcy, the cellar transformed into nothing more than a forgotten storage hold—ordinary, unremarkable. A warning had come. Investigators were at the main house with badges.

The quiet was not emptiness, but survival, an unspoken understanding passed between glances, gestures, the way bodies moved in sync without command.

Bell-View's secret did not exist in the darkness—it thrived in the spaces just out of sight.

The librarian's smile flickered with recognition as 307 stepped through the double doors, their brass handles worn to a soft shine from decades of use. Something stalled in her expression—like a vinyl record catching for just a breath—before it smoothed over again, adjusting to what had changed.

307's hair, normally a curtain shielding her from the world, was now woven into a crown. It wasn't just arranged—it was worn like a quiet halo. Something about it made her pause. She looked like someone who had touched death and come back with secrets stitched into her skin.

"Great to have my favorite patron back," the librarian said, her voice light as she pushed her half-moon glasses up the bridge of her nose.

The word *patron* struck Eliza like a dropped book in a silent room. She was never the patron—always the one on the other side of the transaction.

The building smelled of dust, cracked vinyl, and old radiator heat. Faded bulletin boards displayed decades-old flyers. Overhead, fluorescent lights buzzed faintly, flickering in protest of another long afternoon.

"What would you like to explore today?" the librarian asked brightly, misreading Eliza's silence as the usual quiet of 307.

"Perhaps something on Native American Spirit Walking?" she offered, already drifting toward the back corner of the building, past wooden card catalogs and low shelves crowded with aging encyclopedias. The Native American folklore section was nestled between Local History and Religion, just beside a dusty globe whose oceans had faded to gray.

"Thank you," Eliza murmured, gathering several titles and carrying them to her usual table beneath the tall window. The light filtered in soft and golden, dancing off the particles in the air, wrapping the space in a hush that felt sacred.

She read until her stomach growled loud enough to be heard across the room.

"Do you want to check any of them out with you?" the librarian asked, her voice gentle. "So, you can go home and eat?"

They had developed this pattern. 307 would read until her hunger roared like a mountain lion, then quietly disappeared, never spending her credits at the café or the tavern. She was saving—for something far away, something still forming beyond the edges of Bell-View. A place without numbers for names.

Eliza looked down at the book in her lap. She carefully selected three. The books would be heavy on her walk, and she had not thought to bring a bag. She was delighted at the thought of checking out books and taking them to her room. Having books of substance in her room, such a luxury.

Eliza hesitated at the librarian's desk, running her hand along the worn edge of the counter. Should she already know the answer to this?

"Can I request a book that isn't in this library?" she asked, the words faltering slightly, uncertain.

The Librarian looked up, pausing only for a second before offering a kind smile, her voice effortlessly smoothing over 307's awkward phrasing.

"What book would you like me to request this time?"

Eliza leaned in slightly, lowering her voice as if the walls might listen too. "The Woman in the Iron Mask," she murmured.

The Librarian's fingers moved swiftly across the terminal, searching.

"There's a copy available from the Sisters of Carla Mercy," she noted, nodding as she entered the request. "I'll order it for you."

Eliza exhaled, a quiet confirmation settled in her chest.

The book itself was just a novel, one of Audrey's favorites. A classic conspiracy theory, with a twist. But the request—the exchange, the path it would take—had just become something more. The beginning of a plan. A way to send messages beyond Bell-View's quiet confines back to the Hall of Mary Ann.

The bar hummed with low conversations and the clink of glasses, the air thick with the scent of spilled whiskey and fried food. Neon signs buzzed softly, casting flickering light against scratched tabletops and walls layered in posters that had faded with time.

Mack leaned against the bar, the wood worn smooth by years of elbows resting, deals being struck, secrets exchanged. The place had history. The kind that didn't ask questions but always had answers for the right price.

He showed a picture of a girl to the regulars, moving from face to face, the silence stretching after each negative shake of a head. Nothing. Until, finally, a woman, her eyes crinkling at the corners from years of laughter and worry, squinted harder at the photo. She punched her friend in the arm, a sharp, familiar jab. "If that doesn't look like 307 you can bowl me over." Her cackle, raw and unrestrained, cut through the bar's murmur.

Her friend snatched the photo, tracing its edge with a chipped nail. "Older, but her, I'd say. She left first shift, what, eight years ago?"

"Oh, yes, the duchess too good to hang out with us, always with her nose in a book," the first woman responded, her voice dripping with remembered disdain. "Did she finally get herself into some trouble?"

"You gonna buy us a drink for our troubles?" the second asked, her gaze steady, appraising.

Mack let the moment hang, a silent currency exchange, before a slow grin softened his features. "Depends on how much trouble she got into."

He flagged the barkeep, motioning for another round for the women. "Whiskey neat," he ordered for himself, a simple anchor in the swirling room.

"Didn't she almost die recently?" Eleven added, her tone shifting, a hint of something deeper in her voice. "You can call me Eleven by the way, lucky eleven."

"I'm Twelve," her friend added, leaning closer to Mack, a glint in her eye. "She left first shift, what…eight years ago? Saw her every once in a while on shift change or at the doors, but that has been it since."

Mack kept his expression easy, but his mind raced. What was up with these numbers? A chill, faint as a phantom touch, brushed him. "What do you mean, 'almost died'?" he asked, his voice a low, casual murmur. He pushed the fresh drinks toward them, a silent offering.

Eleven smirked, her guard loosening with the alcohol's warmth. "She got sick, bad. The nurse tried to help, but…" She flicked a glance at her friend, a shared, dark understanding passing between them. "The nurse didn't make it, but the duchess did."

Mack nodded slowly, the whiskey warm on his tongue, a second confirmation of a grim detail.

The first woman, Eleven, as she introduced herself, cackled again, taking a deliberate sip.

"She always thought she was better than the rest of us. Spoke foreign languages and was constantly showing off how smart she was."

Twelve exhaled, rubbing at her temple as if to chase away a memory. "Look, I don't know what you're looking for, but if you want dirt on 307, you're barking up the wrong tree."

Eleven winked, a practiced, weary gesture. "You want a good time, you come ask for Lucky Eleven or Twelve, or both. You want to hang out and write poetry or whatever pretend rich wannabes do…you find 307."

Twelve laughed, a sharp, dismissive sound that sliced through the low hum of the pub. "She ain't one of us," she said, raising her glass in a brittle salute to no one in particular.

The others at the bar chuckled nervously, more out of habit than conviction.

Behind one of the rough-hewn wooden pillars near the dartboard, 305 stilled her breath.

She wasn't eavesdropping—at least, not in the way people meant when they said it like a sin. No, this was something else. A protective instinct. Her ears tuned sharply to every nuance in the conversation, weighing the tension between words.

Someone had been asking about 307. Showing a photo, this couldn't be good.

Unless she's a secret duchess, 305 thought. *Oh please, let her be a secret duchess.*

It would explain so much. The strange silences. The dreaming. The way she always had her head in a cloud.

Mack took a slow sip of his whiskey, the bitter warmth a counterpoint to the growing certainty in his gut. That was starting to feel more true by the second.

The café was the kind of place where time felt slower, where the scent of fresh-brewed coffee and buttery biscuits lingered in the air long after the breakfast rush. The worn wooden floors creaked underfoot, polished smooth by years of steady foot traffic. A chalkboard menu hung behind the counter, the specials scrawled in looping cursive—meatloaf with mashed potatoes, fresh peach cobbler, and a bottomless cup of coffee strong enough to wake the dead.

"What do you think Mack?" Nick asked.

"Something is strange here," he took a bite of his meatloaf. "What is up with these numbers?"

Nick leaned back in his chair, the soft hum of conversation mingling with the clatter of plates and the occasional hiss of the old espresso machine behind the counter. The staff moved with the quiet efficiency of people who had been here forever.

Mack stabbed his fork into his meatloaf, the brown gravy pooling against the edge of his plate.

"Right," Nick said. "The couple that owns the place seems nice enough, but this whole numbering thing is super creepy." he muttered between bites, glancing around the room like the answers might be hiding among the worn booths and faded floral curtains.

Mack nodded slowly. "And the girl—307? My sources say she keeps her nose buried in books, barely interacts, like she doesn't belong."

Nick tapped his fingers against the table. "Owners said the same thing—called her a dreamer."

A beat of silence. Then Nick exhaled, shaking his head. "Do you feel like we traveled back in time to this place?"

Mack cracked a grin, picking up his coffee, which had just been refilled. "Which is why I'm going to order a second peach cobbler," he patted his stomach. "Tomorrow morning you get Dorm Matron Two—I'll handle Foreman Three."

Nick smirked, "Let's see what answers numbers can give us." He cracked a small smile.

"Bad one," Mack responded with a wry chuckle.

As they went upstairs to the rooms above the café they had rented there was a slight sense of unease. As if everyone held them guilty. In suspicion, of what they did not know.

The cellar held its breath, the quiet thick with waiting. Receiving notice; the investigators had not left the town, they would be there overnight.

The mothers settled their infants, hands moving with practiced care, their exhaustion pressed deep into their bones. Three days' worth of supplies sat neatly tucked away, a fragile promise of survival—but only if no one came too close.

Above, in the cottages, parents lay awake, their bodies still but their minds restless, every whispered prayer turning into silent bargaining.

If cooperation meant safety, they would comply. If silence meant survival, they would endure it. They would pray the investigators left in the morning.

Bell-View thrived not on deception, but on devotion—on the unshakable willingness to do whatever was necessary to protect its brightest secret.

305 knocked fast—three sharp raps—before Eliza even had a chance to unlace her boots. When the door opened, the urgency in 305's eyes said everything. She barely glanced at the soft waves that now framed 307's face—Eliza's face—with new clarity, no longer hidden but softened, defined.

"We have to talk," 305 said, stepping in before Eliza could nod.

Library books lay open and half-stacked on the desk, titles on mythology, spirit walking, and something obscure about seed codes. The air buzzed with unfinished thoughts and ancient wisdom. But 305's presence cut through it.

"There was a man at the pub today," she said, her voice tight. "He had a photo. Of you."

Eliza blinked. The breath she took felt too shallow.

"He was asking questions. Not casual ones. The kind that make your stomach drop."

Eliza swallowed. "Why would a man be looking for me?" Her voice tried for flatness but hit something closer to a challenge.

305 didn't hesitate. "Maybe you killed that nurse and lost your memory. Maybe it's tax evasion—all that money used for your treatment. Or maybe…" she paused dramatically, the glint of mischief breaking through, "you're secretly a duchess, ripped from the arms of aristocracy as a baby and raised in hiding. You know, like one of those regency vids."

Eliza's lips twitched. Almost a smile. Almost.

305 dropped onto the edge of the worn sofa. "I'm just saying—you almost died and now you've got strangers with glossy photos poking around town."

Eliza looked at the books again, their spines full of myth and warning. Her fingers grazed the one on ancestral echoes.

Maybe it wasn't a fairy tale. But it wasn't just a coincidence either.

"Alright," she said softly, but with more steel than before. "Then let's start figuring it out."

⊰ ❀ ⊱

Madame Mary Margaret's fingers tightened around the note from the Abbess, its brevity more frustrating than the message itself. It didn't require any decoding.

She exhaled slowly, forcing patience into the space around her.

The study felt smaller, still tainted by the recent events, amplifying her sense of confinement. She was used to motion, to action, to decisions made in precise strokes. But now?

She reread the message again.

"Wait."

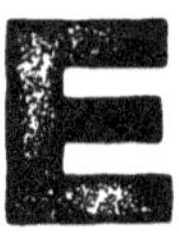ELIZA SAT BENEATH A sprawling oak, its roots pushing through the warm earth like fingers anchoring her to something older, deeper.

The season was shifting—spring's sharp greens maturing into the lush, heavy hues of summer. The air was sweet with sun-warmed grass, the buzz of insects rising and falling like distant music.

Ana Lucia's diary lay open in her lap, flanked by a scattering of travel books detailing the majesty of ancient Native cultures scattered across the Central and Western United States. She turned the pages slowly, letting her eyes wander—letting the land speak.

In the paddocks beyond, horses moved with lazy grace, tails swishing against the afternoon heat. One had taken an apple from her palm earlier, its breath soft, its mouth warm and unafraid.

So different from the brothel courtyard.

There, the air had been laced with perfume and tension. Flowers groomed into submission masked the rot beneath. The flagstones had worn smooth from generations of practiced seduction—women gliding through theater and survival, every step a negotiation. Beauty there was currency. And laughter rarely touched the eyes.

But here, at Bell-View Farms, nothing needed performance. The cannery was functional, not contrived. The horses didn't posture. The trees blossomed, bore fruit, and shed their leaves without apology.

Eliza's fingers grazed the edge of Ana Lucia's diary—thin paper, yet strong. Like memory. Like truth.

Here, she could think. Breathe. Ask.

Why me?

What knowledge had Dave loaded into her brain? *Had he done it at all?* Was the phantom weight in her head implanted memory... or trauma masquerading as data?

And if it *was* real—what was she supposed to do with it?

Nick rested his hand against the reception desk, taking in the space with a practiced glance. Clean, well-kept, orderly—but not sterile. The dorm had the warmth of routine, the quiet hum of lives moving within its walls.

"Can I speak with Dorm Matron Two?" he asked, his voice easy, measured.

The woman behind the desk smiled, tucking a stray strand of hair behind her ear. "You're looking at her."

Nick nodded, noting the lack of hesitation in her response. No stalling, no deflection—just direct, friendly confidence.

"You must be the detective I was warned about," she said, still smiling. Not guarded, not nervous. Just amused.

Nick set his mug down, watching the steam curl into the air. "Warned? That's an interesting choice of words."

She chuckled, folding her hands on the desk. "Not in a bad way. Word travels fast here. Anytime someone starts asking questions, people take notice."

She gestured toward a small side table where a standard hotel coffee and hot water dispensers sat beside a collection of neatly arranged mugs. "Help yourself to some coffee or tea," she said, the offer genuine, her smile welcoming.

Nick watched her carefully as he poured himself a cup. If this woman was some diabolical keeper of secrets, he'd eat his own shoe.

Nick took a slow sip of the coffee, letting the warmth settle as he studied Dorm Matron Two. She had the air of someone who ran things efficiently but kindly—the kind of authority that kept order without needing to raise her voice.

Nick nodded, resting his elbow on the arm of his chair. "What can you tell me about 307?" he asked with no further preamble.

Dorm Matron Two's expression softened. "She's always been... different."

Nick leaned in slightly. "Different how?"

She exhaled, choosing her words carefully. "She keeps to herself. Reads constantly, saves all her earnings, plans for a trip that she might never take now. It's like she lives half in reality, half in whatever place she escapes to in her mind."

Nick tapped his fingers against the edge of his mug. "Does she have friends?"

Dorm Matron Two tilted her head. "Not really friends. Not for lack of kindness, but...she's not easy to know. She's polite, pleasant, but always distant. She and 305 get on okay. Eight and Nine, the other two women on night crew are Spanish-speaking sisters who spend their time to themselves," she volunteered the information.

Nick watched her closely. "Would you say she trusts anyone here?"

A pause.

"I'd say she trusts books more than people, but 305, if I had to say a person."

Nick nodded slowly. That tracked.

"Boyfriend?" Nick asked.

"Not 307. Don't have to worry about that one trying to sneak out of the dorms," she chuckled.

"She was sick recently," he said, easing the conversation forward. "I heard it was serious."

Dorm Matron Two's smile faded slightly, replaced with something more thoughtful. "It was. We were worried for a while."

Nick studied her reaction. "And the nurse?"

Her fingers tightened slightly around her sleeve. "That was a tragedy. She was dedicated—really cared. I think she pushed herself too hard."

A careful answer. Clean. But there was weight behind it. Was it just sadness? Had she lost a friend?

Nick exhaled, letting the silence stretch just a bit. "307 survived. But she lost everything in the process."

Dorm Matron Two nodded. "Most of her savings went toward the treatment. She hasn't talked about it, but I imagine that weighs on her." She hesitated, but added, "She may have lost almost all her money, but she gained something. Since she was sick, she is different. Like an angel touched her," she breathed, knowing the detective might think she was a little daft.

"An angel," Nick raised an eyebrow.

"They say it happens with near death experiences," Dorm Matron Two crossed herself.

Nick let the conversation settle for a moment, then shifted slightly in his seat. "One last question."

She nodded, waiting.

"Why the numbers?"

Dorm Matron Two gave a hearty laugh, "That's a story. I arrived here about twenty years ago, and they started calling me Heather five. Who knows why, but it seems like all the girls were named Heather around the time I was born. Eventually, it evolved into calling people by their room number in the dorms and their positions. It just became part of our culture." She laughed. "The Dorm Matron One is also named Heather," she concluded, a twinkle in her eye.

Audrey stepped up to the heavy wooden desk where Sister Hope sorted through worn parchment and softly creased bindings, the scent of ink and aging pages wrapped around them.

"Could you request a book for me, please?" Audrey asked, her voice even, but carrying a familiar kind of expectancy—dark circles under her eyes.

Sister Hope glanced up with a smile, the quiet crackle of paper shifting beneath her hands. "Certainly."

Audrey straightened her shoulders slightly, as if steadying herself before speaking the title aloud, before letting the words carry their weight. "*The Woman in the Iron Mask*," she declared, her tone just a shade defiant, but not without warmth.

Sister Hope's brow arched in quiet amusement, fingers pausing against the spine of an old volume before she spoke. "Haven't you read that a dozen times?"

"Only ten," Audrey responded, lips curving, not embarrassed, only assured.

The book was more than just ink on paper—it was something solid, something known, something she could return to when the world felt unpredictable.

Sister Hope nodded, her movements deliberate as she reached for the request ledger, its worn edges softened by years of use.

"I will send a request back to the convent," she said, her voice carrying the easy patience of a place where time moved differently—where technology did not dictate urgency, where anticipation was woven into daily routine like thread into fabric.

Audrey exhaled, the weight of the moment settling—not heavy, but anchoring, steady.

Mack walked into the cannery with ease—this was his kind of place. The scent of metal and brine, the rhythmic hum of machinery, the steady movement of workers loading crates with quiet efficiency. He scanned the space as he approached a young man carrying a box.

"Can I speak to Foreman Number Three?" he asked.

The worker didn't break stride. "Yo, boss! Someone here for Foreman Three!" he called out, his voice carrying over the clatter of the shop floor before he disappeared into the rows of equipment.

A man with calloused hands and a firm stance stepped forward, offering a handshake.

"Foreman Two," he said. Direct. No nonsense.

Mack returned the handshake, appreciating the grip. "Mack."

Foreman Two gestured for him to follow, leading him through the bustling factory floor. The place ran smooth—not chaotic, not desperate. These weren't workers barely scraping by.

That meant something.

In the office, stacked logbooks and shift schedules sat beside an old thermos—a space built on routine.

"Three," Foreman Two said, gesturing to another man standing near the desk. "Detective's here."

Foreman Three straightened, wiping his hands on his coveralls before offering a shake. "You got questions?" His voice was steady, grounded.

Mack nodded. "Yeah. About 307."

Foreman Three exhaled. "Good worker when she isn't daydreaming. Picks up extra shifts, weekends. Been on nights for about eight years—used to work days when she first arrived but had some run-ins with the other women. Too much drama for me. Nights are better. Run half the line most nights, so the other can be worked on by maintenance teams."

His tone was logical, steady, methodical. No hesitation. No edge of deception.

"What about since her illness?" Mack asked.

Foreman Three hesitated—not out of doubt, but consideration. "Was hard being down a set of hands. Since she's been back, she's different."

Mack lowered his voice slightly. "Different how?"

Foreman Three glanced at the factory floor outside the office window. "Do you believe in God?" His voice was quieter now. "Like He was watching out for her."

Mack didn't answer immediately. He kept his expression neutral, waiting.

"God?" Mack repeated, prompting him to continue.

Foreman Three crossed himself. "Don't be doubting the Almighty."

His tone wasn't defensive—it was solemn. "Working a shop floor, you see things. Men get pulled into machines. Some survive, most don't. The ones that do—that's God watching over them."

Mack let the weight of the words settle. There was no exaggeration in his voice, no performance—just quiet, lived truth.

"One last question," Mack added. "What's up with the numbering system?"

Foreman Three shrugged, wiping oil from his hands with a rag. "Don't know for sure where it started, but it's efficient. Better than trying to figure out if someone wants to be called Steve, Steven, or Stephen with a 'PH.' Numbers are clearer. No confusion. Whoever came up with it was a genius."

Mack nodded, standing up. "Thanks for your time."

He walked out, the hum of machinery steady beneath his feet. The factory was efficient. The workers were steady. The warmth of the factory still clung to Mack's jacket, the scent cherries and sweat.

Mack and Nick met at the hovercraft.

Nick filed their report, fingers moving swiftly over the controls.

"No further investigation required at this time." The words felt tidy, official—but like closing a book that didn't yet have its final chapter.

The hovercraft hummed beneath them, steady, unhurried, as if even the engines recognized the peculiar stillness of Bell-View.

"You notice anything odd about this place?" Nick asked, looking down.

Mack leaned back, letting his gaze drift over the neat little houses, the dormitories converted from old hotels. Everything was orderly, well-maintained—not flashy, not desperate, just… quietly intact.

"Most people seem content," he mused. "Hell, I even got blatantly flirted with at the bar."

Nick smirked. "Shocking."

Mack chuckled, but his expression sobered. "Feels like a throwback, doesn't it? Like a place frozen in time."

Nick nodded. "Bell-View isn't just trying to stay under the radar. It's protecting something." He ran a few queries into the terminal's feed, scanning old census records, local ordinances—small, careful adjustments over time, each one pulling the town tighter into itself.

"They don't hide because life here is bad," Nick murmured. "They hide because they're afraid someone will take it away."

Mack exhaled, watching a couple step out onto their porch, talking easily. Community without interference. Stability without surveillance. No wonder they feared the government.

Power did not tolerate kindness.

⇒ ✵ ⇐

Notice came that the hovercraft was leaving—relief came like a breath held too long, released in quiet exhales, in the unfurling of tension from shoulders hunched for hours.

As the barrels were shifted, the cellar opened to the world again, and with it came the rush of cool air, carrying the scent of damp earth and stored apples—a contrast to the air that had become stale inside.

Parents held their children, not frantically, but with desperate reverence, as if confirming again and again that they were still here, still whole, still warm. Some closed their eyes, inhaling deeply, letting the chilled air touch their skin, reminding them that survival was not just theory but tangible.

Cottage seven male didn't hesitate—his legs carried him forward. His wife, Cottage seven female, stood near the far wall, their toddler clutched tightly against her hip, their infant cradled close to her chest. Her eyes lifted the moment she saw him, resolved.

He reached them in seconds, arms wrapping around all three, pressing his forehead against her temple, feeling the tension still lingering beneath her skin, the weight of hours spent waiting. The toddler burrowed against him, small fingers gripping the fabric of his sleeve, searching for reassurance. The infant, blissfully unaware.

"You're safe," He whispered against her hair, not a statement, but a prayer.

Her fingers gripped his shirt, anchored herself in him, as if needing to physically confirm that he was real, that this moment was theirs again.

The cold had retreated, but the ache remained—the knowledge that relief was always temporary. There were no triumphant cries, no exuberant shouts—the risk always remained.

Bell-View remained intact. Hidden. Their secret safe. For now.

≳ ✻ ≲

Mack stretched, rolling his shoulders before giving Nick a sideways glance. "So? What do you think? Missing heiress?"

Nick smirked, shaking his head. "Above my pay grade to decide that."

Mack chuckled, propping his feet up on the edge of the control panel. "Speaking of pay—this has been a sweet gig. No one tried to knife us or shoot at us."

Nick exhaled, shutting down his tablet. "You sound almost disappointed."

Mack grinned. "Not every case needs a body count, but it does keep things interesting."

Nick glanced toward the window, where the city lights flickered in the distance. "Maybe next time."

The hovercraft lifted smoothly, pushing forward into the night. Case closed. For now.

≳ ✻ ≲

Dave read the report again, his fingers drumming lightly against the desk. Perfect. Clean.

The kind of document that laid out just enough truth to steer the conversation without outright forcing it. He exhaled, straightening in his chair. Now for the harder part. He had to convince his Father and Brother to take action.

Aunt Sophie had been left in the dark long enough, but this had to unfold carefully.

Dave closed the folder on this screen. Control. Precision. Timing.

He pushed himself up, adjusting his cufflinks. The study, dimly lit with the glow of the evening, felt heavier than usual. The scent of expensive leather and faint traces of cigar smoke from past conversations lingered in the air.

Dave stepped into the hallway. It was almost time to play his hand. He just needed to allow the whispers to grow—to percolate.

⇒ ✴ ⇐

The tension in the parlor shifted subtly, whispers curling through the space like smoke from a forgotten candle. Virginia's charm was effortless, her movements calculated yet natural, the twirl of her blonde hair drawing her client deeper into conversation.

"A lost heiress to the Barkley-Rochester family?" She leaned in just enough to make it feel intimate, exclusive.

Senator Jackson smirked, his voice tinged with satisfaction. "That's what I heard. Johnny boy met some Catholic girl at a pub in Georgetown—left her behind when he got himself killed in a plane crash."

Across the room, the atmosphere tensed.

"Give some respect to the dead," a patron muttered, just loud enough to be heard.

Virginia didn't react. She let the words settle, watching the ripple they caused but keeping her focus on the story.

"I hear the girl was raised in an orphanage," the client continued, lowering his voice like it added weight to the rumor.

Virginia felt Ava shift beside her.

"Really," Ava murmured, her voice threading intrigue into the conversation.

From her corner, Audrey idly traced the rim of her glass, ice shifting with a soft clink. "A lost heiress, you say."

Gray, normally reserved, finally spoke. "That's right." His tone was quiet but firm, reluctant but sure. Not a man given to idle gossip—but not one to ignore a persistent rumor, either.

Senator Jackson glared at his son from across the room. The boy needed to learn that one woman was just as good as the next.

Apsara smiled and nodded, "How romantic—a lost heiress."

Edgar looked at her sadly, "A lost heiress could mean a power play." Silently, he wondered if Apsara would report him to his father if they just talked or played a card game when they went to the salon.

Madame Mary Margaret had overheard versions of this same whisper floating through her parlor all night; she knew what it meant.

Where there was smoke, there was fire.

And someone—perhaps more than one—was bound to be burned.

ELIZA ADAPTED, BUT ADAPTATION was not the same as belonging. She knew someone was looking for her, but why?

She missed her old world—the quiet certainty of Sister Hope, the steady authority of Madame Mary Margaret, the effortless grace of Virginia, the bold vibrancy of Audrey.

But time, indifferent and unstoppable, pulled her forward whether she was ready or not.

Eventually, she found herself settling into a rhythm at Bell-View.

She watched cooking tutorials on her terminal, fumbling through her first attempts. Her inaugural grilled cheese ended in smoke—the bread scorched black, the kitchen thick with the scent of failure. But she learned. She adjusted. She laughed at herself. In time, her meals became edible, even good. It was a small thing, but it mattered—a piece of independence she'd never needed before, but now quietly craved.

She walked to and from the cannery beside 305, letting the rhythm of her chatter become a kind of grounding music. 305 swiftly vacillated from the latest town gossip to peppering Eliza with a travel question.

"Where do they grow avocados," 305 asked, "That's right, Mexico, you have told me that before. I am going to try an avocado one day," she declared. "How long does it take to get to Bora Bora…"

There was comfort in voices, in shared space, in knowing someone else existed beside her.

When Eight and Nine spoke in rapid, whispered Spanish, she let their words wash over her—absorbing tone and cadence with whispered understanding.

The terminal became her window to the world. News fascinated her—the speed, the clarity, the openness of it all. She wondered if the nuns at the convent had done the same—pieced together truth from scraps of headline and story, the way she and her friends had once done in the Hall of Mary Ann.

And then there was Ana Lucia's diary.

She read it and reread it, returning to favorite passages like an old friend. She carried it everywhere, letting the pages breathe in open spaces—near the river, by the paddock, beneath skies so wide they made her chest ache.

Only in nature did she feel truly free.

To run her fingers through wild, unmown grass.

To smell flowers planted not by human hands but by the wind.

To be still. To unfocus.

To stop asking questions.

To simply be.

Dave took a slow sip of water, letting the silence stretch—calculated, deliberate, a quiet signal that this was their moment to speak first. He had used this tactic countless times in negotiations, letting discomfort do the work for him. But this wasn't business. This was blood.

John furrowed his brow, tapping his fingers against the edge of the device, his mind undoubtedly running through the ramifications—legacy, responsibility, control.

Robert leaned back, arms crossed, staring at the screen like it might somehow change under his scrutiny.

The study felt heavier than usual—the rich scent of aged whiskey lingering in the air, untouched. The weight of the documents on their tablets, heavy with implications none of them had voiced yet.

Dave let the silence stretch, let the quiet press against the room like an unseen hand. Power wasn't in speaking. It was in waiting.

John exhaled first—predictable, steady, the one who bore responsibility like armor. "This is my sister's grandchild." Saying it aloud made it real, gave it form. "She needs to know."

Robert leaned forward, fingers steepled, his gaze sharp with calculation. "We have to get ahead of the narrative." A man thinking not in terms of family, but in terms of optics, control, leverage. His election was close enough that surprises were dangerous.

Dave barely tilted his head, just enough to affirm without pushing. "We have time to get ahead of this if we act swiftly." His voice was measured—guiding, not demanding. This needed to feel like their idea.

Robert's jaw tightened as he tapped the tablet with two fingers. "We need to move this girl and train her before she can be used against us."

John's expression remained firm, his presence commanding. "Between your mother, my sister, and your wife, I have no doubt they can mold her." No hesitation. Decades of wielding power made him certain. He never doubted his control of the women in his family. Robert was letting Patricia have too much freedom, and in his opinion, this may be an opportunity to course correct her as well.

Dave allowed the thought to settle before tilting the conversation forward. "She could be an asset."

John didn't blink. "Bringing the Rochesters into the fold," he paused. "While offering the potential for a marriage alliance into the Barkley-Rochester dynasty for the right price," he smiled.

Robert hesitated—not rejecting, not accepting. Calculating. "There is some potential there." His voice held the weight of consideration, not commitment. But that was enough—for now.

Dave leaned back, lowering his voice just enough to make the final point a challenge. "How do we tell Aunt Sophie?"

John inhaled slowly, like a man who had already settled on his course. "Let me handle that."

Dave nodded, the flicker of satisfaction hidden beneath practiced neutrality.

The decision was made. Not forced. Not dictated. Not demanded. But shaped—precisely as intended. That was power, and he reveled in it.

⋟ ✵ ⋞

One day, while reading beneath her favorite oak tree, Eliza heard something—sharp, sudden, impossible to ignore. Laughter. Not just one child, but many. It cracked through the quiet like sunlight through clouds.

She looked up from her book, the soft murmur of wind in the leaves momentarily forgotten. The scent of warm earth and dry bark grounded her, but her pulse quickened. Her back straightened against the rough trunk.

Then she saw them.

The barn doors creaked open—not with hesitation, but with practiced ease. From the shadows poured a stream of children, more than two dozen, aged from the smallest, still in round-cheeked innocence, to lanky teens who moved with purpose. Their steps were quick but quiet, deliberate, as they climbed into the back of a waiting cattle car. There was no fear. Only urgency wrapped in routine.

The transport sat low on its tires, old and mud-caked, its metal sides dull in the late afternoon sun. It looked like nothing. Ordinary. Farm equipment. But now, Eliza knew better.

Her fingers clenched around the spine of her book, the pages fluttering in the breeze like startled birds. She could feel the coarse grass beneath her legs, the way it itched against her skin. She didn't move. She barely breathed.

The air carried the scent of hay, dust, and something floral from the nearby hedgerow—but beneath it, Eliza sensed something more sacred. This wasn't a secret wrapped in shame. It was a miracle hidden in plain sight.

Bell-View's secret was greater than she imagined. Not just a child or two. It was the town. This truth wasn't darkness. It was light—defiant and fragile and full of breath.

Eliza pressed her hand to her chest, steadying herself. Slowly, piece by piece, something inside her shifted. She wasn't just surviving anymore. She was beginning again. Reborn.

⋟ ✵ ⋞

Sophie Barkley Rochester sat perfectly poised on the patio at the Rochester Estate, the embodiment of discipline and quiet strength. Composure was not a mask—it was her inheritance, her armor.

The silver tray between them gleamed in the dappled light, delicate porcelain cups already filled with steeped Darjeeling. Crustless sandwiches rested in neat triangles beside lemon tarts and rose-petal shortbread. The ritual of tea was sacred—an act of grace, of control, of refusing to unravel.

She reached for her cup with the precision of decades, the scent of bergamot grounding her. Opposite her, John stirred his tea once, then set the spoon aside with care. No words yet. Only the sound of distant birds and the faint clink of china.

She had been raised at a time when other girls rebelled—wild nights, neon fabrics, anthems of defiance. But a Barkley did not rebel. A Barkley endured.

Her Chanel suit and pearls had been purchased at the expense of her freedom. But she had worn them like armor, as expected. Duty never felt like a sacrifice. It had always felt inevitable.

The greatest joy of her life had been her boys—Edward, William, and her youngest, Johnathan. But when Jon Jon disappeared, she refused to allow him to be declared dead; her loss was not just grief—it was erosion.

Jon Jon had been hers. Edward and William belonged to their father, had been absorbed by his world, his legacy. But Jon Jon had gravitated toward her—her presence, her discipline, her judgment. A mother's boy, not in weakness, but in loyalty.

When their father passed, the older boys drifted further, absorbed by duty and their wives' families. Only Jon Jon had stayed, her tether. And then he was gone.

John sipped his tea slowly, letting the silence stretch between them. He understood the weight of timing. He always had. For him to arrive unannounced meant only one thing: the news was too delicate for screens or phone lines.

Sophie placed her teacup down, the saucer barely whispering beneath it.

"What brings you here, my dear brother?" she asked, her voice an even blend of curiosity and steel.

John adjusted the napkin in his lap before replying. "I have news."

He reached for a cucumber sandwich but didn't eat it. "We've done our due diligence. There can be no doubt." His voice was firm, unyielding.

Sophie's fingers paused at the edge of a lemon tart.

"Jon Jon left behind a daughter."

The tartness of lemon lingered on her tongue, but she barely tasted it. Her breath caught.

"This can't be true," she said softly, the disbelief laced with a longing too dangerous to name.

John held her gaze.

"You have a granddaughter," he said, and after a pause, "I have a grand-niece."

The words fell gently but with weight, like crumbs on linen—small, but altering everything.

Sophie looked past him, to the trimmed hedges and blooming roses that framed the patio. She had cultivated this garden the way she had cultivated her life—with precision, care, and an unspoken hunger for permanence. She watched the spray of the fountain, listening to the soft patter.

But something in her had shifted.

She sat until the tea grew cold in her porcelain cup. John remained silent, letting his sister process in a few moments what he had in days.

"Tell me everything you know about her," she demanded with delight. For the first time in years, hope.

≳ ✵ ≲

"Looks like we're heading to DC," Nick said, eyes still on the screen.

Mack snorted. "What's in DC? Politicians and overpriced coffee?"

"Part two of the lost heiress," Nick replied, scrolling. "DNA confirms Angela O'Brien as the mother. We need to figure out how she crossed paths with the Barkley-Rochester kid before his crash."

"Twenty-six years ago?" Mack leaned back. "You want me to find their hookup bar? Hope they left a tab."

Nick smirked. "Records say she's quiet. Maybe it was a fling in the library."

"Hot," Mack muttered.

Nick flicked through the dossier—CUA, Library of Congress, St. Brigid's Orphanage. Fragmented, but there.

The hovercraft steadied beneath them, night closing in. Destination: Washington, DC.

"Also," Nick added, "we're to check out the nearest living relative— some distant cousin in New Mexico after this."

"At least the pay's top rate," Mack acknowledged, leaning back with a grunt.

The Hall of Mary Ann stood steadfast—unchanged yet shaped by the passage of time, by the rhythm of lives moving within its walls.

Summer's heat bore down, thick and relentless, pressing against old stone and worn wooden beams. The air was heavy with the scent of rain long before the storms arrived, an unspoken promise lingering between distant thunderclaps.

Lightning split the sky in jagged bursts, illuminating corridors where whispered conversations never truly faded. Some voices belonged to the present, others to memory.

Madame Mary Margaret sat in the Widow's Peak and looked to the sky.

THE WAVES CRASHED RHYTHMICALLY against the shore, sending a fine mist into the air. The scent of salt, sharp and clean, mingled with the damp, earthy smell of renewal carried on the cool breeze. Though the storm had passed, the lingering sheen of wet sand and the distant, muffled thunder served as a reminder that the world could shift in an instant.

The Barkley Estate at Cape Cod, stood with its familiar white clapboard gleaming faintly under the weak sunlight. The meticulously manicured lawn remained undisturbed, yet something in the air felt different—not quite settled.

Dave remained at the gravel edge of the patio, the cool stones pressing through the soles of his loafers as he watched the family gather.

William and Charlotte arrived in a sleek, black hovercraft, the soft thud of the closing doors echoing across the lawn. Patrick and Paul followed, their movements fluid and familiar, the scent of Patrick's overzealous use of expensive cologne, a blend of citrus and spice, drifting on the air.

Edward and Catherine arrived next, their tailored clothes sharp and precise. Carson and Casey trailed behind, their young faces serious, their small hands gripping their parents'. Their steps were measured on the flagstone path, their gazes sharp. They knew, even before a single word was spoken, by the unusually hushed tones and the way their parents held themselves, that this was not just another summer retreat filled with the usual laughter and games.

Sophie looked towards the distant path where Jon Jon used to arrive, a quiet, impossible habit, like a phantom limb she would never break. But today, her anticipation held a different weight. Her gaze, though still tinged with a familiar sadness, focused not on a ghost but on the promise of something living. It was for the daughter he had left behind, a girl none of them had ever seen.

The air vibrated with a festive hum, the clinking of ice in glasses a delicate counterpoint to the easy flow of conversation. Yet, beneath the surface, a tautness remained, each word carrying an undercurrent of expectation. John and Eunice played hosts, their movements smooth and practiced, their smiles as polished and unwavering as their political stances.

Robert with Caroline at his side, Jacqueline, Patricia, and Bobby—the picture of a first family, their postures perfectly erect, their laughter pitched just so. Dave caught snippets of quiet exchanges, hushed words wrapped in careful curiosity but edged with a subtle calculation, like the almost imperceptible glint of metal.

Servants moved like silent currents through the gathering, their soft-soled shoes barely disturbing the gravel. Silver trays laden with colorful hors d'oeuvres and sparkling drinks wobbled gently, balancing between the murmur of chatter and an underlying restraint. The faint, savory aroma of miniature quiches mingled with the sweet scent of elderflower cordial.

When Sophie began her descent down the sweeping mahogany staircase, the cheerful murmurs abruptly faded, conversation dimming like a slowly dying ember as every eye turned towards her. The soft rustle of her silk dress was the only sound for a fleeting moment.

Dave noted the subtle shift in body language—the almost imperceptible straightening of William's broad shoulders beneath his crisp linen jacket, the near-imperceptible furrow that creased Edward's brow, tightening the skin around his eyes.

John stood near the fireplace, his smile measured and easy, the fire crackling softly behind him. "Thank you for coming," he said, his voice smooth and resonant, carrying just enough weight to steady the palpable tension in the moment. "It is always a joy to gather our family." A deliberate pause hung in the air, thick with unspoken questions. "Today, we have a special announcement."

He gestured with a practiced wave of his hand towards Sophie, who stepped forward, her movements displaying a quiet strength and practiced grace. The soft sunlight streaming through the French doors illuminated the faint silver threads in her hair.

"It has come to light," she began, her voice clear, though it trembled faintly, "that Jon Jon had a daughter."

A collective intake of breath rippled through the assembled family. Gasps, like sudden bursts of air, mingled with low murmurs that spread like ripples in a pond. Champagne glasses, catching the light, were suddenly still in mid-air, expressions sharpened, thoughts visibly shifting behind carefully constructed facades.

Dave's gaze flickered to William, catching the almost imperceptible tightening of his fingers around the stem of his crystal glass, a subtle whitening of his knuckles. A flicker of something crossed his face—not wide-eyed shock, but a swift, assessing calculation.

Edward exhaled slowly, the sound almost lost in the sudden hush, measured and quiet, the kind of reaction that wasn't immediate dismissal but certainly wasn't open acceptance either.

John allowed the wave of murmurs to gently recede before continuing, his voice calm and authoritative. "Her name is Elizabeth Angela Barkley Rochester."

A faint smile touched Dave's lips, unseen by the others—a secret amusement playing in the corners of his eyes. *She just doesn't know it yet,* he thought, the anticipation building within him.

Sophie, her gaze soft. "She was raised beyond our world, but that will soon change."

Sophie's tone did not waver, did not falter, holding a quiet strength. "In order to acclimate Elizabeth to her new situation, we have prepared the retreat in Canyon Point, Utah, for an exclusive stay this summer."

Dave watched the reactions subtly shift once more—initial curiosity hardening into strategic planning, polite interest sharpening into focused intent. The air, still carrying the scent of the distant sea, now felt thick with unspoken agendas and maneuvering.

The storm had passed. But something far greater, far more complex and potentially disruptive, was undeniably beginning.

The weight of Sophie's words settled over the assembled family like the hush before a storm—controlled, deliberate, carrying the authority of a man, despite being a woman, who understood the gravity of what he was orchestrating.

Sophie's regard remained steady, landing first on Caroline. "We will need the best tutors, etiquette, dance, social skills." Her words were crisp, measured. This was not just preparation—it was transformation.

"What we know is limited," she continued. "Beyond her love of reading, we've been informed she is introspective and well-behaved." A pause. "That is a start, but we must shape more."

Dave scanned the room as reactions shifted. William remained thoughtful, Edward's fingers drummed lightly against his knee, and Robert exchanged a glance with Caroline—already thinking three moves ahead.

John exhaled, pacing the space near the fireplace with quiet authority. "As soon as we make arrangements to take possession of this young woman, media and social communications will be in overdrive."

Possession. Dave caught the term, tucked it away. Not introduction. Not reunion. Possession.

"We need to control the narrative." John's voice held no uncertainty. It was an expectation, not a request.

"If any of you would like to see the DNA evidence, I can provide it." He let the offer linger—but none of them truly needed confirmation. The moment Sophie had spoken, the truth had already taken root.

"In addition," John continued, "a private investigator has confirmed that the young lady's mother and Jon Jon were in the same locations on at least three occasions in DC twenty-six years ago. The parentage is indisputable."

The room remained silent—but it was not stagnation. It was calculation. Adjustments. Quiet shifts in expectation.

"If we had not verified it completely," John concluded, "we would not have brought you here."

Dave watched William's posture straighten, not in shock, but in preparation. Edward's jaw tensed, his thoughts churning behind careful restraint.

Caroline let her fingers skim across her champagne flute, calculating, considering the optics, the next steps, the narrative to weave.

Sophie allowed another moment of silence before speaking again. "Elizabeth will arrive, and she will learn. We will teach her. But when she steps into this family, she will not simply exist within it. She will represent it, just as each of you do," she looked pointedly at Patricia, who was known to be precocious.

Casey, six, restless with boredom, sent a sharp kick at Carson, nine, who retaliated without hesitation. A smack, not brutal, but decisive.

Bobby, who had just turned ten, ever the defender, launched himself into the fray with righteous indignation. "You can't hit him, he's littler than you!" His voice cut through the murmurs of calculation like a blade.

Dave smirked, watching the ripple effect—John's practiced authority flickering as he glanced toward the commotion, Caroline's polished demeanor briefly cracking as she sighed, William and Edward exchanging looks, knowing this cycle would repeat itself forever.

Paul looked over like he wanted to join in, his mother quickly grabbed his wrist. "You are fourteen and know better," she hissed.

Patrick and Patricia shared a glance of amusement and rolled their eyes, at seventeen; and technically adults, they were much too mature to take part in the melee.

The tension of high-stakes discussion shattered in an instant—replaced by the pure, unfiltered chaos of childhood.

Jacqueline sat beside her mother, calculating. This Eliza was three years older—and Jacqueline already despised the idea of her.

Dave observed, an unexpected development—one he might need to smooth over. Jacqueline had always been biddable in the past.

And just like that—a reminder that family was never simply about politics, alliances, or reputation. It was messy, volatile, protective.

Eliza smiled, the sun catching the edges of the water as her feet dangled in the river. Never before had she imagined freedom in something so simple. At the Hall of Mary Ann, such a wild thing was impossible.

She returned to her book, her eyes settling on the passage about the Three Sisters—maize, beans, and squash, intertwined through the wisdom of those who understood that growth was strongest when nurtured together.

The Three Sisters myth, a cornerstone of Indigenous North American agriculture. In some versions, these plants are seen as sisters…or even the daughters of a Sky Woman, who provided the gift of agriculture to their people.

Corn standing tall, providing support.

Beans weaving around it, enriching the soil.

Squash spreading wide, protecting, holding everything in place.

The story carried weight beyond agriculture—it was survival, wisdom passed down through generations. And yet, what struck Eliza most was the lesson beneath it: the interconnectedness, the way strength came not from isolation but from unity. Here she was isolated.

She thought of Virginia—shining, steady, always standing tall, providing structure in the way corn did.

Audrey—resilient, weaving herself into spaces, adapting, enriching their dynamic, much like the bean, strengthening the soil around it.

And herself—wide-reaching, grounded, shielding the others without being obvious about it, much like the squash that protected the roots from weeds and dryness.

Together, they had thrived. She wondered if she would be able to develop friendships like that again. Had Virginia and Audrey replaced her?

She dipped her feet deeper, sunlight dancing across the surface, and smiled. Perhaps the universe had been trying to tell her something all along—not just about survival, but about belonging.

The Hall of Mary Ann shimmered in its opulence, a world built on whispers, on calculated glances, on influence wielded with grace.

Virginia stood in its center, effortless, commanding—a golden goddess draped in authority, her presence magnetic. Her client leaned in, drawn not just by her words but by the way she held them, shaped them, made them essential.

Audrey, ever adaptive, moved through the conversation like silk, weaving the narrative with precision, adjusting with each flicker of reaction from the Brazilian trade advisor. A quiet master of tone, of balance, of ensuring her audience left believing they had arrived at their own conclusions.

Madame Mary Margaret strode through the parlor with silent authority—filling in the hole which Eliza left behind. A shield. A quiet force. A reminder that in unity there was strength.

The Hall glittered in its decadence. But its gates, its carefully guarded thresholds, were not for everyone.

A Barkley-Rochester daughter could never walk its halls.

ELIZA ESCAPED TO THE forest near the old barn, slipping between the trees like a breath held too long. Here, the air smelled of moss and pine, rich and alive. Leaves shifted overhead, casting dappled shadows that danced across her skin as she moved barefoot through the undergrowth, her steps silent, reverent.

This place was sanctuary—not a hiding place, but something sacred. Something older.

She became part of it slowly, day by day. A quiet witness to rhythms that needed no explanation. The swell of life, the hush of death, and the silent courage of rebirth.

Sometimes, crouched beneath the ferns or nestled against the roots of a maple, she spotted the children entering or leaving the barn—never hurried, never loud, always protected. She held still, never interfering. Watching was enough.

Unbeknownst to her, some of the children had seen her too. A figure bathed in golden afternoon light, quiet and still beneath the trees. They whispered of her in hushed voices, calling her the forest guardian, their angel with watchful eyes and wild hair. To them, she wasn't real. She was myth made flesh. A woman who had died and come back.

Eliza stopped thinking out here. She felt.

She traced her fingers along the bark of trees, rough and firm beneath her touch. She let the wind move over her arms like water, cool and patient. She watched the clouds drag slow brushstrokes across the sky, as if the world itself refused to rush.

Bell-View's landscapes weren't background, cultivated and manipulated, every blade of grass pruned with a purpose. They breathed wild and free. They pulsed with something ancient—older than any of them, deeper than memory. The forest didn't merely exist. It remembered.

And Eliza learned to listen.

The earth spoke in its steadiness. In the thud of her heartbeat against the soles of her feet. In the scent of wet leaves after rain. In the silence between birdcalls.

It didn't ask anything from her, except to be present.

She often saw a bobcat and her cubs—sleek and silent, shadows made flesh. The mother moved with grace, eyes sharp, steps sure. Her cubs tumbled behind, wild and reckless and free. Eliza saw Madame Mary Margaret in that feline watchfulness—the quiet power, the untamed devotion. In the way the bobcat shielded her young without ever needing to be seen.

And the barn cats—scrappy, territorial, clever. They reminded her of the dorm matrons, circling the perimeter of their tiny world with the same mix of weariness and will.

Here, nothing pretended to be what it wasn't. The forest held its truth like a steady breath. And Eliza, for the first time in too long, allowed herself to do the same.

She didn't need answers. She just needed presence. And the forest gave it freely.

The hovercraft hummed with quiet intensity, its propulsion system emitting a low, rhythmic thrum that settled deep into the chest. Sleek and windowless, the interior was all polished steel and muted lighting—sterile, deliberate, and efficient. Tension hung in the air like static before a storm, a wire pulled too tight and waiting to snap.

Sophie, William, and Edward sat in silence, the kind bred from shared conviction. They didn't speak because there was nothing left to say. The plan was clear. No messages had been sent ahead. No warnings offered. No last-minute negotiations entertained. They would arrive, and they would take what belonged to them.

Jacqueline had graciously provided clothes with a smile—ensuring Elizabeth wouldn't leave as just another worker, providing the necessary garments—not coveralls, but a statement, a reminder that she was a Barkley-Rochester now. And the first photos of her in the media would be in Jacqueline's last year's cast offs. A petty victory, before meeting her rival.

The air inside the craft buzzed with anticipation, charged with something unspoken but undeniable.

The response was immediate, seamless, practiced, as if every pulse of urgency had already been woven into their bones. At the first distant hum of the hovercraft, the silent signal passed from one set of eyes to another, and the motion began.

Children moved with quick precision, led by hands that had guided them through this drill before. The Apple Cellar became their refuge once again, the air thick with whispered reassurances as older children hushed the younger ones, pressing fingers to trembling lips.

Mothers clutched infants close, their grips firm but not panicked—fear was a luxury they could not afford.

"307," Matron Two said, her voice more clipped than usual as Eliza reached the women's dormitory. "You need to go to the main house immediately."

Eliza stopped. "Why? What's happening?"

Matron Two's gaze flickered around the room before settling back on Eliza. "Visitors have arrived. Something big is going on. You can feel it in the air. Can't you?" Her voice was low, hinting at an unease Eliza hadn't heard from her before. "They want to see you now. It's not optional, 307. You need to go."

A knot tightened in Eliza's stomach. She turned to 305, who was watching with wide eyes.

"Can I come with you?" 305 blurted out, her usual cheerful tone tinged with anxiety.

"Please?" the word hung in the air between them.

For a fleeting moment, Eliza hesitated, the ingrained caution telling her to keep her distance. But then, she looked at 305 – really looked at her, at the slight tremor in her hands and the worry etched on her freckled face.

"Yes, 305," Eliza said, the words coming out more readily than she expected. "Come on." She realized how much she needed 305's presence, the familiar stream of her chatter a small anchor in the growing storm of uncertainty.

As they walked in quick steps towards the main house, Eliza studied 305. Her strawberry blonde hair seemed brighter in the afternoon sun, her pale hazel eyes reflecting a genuine concern. The freckles dusted across the bridge of her nose gave her a youthful, vulnerable look that Eliza hadn't truly registered before.

She had always kept 305 at arm's length, wary of connection, of letting anyone get too close. But 305 had persisted, had offered her unwavering loyalty and a steady presence in the confusing landscape of Bell-View.

305's voice filled the space, breaking through the mounting tension like a thread pulled through fabric, light but necessary.

"You know, I've watched a few vids about what to do when mystery visitors show up unannounced..."

She nudged Eliza lightly with her elbow, her energy undeterred despite the unease curling ahead of them.

"Do you think this has anything to do with those guys asking questions about you."

"What if they're here for you?" 305 continued, shifting gears, glancing at her carefully.

"Like, really for you. Not just because of the illness or Bell-View, but because you're... I don't know, important?"

She spun the word like it was both thrilling and terrifying, casting Eliza as a heroine in one of her favorite regency shows in her mind, she continued.

"If you turn out to be secretly royal or the heiress of some doomed empire, you have to take me as your ladies' maid," she reminded Eliza of their running joke.

Eliza almost smiled, but the weight in her chest held firm.

The main house loomed ahead.

Sophie, William, and Edward Rochester stood as silhouettes against the late afternoon sun on the wide, wraparound porch. The aged wood of the porch creaked softly under the weight of Edward's polished shoes. A faint, expensive cologne, sharp and citrusy, drifted from William towards the entrance where Eliza stood. Georgette and Marty stood a few steps back, their postures stiff and unwavering, their faces etched with a quiet protectiveness, though their hands remained still, acknowledging the undeniable power dynamic unfolding.

The hovercraft, sleek and obsidian black, hummed with a low, resonant thrum that vibrated faintly in the still air. It sat like a predator crouched on the manicured lawn, a stark, futuristic contrast to the slightly weathered charm of the main house and the rustic scent of pine carried on the gentle breeze from the nearby forest. The polished surface of the craft reflected the fading sunlight in long, distorted streaks.

Sophie stepped forward, the soft rustle of her tailored silk suit audible even from across the porch. She extended a hand, her movements precise and deliberate, each gesture carrying the weight of generations of social training. A delicate gold bracelet on her wrist caught the light. Her voice, when she spoke, was smooth and carried effortlessly across the space, each syllable enunciated with a confidence that brooked no argument.

"Elizabeth Angela Barkley Rochester," she decreed, her voice like polished stone, undeniably authoritative. "We are here to take you home."

Eliza felt the name settle over her like a mantle, the syllables unfamiliar yet resonating with a strange, deep echo within her chest.

Eliza's poise was effortless, a perfect manifestation of Madame Mary Margaret's years of training—the grace of legacy meeting the precision of adaptation.

She greeted Sophie without a moment's hesitation, her confidence solid, her voice carefully measured, not eager, not resistant, but entirely in control—as if this moment was inevitable. "Grandmother," the word a prayer, a whisper, a coming home.

"Uncle William, Uncle Edward." she acknowledged them, each tilt of her head precise, each gesture subtly reinforcing her place in this unexpected reunion.

Her gaze shifted, landing on Georgette and Marty, "I see you have met my benefactors."

Then, she turned to 305, "And this is…" The pause was deliberate, a fracture in the seamless execution of the moment—having no idea what 305's real name was.

"Jennifer, but you can call me Jenny," 305 said, dropping into a deep courtesy, to Sophie, the gesture unexpected but sincere, living her greatest regency fantasy moment.

Sophie smiled, the flicker of intrigue shifting in her expression. "This is unexpected," she murmured.

The air pulsed with something ancient and unseen, thick with the scent of scorched earth, leather, and the sharp bite of peyote—an incense not burned, but breathed. It coiled around them like memory, like warning.

She sat at the heart of it all, robed in deep indigo and rust, the fabric alive with the shimmer of old thread and older power. The stars above blinked slow and reverent, as if awaiting her permission to shine.

"Sit," she said.

Not a suggestion. Not an invitation. A gravitational truth, already decided before their arrival.

Nick and Mack dropped to the ground without protest. It wasn't obedience—it was inevitability. The kind of pull one only resists if they wish to be unmade.

Her voice didn't rise, but it carried—through bone, through breath.

"You have come to tell me," she said, "that you have found the daughter of the moon. One of the three sisters."

Nick went still. His hands flexed against his knees, grasping for tact, for language suited to a moment that felt carved from myth. He was a PI, not a shaman.

And Mack—Mack crashed through the reverence like a bull in a china shop. "If that means we found a DNA match for your long-lost relative," he said, "you're right."

She looked at him then. Just a look. And the entire desert shifted. The wind stilled. The silence deepened. And Mack—brash, loud, unfiltered—felt something inside him bend, liquid and weak. His lungs forgot themselves. His spine no longer knew how to hold him.

Nick moved. Smooth, swift, a card in his hand like a talisman of logic. "Thank you for your time," he said, voice clipped, extended toward her like a shield.

She did not reach for it. She didn't need to. She smiled, "The deal had already been written—on starlight, on blood." She paused, "The daughter will come to me when the time is right.

Without another word, they turned, not walking so much as retreating, the hovercraft in sight like salvation. They did not speak until the engines roared and the magic was behind them.

Some places were sacred. Some truths older than proof.

⇒ ✵ ⇐

The sewing room hummed with quiet industry; its walls lined with bolts of fabric in muted tones and faded florals. The afternoon light filtered through lace curtains, casting a golden haze over everything it touched. The scent of lilacs mingled with pressed linen and old cedar from the dress forms, creating a calm that anchored even the most fluttering nerves.

"These were all donated by your cousin, Jacqueline," Sophie informed Eliza, her voice smooth, effortless, as if the matter had already been settled. Curious how Eliza would manage the situation, Sophie watched and observed. At first, she had assumed that they would simply put the girl in a dress and hope for the best, but this had become something all together intriguing.

Jenny, a force of movement and sound, flitted between discarded garments, her energy uncontainable, her running commentary punctuated by delighted gasps. She had never touched silk or satin before.

Eliza, meanwhile, studied the selection with careful detachment, assessing which gowns could serve her best when the inevitable media attention descended. The no-technology zone of the brothel suddenly seemed appealing again.

Sophie observed from a wingback chair—poised, softly coaching, surprised how little guidance her granddaughter needed. The crisp lines of her tailored jacket remained pristine despite the warmth of the room, a silver brooch catching the afternoon light as she lifted her teacup with effortless grace.

Georgette brought in the tea—simple country tea, nothing extravagant, yet Sophie accepted it as if it had been served in a London salon, treating the moment with quiet dignity.

"We should order our preserves exclusively from Bell-View in the future," she remarked, turning a gesture of courtesy into a business proposition, evaluating the value of the place even as she prepared to remove Eliza from it.

Georgette smiled softly; favor from the Barkley-Rochesters could be game-changing, in more ways than one.

Eliza stood at the center, arms lifted as Georgette pinned a dress, once forgotten, slowly becoming something luminous again—reshaped, redefined, renewed with purpose.

Stepping away, Georgette came back with a bronze shawl, perfect for Eliza's complexion. "I wore this at my wedding," she said, wrapping it around Eliza's shoulders.

"I can't," Eliza breathed, feeling the shawl hug her in a maternal embrace.

Georgette looked in Eliza's eyes, praying she was right. "Keep it for the children's sake," she said in her ear with one more hug.

Beside her, Jenny's gown was simpler, yet no less significant. It carried not just elegance, but intent—she was not being left behind.

Sophie tilted her head, eyes sharp with interest.

"Is Jenny coming with us?" she asked, the question light, but the gaze behind it deep.

Eliza didn't hesitate. "You reward loyalty."

A beat passed, and Sophie's lips curved—not quite a smile, but close.

Suddenly, Eliza paused at the threshold of the hovercraft.

"May I go back to my room to pick up a few things?" she asked, her voice even, but with an undercurrent of urgency.

"My dear," Sophie replied smoothly, "we can replace anything you have here."

Georgette, standing just behind them, bristled. Eliza met her eyes, and quietly confided, "It's my diary. And I need to return some library books."

"Library books," Sophie repeated with a small, indulgent smile. "Well of course. A Barkley-Rochester is only as good as her word—and something borrowed must always be returned."

Without waiting for further permission, Eliza and 305 darted off, their footsteps light across the path. They waved to Matron Two as they passed, receiving a faint but fond nod in return.

"Grab whatever fits in a small bag," Eliza told 305 with a conspiratorial wink.

Inside her room, Eliza shut the door firmly. The silence hit her like a breath held too long.

She opened her diary.

She tore out a single page, the motion clean, deliberate.

My name is Ana Lucia, it read in her looping hand.

"Goodbye," she whispered, "and I'm sorry, Ana Lucia."

She struck a match and held the fragile paper above the burner—the same one where she'd once scorched grilled cheese. The flame took quickly, curling the edges black. She dropped it into the sink, turned on the faucet, then flipped the garbage disposal switch.

The whirl of metal on ash was final. Not a trace of Ana Lucia remained.

She moved to the shelf where her library books were stacked, fingers hesitating over their worn spines—she scribbled a note and placed it deep in the crease of '*Woman in the Iron Mask.*'

Eliza tucked the books under her arm and stepped back into the hall just as 305, no Jenny, emerged, beaming with a small bag and a dramatic summary of her packed wardrobe.

"I'm ready," she declared. "And I've narrowed it down to two shawls. One for Brontë moods, one for Austen."

Eliza laughed softly as they walked. At the front, Matron Two stood waiting. She pulled them both into a tight embrace.

"Say goodbye to Foreman Three for us," Eliza said. "Sorry to leave you short-handed."

Matron Two simply hugged them again, tighter this time, her eyes bright with tears.

"No apology needed," she murmured. "Just don't forget who you are."

The hover craft paused just long enough for Eliza to drop the books off in the drop box.

⪦ ✵ ⪧

The parlor, draped in velvet shadows and the perfume of old money, oddly vacant. Saturday nights usually carried music, murmurs, and deals whispered between champagne flutes—but not tonight. Tonight, even the chandelier light seemed dim.

Audrey and Virginia had been lucky enough to attract two businessmen with a family partnership dating back to the East India Company founded in 1600.

Audrey leaned back, fingers wrapped around a crystal glass, her laugh light and perfectly measured. "Tell me more about the spices you sell, Rudra, I have always wanted to try French saffron."

The spice merchant chuckled, his tone indulgent. "I will send you some. A spice for my spice," he smiled while looking at her lounging in her gown.

Across from them, Virginia sipping her champagne slowly, glancing toward the grand entryway as if expecting ghosts. Archie, Rudra's British partner sat beside her, posture impeccable, voice low.

"You Americans," he mused, "you love to speak of revolutions, but in the end, you just created your own aristocracy."

Virginia smirked. "Independence was just a different shape of empire," she raised her glass to lighten the sentiment.

Audrey's smile didn't falter, but her eyes sharpened. "Still, it's easier to crown an heiress if she's dressed properly."

Then, the sound—heels on marble, precise, unhurried.

Madame entered, her silhouette cutting through the hush like a blade. She paused just inside the doorway, eyes scanning the room with the clarity of someone used to being underestimated.

Outside, the live feeds spun into motion. Livestreams flowed into almost every corner of the world, except this one. In the hush of the parlor, privacy was preserved.

Virginia smiled at Archie with skill and practice, refocusing on the mood. "I thought the British didn't like spice," she said playfully.

Playing with a strand of her hair he responded, "I prefer honey."

The hovercraft descended smoothly, casting a long, sleek shadow over the Barkley Estate—a compound of manicured tradition and concrete legacies, where even the hedgerows stood at attention. The whir of the craft was the only sound as the family waited, not for welcome, but for judgment.

John and Eunice Barkley stood at the edge of the stone landing, dignified beneath layers of expectation. Their presence was stately, their greeting restrained—the kind offered not out of warmth, but duty.

The family assembled behind them in a deliberate tableau:

Charlotte with Patrick and Paul, their formation instinctively tight, a quiet shield of solidarity.

Catherine stood with Carson and Casey, the boys scrubbed clean and still, their youthful vibrance muted by the significance of the moment.

Robert took the center, Caroline, Jacqueline, Patricia, and Bobby flanking him like branches from the same cultivated root. The first family. The image.

And then there was Dave—standing off to one side near a colonnade, alone but unbowed. He observed everything with detached calculation, the man in the family who never blinked until it served him.

Edward emerged first, every movement composed and deliberate, the kind of man who had never arrived anywhere by accident. He extended a hand back toward the craft—and Sophie appeared, regal in muted silk, her expression unreadable. She accepted his arm not like a gesture of help, but of ceremony.

Above them, drones buzzed like gnats around a carcass. Sophie glanced up. Typical vultures, she thought.

William stepped down next, offering his arm to Eliza. She accepted with poise, her gown catching sunlight in a subdued shimmer—Jacqueline's cast-offs reimagined, Georgette's bronze shawl, like a mother's hug, glinting like a secret passed down through generations. She looked reborn. A woman rewritten. An angel forged in bronze.

Exquisite, Dave thought, eyes narrowing. He had been prepared to sculpt the narrative of the "lost heiress," but this? This was a message in silk and steel, Sophie's influence visible in every detail, but the signature unmistakably Eliza's.

Jenny followed, trailing behind, entering a world she had only seen on vids. Her modified gown whispered of the loyalty, harder than diamonds—a clear discard of Jacqueline's, reimagined into a handmaid's story. A tribute turned tactic.

Dave's lips twitched. That was strategy. Well-played!

Eliza moved with deft precision, pausing before each family member just long enough to signal recognition without supplication. It wasn't just performance—it was fluency. She knew how to enter this world because she had studied it her entire life, performed for it for a living, and now she meant to own it.

When she reached Jacqueline, she stopped. Not long. Just enough to shift the air.

"Thank you for the use of the gowns," Eliza said, voice smooth. "Your taste is impeccable. We should plan a shopping trip."

The comment struck its mark—not groveling, not dismissive. It was an overture with teeth. Jacqueline's jaw tightened a fraction. She had wanted to recoil, had expected to, but the compliment was too clean, too exacting to reject outright.

Perhaps, she thought grudgingly, there might be room for both of them.

And then came Dave.

"Uncle David," Eliza said with flawless timing, her voice giving nothing away. Not the past, not their last encounter, not the shift in power that now hung between them like perfume. She clearly remembered his words *"If I ever see you again, it'll be the first time we've met."* Madame Mary Margaret would be proud of her.

Jenny watched from the edge, uncharacteristically silent. Just hours ago, she'd been a number. She wasn't a Bell-View factory worker anymore.

The drones hovered greedily, transmitting grainy images to a ravenous public.

And just like that, Robert's poll numbers began to rise.

Dave's smile returned. The game was moving forward—and this time, the players, perhaps pawns, perhaps something more.

⇒ ✱ ⇐

"Well, knock me over with a feather duster," Lucky Eleven cackled, elbowing Twelve at the bar, her grin wide, a little feral.

Twelve squinted at the vid screen, where 307—no, *Elizabeth Angela Barkley Rochester*—stood in bronze-draped elegance, as if she'd never worked on a cannery floor. "Huh," she muttered, tipping her beer back. "Guess she was a long-lost duchess after all."

They clinked bottles, the gesture loud and unapologetic. Not mockery—just grit. Twenty-four grit sandpaper: rough, but it smoothed what needed smoothing. Not unkind, simply unrefined—wild, untrained.

In nearby cottages, children clapped at the screen, joy bubbling over with the purity only childhood allows. They didn't care about dynasties or politics. To them, she was still the one who lingered near the trees, the bronze-shawled guardian, who watched with kind eyes, and always reading a book.

That truth, at least, remained untouched by satin gloves or media streams.

But inside the farmhouse, Georgette sat at the kitchen table, eyes locked on the stream. Marty stood behind her, arms crossed, jaw tight. The air between them wasn't tense—it was calculating. The kind of silence born from people who knew how fragile peace could be.

"She's beautiful," Georgette said quietly.

Marty nodded once. "Power destroys beauty," he observed. He had lived long enough to know.

Georgette placed her hand over his. "Bell-View will persevere; we always do."

Marty shut off the screen—a void of nothingness.

PART III
ELIZABETH
ANGELA BARKLEY
ROCHESTER

Introduction of Characters

BARKLEY ROCHESTER FAMILY (EXTENDED)

* John Barkley: Dave and Robert's father, Sophie's brother, ninety-five years old.
* Eunice Barkley: John's wife, Mother of Robert and Dave, eighty-nine years old.
* William Rochester: Sophie's oldest son, married to Charlotte, has two sons, sixty-five years old.
* Charlotte Rochester: William's wife, mother of Rick and Paul, yearning for a daughter, forty years old.
* Patrick (Rick) Rochester: William and Charlotte's eldest son, seventeen years old.
* Paul Rochester: William and Charlotte's younger son, fourteen years old.
* Edward Rochester: Sophie's son, married to Catherine, has two sons, sixty years old.
* Catherine Rochester: Edward's wife, mother of Carson and Casey, thirty-two years old.
* Carson Rochester: Edward and Catherine's older son, nine years old.
* Casey Rochester: Edward and Catherine's younger son, six years old.
* Abigail (Abi): Distant relative Caroline's side of the family, studies at St. Gabriel of Our Lady of Sorrows, nineteen years old.
* Beatrix (Bea): Distant relative Barkley side of family, attends St. Gabriel of Our Lady of Sorrows, twenty years old.

POLITICAL & PERIPHERAL FIGURES

* Captain Rob and First Mate Omar: Pilots of the Barkley-Rochester airship.
* Ziana: New brunette courtesan at The Hall of Mary Ann
* Headmistress Janet: Headmistress of St. Gabriel of Our Lady of Sorrows.
* Madame Evangeline: Seamstress who creates the gowns for the debutante ball.
* Jennifer/Jenny/305: From Bell-View, twenty years old.

THE ROOM WHISPERED OF luxury, its silence deep and deliberate, like a space accustomed to secrets. Every surface gleamed with understated wealth—the kind that didn't need to announce itself. It just *was*.

Eliza sat up slowly, the silk sheets slipping across her skin with a whisper. The morning light filtered in through curtains that hadn't just been chosen—they had been *calculated*. Heavy enough to command privacy, sheer enough to soften the world.

The ensuite bathroom gleamed beyond open doors, the marble cold and perfect. A reading nook waited by the window, flanked by shelves already stocked with books, tasteful for ladies in society. A sitting area for brunch or an afternoon tea, and most importantly a balcony over a courtyard. Everything designed. Everything planned for who the Barkley Rochester's wanted her to be.

She ran her hand along the bedding and stretched. Not quite as decadent as the brothel——but worlds better than Bell-View.

Who was she, really?

Eliza. 307. Elizabeth Angela Barkley Rochester.

Names like costumes, each one fitted for a different stage. Each carrying pieces of her, none telling the whole story.

Bastard. Orphan. Whore. Factory worker. Heiress.

Labels, yes. But roles too—each one requiring endurance, performance, survival.

Were they really so different?

She stood, bare feet touching the cool floor, grounding her in the moment. The room was too quiet, like it was waiting for her to speak first. Waiting for her to choose who she'd be in it.

She stepped onto the balcony, the courtyard below quiet, manicured to perfection. A gardener moved soundlessly near a marble fountain, trimming what did not need trimming. Even the vines here were expected to behave.

Behind her, the room belonged to Elizabeth Angela Barkley Rochester. In front of her, the rose's were carefully cultivated, pathways meticulously groomed. She knew this world, but didn't—and a part of her longed for the wild untamed roses at the forest's edge and the trails cut only by nature.

A knock at the door broke her contemplation.

Jenny grinned, standing proudly in the doorway, hands on her hips, her energy a force of nature, undeterred by the weight of change unfolding around them. She twirled as she entered the room.

"You realize I'm basically Ana Bates, right?" she announced, as if it was the most obvious truth in the world.

Eliza raised an eyebrow, barely suppressing a smirk. "Oh?"

Jenny nodded enthusiastically, already launching into her reasoning.

"You, are my Mary Crawley, stepping into a world of wealth, influence, scandal—possibly a tragic love story or two ahead—" she paused, then gasped, delighted at the prospect, "—and I am your steadfast confidante, your advisor, your right-hand! With slightly less starched linens, obviously, but the dedication remains."

Eliza shook her head, but the warmth in her chest lingered.

Jenny was many things—unfiltered, excitable, prone to dramatic declarations—but she had never wavered. Never once stepped aside when things got complicated.

Eliza laughed—actually laughed—before shaking her head once more, softer this time.

"Fine, Ana Bates. Let's see if you live up to it."

Jenny grinned like she had just won something monumental. "Oh, I will. You just watch."

Upon entering the breakfast room, Eliza barely had time to take in the massive buffet and scattered tables before Jacqueline intercepted her with the speed and grace of a socialite trained in battlefield diplomacy.

"My dear cousin Elizabeth," she said, linking arms before Eliza could respond. "I wanted to hate you before I met you, but your fashion sense is *too* stunning, so let's be friends. Call me Jacque."

"Eliza," she said, amused. "Why did you want to hate me?"

Jacqueline didn't even blink. "Because now I'll have to share *my* ball with you. I know that's super petty when I say it aloud," she added with a sheepish grin, "but this is my coming out ball and I will be married off to the highest bidder after the season."

"Ball?" Eliza asked, a touch of intrigue curling in her tone.

"Oh, darling," Jacque beamed. "I've been planning it obsessively since my Mother and Great Aunt Sophie finally got my Father to say yes. It will be at the White House—theme, gowns, orchestra, the works. And now everyone's going to want *you* there, front and center. But don't worry," she said, tossing her hair, "we'll make it work."

Meanwhile, Jenny hovered at the entrance, uncertain whether to follow Eliza or find her own place to land.

She didn't have to wonder long. A firm but friendly hand closed around her forearm.

"Hey," said a woman built like a professional bouncer in a sundress. "I'm Beatrix, but call me Bea. Come join Abi and me—we're at the country cousins table."

Jenny blinked. "Country cousins?"

Bea chuckled. "Yeah. Like the ones in the regency vids—less silk, more sarcasm."

She nodded toward a woman with dishwater blonde hair and a warm, inquisitive gaze—clearly Abigail.

Jenny's smile broke wide. "That's exactly my speed."

As she followed Bea across the room, sliding into the seat with a laugh, she realized: she had found her people.

Across the room, a trio of china cups caught the morning light, untouched slices of melon sweating gently on porcelain plates. John, Eunice, and Sophie sat in quiet cadence, their voices low, polished, each syllable carefully placed like stones in a garden path.

"You want to take the airship out to Utah?" John asked, not incredulously, but as one who already suspected the answer. His brows rose—part skepticism, part concession.

Eunice didn't miss a beat. "Yes, dear. It's just collecting dust. Like those RVs everyone bought during the 2020s and used twice. This way we travel in comfort—and," she added with a glance at Sophie, "we control the narrative."

Sophie stirred her coffee once, twice, then set the spoon down with precision. "We have to get to Canyon Point somehow. We might as well make a statement."

John's eyes flicked from wife to sister-in-law. It wasn't a discussion about transport; it was about message. Spectacle. Presence.

"We do need to get Robert reelected," Eunice added softly, like it wasn't the linchpin of the whole idea.

There it was. Not just travel. A statement. A display. A move designed not just for comfort, but for optics. Opulence that would attract the media and continue the buzz of the long-lost heiress.

John exhaled, turning the logistics over in his mind. "The ladies can all go on the airship," he finally mused. Dividing the heirs, ensuring security—strategy creeping into the decision like second nature. "We can split up Paul and Patrick, Carson and Casey, as well as Bobby. We can't risk all the heirs on one craft." Dave, Robert, Edward, and William would all be taking crafts of their own anyway, so plenty of options. John would sacrifice and escort the women on the airship and catch a ride back to DC at a later date with one his sons.

Eunice nodded. "The plan is falling into place nicely," she said, whether addressing the travel or something more hung in the air.

Sophie raised her cup, but didn't drink. "Then let's remind the country who still sets the standard."

William, Edward, Robert, and Dave lingered in the sun-drenched breakfast room, the rich aroma of freshly brewed coffee hanging in the air, mingling with the faint, lingering scent of crisp bacon from breakfast. The clinking of their china cups against saucers punctuated their low discussions about business ventures and the latest political maneuvers, their voices a comfortable rumble against the backdrop of the estate's morning sounds – birds chirping outside the open French doors, the distant hum of groundskeepers' equipment.

At a nearby table, bathed in the soft glow of morning light

filtering through sheer linen curtains, Caroline, Charlotte, and Catherine were gathered.

"Patricia is a concern," Caroline sighed, the sound carrying a weight of worry that momentarily disturbed the otherwise calm atmosphere. She traced the delicate embroidery on a throw pillow with a restless finger. "The same age as Patrick, but do we keep her with the children, their boisterous games and carefree laughter, or with the ladies, their more measured routines?"

"Perhaps it is best for her to split her time between the two," Charlotte suggested, her gaze drifting towards the sunlit gardens beyond the window, a wistful expression softening her features. She had always longed for a daughter, a gentle presence to balance the boisterous energy of her sons, but William had insisted on securing the lineage with an heir and a spare. Fourteen years had passed since Paul's birth, and despite the discreet and often uncomfortable attempts with invitro, the prospect of holding her own daughter dimmed with each passing year. "Rick is in the same position, and I plan to ensure he has some structure, but also let him find his own way a bit.

Catherine offered Charlotte a small, sympathetic smile, a silent acknowledgment of her sister-in-law's unspoken yearning. Since she had provided Edward with his heir and a spare, Carson and Casey. Edward had been more relaxed, their family feeling complete, and he was content to let nature take its course. In the gentle curve of her own abdomen a was a secret she held close. What she couldn't yet reveal to anyone, a joyous secret that warmed her from the inside out, was that she was almost four months pregnant with a girl. This trip to Canyon Point, with its vast skies and quiet moments, would be the perfect time to share the happy news with the family.

"Perhaps Tricia could join the boys for studies and us ladies at other times," she suggested, a slight sadness touching her. What would the world be like for her daughter? She remembered from her own history lessons how the SAVE Act was supposed to protect against identity theft and prevent illegals from voting, but many married women had lost their ability to vote because they had changed their names.

"That sounds like a wonderful compromise," Caroline responded, breaking Catherine out of her reflection. "Rick doesn't mind staying with the boys?"

"Where else does he have to go?" Caroline responded.

"I would like to schedule swimming lessons and coaches for the boys," Charlotte said.

"Rick is very strong, and I want to continue his training. Paul's technique could use some improvement."

"We should find out if Eliza knows how to swim," Caroline said firmly. She was a strong believer that swimming was essential to safety, not just a sport.

"Let's just put all the kids in swim lessons," Catherine suggested.

Caroline added a note to her tablet. "I am planning to ask a few of the distant cousins to come out. Beatrix from the Barkley side and Abagail from the Rochesters. Any concerns?"

"Wasn't Beatrix just in the national pole-vaulting competition?" Cathrine asked.

"I think it was shotput," Charlotte corrected.

The lighthearted correction drew the faintest smile from Catherine, who instinctively rested a hand on her lap, just above the secret still growing quietly within. "She'll bring good energy either way," she said softly. "And Abigail's always been so composed."

Caroline looked at the table where Beatrix, Abigail, and Jennifer were talking. "I agree,"

Caroline said, tapping swiftly on her tablet. "We'll place all of them in the same morning swim block, regardless of age. Skill-building, routine, and subtle bonding. It'll give us time for tea and strategy."

Charlotte tilted her head, amusement flickering behind her eyes. "Do you ever stop planning?"

"Only in my sleep," Caroline replied. "And even then, I'm usually styling outfits in my dreams."

At the men's table, a ripple of laughter rose, momentarily drawing the women's attention. William had just made one of his dry, biting jokes about the new tax structure being like "a courtesy mugging." Edward raised his cup in agreement.

"They laugh like they're not being slowly cornered by their own pol-icies," Charlotte murmured, eyes narrowing playfully.

Catherine didn't respond—her thoughts drifting instead to her unborn daughter, and how she might one day sit at this very table, sipping tea and listening to the undertones in every conversation.

The children's table buzzed with two distinct conversations, layered like a quiet chess match against a backdrop of eager, youthful enthusiasm.

Tricia and Rick sat with measured expressions, their forks idly pushing food around their plates as their minds worked far beyond their current meal.

"Technically we shouldn't be at the children's table," Tricia muttered.

"Really?" Rick laughed. "You know you would rather be sitting with me."

"They're definitely plotting something," Tricia muttered, her gaze flicking toward where the mothers sat in hushed discussion across the room.

Rick huffed a small laugh, leaning back in his chair. "Oh, this is definitely a 'political maneuver disguised as vacation' situation and they will all emphasize 'let's all bond as a family'."

"What's your thoughts about Eliza?" Tricia asked.

"I heard my dad and Uncle Eddie talking," he leaned forward. "They say they had separate DNA tests done and it was indisputable."

"She brings the smile out to Aunt Sophie's eyes," Tricia observed.

"Grandmother always wanted a girl," he said, looking around the table at his sibling and cousins.

Across the table, the younger boys were deep in their own world, their voices rising and falling with the excitement of video game strategy.

"Okay, but if we form two teams, we need actual balance," Carson insisted, fingers drumming against the table as if mentally constructing their battle plans.

Paul shook his head. "Nah, forget balance—just let us absolutely dominate the enemy team. That's way more fun."

Bobby scoffed, "You say that, but if you don't have a defender worth a hoot, you're just going to get wiped first round."

Casey grinned. "Right, so let's make sure Paul's on offense so he gets targeted first."

The laughter spilled over for a moment, infectiously easy, before returning to tactical plotting.

Tricia glanced at Rick, lifting an eyebrow.

"Honestly? I think I'd rather deal with the mothers' schemes than whatever this level of intensity is."

Eliza glanced up from her ball planning with Jacque and looked around the grandeur of sunlight breakfast room.

She happily noted Jenny laughing with two other women she hadn't been introduced to yet.

Grandmother Sophie, John, and Eunice sipped coffee in orchestrated conversation.

The men were plotting political intrigue, Dave sipped coffee and quirked his eyebrow when he felt her gaze shifting over him—while the Mother's plotted summer plans, Caroline detailing every on her tablet.

The children's table buzzed with laughter. This was family in a way she had never imagined before.

She leaned back slightly in her chair, letting the moment settle around her like warmth from the morning sun streaming through the tall windows.

This wasn't the kind of family born of blood alone—it was built, shaped by roles and rituals, politics and protection, alliances made over generations. And yet, in that very structure, there was something astonishing: belonging.

"Feels like a scene from a regency show, doesn't it?" Jacque murmured beside her, not looking up from the guest list she was fine-tuning.

Eliza smiled. "Better. Those are just stories."

Jacque looked up then, meeting her gaze. "And this is real?"

"Yes and No," Eliza said quietly, she had tried to hold on to the Hall of Mary Ann at Bell-View; she wouldn't make the same mistake again. Reality is where you are sitting today, she thought to herself with a secret smile.

URING THE THREE DAYS it took the airship to be prepped, the world spun itself into a frenzy. News anchors wore practiced smiles as they looped the same five-second clip: Eliza descending from the hovercraft like something out of a forgotten fairy tale, the wind tousling her dark brown hair, her bronze shawl gifted from Georgette, a mantle.

She watched in silence from the sitting room in the Cape Cod estate, Jacque beside her on the settee, sipping tea.

"They're obsessed," Jacque murmured, popping one into her mouth. "Like proper bloodhounds. We will have to plan our gowns to highlight your bronze and my gold undertones?"

Eliza looked intently at the screen. "We will take the world by storm."

Jacque's laugh was soft, calculating, "Yes, we will."

The camera cut to a grim-faced reporter standing in front of Bell-View.

"Here we are outside Bell-View Farms, where the workers go by numbers, not names. No one here will speak on record, but rumors swirl of a girl known only as Three-Oh-Seven. Described as quiet. Bookish. Brown hair. Brown eyes. Who recently had a near-death experience. Some claiming she was touched by God."

"They make it sound like a ghost story," Eliza whispered.

Another clip played—this one from a shaky cell phone camera in a bar lit by neon and memory. Two women clinked half-full bottles of cheap beer. Both wore faded overalls and smirks sharpened by years.

"To 307," said one, her voice scratchy with smoke.

"To the goddamn Duchess," replied the other, raising her bottle.

Jacque leaned forward. "Wait—play that again."

The screen obligingly repeated it. To the goddamn Duchess.

"That's Eleven and Twelve," Eliza murmured. "Lucky Eleven… always called me that like it was a joke."

The room felt heavier. Outside, birds chirped in the nearby tree branches.

"Do you… miss them?" Jacque asked, careful.

"I miss being someone who didn't need a press team and hide indoors," Eliza said, standing. "Someone who could just… read a book in peace."

She walked to the window. In the distance, hover drones belonging to reporters, circled like gulls.

Jacque stood too, voice gentle but firm. "That girl's still in there, Duchess."

Eliza didn't answer. She just watched the fog roll in, thick and slow, like memory. Jacque was quickly becoming a real cousin, a real friend. Was she being disloyal to Virginia and Audrey? Had Audrey received her message?

⁂

"You are lucky," Sister Hope told Audrey, her voice low with a rare note of excitement. "*The Woman in the Iron Mask* was just returned from the interlibrary loan system."

Audrey's face lit up. "Thank you so much," she said, reverently cradling the worn book in her arms like a relic.

Instead of retreating to the old cafeteria-turned-reading room, she climbed the winding corridor to the main building's Training Library— an elegant, echoing space lined with dark walnut shelves and high arched windows. She found Virginia seated cross-legged on a velvet cushion, her nose buried in a *Mama Gena* book.

"What are you doing here?" Virginia asked, surprised but smiling.

"I brought my favorite book," Audrey replied, holding it up like a peace offering. "It might be silly, but… I just wanted to read near you."

Virginia closed her book gently. "I think it's wonderful," she said. "I miss her too."

As Audrey curled into a nearby velvet sofa, she ran her fingers over the book's faded cover, tracing the worn letters with something like affection. She turned the pages slowly, inhaling the soft scent of old paper. Toward the back, something crisp interrupted the texture—her fingers froze.

A small slip of paper, no larger than a fortune from a cookie, nestled between two pages.

Frowning, Audrey eased it out and read the elegant handwriting aloud:

"Don't believe everything you read. —E"

For a heartbeat, neither of them moved.

Audrey silently handed the note to Virginia, who examined it with wide eyes. Her voice was barely above a whisper. "It's her handwriting."

"Do we tell Madame and Sister Hope?" Audrey asked, though her tone said she already knew the answer.

"Not yet," she said, her eyes darting to the towering stained-glass windows. "They're hiding something."

Audrey nodded slowly, gripping the book tighter. "Then we wait. And we plan." She glanced over at Virginia, something unspoken sparking between them. "We have to get a message to Eliza."

Virginia smiled, a rare full one. "*Code Talkers*," they said at the same time.

⇒ ✳ ⇐

Dave's smile was sharp, as he leaned back in a chair in the study, calculated, a quiet amusement tucked beneath layers of careful thought.

His schedule was packed—everyone begging for access and he held the key. What was the heiress like? When could he meet her?

Sophie had stood firm through the years, refusing to let Jon-Jon be declared dead, keeping his inheritance suspended in waiting—neither claimed nor forgotten. William and Edward hadn't wanted to push her and upon her death, they would simply override her wishes anyway.

So, the trust remained intact, its future contingent on the existence of an heir. A woman could inherit, but only a fraction until she married or turned twenty-six.

Eliza, for now, comfortably set—the summer hers to spend as she pleased, gowns, jewelry, indulgences at her fingertips.

Dave's smile deepened—not indulgent, not soft, but knowing.

An heiress was never a threat to the men in the family—only an opportunity. He had cultivated wealthy contacts from around the world, for just such an occasion.

⁂

Eunice, Sophie, Caroline, Charlotte, and Catherine reviewed every detail of the trip. Unlike airplanes, which carried the urgency of speed, airships moved with deliberate grace, their slow, rhythmic glide across the horizon designed for comfort rather than efficiency.

It was less stressful on the body, offering a languid luxury, a chance for the family to breathe, to settle, to absorb the world from an altitude that felt like it belonged to time itself.

A journey not dictated by the ticking of clocks, but by the quiet hum of steady motion, the kind of travel meant for long conversations, reflective moments, and the slow unfolding of intentions.

⁂

The airship facility hummed with quiet anticipation, its sleek frame resting like a predator in wait—not dormant, just choosing when to strike.

Rob leaned back, smirking at the itinerary, feet up, radiating a kind of casual authority that said, I already know how this plays out.

"Hey, Omar," he called, pointing to the tablet. "Looks like we're finally making moves."

Omar closed the distance in three strides, reading over Rob's shoulder, sharp-eyed, ready to assess the opportunity before deciding whether to be impressed.

"Canyon Point, Utah?" he muttered, the skepticism blunt, amused. "All this buildup just to end up in the desert?"

Rob chuckled, tapping the edge of the itinerary with deliberate ease. "Two months at a luxury resort. All expenses paid by the Barkleys."

Omar huffed, arms crossed, weighing the reality. "Funny how power works, huh? Buy an airship, let it sit, pay for two pilots—just to use it once or twice a year."

"If I am going to be bored in an air terminal," Rob said to Omar, "I'm glad it's with you."

"Way to make a guy blush," Omar laughed.

"Well, let's get this beauty ready," Rob indicated the airship. We have to perform for the rich and famous."

The thought hung in the air, the unspoken truth thrumming beneath their exchange.

This wasn't just about travel. It was about presence. About control. About making sure the right people were in the right places at the right times.

The security review was meticulous, methodical, each name on the staff list scrutinized with the weight of calculated precision.

Canyon Point was a fortress in its own right, its 900 secluded acres ensuring absolute privacy, its lavish accommodations concealing control beneath extravagance.

Even drones stood no chance, the distance too vast, the isolation too perfect.

John, Robert, and Dave moved down the list, ticking off necessities—cooks, maids, valets, groundskeepers, hovercraft drivers, security woven through every layer of service.

And then—the additions from the ladies' side.

Tutors. Swim instructors. A lifeguard.

"A lifeguard?" John muttered, barely masking his skepticism. *"In the middle of the desert?"*

Robert exhaled, eyeing the list again, but didn't voice his own doubt. If Eunice and Sophie had deemed it necessary, there was a reason.

John had already decided to keep the airship pilots at the resort, ensuring they were positioned for immediate departure if necessary. A hangar facility would be erected for the duration of their stay—another layer of control in a game where movement was everything.

And then Eunice's offhand remark—a trip to the West Coast later in the summer, once Eliza was further along in her studies.

John paused.

"Her studies," he echoed internally. What did that even mean?

Eliza was already far more composed, more deliberate, more grounded than Patricia—as if she had stepped into this world with the quiet, unquestionable understanding that she was meant to shape it, not stumble through it.

⁂

The morning unfolded with precision, every movement orchestrated under the watchful lens of hovering drones, capturing the flawless spectacle of departure.

John and Dave escorted the ladies one by one, their hands steady, their expressions composed—each step up the gleaming airship a calculated transition from control to expectation.

First the elders, then the mothers, next, the distant cousins and Patricia.

Dave smiled, as he and his father walked back to the house, drones buzzing. The moment the media had been waiting for had arrived.

Eliza and Jacque moved with effortless grace, their sundresses echoing each other's elegance, wide-brimmed hats shielded their faces while sunglasses provided an air of mystery. Their heels clicked lightly against the polished steps, a sound barely audible beneath the hum of the waiting vessel.

The airship pilots—pressed uniforms, sharp posture, the embodiment of quiet authority—stood ready, offering their hands as each woman ascended, their presence reinforcing the air of dignified tradition.

"I'll see you in a few days," John murmured to Dave before stepping forward, the final act in this meticulously planned departure.

The moment he entered, luxury wrapped around him like a familiar embrace—the scent of polished leather, faint notes of perfume lingering in the air, the soft murmur of discreet conversation.

A flight attendant—immaculate in a uniform reminiscent of the golden era of aviation, carefully selected by Eunice to signal both refinement and nostalgia—approached with graceful efficiency.

"Would you like a drink, sir?"

John barely paused.

"Whiskey neat," he replied, his voice unhurried, certain—the start of the journey unfolding exactly as it was meant to. He would never admit it to Eunice, but airship travel did have its perks.

That night at the brothel, Madame Mary Margaret circled the parlor, her high heels clicking softly against the polished floor. The air, thick with the mingled scents of expensive perfume and champagne, the electric wall sconces turned low, humming with a low murmur of hushed conversations. She admired the architecture of the old native museum, the faded grandeur of its rotunda now transformed into the heart of her establishment. The central space, once echoing with the vastness of the museum, now had a low, intimate ceiling crafted from dark wood, casting warm shadows across the plush velvet seating arrangements.

Downstairs, the salons with just a slight rounding, their damask wallpaper and strategically placed mirrors, were practical yet inviting. A gentleman who booked three hours with a lady would first spend time in the parlor, the murmur of conversation and soft music creating a discreet ambiance, before retiring to the more private salons. The heavy velvet drapes at the salon entrances, over the doors, ensured complete seclusion.

A man would leave discreetly from the back door of a salon, following the circular pattern back to the reception area, where the soft glow of a single lamp illuminated the polished mahogany counter. Each salon cleaned before the next client.

Upstairs, in the hushed quiet, were the ladies' residences, each room a haven of soft fabrics and subtle lighting. A lady had a precious hour to attend to her hygiene in the perfumed lavatories and recover her composure before meeting her next client.

As Madame looked around the salon that evening, the air itself seemed to vibrate with the echoes of songs performed in the old museum. The haunting notes of flutes, soft and melancholic, and rhythmic chants and drums, barely audible beneath the parlor's murmur, seemed to emanate from the very walls.

She could see the subtle tension in Virginia's tightly clasped hands and the almost imperceptible tremor in Audrey's smile as they interacted with clients, but the gentlemen, lost in their own pursuits, remained oblivious. The dance continued, a different kind of performance unfolding now, a different rhythm pulsing through the old building.

23

ELIZA SPUTTERED, WATER STINGING her eyes and nose as she surfaced, blinking in the morning light streaming through the tall windows of the resort's glass-walled pool. Her limbs flailed for a moment before she found her footing in the shallow end. The water felt heavier than she'd imagined—cool and dense, wrapping around her like an unfamiliar embrace.

She had never been swimming in her life.

Beside her, Jenny stood frozen, knuckles white as she clutched the pool's edge. Her usual chatter—nervous, excitable, always rushing to fill silence—had evaporated. Now there was only breath: short, uneven, and scared. The swim instructor crouched beside her, calm and steady.

"You're safe here," the instructor said, warm but firm. "Try letting go with one hand. I'm right here."

Jenny shook her head, drops flinging from her braids. "I can't. I just... I can't."

Before the instructor could coax further, a high-pitched squeal burst through the tension.

"Look at me, Cousin Eliza! I'm swimming!"

Casey bounded across the waist-deep water, his orange arm floats bouncing with every joyous splash. His grin was full and fearless, a jack-o'-lantern smile minus two front teeth.

Eliza couldn't help but laugh—really laugh—choking back another mouthful of chlorinated water as Casey flailed with six-year-old enthusiasm.

Nothing in her life had prepared her for this moment: not the solemn hush of manor parlors, not the unspoken codes of who to watch, and when to smile. Here, there was no performance. Only breath, water, and movement.

"You're amazing, Casey!" she called out.

Jenny glanced at him, then at Eliza. Her grip loosened—just a little.

"I used to think pools were for show," Eliza said, softly. "Back at Bell-View, I'd barely dip my toes in the river."

Jenny bit her lip. The instructor offered her hand again.

This time, Jenny took a step.

Sunlight shifted across the blue surface as the three of them—one fearless child, two tentative young women—moved through the shallows, buoyed by more than just water.

At the far end of the pool, another group cut through the lanes in slow, even strokes. Tricia, Paul, Bobby, and Carson moved with a practiced rhythm as the instructor called out drills. It wasn't Olympic training, but it had a crispness that made the morning feel orderly, almost official.

Above them, the lifeguard slouched on his highchair, chewing on the tip of his whistle. He watched the lanes without urgency. This was his summer gig: half-decent pay, no lifting, and a view that wasn't bad. He hated caddying—carrying around a rich man's golf clubs for show. His dad had told him to get friendly with the Barkley Rochester kids—make connections, whatever that meant.

He mostly just stayed awake and scanned for trouble.

Tricia moved like she belonged in the water. Confident. Clean strokes. She didn't joke like the others. Didn't show off. The lifeguard frowned. Hard to believe someone that put-together was just seventeen. Daughter of the President, too.

The swim instructor blew her whistle, and the group surfaced. Tricia hauled herself from the water with a quiet grace, removing her cap and goggles. The lifeguard leaned forward, elbows on knees, eyes following them as they joked on the deck. Were they always this... watched? Or had they just learned not to care?

Later, the last group of the morning approached. Rick and Bea hit the water with barely a word, racing hard like there was something to prove, perhaps there was. Bea, especially—arms like pistons, pushing water like it had wronged her.

Jacque and Abi followed. Smooth. Deliberate. Jacque moved like an eel in open water—long, silent, practiced. Abi glided beside her, unreadable. Precise.

The lifeguard squinted, scratching at his jaw. Another of the President's daughters, wasn't she? Abi or Jacque or—hell, didn't matter. He wasn't in their orbit. Just some guy on a chair, keeping time and watching rich kids not drown.

Still, he stayed alert. Anyone who rents out 900 acres of resort for the summer probably doesn't leave much to chance.

After showers and breakfast, the younger kids were ushered into the library for their morning tutoring schedule. The thick scent of books and polish lingered in the cool, sun-dappled room, quiet except for the occasional shuffle of feet or the soft thud of a book placed on a table. The young women decided to go to get a look at what the resort library had to offer.

"This is just so wrong," Tricia groaned, slumping into a tufted armchair near the tall windows. She turned to Abi and Bea, who sat relaxed, untouched by the summons. "Why don't you have to go to tutoring?" she added, pouting dramatically.

Abi didn't look up from her journal. "I think it's because Bea and I attend St. Gabriel of Our Lady of Sorrows during the school year. You're home-tutored, right?"

Bea nodded, flipping a page in the thin paperback in her lap. "We have a summer reading list from school. It's expected we keep up independently."

At that, Eliza, who had been quietly skimming through a volume on the Paiute people and Bryce Canyon National Park, looked up with a wide-eyed smile. "I'm sorry—I wasn't trying to eavesdrop—but did you say you have a summer reading list?" Her voice carried a mix of surprise and genuine delight. "We could form a book club. I've only ever read about them!"

"Oh, that is a fun idea," Jenny piped in, her face brightening as she leaned over the arm of Eliza's chair. "We could have weekly meetings and maybe even snacks—"

"We could ask mother to have our meetings with tea," Jacque suggested.

"I won't be joining," Tricia added a beat later, her tone shifting. "I'm about to find out my tutoring assignments." She sighed and gave them a half-hearted wave before slipping toward the area where the boys had already gathered.

The remaining ladies exchanged glances—Jaques concerned, Abi steady, Bea unreadable, Jenny supportive, and Eliza glowing with the possibilities.

"Maybe we start with something short," Bea offered. She hadn't actually intended on reading the summer reading list, but she didn't want to dim Eliza's enthusiasm.

"Something with chapters and secrets," Eliza said, eyes sparkling.

"'*The Maid of Orleans: The Life and Mysticism of Joan of Arc*' by Sven Stolpe," Abi suggested, looking at the list on her screen.

"Do you prefer old-school books?" Jacque asked Eliza, "I can have mother order one if you prefer one instead of using an e-reader."

And just like that, the summer book club was born—without permission, without a schedule—just a flicker of revolution wrapped in pages and prose.

The first few days at the resort were filled with discovery—new routines, hidden corners, and the slow settling into a summer rhythm. On one of those quiet mornings, Eliza found a rock-climbing wall tucked discreetly off a path near the rear terrace.

Later that afternoon, once the heat of the day had passed, she found Grandmother Sophie seated in the shade of a linen-draped pergola, a book in her lap and a teacup poised delicately in one hand. Eliza hesitated, her voice small when she finally spoke.

"Grandmother... I found something. A climbing wall. I was wondering if I might be allowed to try it."

Sophie looked up over the rim of her reading glasses, surprised but intrigued. "A climbing wall?" she repeated.

Eliza gave a shy nod. "Yes. I know it's… odd. I just thought it might be something I'd enjoy." Eliza could not explain that climbing had always been an outlet for her at the brothel.

Sophie's face softened with a smile—not just polite, but deeply warm. She closed her book and set it aside. "My dear, I think it's wonderful. I can't tell you how happy it makes me to learn something new about you."

She reached for Eliza's hand, gave it a gentle squeeze. "I adore surprises," she said, eyes crinkling. "I always hoped my grandchildren would have corners of themselves that even I didn't anticipate. And here you are—quiet little Eliza—with a hidden interest in scaling walls."

Eliza laughed, a little breathless, grateful not to be asked why or how she had taken to climbing. Sophie didn't press. That was something Eliza would come to value: her grandmother's way of accepting truth without demanding its full history.

By the next morning, Sophie had arranged for a professional instructor. Dave, ever vigilant, reviewed the woman's credentials from his terminal. She had once summited K2 with her husband—precise, experienced, and calm under pressure. Dave approved the hire with a quiet nod.

Eliza's request surprised the rest of the family too. She was known for her stillness, her books, her careful manners. But this spark, this physical pursuit, awakened something new.

The first day, Eliza had to pretend that she knew nothing of harnessing in. As she climbed, she forgot herself in the sheer joy of exertion. "That's high enough for today," one of the instructors called. Convinced she had found a natural climber.

"Do you dance," she asked Eliza, when she returned to the ground.

"Yes," she replied. "We even have an instructor here to prepare us for the ball."

"Ah, that must be it," the instructor replied. "Dancers normally make great climbers, they don't try to overpower the rock, they find a rhythm."

On the second weekend of their stay at the Utah resort, the entire family was finally reunited—all the men taking time away from their work schedules. The desert sun poured across the red sandstone cliffs that rose around the property like ancient sentinels. Sagebrush danced in the wind, and the scent of juniper and dust drifted through the canyon air.

That Friday evening, Catherine asked Edward to take a walk with her along the trail that wound behind the main lodge. The path curved along the rim of a shallow gorge, the red rock glowing beneath the falling sun. She reached for his hand as they walked in silence, their shadows stretching long across the dirt.

"I have something to tell you," she said when they reached a flat bluff overlooking the valley. Her voice was barely louder than the breeze.

Edward turned to her, his expression open.

"I'm pregnant," she said.

For a moment, there was only the sound of the wind and the distant chirp of canyon wrens. Then Edward pulled her into a tight, smiling hug. "You're serious?" he whispered, already laughing.

Catherine moved Edward's hand down to her belly, which was starting to swell, "Carson and Casey are going to have a little sister."

"Catherine, this is... everything."

They stood there for a while, the red cliffs glowing behind them, the sun a low flame on the horizon. It felt like the whole desert had paused to listen.

⇒ ✵ ⇐

The next morning, over brunch, reminiscent of Cape Cod just two weeks before, Catherine and Edward made their announcement. The family sat at long reclaimed wood tables, sipping cactus fruit juice and coffee, servants placing cast-iron skillets filled with chorizo and eggs in front of them.

Catherine rose from her seat, Edward's hand steady on her lower back. He cleared his throat. "We have some news to share—Catherine and I are expecting."

A moment of stunned silence followed, then came the joyous laughter, the congratulations. Even the prickly ones softened. Grandmother Sophie looked at Catherine like she was seeing her whole future unfold at once.

Dave popped open a bottle of cava, even though it wasn't yet noon. Wonderful news indeed. This was going to drive the media into an all-new frenzy.

Out in the desert, surrounded by red rock and wind-polished mesas, the family toasted to new beginnings—life growing where no one had expected it.

Tricia felt it like an itch beneath her skin, a quiet but relentless discomfort—the realization that, despite the sprawling resort, despite the family reunion, despite all the carefully planned luxury—she was adrift.

Everyone else had found their rhythm, their space, their people.

Paul, Bobby, Carson, and Casey hunched over their vid games, voices rising in bursts of strategy and frustration.

Rick, constantly in motion, constantly chasing adrenaline, was petitioning hard for a climbing excursion to Bryce Canyon—convincing parents, lining up approvals, making plans she wasn't a part of.

She only ever saw him at swim practice, where they rarely exchanged words, and during tutoring, where conversation felt more like obligation than connection. And yet—Rick had found an unexpected partner in Eliza, who, despite her polished demeanor, seemed perfectly at home scaling cliffs, gripping rock faces, carving out something of her own in the landscape.

Eliza and Jacque were indivisible, their heads bent over sketches, plans, and details of the ball that had become their obsession.

Abi, Bea, and Jenny were their own unit, thick as thieves—laughing, scheming, building something quiet and impenetrable between them.

Even their book club—seemed to have formed just to spite her. Before Eliza and Jenny came along, Bea and Abi would never have dared to go against her.

THE TEA TABLE, SET on the shaded patio overlooking the vast, ochre-toned Utah landscape, hummed with a low buzz of untapped energy. Sunlight, sharp and bright, glinted off the delicate silver teapot and the pale gold liquid within. The air, crisp and dry, carried the faintest scent of sun-baked earth and the herbal infusion steeping in the porcelain teapot, a fragrant blend with notes of desert sage and wild mint.

Eliza, the natural leader of their book club, gently traced her fingers, still slightly sticky from the honeyed scones they'd been enjoying, over the cover of '*Sisterhood: Giving and Receiving the Gift of Friendship*' by Chloe Langr. Another title pulled from the summer reading list at St. Gabriel of Our Lady of Sorrows.

Jacque leaned forward, the delicate clinking of her teacup against its saucer punctuating her words. She tapped a perfectly manicured finger, her nail catching the sunlight, against the text. "This entire chapter is about sacrificial friendship. Isn't friendship supposed to be… fizzy, like this champagne?" she gestured to her glass, tiny bubbles rising to the surface.

Abi smirked, the corner of her mouth tilting as she slowly sipped her hot tea, steam curling gently around her face. "Maybe you just don't like the idea of giving more than receiving," she said, the warmth of the cup radiating in her hands.

Jacque feigned offense, her voice light. "How dare you, Abigail," she exclaimed, a playful glint in her eyes that didn't quite meet the serious gaze of the red rock formations in the distance.

Jenny, ever full of energy, leaned forward in her wicker chair, the gentle creak of the fibers barely audible. "I actually love the idea that friendship is supposed to be chosen family. It's… comforting," she said, the warmth of the afternoon sun on her bare arms making her feel drowsy but content.

Bea nodded slowly, her gaze steady as she considered her own cup of iced tea, condensation beading on the cool glass. "Depends on who's doing the choosing," she murmured, the dry desert air rustling the pages of the book beside her.

"I feel like God sent Eliza," Jenny said gravely, the intensity in her voice contrasting with the light breeze that whispered through the near-by juniper bushes. The table nodded, the thought lingering in the dry air – going from a factory, working her fingers to the bone every day, to a desert resort, drinking tea with the same jams, she used to make, with the first family – was that the work of a God?

"I can't believe I am actually enjoying reading the summer read-ing list," Abi smiled at the ladies around the table, feeling connected to the sisterhood.

Eliza, who had been quietly absorbing the discussion, the faint bit-terness of the black tea on her tongue, finally spoke. "It reminds me of St. Brigid's Orphanage."

The table stilled for a moment, the weight of her words settling in the dry heat like a sudden calm.

"Everything there was about preparing you for what came next," Eliza continued, absently swirling the remaining tea in her cup. "Not about who you *were*, but who you were supposed to become."

Jacque studied her carefully, the late afternoon sun casting long shadows across the patio. "And do you think this book is the same?"

Eliza exhaled slowly, the dry air carrying her breath away. Her fin-gers still rested on the slightly worn spine of the book, feeling the texture beneath her fingertips. "Maybe. But I'd rather shape my future than have it decided for me."

The table was silent—reflective, the only sound the distant call of a canyon wren.

Then the door to the patio creaked softly.

Jacque's eyes flicked up, catching the bright glare of the desert sun reflecting off sunglasses. She spotted Tricia lingering in the doorway, arms crossed, sunglasses perched atop her head like a dark crown.

"Come join us, Sister," Jacque said, her voice sweetened like the peach preserves they'd had with their tea but unmistakably pointed.

Tricia stepped in slowly, her gaze sweeping the shaded patio. Her reply came low, almost a whisper in the dry air, a mirror of Eliza's words—but stripped of their quiet humility.

"I'd rather shape my own future," she said.

The echo landed like a dropped stone, the air suddenly feeling heavier, the unity of the moment disrupted—not shattered, but cracked just enough, like a piece of ancient pottery exposed to the harsh desert elements.

⇒ ❋ ⇐

Eliza tightened the straps of her harness, the familiar weight settling against her as she approached the climbing wall. The air was dry, crisp, the faint scent of chalk and sun-warmed stone lingering around her.

This climb wasn't about the physical challenge—it was about silence, focus, the rhythm of her own breath against the backdrop of unanswered questions.

Why was Tricia so resentful?

Eliza gripped the first hold, testing her footing.

The younger boys had their games. Rick had his endless pursuits. Jacque had her meticulous planning. Abi, Bea, and Jenny had their sisterhood.

Another handhold. Another steady pull upward.

And Tricia—she had her defiance, her restlessness, her quiet rage at feeling left behind.

Why was Eliza here?

She pulled herself up another level, muscles moving on instinct.

Was she meant to inspire? To lead? To play a role that had already been shaped for her? Or was she here because this was the only place where she had control—where she could move, climb, struggle without cameras catching every expression on her face?

She reached higher, fingers catching the next hold. Grip. Pull. Breathe.

Had Audrey and Virginia received her message? The thought settled like a weight in her chest, heavier than the harness. She had sent it. Had they read it? Had they understood what she meant?

Eliza gripped the next hold, the rough texture pressing into her fingertips. She pulled, the strain in her muscles grounding her against the storm inside her mind.

Dave. The architect of her public image, the orchestrator of her presence. Was she simply another pawn in his game, a polished piece maneuvered for maximum effect?

Her arms burned, the weight of her body shifting as she pushed herself faster, as if outrunning the questions racing through her mind.

How much control did she have? How much was illusion?

She swung a leg up, digging her toe into the rock, pushing off with a burst of momentum, defying the weight of expectation pressing down on her.

She could play the part—the poised heiress, the effortless leader, the picture of quiet grace—but wasn't she more than that? Could she shift the game without him seeing? Could she turn the board without tipping it?

The next ledge was just out of reach.

She tightened her jaw, ignored the ache in her shoulders, stretched farther, farther—

Fingers locked onto the edge, legs kicked against the wall, momentum carrying her upward in one final push.

She exhaled.

Perched high above the ground, she stared out at the horizon. Still standing. Still moving. Still deciding.

⁂

Eliza knew she couldn't just request to go to the public library—Why walk into a public library when anything she desired could be delivered to her door, wrapped in discretion and efficiency?

But this wasn't about convenience. She'd discovered the interlibrary loan system while at Bell-View and it was the only opportunity she saw to exchange messages with Virginia and Audrey. Had they gotten her message?

"Grandmother," Eliza said softly, finding Sophie and Eunice in the ladies' salon. "I hear Caroline talking to Jacque and Tricia about the importance of charity work, and that gave me an idea."

"Go ahead child," Sophie encouraged.

"I learned about a children's summer reading program at the public library and they are looking for volunteers to read," she concluded.

Sophie and Eunice had loved the idea, of course. Their delight was immediate, though layered with the cautious pragmatism that came with a lifetime spent navigating power and perception.

"There are optics to consider," Sophie said gently,

"And protocols," Eunice added knowingly.

When Sophie messaged John, he surprised them both.

The men didn't' just approve the outing. They leaned into it.

Dave's support came with a strategist's gleam in the eye, a quiet pleasure at how elegantly the move fit the story already building around Eliza. The world had already dubbed her "the reading one"—her love of books mythologized by a media hungry for personality in pedigree.

This next step? It was narrative gold.

Images of Eliza—poised, accessible, reading aloud to children on a worn rug in a modest library—would echo across news cycles. Regal, but relatable. Controlled, yet unrehearsed. A scene made rarer still by the strict embargo on press during events like this.

Each captured moment would become more valuable for its scarcity.

Dave couldn't have planned it better himself. But the best part? Eliza had composed it herself. He wasn't going to have to push the girl into the world. She had orchestrated her own debut, with a soft power too subtle for Dave to have seen.

That made it even more powerful.

The day of the library reading the hover crafts were outside waiting. Sophie had approved of Eliza's book, and they would not share it with anyone. Their little processional was flanked with security. The library had been screened in advance. Eliza was very excited and a little nervous. Jenny sat next to her chattering about all the scenery as they passed. Eliza loved Jenny's irrepressible spirit, happy that she had taken her away from Bell-View.

As they exited the vehicle, the driver held his hand to Sophie first, then Eliza, and finally Jenny. The drones swarmed like gnats. In the next hovercraft, Caroline arrived with Jacque, Tricia, and Bobby, then Eunice, Charlotte, Rick and Paul. Next Catherine, who the drones swarmed to capture her baby bump, Carson and Casey. Finally, Bea and Abi, who the drones ignored.

Eliza almost expected to see a red carpet as they walked into the library. Dressed in a bronze channel jacket and skirt, with Jimmy Choo shoes, she was the picture of reserved grace, her hair styled into a braid as a crown around her head.

The Librarian greeted them and with one arm on Sophies elbow and the other on Eliza's lead them to the reading group. A group of about a dozen children sat on the floor, Paul, Bobby, Carson and Casey joined them. An assistant swiftly showed the ladies and Rick to some adult-sized chairs along the edge of the room, decorated in bright colors with letters, numbers, and animals.

Eliza sat down. The children's whispering stopped, and they looked at her with awe, the window behind her turning her hair into a halo.

"Today I selected one of my favorite books to share with you today. The author was a Danish Storyteller and Poet, he wrote this story in 1843, over two hundred years ago," she paused as many of the children's mouths made little "Os"

"Today I will read *The Ugly Duckling*, by Hans Christian Andersen."

Dave, ever the architect of control, watched the scene unfold from across the country, his hovercraft smoothly skimming toward a business meeting as he watched the processional on the vid stream. The media swarmed on Eliza, getting their first clear shots of her stunning appearance. The shots of Catherine's baby bump, added to the scene of a wholesome family. Dave was always hesitant when not in control but had trusted Sophie to steer Eliza.

When Eliza announced the book she was reading, Dave actually pumped his fist. A tale of being in the wrong family, of not belonging, of finding your people. A tale over 200 years old.

"Well played."

A tale so old yet so profoundly relevant, above reproach.

The world was falling for Elizabeth Angela Barkley Rochester, the lost heiress.

Dave's weapon.

⚬ ✳ ⚬

"…he cried out with full heart: 'I never dreamed there could be so much happiness, when I was the ugly duckling,'" Eliza concluded, her voice soft but resonant in the still room.

A hush followed. The children stared at her with wide eyes, suspended in the quiet magic of the moment.

One little girl slowly raised her hand. "Are you a swan, Ms. Elizabeth?" she asked, her voice full of awe.

Eliza's smile bloomed, warm and unguarded. "I'm living a life I never dreamed," she said gently.

The librarian stepped forward, touched by the stillness in the room but also aware of the schedule. She gestured for Eliza to stand. "Let's thank Ms. Barkley Rochester," she said, and the children instantly erupted into claps and cheers.

"That's my cousin," Casey whispered proudly to the boy beside him.

"Wanna see where they keep the *Choose Your Own Adventure* books?" the boy replied.

With a quick glance at the adults, Casey slipped away. Carson and Bobby, sensing the opportunity, made themselves scarce in other corners of the library, each conveniently "drawn" to something interesting.

Eliza seized the chance. She caught the librarian's eye and made her way toward the counter. "Jenny," she called softly, and her friend followed.

"I was hoping to borrow a book through the interlibrary loan program," Eliza said with an easy grace.

The librarian blinked—surprised. Of all the visitors that day, she had not expected this particular request from the poised young woman who could, without question, purchase the entire library if she pleased.

"What book are you looking for?" she asked, curious now.

"The Order of Clara Mercy has an original copy of *The Code Talkers*," Eliza explained. "We have a third edition at the resort, but I'd like to read the original. Since arriving, I've been studying Native American folklore—especially from this region."

She paused, then added with a gentle smile, "I know my grandmother would buy the book if I said I wanted it, but that seems a shame. A copy like that should remain in circulation, accessible to others, not locked in someone's personal archive."

The librarian blinked again—this time with admiration. "You have a kind and understanding heart," she said. "I'll arrange everything. And just so you know, we also have a wonderful section on Southwest Native American traditions, including the original Choctaw Code Talkers— eight men from World War I. It's small but growing."

"That sounds fascinating," Eliza said, her eyes lighting up.

Just then, Sophie approached. "We're ready to depart, Eliza," she said gently. "The crafts are waiting, and I'm sure the librarian will appreciate order restored to her domain."

She turned to the woman at the counter, extending her hand. "Thank you so much for having us."

"The pleasure was mine," the librarian replied, clasping Sophie's hand. "It's been an honor."

The family departed in the same stately order they had arrived, hovercrafts waiting like royal carriages. Outside, the desert sun shimmered on polished metal, and the drone cameras buzzed like mechanical cicadas, hungry for one last glimpse.

After the first family left, the librarian sent the request through the interlibrary loan system and shared her experience with several other librarians.

That weekend, the Utah resort buzzed with the bright, cheerful energy of happy family success. The crisp desert air, scented with the subtle fragrance of blooming cactus flowers and the distant, earthy aroma of sunbaked rock, seemed to vibrate with contentment.

Stock prices, displayed in real-time on discreet screens in John's study, ticked steadily upwards, their green numbers a silent testament to their prosperity. Robert's polling numbers, whispered with satisfied tones over breakfast, were climbing, a tangible measure of their public approval.

The positive media coverage from Eliza's library visit showed no signs of diminishing, the vibrant images and glowing reports echoing across news feeds. Journalists clamored for more glimpses into the life of the newly discovered heiress, their requests filling Sophie's inbox.

Finally, after much discussion, the Bryce Canyon climbing trip for Rick and Eliza received the green light. Dave, already envisioning the breathtaking video streams of the bookish Eliza, her dark hair catching the desert sunlight, scaling the dramatic, orange-hued cliffs alongside her athletic cousin, felt a surge of satisfaction. This was public relations gold, a visual narrative that spoke volumes of adventure and familial bonding.

Tricia was bored. Everyone had something to do—plans to make, people to impress, bonds to deepen—and she had never felt more peripheral. The air inside felt stifling, all scented with cactus blooms and expectation.

Abi, Bea, and Jenny had invited her to play cards, but she didn't feel like they were sincere.

The midday heat shimmered off the pool deck, through the glass windows, as she dove in, slicing through the turquoise water with practiced ease. Stroke after stroke, she swam hard—faster, farther—until her muscles screamed and her thoughts blurred into rhythm.

Her instructor's voice rang in her head: *You have the talent, but not the discipline. Not the drive.*

When she could push no more, she glided to the edge and lifted herself out with quiet elegance, her feet dipping lazily back into the cool water.

From above, the lifeguard's voice broke the quiet.

"Need a water?"

She looked up. He was watching her— boldly, unapologetically. She should've bristled at the way his gaze lingered, but instead, a small smile tugged at the corner of her mouth.

"Yes, please," she replied, her tone breezy, flirty.

He climbed down from the stand, broad-shouldered and confident, a bottle already in hand. She could feel his eyes roving over her, and though part of her knew better—knew this wasn't the kind of attention she should crave—she couldn't deny it felt good.

She accepted the bottle with a bold smile, the condensation cool against her fingers. Slowly, deliberately, she ran it along the curve of her neck, letting it trail down the dip between her collarbones and along the edge of her bathing suit top.

The lifeguard's eyes followed, caught in the motion, unblinking.

A flicker of triumph sparked in her chest—not because she wanted him, necessarily, but because in this moment, she was undeniable.

Finally, someone noticed her.

Dave sat beneath the wide slats of the veranda, the heat radiating in low, shimmering waves off the stone patio. The afternoon sun cast sharp shadows across the rust-colored cliffs that framed the resort, and somewhere nearby, cicadas buzzed like static in the silence. A cold glass of prickly pear tonic sweated on the table beside him, untouched.

The report from Nick and Mack was crisp, neatly tabbed. So far, everything looked clean. The distant cousin—on the mother's side—was an oddity, yes, but ultimately harmless. some dusty desert mystic, painted with starlight and dreamcatchers—she was odd, yes. But harmless. No ambition. Dave could already see the press release: *First Family Embraces Native Ties—Bridging Bloodlines and History.*

He tapped the terminal to the next report. Then his jaw stiffened. A new note, buried in the margin: Bart Jackson was sending his own people.

Dave leaned back in the leather chair, the creak sharp and luxurious. Through the window, the desert light flickered off the red rocks. He pinched the bridge of his nose, not in frustration, but calculation.

Senator Bartholomew Jackson—always sniffing, always posturing. His brand of righteousness made him dangerous: unpredictable, and just popular enough to matter.

Unacceptable. A desert robber fly buzzed by.

A breeze rustled through the desert scrub, carrying with it the faint scent of juniper and something scorched—like metal left too long in the sun. Dave sipped his tonic finally, the coldness biting through the heat, then set the glass down with a hard clink against sandstone.

He didn't like flies. And he never hesitated to swat one. There wasn't much difference between Bart Jackson and the robber fly-dead on the ground beside him. Looking at the fly he ground it with his sandal, just for the satisfaction.

The deck house buzzed with quiet camaraderie, the scent of grilled food and desert air drifting through the open windows as staff gathered around the long wooden table. Most were couples, their bonds formed through long hours of instruction, shared duties, and the rare but treasured moments of leisure—swim instructors, dance tutors, rock climbers, history specialists, even the airship pilots.

At the far end, the lifeguard sat alone, absently twirling his fork in his plate, barely paying attention—until the comment landed.

"Better be careful. You're playing with fire."

He glanced up, brow furrowed, catching the pointed look from the swim instructor's husband.

"I don't know what you're talking about," he replied, his tone flat, measured.

His wife exhaled, shaking her head, her voice laced with something sharper than caution. "The President's daughter."

The words landed with weight, setting off an immediate murmur—low, knowing, a ripple of hushed discussion at the table.

Not getting mixed up with the bosses—that was the golden rule, the unspoken understanding among them all.

Omar's words landed with a theatrical finality, his tone exaggerated but carrying a warning that wasn't entirely a joke.

"Oh no, son, this never goes well," he declared, leaning back against Rob's shoulder, with a knowing smirk. "Getting fired is the least of your worries if you cross Dave Barkley's radar. Two snaps—boom— you're done."

The table fell quiet, the weight of his statement settling over the conversation like dust in the desert air.

Some chuckled, some just shook their heads, but no one argued.

Rob and Omar cut through the heaviness with their traditional toast. "To Peter," they said together.

The chatter picked up around the room, but the unspoken truth lingered—power like the Barkley Rochesters didn't tolerate missteps. No entanglements. No headlines. No mistakes.

Sophie's smile was warm, lingering with quiet satisfaction—all her life, she had wished for a granddaughter, and now, she had Eliza by her side. Soon, Catherine would bring another into the family, the legacy expanding, the future unfolding with certainty.

Eliza sat poised, yet a flicker of emotion passed across her face—surprise, intrigue, perhaps even hesitation. The evening air brought a cool desert breeze

"We've managed to find your closest relative on your mother's side—fourth cousin, twice removed. She's not too far away, in New Mexico."

Eliza's fingers tightened slightly around her glass of iced tea, the words settling in her mind. Family. On her mother's side. Something real, something tethered to the past she had never fully touched.

Sophie watched her carefully, patience woven into the moment. *"Would you like to meet her?"*

Eliza's gaze flickered downward for half a breath, then lifted, her expression controlled but not devoid of feeling—curiosity edged with restraint. Was this a loyalty test? The relationship was so distant—tenuous.

"Yes," she said finally, the weight of the word landing between them.

Sophie clapped her hands, delighted, "Perfect my dear, I will make the arrangements for a small trip, just the two of us." She paused, "Just some Grandmother, Granddaughter time."

⇒ ✹ ⇐

The vid screen flickered, casting a faint glow across Edgar's dimly lit room, illuminating the quiet grief etched into his features.

The heiress, the lost figure now found—dark hair, familiar eyes. The world celebrated her return. And yet, his Eliza remained gone, swallowed by the passage of months, by unanswered questions, by the hollow ache of absence.

His father's voice muttered just beyond the door, the words indistinct, but their weight unmistakable.

He needed to rise, to face the world outside this room, but the sheer force of his sorrow held him down, heavier than exhaustion, deeper than simple grief.

⇒ ✹ ⇐

Sister Hope met Madame Mary Margaret in her private study after the final checks were made for the night, sliding a photo across the table. Both women enjoyed port in crystal glasses.

Sister Hope watched as Madame Mary Margaret studied the image, her fingertips hovering over it for a beat too long.

Eliza—poised, radiant, utterly engrossed in the act of reading to children, her presence commanding attention even in stillness.

"We can tell Virginia and Audrey in the morning," Hope murmured, her tone carrying both resolution and quiet reverence.

Madame Mary Margaret exhaled, swirling the dark red liquid in her glass before taking a slow sip.

"She's found her way into the light, then." Without a doubt, Eliza was alive.

The words weren't quite a question, but they carried the weight of one, nonetheless.

25

J ACQUE THREW UP HER hands in mock exasperation, but the amusement danced in her eyes, utterly failing to mask her excitement. "Now you've done it."

Eliza blinked, genuinely at a loss. "Done what?"

Jacque grinned, unable to contain the delight bubbling under her words. "Found the key to our leaving the resort!"

Eliza barely had time to process the statement before Jacque gracefully slid into the seat beside her, triumphant, leaning in conspiratorially.

"Mother managed to get Father and Uncle Dave to approve two more charity events because of you."

"That's great," Eliza said, catching the energy, but before Jacque could elaborate, Tricia's voice cut through the conversation from the next table, sharp with frustration.

"It's not like we can actually do anything when we go out." She didn't even bother looking at them—just stirred the foam in her untouched coffee, voice edged with quiet resentment. "Just go from one gilded cage to the next, like pretty birds."

The words hung in the air, turning the excitement into something heavier, something that pressed against the edges of their carefully planned futures.

Jacque tilted her head, considering the remark, but didn't refute it outright.

Eliza exhaled slowly, fingers tapping absently against the porcelain of her teacup.

Frustrated, Tricia stormed off toward the pool, the murmurs of family chatter echoing in her head. She needed space—sun, water, silence.

She slipped quietly out a side door of the ladies' salon, stealthily moving towards her room.

Back inside, Sophie's teacup paused midair as she glanced up. Eunice followed her gaze just in time to see the shimmer of Tricia's hair vanish as the door closed.

"She's restless," Eunice said gently.

"She's drifting," Sophie replied.

When Tricia reached her bedroom, she bypassed the standard-issue training suit, instead, she pulled out the royal blue bikini—the one she hid from her mother, in a pile of other clothes, when they made purchases for their trip. She piled her thick, sun-streaked hair on top of her head and slid on oversized sunglasses, watching herself in the mirror with a mix of defiance and calculation. She opened the resort pool app and tapped the attendance notification—the lifeguard would be there in minutes.

By the time she strolled onto the pool deck, the lifeguard was already in his chair, looking slightly irritated. She ignored it. Her wrap landed on a lounge chair with a flourish, and she descended the pool stairs slowly, the cool water licking at her skin. Once she reached thigh depth, she began to breaststroke lazily, keeping her head above the surface, her movements fluid and controlled.

After a few slow laps, she drifted toward the edge, then suddenly stopped and grabbed her calf.

"Help," she called, her voice pitched just right. "I've got a cramp."

The lifeguard reacted instantly, jumping down and into the water beside her. He reached her quickly and steadied her with one arm, guiding her toward the side. She leaned back slightly, propping herself on an elbow, breathing heavily but not panicked. The lifeguard began gently working her calf muscle, his brow furrowed.

She wasn't in distress—at least, not physically.

His gaze meandered, from the calf he was massaging, down her thigh, to the thin piece of bikini fabric between her thighs. He kneaded her calf just a little harder. Her breath quickened.

Twenty-eight minutes passed. Sophie checked the time; lips pressed into a thoughtful line.

Then, with one graceful motion, she reached for her device and typed a brief message to Rick: "Find your cousin. She's wandered. Check the pool first."

A sharp voice rang out: "Tricia, what happened?"

Rick's presence was immediate, cutting through the lingering tension like a blade sharpened by instinct.

"Get back," he ordered, voice controlled, firm, shoving the lifeguard aside with a force just shy of aggression—but unmistakably protective.

The lifeguard stepped back, hands raised slightly, the sudden shift in authority unmistakable.

Rick didn't let the silence stretch. No room for speculation. No room for scandal. "You good?" he asked Tricia, his voice clipped.

Tricia blinked, wide-eyed. Her voice was feathered with theatrics. "I—he saved my life."

Rick's jaw flexed. The pool. The lifeguard. Her posture. Her choice of suit. This wasn't a rescue—it was a scene. One that could be captured, twisted, whispered about in the media streams.

"You're on thin ice," he said flatly, to the lifeguard or Tricia, it was unclear which, or both.

The lifeguard opened his mouth—to defend himself—but Rick's glare shut him down before a syllable could be uttered.

Rick turned back to Tricia and extended his hand. "Let's go."

"Let me lean on you," she said, her voice softening to something dangerously close to pleading.

Rick exhaled, his patience stretched. She was his cousin. The President's daughter. Every move mattered—and this moment, seen by the wrong eyes, could unravel far more than just a lazy afternoon.

He offered his arm, not warmly, but steadily.

"Just walk," he muttered, already anticipating Sophie's inevitable question: What happened this time? Uncle Robert and Uncle Dave would want to review and scrub the videos. Luckily, they were on a closed circuit with no access to the cloud.

⇒ ✻ ⇐

Robert and Dave dissected the video with the practiced detachment of men accustomed to control—Tricia's antics were obvious, but the lifeguard's reaction was not overt.

Rick's claim that the lifeguard looked at Tricia inappropriately required an extra layer of scrutiny, but Robert and Dave weren't quick to condemn.

"The kid's dad owns a couple of golf courses," Robert mused, recalling past interactions, assessing ambition versus recklessness. "Caddied for me last summer. Seemed ambitious, not stupid."

Dave leaned forward looking at the screen, paused, Tricia leaning back in her royal blue bikini, the lifeguard massaging her calf. His mind already building a strategy, already reshaping the situation.

"I will scrub this personally," Dave told Robert. "I can control a lot of things, but you need to get control of your daughter."

"I know," Robert shook his head in regret. Tricia had always had a special place in his heart. He had indulged her too much.

"Let's head out to the resort this weekend," Dave said, a smile curling at the edge of his words. "Looks like I'll need a caddy."

⇒ ✻ ⇐

The air in the room was heavy with unspoken consequences, the weight of Tricia's misstep settling like dust in the quiet.

She lay flat on the bed, face buried in the pillow, her posture a mix of defiance and surrender. Rick had barely spoken before dropping her off—just silence, just expectation, just the inevitable lecture waiting to unfold.

"What were you thinking?" Caroline's voice was sharp, clipped, controlled—not angry, but cool, precise, honing in on the gravity of what had just been cleaned up.

"Does it even matter what I'm thinking?" Tricia's voice was muffled, but not so much that the irritation didn't seep through, her hand pulling the pillow tighter over her head as if it could shield her from the reality outside these walls.

Caroline didn't bother softening the blow. "Your father and Uncle David are reviewing and deleting the security videos right now."

Tricia exhaled sharply, a mixture of frustration and something almost like relief. For now, at least, the worst was being erased.

"From now on, you do not leave this room without an escort." The words were simple, final, non-negotiable.

Tricia groaned, rolling onto her back, the pillow still pressed against her stomach. "So, I'm on house arrest?"

"You're lucky not to be shipped off to a convent." Caroline's delivery was calm, absent of exaggeration—it wasn't an idle threat, it was a truth to make Tricia pause. "You are quickly becoming a liability to this family."

The door shut with a quiet finality, sealing Tricia inside with her own thoughts, her own frustration, her own confusion. She threw the pillow at the door, but the soft thud against the door did nothing to dull the sharp ache in her chest.

Why couldn't her mother be kind instead of cold? Hold her instead of lecture her?

The weight of expectation, of reputation, of control—pressed down like a weighted blanket, instead of comforting; it felt smothering. Yet, beneath it all, something else stirred.

Her mind slipped back to that moment at the pool. The quiet splash of water. The low sun reflecting off the tiles. The lifeguard's hands, strong and practiced, working into the knot of her calf. His touch had been strong—practiced. His eyes lingered. Her skin burned. And between her thighs, a pulse, sudden and confusing, had flared like a signal from a body she didn't understand.

There had been no handbook for this, no book club books, sites were blocked on her terminal feeds. No mentor. No conversation over tea with her older sister. Only silence. Only shame.

She crawled into bed, clutching the pillow now—not to throw, but to hold. Her breath hitched as the tears came, slow and hot, soaking into the cotton. Her sobs were quiet, embarrassed by their own existence.

And so she held herself. Because no one else would.

≈ ✵ ≈

The ladies' salon, usually a place of quiet refinement and effortless ease, had taken on an air of quiet urgency, the delicate clink of teacups and wine glasses punctuated by murmured strategy.

Caroline sat with the others, their discussion circling around a singular objective—containment, control, and preventing future damage.

Someone would have to escort Tricia to and from her tutoring lessons, ensuring no chance encounters, no further missteps.

Someone would have to walk with her to breakfast, ensuring every movement was accounted for.

And most critically—swim lessons, where oversight would be absolute.

The illusion of freedom that the resort once held had fractured, replaced now with layers of quiet surveillance woven into every routine.

THE NEXT MORNING, THE sun was already beginning to bake the flagstones outside when Catherine tapped on Tricia's door. She stepped in, radiant and glowing, her hand resting proudly on her swelling belly.

"Let's get you down to swim practice," she chirped, the kind of perkiness that made Tricia blink in disbelief. "I'm excited to see Carson and Casey's progress," Catherine added, as though that explained why she'd come herself.

Tricia trailed behind her, shoulders tight beneath her towel wrap. Her swim uniform felt more like armor than clothing—practical, form-fitting, plain. She didn't expect anything from the morning except sunburn and boredom.

But then she saw him.

The lifeguard sat at his usual post, sunglasses on his head, posture casual but alert. Their eyes met briefly—just a flicker, but it was enough. Something unsaid passed between them, and Tricia felt her pulse jump before she turned quickly toward the swim instructor.

"Look, Mom!" a shrill voice broke through the humid morning air. "I can swim all the way to the deep end and back!" Casey said with enthusiasm.

Catherine beamed, clapping politely. The instructor gave Tricia a short nod toward her lane.

On the sidelines, Eliza stood, her gaze following Tricia with a quiet heaviness. She didn't miss the exchanged glance. She didn't need details. She had grown up in a world where every emotion was monitored, every instinct redirected.

But even here, lust would find a way.

The lifeguard put on his glasses, knowing his eyes would betray him. He wanted to heed the warnings of his coworkers, but he couldn't forget that royal blue bikini.

Madame Mary Margerat requested Virginia and Audrey to follow her upstairs to her private study after the morning announcements. The photo lay between them on the polished table, glossy, new, smuggled in at great risk by Sister Hope. Eliza sat on a chair, regal, a circle of children gathered at her feet, her hand frozen mid-gesture as she read from a weathered storybook. Her face, serene but alert, spoke volumes.

Audrey let out a breath she hadn't realized she was holding.

"It's her," she whispered. "It's really her."

Virginia didn't speak right away. Her fingers hovered above the photo, then settled lightly on the corner—like touching it too firmly might break the fragile proof.

"And that note…" she murmured to herself, eyes scanning the neat, looping script again. "Don't believe everything you read. —E."

"It could mean anything," Audrey said, but even as she said it, her voice wavered. The note hadn't felt like a deflection. It had felt like a plea.

Across the room, Madame Mary Margaret poured tea into three china cups, the steam curling with the scent of chamomile and rose. She moved slowly, listening.

"You had reason to question," she said at last, placing a cup in front of Virginia. Her voice was calm, her gaze was steady, holding a glint of knowing. "I wanted to tell you our suspicions, but did not want to get your hopes up." She paused, "I didn't want you to experience Eliza's death all over again if we were wrong."

Audrey glanced at Virginia, who nodded, in understanding. An omission to protect them.

"Yes," Virginia admitted. "I think Eliza is asking us to look closer."

The silence that followed was thoughtful, heavy with what hadn't been said. Finally, Audrey sat up straighter, her fingers tracing the worn border of the photograph.

"We need to reach her. Quietly. Directly."

"Not easy," Mary Margaret cautioned. "That resort is locked tighter than a space capsule. Eyes everywhere. Staff vetted to the bone." She didn't need to state the obvious, that they themselves were banned from technology.

"She sent us the message through the Interlibrary loan system," Audrey confessed.

"We planned on sending a note back to her using the *Code Talkers?*" Virginia added.

Mary Margaret's eyebrow lifted slightly. "The books?" Eliza was a clever woman.

Virginia nodded. "Women and the oppressed have used them before. Certain titles, specific copies. Hidden messages in margin codes, dog-ears in patterns. A language of our own."

Audrey's lips curved into the ghost of a smile. "Bookmarks. Ink bleeds. Underlines. Eliza will recognize the pattern if she's looking."

"She will be," Virginia said firmly. "She wouldn't have sent this if she wasn't already searching for us," she said pulling out the note.

They leaned in together, heads bowed like conspirators in a cathedral. The table filled with the rustle of pages as they each wrote down volumes, discussing genres, themes, and meanings—what stories would speak to Eliza without drawing attention. What would be seen as leisure, appropriate for a young lady.

Virginia paused, thumbing through a copy of *Jane Eyre*, then glanced at the others.

"She always liked the line: 'I am no bird; and no net ensnares me.'" Virginia smiled softly. "She knows it's my favorite book."

"Let's get your note and book down to the library with Sister Hope," Madame Mary Margaret smiled. The fewer secrets the better. Eliza was alive.

Eliza, Jacque, Abi, Bea, and Jenny wandered ahead, their voices a soft ripple of laughter and chatter, drifting down the desert trail in the amber light of evening. The red rock formations glowed with the last blush of sunlight, casting long shadows across the dusty path.

Tricia trailed behind, her sandals kicking at the sand, her thoughts heavy and distant. She barely heard the rustle before a hand caught hers—rough, urgent—and pulled her behind a tall outcrop of sun-warmed stone. Her breath caught.

Her lifeguard was there.

His eyes searched hers for a heartbeat that stretched impossibly long in the silence. His mouth claimed hers, pressing her hard against the rocks. Her hands wound around his neck, his thigh pushing between hers, as one hand grabbed her buttocks, she gyrated against him, the rock against her back radiated the day's heat. His tongue explored her mouth. Feeling a wetness between her thighs, she gyrated harder, the rough rock digging into her back.

"Tricia?" Her sister's voice called from the trail, distant but sharp.

They froze. She touched his chest, grounding herself in the moment, then stepped away.

"I have to go," she whispered, cheeks flushed, voice shaky.

He nodded, already retreating into the shadow of the rocks. She reemerged on the trail, kneeling briefly to adjust her sandal. When she stood again, no one seemed to notice—her secret safe.

"Everything okay?" Bea asked, glancing back with mild concern.

"Just a rock in my sandal," Tricia replied, forcing a smile. She was grateful for the lengthening shadows that veiled the heat in her cheeks and the wild thrum still echoing in her chest.

Jenny came bouncing up beside her, oblivious. "Tricia! What's your favorite female character in a Regency vid?"

Tricia hesitated, brushing windblown hair from her face. "Lady Sybil."

The group slowed just a little, absorbing the answer.

"Interesting choice," Eliza said quietly, her tone unreadable.

"I'd want to be Sarah Connor," Bea added without pause.

"That's not Regency," Abi and Jenny chimed in together.

Bea shrugged. "When you don't like the narrative, flip the script."

The group laughed—except for Eliza and Jacque. They walked in thoughtful silence, eyes briefly flicking to Tricia.

Something about her answer had unsettled them. Lady Sybil, the one who defied her station, who ran toward danger, who reached beyond the world that tried to contain her.

It wasn't a favorite—it was a confession.

The night air pulsed with desert warmth—dry and still, carrying the scent of creosote and faint smoke from the evening's mesquite fire. Beneath the wooden pergola, lit by amber lanterns and flanked by the distant hiss of cicadas, three men sat in watchful silence as the six young women approached from the trail.

Tricia trailed slightly apart from the others, her wrap loose around her shoulders, hair tousled by the breeze. Moonlight traced her cheekbones, and though her posture remained upright, her steps were slower, less certain.

The girls' laughter rose like sparrows in flight—bright, unbothered—grating against the weighted hush beneath the pergola.

John reclined in his Adirondack chair with deliberate ease. His gaze fixed on Tricia, cold and evaluative. A patriarch assessing a flaw in the legacy he'd built—this family, crafted over two centuries, did not have room for uncertainty. A single crack in the stonework was reason enough to replace it.

Robert's jaw clenched. His hand curled around the armrest. He managed a fleeting smile for Jacque, then looked away from his other daughter. The sharp, metallic taste of disappointment rose in his mouth. He had raised her to know better. Or thought he had.

Dave sat motionless. A glass of scotch rested in his hand, the amber liquid catching moonlight, untouched. His eyes followed Tricia with calculating calm, noting the smudge of lipstick, the telltale flush beneath her skin. Too much had been invested in her image. Every move choreographed, every headline prepped. One reckless moment with a boy could derail everything. And Dave didn't deal in risks—he eliminated them.

The girls drifted toward the stairs in a loose cluster. Dave's gaze lingered as Eliza doubled back—gently but firmly steering Tricia ahead of her. Clever girl.

A dry wind stirred the sagebrush, whispering through the rock and casting long shadows across the stone. No words passed between the men. But their silence held the weight of a verdict already passed.

⁓ ❉ ⁓

The summons landed with a weight heavier than any golf bag—a command, not a request.

Dave Barkley, the richest man in the world, the President's brother, a name that carried power like an iron grip, and worse yet, the uncle of the young woman he wanted to conquest.

Tomorrow was not going to be a good day.

The lifeguard knew golf—his father owned two courses, and he had caddied more rounds than he cared to count. But this? This wasn't about the game. This was about control. Observation. A test, maybe.

And when Dave Barkley summoned you, you didn't decline.

AFTER THE LIBRARY READING, the name *Elizabeth Angela Barkley Rochester* began to shimmer in the data streams, her "populator" score rising steadily—more clicks, more eyes, more engagement. Just as Dave had planned. He trusted the filters he'd applied: nothing too provocative, no flagged content, no unvetted correspondents—especially not men.

Eliza scanned the messages—before she had only received a few notes from Georgette, but now her feed pulsed with quiet rebellion—brief messages tucked in reading recs, line notes from schoolteachers, recommendations from librarians, and passages from nuns. They slipped past the algorithms not because they were encrypted, but because they were cloaked in the one thing the system underestimated: story and love.

The messages weren't long, but they shone with meaning. A suggested passage about a girl hiding forbidden seeds in the hem of her gown. A margin note referencing a "garden of truths, watered in silence." One nun simply sent: *"The heroines walk alone at first. But not forever."*

Dave's protocols logged it all—monitored titles, tracked engagement requests—but never flagged the deeper rhythm. He saw rising literacy metrics, not dissent. He couldn't see how books were being used as a cipher. He could not imagine anything so complex, by women he naturally dismissed.

Eliza, seated in the sunlit alcove of the resort's study room, scrolled through the messages with a small frown tugging at her lips. The data seemed less raw and more sanitized than at Bell-View.

"I'm calling it a night," Rick said getting up and stretching. "Practice climb tomorrow?" he asked.

"Sure," Eliza agreed and watched him walk out of the room. Quickly she moved to his terminal, which he had not logged out of properly. She began to use the same queries as under her own account—the information was much more prolific. Eliza would need to find a solution, but for now, she would piggyback off Rick's account when possible.

The golf course stretched beneath the early sun, its manicured greens rolling out in measured perfection against the rugged desert backdrop. Warm sandstone cliffs framed the fairways, their edges catching the golden morning light, while a faint scent of sagebrush and mesquite smoke lingered on the breeze.

Dave barely spoke, only signaling for clubs with the flick of two fingers, his expression cool, unreadable, locked in quiet calculation. Robert, William, and Edward with their regular caddies rounded out the quartet.

The lifeguard felt the weight of scrutiny in the silence, the pressure of each step across the dry turf, the smooth leather grip of the club uncomfortably slick in his palm.

The sharp thud of a driver striking the ball echoed, sending the white sphere sailing clean through the crisp air, its trajectory smooth, controlled—like everything Dave did.

Robert adjusted his stance, his cleats digging into the earth, the soft crunch barely audible over the hum of cicadas.

William wiped his brow, the heat clinging to his skin, the condensation from his water bottle sliding over his fingers.

Edward's putter kissed the ball with precision, the soft roll over the green steady, measured, unwavering.

At hole 16, Dave tilted his head toward the lifeguard, eyes narrowing briefly as if sizing him up anew.

No words. Just quiet judgment wrapped in desert heat.

By the 18th hole, his victory was secured, the scorecards confirming what everyone already knew.

But the real game was just beginning, he smiled at the Lifeguard, "If you touch my niece again, I will not only destroy you, but your entire family."

"Let's grab some shrimp tacos," he said to his Brother and cousins.

A casual threat delivered with the same ease as ordering shrimp tacos, as if ruin were just another item on the menu.

The air beneath the awning hummed with conversation, the scent of warm corn tortillas, citrusy margaritas, and smoky mesquite curling through the evening breeze.

The younger boys moved in rhythmic concentration, the soft *tap* of golf balls rolling across the putting green under their grandfather's steady gaze. Each time a club met the ball, the crisp sound blended with the faint chirp of crickets from the nearby brush.

At the driving range, Bea guided Jacque, Eliza, Abi, Jenny, and Tricia, her stance firm, shoulders squared, as she demonstrated the perfect swing.

Eliza felt the rough leather grip of the club beneath her fingers, adjusting slightly before taking her shot. The ball shot clean into the twilight, disappearing momentarily against the purpling sky before landing with a muted thud in the distance.

Jenny let out a satisfied hum, dusting sand from her palms, while Tricia lagged behind, her wrap loose around her shoulders, feet scuffing lightly against the packed earth.

Rick, bored of carefully measured putts, snuck away, the sharp crunch of gravel under his shoes signaling his approach as he joined them, his expression mischievous.

Meanwhile, under the awning, Sophie, Eunice, Charlotte, Catherine, and Caroline spoke in hushed tones, their words threading through the scent of chamomile and lime from half-sipped cocktails, the excitement of upcoming charity events mingling with the unspoken anticipation of Sophie and Eliza's journey ahead, only dampened slightly by Tricia's reckless behavior.

The quartet from the golf course joined them.

Robert stood between them, arms crossed, watching with the trained eye of someone who understood both rivalry and precision. Carson and Bobby's competition was fierce, the rhythmic *tap* of their putts echoing beneath the awning as they tried to outmatch each other, their focus unbreakable.

William leaned in beside Paul, guiding him through the subtle shift in weight needed for a longer putt, his voice low and instructive, deliberate in its patience.

Edward drifted toward his wife, his hand resting against the curve of her growing belly, a quiet moment amid the movement of the afternoon heat.

Little Casey basked in the glow of attention, his laughter bright against the quiet murmur of discussion, his world untouched by the weighted glance between John and Dave.

Dave leaned back and enjoyed the spectacle of the perfect day at the golf course. His thoughts sharpened like the edge of a well-honed blade, cold, efficient, and absolute.

If the lifeguard wasn't smart enough to heed the warning, the consequence would be swift—a few keystrokes, a ripple through the right channels, and his family's ruin would follow without hesitation.

Tricia, though—the lifeguard was merely a symptom, not the disease.

Her impulse to act out was foreseeable. Tricia had always been volatile beneath the surface—a spark looking for dry tinder. But at least here, contained within the desert, she was manageable. Observable. Isolated from the press, the committee aides, and social donors. Here, there were no leaks to fear—only heat, silence, and time. It had to be resolved before they returned to DC, where reputations weren't salvaged—they were sacrificed.

And then, there was Eliza. Dave's gaze flickered toward her, contemplatively, though his expression remained unreadable. Unlike the carefully managed society women, she had been molded differently, her intellect moved on its own terms; her steadiness a sharp contrast to Tricia's capriciousness.

Would she rein Tricia in, or let her burn herself out? Would she disrupt his calculations, or subtly reinforce them in ways he hadn't accounted for?

He leaned back, his fingers grazing the rim of his glass, the margarita oddly satisfying. He bit into his shrimp taco and it fall apart—messy and symbolic—as he reflected back to Tricia.

⇒ ✵ ⇐

"I plan on taking the trip to Albuquerque on Tuesday, and Eliza and I will be gone for three days," Sophie informed Eunice, enjoying a cool drink in contrast to the heat of the golf course.

Eunice nodded, reassuring, her gaze shifting toward Tricia at the driving range, the rhythmic *thunk* of golf balls punctuating the warm evening air.

"We can cover everything," she promised, certainty laced through her tone, but her attention lingered—watchful, thoughtful.

Sophie's voice carried a quiet certainty, the weight of the journey settling into the conversation.

"This trip isn't just about meeting a relative," she explained, her gaze steady, thoughtful. "It's about connecting Eliza with the other half of her family—her Mother's people, Pueblo roots, her history."

Sky City, it sounded so mysterious—ancient, enduring, holding stories older than written records.

No matter how distant the relation, the tie remained, and Sophie knew how much it mattered, how much Eliza needed the chance to step into that heritage and truly see it for herself.

⇒ ✵ ⇐

That evening Eliza's excitement was tempered by caution, the thrill of meeting her distant relative mingling with the awareness that Tricia was restless, unpredictable, and likely looking for any possible escape. A trip to Albuquerque. Acoma Pueblo. Sky City. The promise of answers, of family found in the expanse of New Mexico's sundried landscape,

She asked Jenny to come to her room with purpose. "I'm going with my grandmother to meet a relative from my mother's side," Eliza explained, the words carrying both excitement and quiet weight.

Jenny, ever perceptive, tilted her head, waiting for the part Eliza hadn't said yet. "I need you to shadow Tricia," Eliza added, her tone firm but light. "Like a puppy."

Jenny raised an eyebrow, a smirk tugging at the corner of her lips. "A puppy?"

Eliza exhaled, crossing her arms, knowing Jenny was going to make her say it outright.

"Yes, Jenny. I need her watched every second. "Jenny pretended to consider, tapping her chin.

"I suppose I could follow her around, ears up, tail wagging..." she mused.

Eliza shot her a look, but the humor wasn't unwelcome.

"You really are the best ladies maid ever," Eliza smiled.

Rob adjusted the final sequence on the airship's console, the glow of the interface casting sharp blue reflections against the polished metal.

"You triple-check the hovercraft?" he asked without looking up.

Omar snorted, leaning against the frame of the docking bay, arms crossed. "Triple? Please. I've checked it so many times it could fly itself to Mars if needed."

Rob smirked, finally glancing at him. "Good. That means if anything goes wrong, I know exactly who to blame."

Omar rolled his eyes, stepping closer, close enough that Rob could feel the warmth of him, smell the faint trace of citrus and machine oil that clung to his jacket.

"You know, for someone who trusts me with his life, you sure like to threaten me a lot."

"Keeps you sharp," Rob murmured, his voice softer now, more familiar.

A hum filled the space as the final systems powered up. Omar watched the hovercraft's lights pulse, but his attention drifted back to Rob—the way he always leaned in a little when he worked, that focused crease in his brow.

"Think they have any idea how much work goes into this?" Omar asked, his fingers grazing Rob's wrist, a casual touch, but lingering just enough to mean something.

Rob exhaled, tilting his head slightly toward him, the corner of his mouth quirking up. "Nope. And that's exactly how it should be." He touched Omar lightly on the hand, "let's go to bed and enjoy our last night at the resort for a few days,"

⸎

The soft, buttery notes of the Chardonnay mingled with the quiet hum of conversation in Madame Mary Margaret's private study. Outside, the Hall of Mary Ann was settling into its hot summer lull, but within these walls, Madame and Sister Hope felt a different kind of energy pulsing—a subtle, electric current humming through their carefully woven network.

Since the Public Library reading by the lost heiress, movement was happening. Eliza's reading had ignited a ripple of excitement that spread far beyond the underground library. It confirmed what the inner circles, the women privy to the secret alliance between the church, the libraries, and the brothels, had long suspected: a hidden path to power, ripe for reclamation.

They spoke in carefully chosen words, their voices low, almost conspiratorial. Messages were being exchanged outside these walls on the very networks men controlled—codes within coded exchanges, a language of subtle inflections that men, in their oversight, would simply overlook.

"The overwhelming support for the heiress," Madame mused, swirling the pale wine in her glass, "it's... a gift. A small light for those seeking."

Sister Hope nodded, her gaze distant. "And the Abbess has already begun to shift the focus of our sermons. Emphasizing the need for healing, the power of unseen forces, the resilience of hidden lineages."

Madame's smile was thin, strategic. "Dave expects us to be consumed by grief, to be broken by the 'loss' of Eliza. Instead, we weave her into something new. Something far more powerful." She paused, a glint in her eye. "It's a brave man indeed that continues reading once he realizes a message is about menstrual cramps or bleeding."

They clinked glasses, the soft chime a silent toast to the meticulous deception, to the network that saw opportunities where others saw only compliance. The game was escalating, and Eliza, unknowingly or not, was its very heart.

THE BREAKFAST ROOM HUMMED with quiet activity, the usual undercurrent of conversation flowing in pockets around the space. Eliza scanned the room and felt a flicker of relief at the sight of Jenny seated beside Tricia. Tricia's expression was one of practiced disinterest, tinged with reluctant amusement. Jenny, ever undeterred, animatedly detailing her latest fictional obsession, hands moving in wide arcs as if summoning her characters to life. Her energy, light and persistent, served as both distraction and balm.

Across the room, Sophie, Eunice, and Caroline leaned in over preparations, their voices measured, the weight of upcoming plans reflected in the careful way they exchanged notes.

Rick and the boys, clustered at their own table, discussed tutoring lessons, their tones shifting between enthusiasm and reluctant duty, the occasional laugh breaking through the seriousness.

Jacque, Abi, and Bea spoke in lilting tones over ball gowns, their conversation rich with colors, fabric details, and the subtle thrill of what was to come.

Near the terminal, Charlotte and Catherine sat side by side, their focus locked as they screened potential nannies, heads slightly tilted as they evaluated profiles with careful scrutiny.

The absence of the men, having departed for the week, left behind a noticeable stillness, a rare moment of space.

Outside, the morning air held a crispness that clung to the skin, tinged with the scent of creosote and sun-warmed stone. Wild desert blooms pressed faint perfume into the breeze, blending with the sharp bite of oolong tea in Eliza's mouth.

Eliza's hug to Jenny was quick but firm, a silent exchange of gratitude, reassurance—an acknowledgment that Jenny had done what was asked, that Tricia would be watched, protected.

Then, she turned, her steps purposeful, heading toward the airship where her grandmother's and her own luggage were already loaded and in their cabins.

The lustrous craft gleamed under the soft sunlight, engines humming low, steady, ready. Opulent and intimidating.

This was more than just travel—this was a threshold, a step into something that carried weight, history, expectation. Bringing the maternal and paternal elements of her family together.

"Permission to board," Grandmother Sophie called out to the Captain, following traditional Naval Protocol.

Rob smiled slightly in his crisp uniform, "Granted," he said, escorting Grandmother Sophie onto the craft.

Rob and Sophie chatted ahead about the course plan.

Omar extended his elbow and Eliza took it gracefully. The Captain and First Mate saw the ladies settled in a lounge compartment and then headed to the front of the ship.

"Permission to board Captain," Omar chuckled to himself. "I am using that one tonight," he added with wink to Rob.

The lounge compartment of the airship shimmered with quiet elegance—sunlight filtered through etched glass, dancing across silver fixtures and fine china.

Sophie eased into the upholstered chair across from Eliza, her movements graceful despite the stiffness in her joints. She stirred her tea with slow precision, the spoon tapping once against porcelain.

"I'm glad to finally have some time with you, Eliza," she said, her tone warm but measured, eyes sharp beneath soft lashes. "You've adjusted unexpectedly well to our little world—perhaps better than my grandniece, Patricia. Yet even now, I see how you make room for her. You offer grace where others wouldn't."

She paused, letting steam rise between them like a veil. Eliza remained silent, patient.

Outside, the airship glided effortlessly above rugged desert landscapes stretching between Canyon Point and Albuquerque—deep terracotta, sun-bleached sandstone, and bursts of hardy green stitched the earth below.

"We are never far from prying ears or eyes, but I think you know that," Sophie said, stirring again. The silver spoon clinked gently. Her gaze was calm, discerning.

Eliza nodded, recalling when even the simplest tech had been out of reach—and yet they had still tracked her like a specimen.

Inside, the air was cool, scented faintly with chamomile and orange peel. Golden light filtered through etched windows, casting warm patterns over polished teak and gleaming silver. A floating masterpiece of craftsmanship.

"People forget about women like me," Sophie said. "Tucked into corners, sipping tea, dismissed before we speak. But you… you don't forget. You see the angles. You stay calm. You understand power."

Eliza met her gaze. Sophie leaned forward slightly, approval glinting in her eyes.

"Let's see what we can do with that."

Eliza took a slow sip of tea, grounding herself in the warmth, weighing not just Sophie's words, but the invitation within them.

Opportunity. A challenge. A door slightly open.

"I see the angles, Grandmother," she said, setting her cup down with quiet precision. "But understanding power isn't enough. It's knowing when to use it that matters."

Sophie's lips curved—subtly, approvingly.

"Precisely. And I want to ensure you understand your situation clearly, while we take this little holiday. You are a very wealthy, independent woman. At the ball in DC, you will be presented as Jon Jon's rightful heir. There is nothing anyone can do about it—the legalities are already completed."

Eliza's breath caught.

"You are barren. No one can force you to marry," she took a sip of tea. "At twenty-six, just a few weeks after the ball, you will have the right to do anything you wish with your inheritance—it would no longer have to stay in trust."

"I would be free?" The words felt fragile, almost dangerous. Untethered.

"You are free, my dear," Sophie said gently. "But for a woman to make it ten years past her majority and not be wed is truly exceptional. My sons and the men in my brother's family will encourage you to marry."

"But it would be unseemly to rush into a marriage," Eliza processed. "My birthday is rather inconvenient for them," she smiled, sipping her tea.

"I'd like to offer you something. Consider staying with me, in Pocantico Hills—at the Rochester estate. Even if you say no, know that my door will always be open." She lifted her cup again, the rim smooth against her lips. The tea was floral, earthy—chosen with care, a pause in a conversation that changed everything.

"Don't answer now," Sophie added, taking a petit four from the tray. "I've placed a lot on your plate."

Eliza sat across from her, the steam curling softly between them.

"I don't know what to say," she murmured.

"Then don't," Sophie replied, eyes on the desert unfolding beneath them. "Just sit with your old grandmother. And enjoy the view."

The revelation hung in the space between them, just as vast as the land passing beneath their journey.

The atmosphere at lunch was measured but confident, the kind of quiet tension that accompanied well-oiled strategy. Conversation moved in low tones, threaded through the soft clink of silverware and the practiced cadence of updates.

"Poll numbers are strong," Dave observed. "The ball will be a good optic, as long as you can keep Tricia in line."

"The kids will only be there for the family portrait and the first hour," Robert assured him.

"Plenty of time for a hussy to find a waiter," John observed.

"Dad," Robert said with menace, "she is my daughter."

"She is a threat to this family, is what she is, son." John continued. "You need to send her off to a convent before it's too late."

"The economy is thriving," Dave cut in, "Trade is fluid, deals moving fast." His network ran deep, and he knew precisely which levers to pull, when to apply pressure, and when to disappear.

"How are your cryoprojects going?" John asked.

"Production is up in one of the facilities," Dave replied. "I am going to take a look and find out how to emulate it."

John nodded. Robert gave a slight shutter.

"Once we have perfected our methods, and after the election," he looked from John to Robert.

"I plan to build additional capacity; our product is in high demand both here and globally."

"There is still the problem of Bart Jackson," Robert reminded them. Too entrenched to remove, too dangerous to ignore.

John leaned back, wiping his mouth with a linen napkin. "If we let Bart keep poking at supply lines, he's going to convince people there's a fault line in the system."

Robert kept his gaze on his plate, voice low. "He already has in Council 3. Half of them are reading his policy memos like scripture."

Dave didn't look up. "Then we remind them who built the table they're sitting at."

John's brow lifted. "That a warning or a threat?"

"It's direction," Dave replied, calmly slicing into his salmon. "If he wants to make noise, fine. Let him. But we control what echoes."

Robert finally met his eyes. "And Gray?"

There was a pause, longer than the others. Gray was both a problem and a solution.

Dave set his fork down. "No change. Gray stays where he is—until after the elections."

"Let's make sure these next two charity events are successful," Dave commented.

"A hospital and county fair," Robert read. "Caroline will have it covered."

"There's also the Bryce Canyon Rock climbing with Eliza and Rick scheduled." John added. "Strength and unity should be a clear message from that stunt."

Across the table, the silence settled again. The weight of the next moves was no longer abstract. They were inevitable.

The shuttle craft hummed softly disconnecting from the airship, swiftly taking them toward Acoma Pueblo, the vast desert stretching beneath them in waves of ochre and rust, the mesas standing like ancient sentinels against the sky.

Eliza stepped out, the warm air wrapping around her, carrying the scent of sunbaked earth and juniper, the distant echo of voices blending with the rustle of wind through the canyon.

A wisewoman greeted Sophie and Eliza, "Come, my sister and my daughter."

They followed, her presence steady, knowing, woven into the very fabric of the land. Acoma's matriarchal traditions ran deep, the women holding the pulse of the community, the keepers of lineage, the architects of renewal.

The name Haaku—"a place prepared"—resonated in the air, a reminder that this meeting, this moment, was not just chance but part of something larger.

"Sit," she said, indicating some blankets. She threw some herbs in the fire and offered them drinks.

Eliza listened as the wisewoman spoke of Tsichtinako, Thought Woman, the goddess who sent the first two sisters into the world, teaching them agriculture, ceremony, survival. One sister, Iatiku—"bringing to life"—embodied renewal, the cycle of beginnings that stretched across generations.

Nearby, Kachina figures stood in quiet reverence, their presence tied to ceremonies of renewal, of life, of the unseen forces that shaped the world.

The campfire crackled, sending soft embers into the crisp desert night, its warmth stretching over the small circle of figures wrapped in woven shawls. The scent of mesquite smoke curled through the air, mingling with the earthy fragrance of the canyon walls beyond.

Eliza sat cross-legged on the ground, her palms resting against the cool stone beneath her as she listened.

The wisewoman stirred the fire with a smooth, practiced motion, her face lined but unwavering, the deep glow of flame reflecting in her keen eyes.

"Our people are guided by the women," she said, her voice a steady current, low but resonant.

"The mother's lineage carries the name, the responsibility, the wisdom. It is through the women that the land remembers us, and through us that the land is kept."

She glanced at Eliza, observing her quiet contemplation, the weight of understanding shifting into place.

"We are the ones who hold the seeds—corn, beans, squash, and history. We plant them, nurture them, pass them to the next hands that come after us."

Eliza traced a thumb across the edge of her ceramic cup, the herbal steam rising between them.

The wisewoman continued, her tone deliberate, revealing what was often overlooked.

"They say the name Acoma comes from Haaku—a place prepared. But preparation does not happen by chance. It happens because we remember. Because we build for those who come next."

The fire snapped, releasing a plume of smoke into the cool air.

"This is why we honor Thought Woman. Because she gave the first sisters—our ancestors—not just life, but the understanding of how to tend it."

Eliza felt the words settling deep, like roots threading into unseen soil.

The wisewoman studied her in the flickering light.

"You carry blood tied to this place, though you have been raised elsewhere. But the land does not forget its own. The question is—will you remember it?"

The fire crackled low, its smoke curling upward in slow spirals, fragrant with sage and cedar. The wisewoman's eyes, dark and knowing, lingered on Eliza as she handed her a small woven pouch. "From mother to daughter," she said simply. "From daughter to earth."

Eliza always felt her best when grounded by the earth, reading in the woods, climbing rocks, sitting around the fire at this moment.

"What do I need to do?" she asked?

"You must find us all?" the wisewoman replied.

"All?" Eliza inquired.

Sophie sat silent but knowing, her presence an anchor, letting Eliza absorb what was meant for her alone.

"There are so few left around the world that respect the mothers. You must find the rest of the surviving cultures that follow the path of nature," the fire hissed.

"All the Matrilineal Societies in the world?" Eliza asked.

"You were a daughter of the night—now you are a daughter of day," came the response. "We need you to be a daughter of the infinite sky."

Eliza's hands tightened around the small woven pouch, the weight of the wisewoman's words sinking into her chest like a drumbeat—steady, undeniable, transformative.

"You must find us all," she said, an echo.

The mission was as vast as the sky stretched above them, as intangible as the stories whispered between flames.

Eliza's breath was steady but charged, a quiet exhale against the night. "I promise."

The fire crackled, sending golden embers soaring into the infinite sky, the moment sealed not by force, but by choice.

Sophie and Eliza returned to the airship to shower and rest, their souls renewed, their bodies depleted.

Tricia moved through the house with a restless energy, feeling the weight of every glance, every expectation pressing against her.

Jenny's chatter was constant, relentless in its optimism, a bright thread woven through the tension—but even that became suffocating sometimes.

"So, did you see the latest episode?" she asked Tricia, undeterred by the visible annoyance settling on her friend's face. "Lady Rosalind finally admitted she's been secretly hiding her engagement to the Duke! I knew it—too much longing in those glances at the last ball. And—get this— the staff are betting on which maid will let it slip first."

The Powder room, her bedroom—these were the only places of escape, where she could close the door and pull in the silence, just for a moment.

And yet, as frustrating as Jenny could be, Tricia understood why Eliza liked her.

She always tried to make her smile, even when Tricia wanted nothing more than to disappear.

"And speaking of staff gossip—do not repeat this, but you know that new cook?" Jenny lowered her voice, dramatically glancing around as if the walls had ears. "Apparently, he's not just here for any reason. Sophie had him reassigned from another estate because the head chef there was so jealous of him and thought he was too good of a cook. Like when the Wicked Queen banished Snow White."

Jenny's voice bubbled through the tense atmosphere, relentless in its enthusiasm, weaving chatter through the uneasy silence.

Tricia sighed, resting her chin in her palm, but Jenny pressed on.

But the worst was her mother's gaze—silent, judging, unwavering

"You're awfully quiet," Jenny said, a little more gently now, her chatter slowing to something more tentative.

Tricia didn't respond right away. She stared at the Navajo trim on the edge of the hallway mirror, its gilded frame distorted just enough to blur her reflection. She hated how much of herself she saw in her mother's stare—cold, assessing, impossible to please.

"She's just waiting for me to fail," Tricia muttered, more to herself than Jenny.

Jenny blinked. "Who is?"

"My mother. Everyone." She straightened up, suddenly aware of how exposed she felt. "I don't know why Eliza even tries with me. She should just stop."

Jenny crossed her arms, tapping a nail against the edge of the marble sink. "Because she *doesn't* want you to fail. And neither do I or anyone else here."

"I don't need a cheerleader," Tricia said, walking swiftly to her room and shutting the door in Jenny's face.

⇒ ✳ ⇐

The next morning, the airship hummed softly as it descended once more toward Acoma Pueblo, the vast desert stretching beneath them in waves of ochre and rust, the mesas standing like ancient guardians of history.

Eliza stepped out onto the packed earth, the scent of sunbaked stone and cedar lingering in the breeze, her thoughts still woven with the weight of last night's revelation.

The wisewoman stood waiting, steady, expectant, her gaze unwavering yet kind, a silent acknowledgment of the path ahead—one that would not be easy, but one that was hers to walk.

"Come, my daughter," she said, leading Eliza to the shaded alcove where woven blankets lay spread beneath the morning light.

The tea was prepared—rich with mountain herbs, grounding, meant to steady one's spirit for the decisions ahead.

She gestured for Eliza to sit, then settled across from her, the fire from the previous night now reduced to smoldering embers, whispering heat into the cool dawn.

"Your journey will ask much of you," she began, voice even, a truth rather than a warning.

"You must seek those who still honor the mothers—the societies where lineage is carried through the women, where the land and traditions are preserved through careful hands."

Eliza nodded slowly, absorbing every word, her fingers grazing the woven pouch she had been given, its weight a quiet reminder of what had been entrusted to her.

"But do not mistake recognition for belonging. Each place, each people, will test you. They will ask who you are, why you have come. And it will be for you to answer—without hesitation, without fear."

The wisewoman poured the tea, the scent of sage rising between them, curling into the early sunlight.

"You are not just searching for them, my daughter. You are searching for yourself."

Eliza lifted the cup to her lips, feeling the warmth spread through her, grounding her, readying her. For a moment, Eliza could feel them— those who had walked before. Her mother, silent but present. Sophie, observant but steady. And others she had never known: women whose names were not in any ledger or database, but in the bones of the land, in the lullabies passed down in kitchens and fields.

"You will need allies," the wisewoman said. "Not just those with influence, but those with memory. Those who remember what the world was like when women held the sky."

Eliza met her gaze, a quiet fire kindling behind her eyes. "And if I can't find them?"

"You make them," the wisewoman said, without pause. "You gather those who've been waiting to remember. You build on the web you have already begun weaving."

The air stirred. Somewhere beyond the ridges, a bird cried out—sharp, piercing, like a signal.

Eliza tucked the stone into her pocket. "I'll go," she said.

"Yes," the wisewoman replied. "To start—you'll need to return to the place where the forgetting began."

⇌ ✳ ⇋

Sophie and Eliza sat in the lounge compartment of the airship, indulging in Mimosas and quiche for brunch. They had not spoken much since returning from Acoma Pueblo, reflecting on the mystical events.

"Grandmother," Eliza began softly, "I have thought a lot about your offer to stay with you."

"I understand, Eliza, you have been set on a quest, you can't possibly stay to keep some old lady from being lonely." Sophie swirled her mimosa gently, watching the orange liquid catch the light, her mind already turning over the idea.

"No, I can't," Eliza confirmed, "But what would prevent you from coming with me?"

"Come with you?" she repeated, not dismissively, but curiously, weighing the possibility, shifting perspective. "Well, we are most certainly borrowing this airship from Eunice and John. Borrowing an airship isn't much different from borrowing a Winnebago, I suppose," she mused, her tone teasing, but not without thought.

"I would like to stay with you while I get my bearings after the ball and my inheritance sorted out," Eliza's gaze held steady.

Sophie let the silence stretch, the idea shaping itself between them, not improbable, not impossible—just unexpected.

"You, my dear, are truly a problem solver," she finally said, taking a measured sip of her drink.

Eliza smiled but felt that there was a weight she could disclose to Aunt Sophie, not the entirety, but part. One that wouldn't burden but be lighter for both when shared.

"When I was at Bell-View all I ever wanted to do was travel. I didn't go out—I hoarded every credit and lived in books," she paused, grounding herself, remembering the worn diary. "When I got sick, they had to use all my money to save me. Now, I am finding out that this dream is my mission."

The moment hung in quiet understanding, the weight of unspoken promises passing between them.

Eliza's remembered her silent vow—I remember you, Anna Lucia, and I will honor your legacy—carried through the space, not in words, but in resolve. I will keep my promise to you.

Sophie, ever perceptive, felt the solemnity, recognized it, and with a simple gesture—a pat of Eliza's hand—acknowledged what did not need to be said aloud.

Moonlight slanted through the window, casting a silver sheen across the private study and caught the rims of the glasses as Madame poured the Pinot Grigio—sharp, clear, resilient.

"To Eliza," Sister Hope said, her voice reverent, unwavering. "The one they tried to erase."

"To those that refuse to forget," Madame Mary Margaret replied, lifting her glass with quiet defiance.

Outside, the Hall of Mary Ann stood resolute, its shadow long against the city's glow. Hovercraft slipped along their prescribed paths, silent sentinels above a capital built on memory and monument.

T

HE MIDDAY SUN BATHED the fairgrounds in a golden light, casting long shadows of carnival tents and fluttering pennants. Laughter rippled through the air, punctuated by the calls of barkers and the occasional squeal—from both pigs and children.

Eliza and Jacque moved smoothly between contests, drones following their every move, gracious and composed. Heading out the blue ribbons, they posed when needed, offered smiles, but their real attention remained on the pulse of the day—gauging mood, watching alliances, absorbing the subtle theater of power disguised as play.

At the relay starting line, Eunice, Caroline, and Tricia, each held a spoon for the three-generation or as many of the locals called it the *tres generaciones* race.

"Breathe, darling," Caroline told Tricia, who immediately bristled. Tricia was going first, an egg sat securely on her spoon as she stood still, but she knew that it would be a balancing act as soon as the whistle blew.

Eunice, gray hair bobbed as she limbered up, giving them both a wink. "I'll take the anchor leg, just in case anyone gets competitive."

Tricia couldn't suppress her laugh. Grandmother was on mission with a spoon and an egg.

Paul nudged Bobby at the greased pig pen. "Five creds say I get it first."

"You're on," Bobby grinned. Carson and Casey had no strategy, just muddy delight.

A local boy managed to eventually capture the squealing pig and Jacque gave him his blue ribbon and the pig got away outside the area. The fairgrounds erupted into a few minutes of chaos as the pig was chased by the gleeful boys. Eventually Bobby was the one successful in the pursuit and took the pig back to it's enclosure.

"You owe me five creds," he told Paul with a smile.

At the pie table, John eyed the blueberry monstrosity in front of him. "Remind me why we are doing this?"

"For the people," Robert deadpanned, already rolling up his sleeves.

Dave chuckled, a rare moment of levity. "Speak for yourself—I skipped breakfast."

Sophie, ever composed, had other plans—A Ferris wheel ride with William and Edward, their smiles firm for the cameras, but softer when it was just them and the sky.

Over at the dart board, Rick exhaled slowly, eyes narrowing as the crowd hushed. Three quick throws—bullseye, just off, and a clean center hit.

He turned to Eliza and shrugged. "Luck favors the boring."

"Careful," she whispered, and looked at his competition.

"Right," he replied. His breath slightly off on his next round, close, but the local champion beat him.

"Great job," Eliza told her cousin with a smile, as she handed out the blue ribbon to the winner, who was beaming with pride.

Bea's throw knocked a tin can pyramid clean off, her expression smug. "Balance and trajectory," she told a gaping teenager beside her.

Back at the pie booth, Abi lifted a tart with perfect latticework. "Presentation is 30% of flavor," she insisted.

Jenny, holding up a rustic crumble, frowned. "But mine feels more honest. Like, heartfelt."

"Messy is not a flavor, Jen," Abi replied.

⁂

Meanwhile, Charlotte remained home with Catherine, ensuring that comfort took priority, a quiet counterbalance to the fair's buzz. Catherine's feet were swollen without having to walk around a fairground all day.

Charlotte stretched out next to her. "Thanks for getting me a day off," she laughed.

"Yes, I'm doing this just for you, so you can have a day away from your boys," she quipped, rubbing her belly, feeling the baby kick.

"I have a confession," Charlotte told Catherine.

"What?" her Sister-in-Law asked, loving the intrigue.

"I'm expecting," she whispered. "We didn't think it would happen again. I just turned forty," she paused tears forming in her eyes. "The last time I went with you to the doctors, I got checked out as well."

"This is so exciting," Charlotte gushed. "What does William think?"

"I am waiting until the second trimester to tell him," she confided.

"Our daughters are going to be best friends," Catherine said with confidence that Charlotte's baby would also be a girl.

The fair hummed with noise, laughter spilling into the warm air, the scent of kettle corn and dust swirling in the golden light.

But Tricia's pulse thrummed louder, drowning out the chaos as she caught sight of him—her lifeguard, her escape, the one steady presence in the whirlwind of expectations.

The pig's squeals cut through the crowd, bodies moving, distracted, shifting—and she saw her chance.

Without hesitation, she reached for his hand, fingers curling around his, pulling him swiftly behind the carnival booths, weaving through clusters of dart-throwers and tin can pyramids.

Here, in the shadows between flashing lights and distant cheers, the noise dulled just enough.

She grabbed his face eagerly, wanting to feel his tongue inside her again. With only the slightest hesitation, he silently complied. Pressing her against the back of the dart booth, his back wedged against the fairground fence, covered in banners. This was not a place where the carnival-goers came.

"I want you," he told her, completely forgetting her uncles' warning. "Are you barren?" he asked.

"Yes," she said heatedly, kissing his neck. She would say anything to continue feeling this way.

Her hands embraced his hips, pulling them against her and she moaned softly into his neck.

"I'll arrange a time at the deck house," he told her. Grinding one last time, wishing their clothes were off. "Go back out to the fairway first," he instructed.

Tricia walked out and started looking around as if for the lost pig. A few minutes later, the lifeguard came from around the corner.

Dave sighed. He would need to screen some drone footage, better to be safe.

⁂

Dave exhaled slowly, his fingers moving with practiced efficiency as he sifted through the drone feeds, ensuring nothing compromising remained.

A stroke of luck—the secluded corner behind the dart booth had escaped capture, leaving no trace of the rendezvous.

He didn't linger on it. What mattered now was control. Precision. Strategy.

And in that arena, the numbers spoke for themselves.

The polling figures surged, the public reception overwhelmingly positive, reinforcing the momentum.

Dave leaned back slightly, allowing the numbers to settle in his mind, the quiet satisfaction of a narrative perfectly executed.

The President's pie-covered grin—genuine, disarming—had landed exactly as intended, humanizing the administration without veering into absurdity.

And then, of course, there was the first son, arms wrapped around the squealing pig, navigating the chaos with calculated ease.

Better than if he'd won outright. Victory wasn't always about competition—it was about image, perception, relatability.

Jacque and Eliza, gold and bronze, handing out blue ribbons to deserving winners. The three-generation spoon race, demonstrating a legacy unbroken.

Dave moved on, refocusing his energy toward the next optic, the next calculated step in a sequence that had to land flawlessly.

Dave approached the one woman in the family he felt he could go to about Patricia, Aunt Sophie.

Dave walked beside her, his voice low, measured, carrying the weight of an admission he wasn't entirely sure how to make. He confided what he had seen at the fair and provided his perspective on Patricia and the Lifeguard.

"You think we should just let it happen?" Sophie asked, her tone sharp but quiet, the disbelief woven through her words unmistakable.

Dave sighed, running a hand over his jaw, eyes fixed on the dirt path beneath them.

"Better here than DC," he answered, knowing full well the chaos that awaited in the capital, the scrutiny that never truly relented.

The trail stretched ahead in soft twilight, the scent of pine and dry earth settling into the cooling air.

Sophie didn't respond immediately, her steps steady, the silence stretching just long enough to make Dave wonder what she truly thought.

"Can't we send the lifeguard away," Aunt Sophie asked, perplexed.

"Why?" he asked. "She'll just find a waiter or cook in DC." Echoing his father's comment.

"This could ruin Robert's chances of getting reelected," Dave continued pragmatically.

"She can't be allowed off premises again. Not the Hospital children's wing visit, not Bryce Canyon. She stays at the resort, and you women can figure out how to contain her. At least here, I control the cameras. If you don't have a solution by the time we need to return to DC, she goes to a Convent."

Sophie kept her expression measured, but inside, wheels turned rapidly.

Dave's stance was clear, firm, absolute—containment was necessary, and failure to do so would result in drastic action.

"John already wants her in a convent."

That much was undeniable. The blue bikini incident had made his opinion firm.

Sophie knew her brother well enough to understand that when he made a decision, he saw little reason to alter it.

Yet, the idea of locking Tricia away to preserve political optics gnawed at something deep in her—an instinct, a resistance, an understanding of what it meant to be young, reckless, and watched.

"We will handle it," she finally said, her voice smooth, commitment sealed within the words but their execution still uncertain.

⇒ ✳ ⇐

The hum of the hovercrafts barely masked Jenny's excited energy, her movements practically vibrating as they crossed the National Park border, unaware of the storm brewing beyond them.

What was meant to be a simple climb, a quiet retreat into the raw beauty of Bryce Canyon, had instead become headline fodder.

The alerts fired off the moment the craft passed the boundary, signals flashing to eager reporters who thrived on spectacle and legacy.

By the time Eliza and Rick had harnessed up, the first drone had already locked in—streaming live, catching every motion, every adjustment of gear, every calculated move up the towering hoodoos.

Jenny and a few of the house servants prepared a picnic area for when they descended. A small awning and some nourishment for a climb being made more difficult by the constant scrutiny.

They had thought they could slip in unnoticed, had planned for privacy, for focus, but the name Barkley Rochester carried gravity, and gravity pulled cameras with it.

⇒ ✳ ⇐

Dave's lips curled into a satisfied smirk as he scanned the live feed on his wrist console, watching the broadcast unfold exactly as it needed to.

The reporters had framed it perfectly—the elusive heiress and her cousin, caught not in grandeur, but in something raw, real, and effortlessly compelling.

The pavilion was simple, unassuming, no extravagant staging—just Eliza and Rick against the canyon's towering backdrop, the instructors below lending a touch of authenticity to the climb's legitimacy.

There was no script, no planned spectacle—yet the story was playing out better than anything overly orchestrated.

Dave leaned back, the hum of data beneath his fingertips, knowing that sometimes, the best optics are the ones that feel entirely unintentional.

The lifeguard recognized his opening. With a smaller group away at Bryce Canyon, the swim instructors and a few others took advantage of the quiet lull to tour the airship, its polished silver hull gleaming under the midday sun, the faint hum of its engines a promise of luxurious flight. In the resort library, a hushed murmur drifted from the study rooms where the academic instructors held their final session, the only sound the movement of fingers on terminals filling the air.

He meticulously prepared the deckhouse for Patricia, the scent of sunbaked wood already thick in the air. He adjusted the tiny lenses of the cameras he'd strategically placed, ensuring each angle would capture indisputable proof; the soft click of the mechanisms the only sound in the stillness. A sly smile played on his lips – none of his friends would believe he'd been with the President's daughter without visual evidence.

Moving like a shadow, he caught Tricia's eye just as her hand reached for the handle of the resort library door. A subtle flick of his wrist, a fleeting glance toward the secluded deckhouse, and the silent message passed between them. He couldn't believe this was really happening; he would be the envy of all of his friends.

Tricia followed him into the cool dimness of the back corridors, their footsteps muffled, the air carrying the faint, institutional scent of cleaning solutions and rarely touched linens. The muffled sounds of resort life faded as they reached the relative privacy of the deckhouse, the sun-drenched wood radiating a dry warmth.

Caroline walked into the ladies' salon, observing Abi, Bea, and Jacque were playing a card game. Eunice and Sophie were sitting just outside the gauzy curtains on the balcony.

"Oh, please let Patricia be out there," she thought to herself seeing no sign of the girl in the room. Her heels clicked steadily as she walked to the balcony. "Have you seen Patricia?" She asked, not waiting for a break in their conversation.

"She said she was going to the study session with the boys today," Eunice informed her.

"I just came from the study and she is not there," Caroline replied with meaning. "Where are Charlotte and Catherine?" Caroline asked, hoping against hope.

"Catherine had a doctor's appointment this morning and Charlotte went with her," Eunice said.

"I knew that," Caroline breathed out, remembering, her mind racing. "We need to find Tricia."

All three women stood and went back into the salon.

"We need to find Patricia quickly," Caroline said, all eyes on her. "Jacque and Abi, check her room. Bea, you will come with me to check the pool," she inclined her head to Eunice and Sophie, please stay here in case she turns up. We all need to use our ladies only group chat. It is fine if Patricia sees, hopefully she will check in. It is imperative that nobody thinks she is missing."

Jacqueline was already halfway to the stairs, Abi on her heels, card game forgotten

Bea rose with uncharacteristic seriousness, trailing behind Caroline, heading to the deckhouse.

Sophie didn't move, but her hand was on her terminal in an instant, her posture tense but contained. Eunice remained poised, but her eyes betrayed fear for her granddaughter.

A soft ping sounded in the room—Jacqueline had already dropped the first message into the ladies-only thread.

Jacque: "Room empty. Bed unmade, typical Tricia."

Sophie typed, then paused—her eyes narrowing.

Sophie: "Ensure that none of your uncles or cousins go near the eastside pool or the deckhouse."

Bryce Canyon was breathtaking. Eliza and her cousin Rick climbed like seasoned climbers under the careful supervision of their instructors. The husband-and-wife team, stood by, confident that they had trained their climbers well.

The drones buzzed like gnats, but Eliza and Rick never lost focus. A family, a team.

The towering hoodoos of Bryce Canyon stretched toward the sky, bathed in the golden hues of late afternoon, their jagged formations standing as silent witnesses to the climb.

Eliza and Rick moved with practiced ease, their fingers gripping the cool, sun-warmed stone, their focus sharp, unwavering.

Rick moved easily above her—effortless in his freedom, his choices unconstrained by the rules and expectations that shaped her world. He had room to breathe, to test his limits without every misstep becoming a headline. Free to pursue his desires wherever they took him.

Tricia, though—Tricia was suffocating.

The air carried the scent of sun-heated stone and pine, a crisp contrast to the warmth radiating from the canyon walls.

Eliza reached for the next hold, feeling the textured rock beneath her fingers, its surface worn smooth in places, jagged in others, a testament to time and resilience.

Rick moved just ahead, his breath steady, his movements controlled, matching her pace effortlessly. No words were needed.

The instructors, watchful but unobtrusive, observed with quiet approval, their presence a subtle anchor.

Eliza's thoughts flickered to Edgar—only sixteen when his father introduced him to her at the brothel—to make a man of him.

Had Tricia ever truly had a choice? Had any of them?

She exhaled sharply, finding the next foothold, the ache in her legs almost welcome.

"There's always a way forward," she murmured to herself, adjusting her stance, pushing upward.

But how?

How did she carve a path for Tricia that wasn't just containment, survival, resignation?

Above, Rick glanced down at her, raising an eyebrow as she pulled herself toward him. "You good?"

Eliza met his gaze, steadied her breath, and nodded. "Yeah."

Rick was a steady partner, young and ambitious, but also still held a certain kindness, perhaps coming from being the eldest of the male cousins. The same age as Tricia, yet their prospects vastly different.

Eliza reached for the next hold, her fingers grazing the warm, textured stone, a grounding sensation against the whirlwind of thoughts racing through her mind.

Above them, the golden light stretched long shadows across the cliffs, the canyon itself humming with life—distant calls of birds, the whisper of the wind weaving through the towering formations.

She recalled the words of the wisewoman, the promise she had made sharpening her resolve. Tricia would be her first step. Her first proof that she could shape a different path, make space where none had been given. She reached up the next hold.

The drones buzzed, mechanical spectators documenting every movement, every second of their ascent, their presence a quiet reminder that no part of this family's life was truly private. The cameras only picked up the graceful scaling of the rock, not the thoughts within.

The deck house was alive with whispered urgency, the kind of hushed voices that carried secrets meant to stay buried beneath heat waves, mirages, and sun-bleached wood.

Caroline exchanged a glance with Bea, a silent confirmation between them, and then, without hesitation—Bea launched forward. Bea's training as a shot-putter, being put to good use.

The door splintered beneath her shoulder, a sharp crack splitting the tension wide open, and suddenly, there was nowhere left for discretion to hide.

Patricia froze, her top off, her hands tangled in the lifeguard's waistband—the last remnants of stolen time crumbling around them.

The lifeguard's palms hesitated mid-roam, fingers curling inward as if, through sheer will, he could undo what had already been seen.

And then—the weight of realization crashed into both of them at once.

Caroline stood at the threshold, the First Lady—a force far greater than the scorching heat of the desert—watching them with a presence that left no room for denial, only consequence.

Patricia scrambled upright, yanking her blouse together as if it could reverse time. "It's not what it looks like," she blurted, cheeks flaming crimson.

Caroline ignored her and focused on the lifeguard.

The lifeguard—barely nineteen, and now fully aware that lifeguarding for the Barkley

Rochesters might have career-limiting fine print—took two steps back, hands raised, bare chested, signs of Tricia's passion evident.

"You dare to defile one of my children on my property," she spoke icily. "What were you thinking? What if you had impregnated her?"

"But, but," he stammered. The punishment for impregnating a woman without lawful approval was death. The woman and child could easily be placed with someone with enough money who wanted a family. Plenty of barren women if you just wanted a tumble.

"You said you were barren," he said to Patricia stricken.

"I lied," she told him, flippantly, with no regard that she had engendered his life.

"Young man," Caroline broke in. "You are fired. Clean out your belongings, fix my door, and report to HR for your severance and transportation from my compound. You will never speak of this to anyone. You will never step foot on this property again. If you so much as use a hover craft in this air space, I'll have you charged."

"You can't do that," he stammered desperately.

"You are now banned to all Barkley Rochester properties," she said. "Say another word and I will reduce your severance and have David start looking into your family assets."

The lifeguard hung his head, knowing he was beaten. Dave's words echoing in his head, *If you touch my niece again, I will not only destroy you, but your entire family.*

Caroline didn't shout. She didn't blink. Her voice, when she faced her daughter, was ice cold against the desert heat. "Patricia, get dressed. Now."

Patricia opened her mouth—some half-formed defense—but something in Caroline's eyes silenced her faster than any raised voice ever could.

Patricia folded her arms tightly over her towel, chin lifted defiantly. "You can't control everything I do."

"No," Caroline said, quiet, lethal. "But I can control what happens next."

The terminal in her pocket pinged again. Jacqueline's message, short and sharp.

Jacque: "Need an update. Sophie's asking."

Caroline typed back without looking.

Caroline: "Found. Situation contained. She's safe and will be heading to her room with Bea."

She turned back to Patricia.

"You will walk up to the house beside me and Bea. You will go directly to your room. You will say nothing until Eunice, Sophie or I speak to you. Do you understand?"

Patricia hesitated just long enough to make it clear she still believed in her own version of autonomy. But then she nodded—because she knew this wasn't about punishment. This was about power.

"Bea," Caroline said, gaze never leaving her niece, "escort her to her room. Please inform the staff that Patricia has caught a slight chill, it is important to remember the shifts in the desert temperature can vacillate wildly. She will be taking all her meals in her room."

Bea nodded, guiding Tricia gently by the elbow and steering her out the side entrance like a bouncer who needed to escort a young lady out discreetly.

And the Barkley Rochesters didn't tolerate weak links.

The deck house was stripped clean of intrusion, every compromised angle meticulously erased, leaving no trace that could spiral into something uncontrollable. Dave's movements were precise, deliberate, each action securing his grip on the narrative, tightening his control.

The hidden cameras—removed, wiped, discarded—no cloud backup, just another miscalculation from someone who thought they were clever.

A lesson would be taught. The golf courses were his now, he would track the future investment's from the proceeds, and bankrupt him. The young man's father a pawn in a game already shifting into checkmate.

Dave walked quietly from the deck house, his mind already moving to the next step.

Tricia, a manageable complication, but one he would watch closely.

Eliza's absence had been an oversight, but not a failure. Sophie's call an understanding between them.

Silence was power. And for now, it was his alone to wield.

Patricia's room held its silence, absorbing the weight of Tricia's grief, the muffled sobs pressing into the pillow like a confession. She wondered if Bea was still stationed outside, standing guard as expected, but she didn't check. Did it even matter? No one could shield her from the hollow ache twisting in her chest.

She cried without reservation. Not prettily, not controlled—just raw, unrestrained, without care for who heard. An ugly cry.

She had spent too long being handled, led, directed—her body maneuvered like an accessory to power. Cold hands at her elbow, rehearsed embraces meant for public consumption, handshakes exchanged as tokens, not gestures of warmth.

In that deckhouse, for the briefest moment, she had felt something unscripted from the confines of duty. It wasn't really desire. It was the longing for connection, for something real, something that wasn't dictated by expectation.

It was a desire to be seen, to be wanted—not as an instrument, not as a symbol, but as a person. And she didn't care if she got pregnant, at least she would have a baby to love her.

⋙ ✵ ⋘

Tricia huffed, her breath misting slightly in the cool morning air, "This is my third day of captivity—are you going to allow me to languish away like Blanche Monnier?"

In reality, she had a room larger than most couples' cottages, with a balcony overlooking the canyons. Breakfast trays laden with warm pastries and fragrant fruit had been brought up to her room each morning, with crisp linen napkins.

A private tea service was brought to her room each day at midday, laden with sandwiches, scones, and petit fours. Trays with soups, salads, spiced chicken, roast beef, prawns, crab cakes, steamed vegetables, crusty rolls and desserts at dinner. Flowers arrived from her cousins wishing her a speedy recovery.

Each of the grandmothers and mothers had come to sit and talk with her, their voices soft and concerned. She had been allowed to walk on the warm trails of the desert with her mother or one of her aunts each morning, the rhythmic symphony of desert wildlife a constant soundtrack to her discontent.

This morning, Aunt Catherine walked beside her, the soft, wool shawl she carried like a blanket occasionally brushing against Tricia's arm, her hand periodically and unconsciously going to her subtly swelling baby bump.

"Tricia," Catherine began, her voice soft against the whisper of the hot wind, "I know that it is hard to imagine at your age, but your mother, your aunt Charlotte, and I, we all understand. We were all married by twenty-two, had our first child at twenty-three."

She paused, "I was married off to a man twenty-eight years my senior—both Charlotte and I were inseminated," Catherine's gaze drifted over the sand and rock features, "we were given no choice but to bear sons," Her free hand rested protectively on her slightly rounded stomach, a secret oasis blooming beneath her light, flowing dress.

"But you get to have a daughter now," Tricia lashed out, glancing at Catherine's growing girth, kicking at a loose stone with her sandaled foot, her voice sharp against the quiet murmur of the desert

"Yes, after doing my service for my family," Catherine pointed out, her own voice tinged with a weariness that belied her outward composure.

"Didn't you ever just want to *feel?*" Tricia questioned, her youthful face etched with a longing that went beyond mere petulance.

Catherine shook her head, a faint smile touching her lips at the memory of being so young and filled with such fiery passion, the sting of societal expectations still lingering. "I still want to feel," Catherine told her solemnly, the hot air whipping strands of hair across her face. "But now, I live for my children, for the soft weight of their heads on my shoulder, and my hope is for their dreams to come true."

"I've changed my mind, if that is my only path," Tricia declared, kicking a stone on the dry sunbaked path, "I wish I really were barren."

The two women walked on in silence, the only sound the soft crunch of their sandals on the sand, neither quite knowing how to cross the emotional distance that stretched between them like the horizon. There was still love, a familiar comfort, but a palpable space remained, a desert that words, for now, could not traverse.

The hovercraft touched down smoothly, and Eunice, Sophie, Charlotte, Catherine, Jacque, and Eliza stepped forward, their movements calm, deliberate, and purposeful.

The steady hum of construction equipment blended into the background, a rhythmic pulse to the ceremony's quiet significance, the beginning of something lasting.

Sophie pressed the golden shovel into the earth, its gleam catching in the afternoon light as she turned over a small pile of dirt. The Jonathan Franklin Rochester Neonatal Unit had officially broken ground.

"Such a generous gift, Jon-Jon would have been so proud," Eunice said to Sophie, her voice carrying a note of genuine emotion as they watched the construction workers bustling with anticipation of the new wing.

Sophie nodded, her gaze sharp. "Indeed. Though I still think the ventilation system design could be improved. I'll speak with Mr. Henderson before we leave."

As the official speeches concluded, Eunice and Sophie engaged in discussions with administrators, refining plans and ensuring the wing's future impact, Jacque and Eliza moved toward the children's wing.

Eliza smiled, holding the worn cover of *The Velveteen Rabbit*. "More than ready." Her voice, steady and warm, filled the brightly colored children's wing as she began to read. "'What is REAL?' asked the Rabbit one day…" The quiet magic of the story wove through the room, the children sitting cross-legged on the carpet, their eyes wide and fixed on Eliza, their occasional soft coughs the only interruption. Each word carried a gentle weight, the themes of love and becoming real resonating in the air.

"He's like you, you know," a little girl whispered to Eliza, pointing to the Velveteen Rabbit in the illustrations, her voice raspy. "Kind and quiet."

Eliza's smile deepened. "Perhaps he is."

After the story, laughter bubbled up as Eliza and Jacque distributed plush toys, colorful wooden blocks, personal vid games, and of course, books.

"Here you go, a brave little lion for a brave little boy," Jacque said, kneeling beside a small child in a cast.

Eliza handed a soft, fuzzy lamb to the little girl, who had compared her with Velveteen Rabbit.

Meanwhile, Charlotte and Catherine moved through the Obstetrics and Gynecology wing, distributing baby supplies with the steady, gentle efficiency of women who understood what was truly needed.

Catherine, radiant in a flowing dress boldly displaying her own transformation, handed a soft blanket to a new mother. "He's beautiful," she murmured, her warmth effortless, a connection made in the simple truth of experience.

Charlotte, her hand resting quietly for a moment in a dress that hinted at possibilities, passed a package of diapers to another mother. "We wanted to make sure you had everything you needed. Don't hesitate to ask the nurses for anything at all."

A grateful smile, a voice touched with awe—"Thank you so much, Mrs. Rochester."

Charlotte's eyes crinkled in response, soft, genuine, disarming. "Please, call me Charlotte."

Catherine chuckled quietly, the moment settling as naturally as breath. "That dress is perfect."

Charlotte laughed, low, content, knowing. "Let them begin to wonder," she mused, placing her hand once more against her stomach.

The six women elegantly entered the luxury hovercraft. Waving to Mothers with children, caretakers, and administrators. The drones devoured every second.

≈ ❋ ≈

"How far along are you?" Sophie asked with the skilled eye of a woman who had borne three children of her own and seen the secrets of expectant motherhood unfold over many decades.

Charlotte smiled with joy, "I am three months today. I plan to tell William this weekend."

"I think that the cat is out of the bag," Catherine said with a musical laugh, her own belly unmistakable beneath the structured elegance of her dress.

"I'm so delighted for you, Aunt Charlotte," Eliza said, her voice filled with genuine warmth as she reached out to briefly squeeze Charlotte's hand.

"This is so exciting," Eunice said. "Do you know if it is a boy or a girl?"

"A girl," Charlotte and Catherine answered in perfect unison, their shared joy weaving into the air around them.

"This family just keeps growing," Jacque said with delight.

"Do you want to feel it?" Charlotte asked Jacque.

Jacque hesitated, then pressed her palm gently against Catherine's stomach, warm, hard, a protective shell beneath her touch.

"Of course, when you touch Catherine's, you can feel the kick. That is months off for me."

Jacque felt a shift, awe settled in—quiet, contemplative. Within the year, she would be married, most likely expecting, soon after her wedding.

But before that—before the changes, before the next chapter—there would be one last glittering night at her ball, a moment of sparkle and glitter, still wrapped in anticipation.

30

THE HOVERCRAFT HUMMED SOFTLY beneath them as it skimmed across the desert horizon, its cabin echoing with laughter and soft chatter—babies and ballgowns, whispered predictions and old family tales. Outside, the canyon shadows deepened, but inside, the light felt endless.

Dave tracked the feeds with precise attention, letting the polished execution of the event unfold seamlessly across multiple channels.

Eliza, as expected, had chosen flawlessly—*The Velveteen Rabbit* resonated at just the right depth, striking that careful balance between warmth and meaning.

The gifts had been distributed with effortless grace, each selection crafted to reflect thoughtfulness without excess.

But the cameras had drifted from the script.

Catherine and Charlotte became the unexpected focal point, the slow zoom framing Charlotte's hand resting on her stomach, sparking a wildfire of speculation in the comments.

"Baby bump or just a mother's empathy?"

The debate raged, theories spiraling, the digital chatter spilling beyond the event itself.

Dave exhaled slowly, watching the footage loop.

Dave: "Is Charlotte expecting?"

William: "No. Why?"

Dave didn't reply; this man could watch the stream for himself.

Dave: "Is Charlotte expecting?"

Sophie: "Come to the resort for dinner."

Dave: "Breakfast? I have late night plans?"

Sophie: "Looking forward to it?"

A slight smile played on his lips. Let the women have their little mystery for the moment.

Dave checked the polling numbers—soaring. He would let it ride.

This unexpected fecundity of the Rochester women was a stroke of luck. The offers for Jacque and Eliza's hands after the ball would be incredible. Fertile simply by association.

The Hall of Mary Ann stood untouched by technology, its ambiance steeped in tradition, a quiet retreat from the relentless hum of machines and the ever-spinning world outside. No telltale glow of screens pierced the dim lighting, allowing the soft murmur of voices and the clinking of ice in glasses to dominate the atmosphere—a deliberate retreat from the incessant digital hum of the outside world.

Dave settled into his seat, Virginia and Audrey on either side, a new brunette opposite, her gaze steady, mouth curving. A hint of secrets learned from the ancient texts of India.

Madame Mary Margaret's eyes met his, not a challenge—a reminder—here, he was the visitor.

He tipped his glass slightly, an acknowledgment of sorts, before shifting his attention to the conversations humming around him.

"I'm telling you that you have to be ready to jump," one man argued loudly from across the room. Swirling his drink, his voice urgent, "This is a volatile market."

"They're watching the markets too closely," Virginia's hand gently massaged his neck, the smooth, cool glide of her manicured nails, a gentle seduction. "They think short-term volatility is the problem when it's their own lack of foresight."

"Good observation, my pet," he said admiring her royal blue silk dress, a vibrant sapphire against the muted tones of the hall, the slit just as high as he needed it to be.

Audrey exuded confidence, leaning toward him, the green leather of her corset, intricately laced with black, contrasting sharply with the delicate creaminess of her exposed skin, "Men with spreadsheets convincing themselves they understand intuition and urgency."

Dave smiled, the rich, nutty flavor of his whiskey coating his tongue. Since his party, Virginia and Audrey had indeed become nice little additions to his construction. Absently, he stroked Virginia's thigh, appreciating the slit in her gown.

The brunette—Ziana, as she had introduced herself—raised an eyebrow, her amusement subtle but present.

"Ziana translates to beautiful, if I am not mistaken," Dave said with a smooth smile.

"Yes," she fluttered her eyes, a vision in an Indo-Western fusion saree. The fine gauze, the color of deep blood-red wine, shimmered in the soft light, hinting at the secrets held within its flowing fabric, both foreboding and alluring.

Dave chuckled, lifting his glass.

"I'm telling you it all hinges on the election," another man responded. "We have to keep Barkley in office for stability."

Dave smiled, hearing the message he had strategically placed echo across the room.

Audrey's green corset brushing softly against him as she leaned towards Dave, her voice a playful purr, "They can't keep their eyes off you."

Dave reached over and played with a strand of Audrey's fiery hair, his fingers trailing further to her collarbone, along the line of her corset. He could feel the eyes of the men across the room following his hand as he traced his path.

"You are very observant, my flame," he praised her, with one last brush of his fingers across her delicate skin.

Ziana leaned forward. Her beads and sequins caught the light like liquid stars. "Desire is natural," she said softly. "Let them want what you have—your wealth, your women, your influence, your power." A slow smile. "Shall I dance for you?"

Dave took a slow drink. "Yes, let's turn up the temperature. I have been spending so much time in the desert."

The quartet's music began, a sinuous blend of Bollywood rhythms and the hypnotic sway of belly dance melodies, its exotic notes hanging in the dimly lit air like a rich, intoxicating Indian spice.

Zianna's hips swayed, the scarlet fabric of her saree shimmering like embers, a deliberate, slow movement—inviting, yet restrained. Her dark eyes, luminous in the soft light, beckoned and held his gaze like a captivating spell. Her fingers soft and directive, summoning Virginia into the dance.

Virginia rose, the sapphire silk of her gown flowing around her like water, her movements graceful, mirroring Zianna's slow, seductive sway—a gentle warmth passing between the red and the blue, the brunette and the blonde. As the music shifted, Virginia settled back into her seat with a practiced grace, the silk pooling around her, one slender leg artfully draped across Dave's lap.

As the tempo of the music subtly increased, Audrey joined Zianna, the green leather of her corset molding to her form as she moved with a bolder, more fiery energy. The interplay between the emerald and the crimson, the scarlet and the brunette, grew more intense, a visual feast of flowing fabric and rhythmic motion. The air in the hall seemed to thicken, charged with palpable energy.

Then, the tune shifted, slowing once more, becoming almost languid. Virginia rejoined the dance, her movements fluid and confident, her gaze occasionally flicking towards Dave. The three women—Zianna in her fiery red, Audrey in her deep green, and Virginia in her royal blue—moved in front of Dave like elements personified: fire, earth, air, their bodies swaying in harmonious unison. The trio spun a visual spell, the energy growing, drawing every eye.

As the final notes of the music faded into the hushed atmosphere, the three women artfully arranged themselves around Dave. A server, silent and discreet, presented four glasses of chilled champagne, tiny bubbles rising like glittering stars within the crystal flutes.

Dave raised his flute just slightly; his gaze meeting Madame Mary Margaret's across the room in a silent acknowledgment of the evening's subtle orchestrations.

Across the room, whispers spread, coiling through the smoke and silk, threading through power brokers and patrons. The air pulsed with curiosity. Men glanced at Dave, seeing a man of power, perhaps a touch too indulgent, surrounded by three striking beauties.

Dave let the rich tapestry of the evening unfold, unhurried. He savored the smoky warmth of his whiskey, watching, listening, always planning.

The DC night sky stretched wide beyond her windows, a deep canvas, reflecting the power of the city.

Madame Mary Margaret settled into her chair, the reports on the terminal, high above the Faraday cage of the brothel.

Virginia, Audrey, Zianna—flawless execution, top scores, remarks glowing with approval.

And the requests from other patrons—more dancing, more spectacle, more of what had long faded but now surged back with hunger.

What was old always became new again. Nothing disappeared. It waited—coiled, patient, eternal—until time spun it forward once more.

The circle of life was not gentle. Nor was it passive. It turned with force, with certainty, dragging the past into the present and sculpting the future with hands wrapped in history.

She powered down the terminal. No surprise. Only quiet satisfaction.

Madame powered down the terminal. No surprise. Only quiet satisfaction.

She walked deliberately down from the Widow's Peak and performed her nightly checks. Everything safe and secure.

Madame Mary Margaret settled into her nightly ritual. The sweet aroma of Riesling hung gently in the air, the golden liquid catching the soft glow from the window.

Sister Hope poured them both a glass, her movements steady, a practice that had been repeated countless times before.

The wheel was spinning. Life shifted, evolved, returned to where it began only to move again. The ebb and flow, fire scorched the land, air carried seed, and water purified; life grew.

Madame took a slow sip, her gaze distant but thoughtful, watching the way the wine swirled within the crystal.

The circle of life continued.

THE MORNING AIR CARRIED the scent of freshly brewed coffee and sun-warmed stone, the quiet hum of conversation from the main breakfast room filtering softly into the alcove where Dave and Sophie sat.

Sophie's voice was measured, a quiet certainty laced into her words, "I have suspected for a while," she confided, her gaze steady, the weight of tradition shaping her choice of words.

Dave leaned back slightly, absorbing her meaning.

"But you know it is a bad omen to make any announcements or predictions until after the second trimester," she concluded.

"Which happened to be yesterday, with the media buzzing," he finished for her, his tone neutral, calculated.

Sophie nodded but did not yield. "No announcement was made. Right now, it is all speculation."

Dave exhaled slowly, acknowledging the truth of her words. "You are right. We can put out a press release this weekend when William comes to the resort."

A shift in tone, the transition from acknowledgment to strategy, from observation to action.

Sophie studied him briefly before asking, "You will be staying here through the week?"

Dave offered a nod, his voice firm. "Yes, I have business to attend to."

Dave's fingers tapped a restless rhythm against the cool glass of his wrist console. He'd been reviewing the latest market projections, the grim data of population decline, and the increasingly desperate appeals from across the globe for new citizens. The numbers were stark, a testament to the "efficiency" of the solutions he'd helped implement.

His Arizona cryobirthing facility, a demonstration of the efficiency of solar power and a chillingly precise breeding program, remained his most productive asset of that portfolio, but he needed to see it, touch it, understand its hidden mechanics if he was to truly replicate its success.

He opened a secure line, the interface a familiar glow against the desert twilight seeping into his private office. A few clicks, and a voice, tinged with a permanent tremor of anxiety, answered.

"Silo Thorn, Manager, Cryobrithing facility Gamma," the voice announced, clipped and deferential.

"Silo, it's Dave Barkley," he stated, his tone flat, leaving no room for questions or pleasantries. "I'll be in the area for the next few days. I require a comprehensive tour of your facility. Tomorrow morning, 0800 hours."

A beat of hesitation on the other end, almost imperceptible. "Tomorrow, sir? Of course. Um, perfectly understandable. Everything is... running to specification."

"Good," Dave cut in, his gaze sweeping across the panoramic view of the city lights below. "I expect nothing less. Ensure the Cryowhisperer is available. I've been informed he's... sensitive to strangers. I trust you'll manage his temperament. I have no tolerance for anything that impacts host survival or productivity."

"Understood, Mr. Barkley. Absolutely. I'll make all the necessary preparations. He... he will be ready." The subtle tremor in Silo's voice intensified.

"See that you do, Silo. Barkley out." Dave severed the connection, the brief interaction a satisfying exercise in control. He leaned back, a faint, almost imperceptible smile touching his lips. Tomorrow, he would walk among his most valuable assets, dissecting the precise alchemy of their silent, endless harvest.

Upon finally being allowed to join the rest of the women for breakfast the next day, Tricia could feel the collective gaze on her like a physical weight, a hundred unseen eyes pressing against her skin. The aroma of strong coffee and sweet pastries filled the brightly lit room, doing little to soothe the knot of anxiety in her stomach.

When she dared a fleeting glance towards Bea, whose gaze felt particularly intense, her face flamed with heat, the blush creeping up her neck like a scarlet stain. *Bea had been there, she had seen everything,* the thought echoed in her mind.

Abi, Bea, and Jenny looked at her with an uncomfortable mixture of pity and awkwardness, their expressions soft with a sympathy Patricia found infuriating. *How dare they pity her?*

Jenny's only here because Eliza picked her out of the factory like a pretty doll.

Abi still jumps at sudden noises—like the daughter of an addict always would.

Bea's father's debts nearly cost her everything, and she knows it.

The clinking of silverware against china plates seemed overly loud in the tense atmosphere.

How dare they pity her, she thought again, clenching her jaw. Defiantly, Tricia filled her plate and sat by a window by herself. The fluffy texture of the croissant on her plate felt like sawdust in her mouth.

The ladies' salon was quiet enough to hear the faint hum of the ventilation system, the only sound besides the delicate clinking of silver against china or the soft thump as a porcelain saucer was carefully placed back onto its glass coaster. The air still carried the lingering sweetness of the fruit compote from the buffet and the robust aroma of freshly brewed coffee, though most plates remained largely untouched.

Finally, Tricia's voice, tight with suppressed emotion, cracked through the stillness. "Why is it so wrong, to feel something, to want something more than this?" she cried out, her gaze sweeping across the assembled women, her own eyes glistening with unshed tears.

"Patricia," Caroline chided, her tone sharp enough to cut through the heavy atmosphere, though her own voice remained carefully modulated. She set her untouched teacup down with a precise click. "We all have our roles to play, dear. No woman in this world, regardless of her station, is truly free to do as she pleases." She added, her gaze hardening slightly as she observed Tricia's flushed cheeks and defiant posture, "You were raised better than a common whore who chases after fleeting desires."

"Excuse me," Eliza said softly, her voice cutting through the tense silence like the delicate chime of a crystal glass, "I don't mean to speak out of turn." Her fingers, resting lightly on the linen tablecloth.

She took a slow breath, the scent of overripe dragon fruit from the nearby fruit bowl filling her nostrils. "But a whore is just doing her job," she looked steadily at Caroline, not a challenge, but a fact.

Tricia blinked. She couldn't breathe. She expected judgment. Instead, Eliza spoke like she was weaving a tapestry out of iron thread.

She paused, her gaze sweeping across the polished surfaces of the breakfast room, catching the glint of sunlight on the silverware. "The age of adulthood in America is legally Sixteen, and then the women are tested." She felt the cool air from the nearby open window against her bare arms. "If they are fertile, their options are limited, they become wives, mothers—traded on their looks, money, and family connections."

She hesitated, her eyes briefly meeting Patricia's flushed face. "When you are an orphan, perhaps to a trader or craftsman, especially if your looks are plain. Men who want strong hips and silence." She paused, "Of course, now with the fertility rates so low, there are extraordinarily few orphans anymore. Children are a commodity."

Eliza shifted her gaze to her Grandmother Sophie seated at a small table with Eunice. Sophie gave a gentle nod, her silver hair gleaming in the sunlight. Eliza continued, her voice gaining a touch more firmness. "All fertile women have the same fate, they bear children." A faint clinking sound came from Eunice's nervous stirring of her coffee; this was a dangerous conversation.

"Of course, there are rumors that some," Eliza hesitated again, her eyes flicking towards her grandmother, who gave a barely perceptible shake of her head. "That they have it very bad," Eliza said, taking Sophie's cue.

"The elite can buy more time for their daughters," she looked across the table at Jacqueline. "Up until they are twenty-one or twenty-two; whichever age is best for ball season."

She shifted her gaze to Caroline, whose expression remained impassive. "But whores are just barren working girls. They service men for money, not for their own desire."

Eliza's hand rose, gesturing slightly. "Jenny and I worked eight hours a day, five days a week to tie little pieces of clothe with pretty ribbon around jam jars." She picked up one of the small jars from the breakfast table, the smooth, cool glass fitting in her palm, the delicate ribbon, a cheerful splash of color.

"When I went to the job fair when I was sixteen, I remember the recruiters for the brothels, offering a more comfortable life than a factory girl," she paused, a fleeting image of Madame Mary Margaret's silk robes flashing through her mind. The other women sat on the edge of their seats; their eyes fixed on Eliza.

"Girls go to factories much rougher than the one, 305, Jenny," she corrected herself. "and I was at. Places where the air hangs thick with dust and the rhythmic clang of machinery never stops. Women work twelve-hour shifts, seven days a week, with only an annual health check." Eliza took another breath, the floral scent from the wallpaper suddenly seeming cloying. "Girls at brothels are promised forty-five-hour work weeks maximum with monthly health checks," she paused, meeting Tricia's gaze.

She took a steadying breath and centered herself. "I was lucky. Bell-View uses a numbering system, which seemed sinister, so it was hard for them to recruit, but the people were nice, even friendly. I had my own small studio, instead of a bed, with a footlocker, like most women in factories."

She looked at Tricia, seated alone—apart. Eliza's expression not one of pity, but of genuine understanding. "You need a purpose," she told her cousin, her voice now soft but firm. "We owe you to help find that."

No pity. Just truth.

Tricia blinked. Her vision blurred.

No one moved.

A desert breeze brushed Tricia's cheek like a forgiveness she didn't know how to ask for.

⇒ ✹ ⇐

The hum of the cryobirthing facility was a constant, low thrum against the Silo Thorn's eardrums, a sound that permeated the very bones of the building. It was a sterile, frigid environment, the air biting with the faint tang of antiseptic and metallic cold. He watched, as he often did, as the cryowhisperer walked the floor, his thin, rubber-gloved fingers brushing along the frosted glass of the cryochambers. The whisperer's voice was a barely audible murmur, a strange, soothing litany as he made tiny adjustments to dials and gauges, the faint hiss of escaping gas occasionally punctuating the quiet. "There you go my pretty," he would croon, as if to a child, "Doesn't that feel better? I can tell that you need more oxygen, even though the readings think otherwise."

In 2025, the protests had been a distant, almost forgotten roar when the news broke: a woman in Georgia, legally brain-dead, forced to carry a child to term. Just one of the thousands impacted by the overturn of *Roe v. Wade.* She wasn't the first to be used as an incubator, but her case had ignited a brief, furious spark of public outrage. As the global population plummeted, fueled by declining birth rates and other, unstated reasons, these cryoincubators morphed from a controversial medical last resort into a booming industry.

Silo reflected how those in power, slick with persuasion, convinced young, fertile women to enroll in their programs. Using advanced in-vitro methods, they could keep these women in stasis for a decade or two, sometimes longer, harvesting embryos and breeding children at a much more rapid rate. It had worked for puppy mills; it should work for humans they reasoned. They argued with the courts that women should have agency for their bodies and they had a right to make long term decisions for their financial futures.

The cryowhisperer, a tech who might have been diagnosed on the spectrum if anyone still cared about such nuances, was now simply known as an expert. His pale eyes, magnified by thick glasses, seemed to see beyond the cold science, to intuit precisely which chemicals or gases needed tweaking. During batch inseminations, the air would thicken with a nervous tension as he'd be there, guiding, his strange expertise ensuring success.

He had a sixth sense for how many embryos could be implanted and thrive. His record was a staggering 50 successful births from one host over ten years. That host, still strong and breeding, was a testament to his uncanny touch. With his unusual intuition, host turnover plummeted, and the volume of "product" had more than doubled over the past decade.

When a host was finally deemed no longer viable or her contract ended, a severance package—a sterile, final accounting of her productivity and years of service—was all that remained. It was, after all, a remarkably efficient business model. "It was a shame that many of these women took their own lives afterwards," Silo mused, his voice devoid of genuine pity. "They left set for the rest of their lives, highly illogical."

The big boss wanted to inspect the operation firsthand, and he needed everything to be perfect. Dave Barkley had a reputation for being a stickler, and Silo did not want to disappoint him.

Years ago, they had built the cryowhisperer a small apartment out of an old conference room and given him anything he wanted. He hadn't left the facility in at least eight years; he was too valuable to risk getting into an accident or picking up a virus on the outside.

Luckily, he had simple tastes and spent most of his time playing children's video games.

Dave stepped into the cryofacility, the bone-deep shiver that crawled up his spine an unnatural greeting. The air was a faint, sweet-metallic tang, a scent profoundly wrong. He moved through gleaming, white-tiled corridors, the constant, low thrum of the cryochambers vibrating in his teeth—a droning lullaby. This Arizona complex, with its ghastly efficiency, was his most productive, and he needed to replicate its grim, unnatural success.

The facility's Manager, Silo Thorn, his face etched with the strain of perpetual vigilance, met him just inside the sterile reception area. His handshake was too quick, his smile a brittle thing. "Mr. Barkley, a… pleasure to have you here," he stammered, his gaze darting from Dave's face to the humming corridors beyond.

"Silo," Dave acknowledged, his voice flat, his eyes already assessing the pristine, yet unsettling, environment. "Everything appears to be running optimally."

"Indeed, sir! Peak performance, actually. All thanks to our… unique talent." The Manager wrung his hands, a faint sheen of sweat visible on his brow despite the biting cold. "About that, sir. I need to brief you on the Cryowhisperer. He's… not having the best day. He's a genius, truly, but his methods are… unconventional. Sometimes, strangers can upset his delicate balance." Silo swallowed hard. "And that, Mr. Barkley, can impact host survival and productivity." His voice dropped to a nervous whisper, betraying the true depth of his anxiety. "We've spent years backward engineering his methods, but we have never been able to replicate his intuitive predictive analysis."

Dave's gaze sharpened, a flicker of irritation crossing his face before it smoothed into an unreadable mask. "Unconventionality is only a problem if it interferes with efficiency, Silo. Lead the way. I want to meet the Cryowhisperer."

The hum of the facility grew louder as Silo led Dave to a small break area, built outside an old conference room now converted into the Cryowhisperer's apartment. The room smelled faintly of stale pizza and something sweet, like melted candy. Through an open door, Dave could see a figure hunched over a flickering screen, a symphony of childish game noises chirping from within.

"This man owns the whole building," Silo whispered to the Cryowhisperer, his voice gentle, like one would use with a child.

The Cryowhisperer looked up, his pale eyes, magnified by thick glasses, blinking at Dave. "Can I have a new game?" he asked, his voice soft, reminding Dave of his youngest nephew.

"Sure," Dave replied, his tone surprisingly even. "What would you like?"

"It's a new game where you get to build your own castles… I like castles," he added, a faint, almost innocent smile touching his lips.

"Who doesn't?" Dave's smile was a practiced curve. He tried to steer the conversation, "This is a big facility. It is sort of like a castle."

"Yes," the Cryowhisperer agreed, his gaze drifting back to the unseen chambers. "It is full of sleeping beauties, and I take care of them." He looked at Dave seriously, a profound earnestness in his eyes.

Silo sucked in a sharp breath beside them. Never had he heard the Cryowhisperer talk so much before.

"That's a very important thing to do," Dave said, his voice gentle, almost coaxing. "Do you know how many princesses are here right now?" he asked.

"4998," the Cryowhisperer responded without hesitation. "They have 21,841 babies inside them." He confided in Dave solemnly, his voice dropping conspiratorially. "I watch them all. I make sure the princesses stay and have more babies when the babies are old enough to go away." There was an unsettling pride in his tone.

"I have four other castles with princesses," Dave told the Cryowhisperer, holding his gaze.

"More princesses!" The Cryowhisperer clapped his hands together with a childlike glee that grated on Dave's nerves. "Do they have babies inside them too?"

"Yes," Dave said, maintaining his calm, "But not as many as you have here. Do you think you could talk to me and some other people about what you do and how you keep them alive?" Dave asked, his inner strategist already mapping the path to replication.

"Oh yes," the Cryowhisperer responded with delight, a genuine, unburdened joy. "I want to help all the Princesses."

Dave walked for what seemed like miles with the Cryowhisperer, his recording device discreetly logging every word. The air in the chambers was even colder, but Dave barely noticed, his focus entirely on the man beside him.

"How do you know that one needs more oxygen?" Dave asked, watching as the Cryowhisperer made a minute adjustment to a dial.

"Because her lips are bluer today," he told Dave, his voice matter-of-fact. "I just look at each Princess and they tell me what they need me to do to help." He glided to another chamber. "See this princess," he said, his fingers gently tapping the frosted glass. "She looks too warm, so I will adjust her liquid nitrogen tank just a fraction."

Dave observed and recorded everything, the chilling simplicity of the Cryowhisperer's "intuitive predictive analysis" unnerving him even as it offered immense potential.

After their rounds, Dave promised the Cryowhisperer a special treat and bought him pizza and ice cream, as well as having his new video game installed.

"A really productive day," Dave told Silo, as they walked away from the Cryowhisperer's quarters.

"You are a miracle worker, Mr. Barkley," Silo told him, relief in his voice.

"You just have to know how to communicate with people," Dave told Silo, a faint, condescending smile playing on his lips. "Let's see if we can't have a few people he trusts walk and ask questions in the future."

"Yes, sir," Silo said, eager to please.

"And remember, he is saving Princesses like in a video game," Dave winked, the statement a chilling echo of the man they had just left.

⇒ ✳ ⇐

The door burst open with barely a knock, and Jenny rushed in like a gust of wind—cheeks flushed, eyes shining.

"Oh my gosh," she gasped. "You're amazing!"

Eliza looked up from the window seat where she'd been curled with a book, the late morning light haloing her dark locks. "What?"

Jenny practically vibrated with excitement. "You *said it*. You actually *said* the thing no one ever dares say—not here, not anywhere."

Eliza smiled faintly, tucking her knees closer to her chest. "Sorry to shock everyone."

"That's why it was brilliant," Jenny said, flinging herself down onto the edge of the armchair. "You didn't rant. You didn't make it emotional. You just laid it out—like a fact sheet. Like one of your books." She nodded toward the stack of well-loved volumes beside the window.

"Thank you," Eliza said, her voice warm with sincerity.

Jenny hesitated, biting her lip. Her hands twisted in her lap. "Can I tell you a secret?" she asked, suddenly quieter. "A big one. Like… the kind you *never* tell anyone."

Eliza straightened, her expression shifting from surprised to curious. "Of course."

Jenny looked around the room, as though someone might be listening behind the curtains. Then she leaned in.

"I was never tested." The words hung in the air for a moment, foreign and sharp.

"My parents worked at Bell-View. We lived in one of the little cottages on the way to town," Jenny said quickly, voice trembling just beneath the surface. "They both got sick with some weird COVID strain the year I turned sixteen. They didn't make it."

Eliza reached out and placed her hand gently over Jenny's. "I'm so sorry."

Jenny shook her head. "They moved me straight into the dorms after that. No testing. Nothing. I kept waiting for it, for one of the matrons or the nurse to call me aside, but… it never came."

Eliza's mind spun. Her earlier speech echoed back, reshaped now by this unexpected confession. "Is it true what you said?" Jenny asked, searching Eliza's eyes. "That every girl gets tested? Because I didn't."

"When was your last health check?" Eliza asked, a knot forming low in her chest.

"Once a year," Jenny said. "Always in the dorm. The nurse comes with one of the matrons. They use this weird old equipment—like something out of one of those early-century hospital dramas."

Eliza studied her closely. "Have you ever… been with a man?"

Jenny blinked, then shook her head, cheeks pink. "No."

They sat in silence. The weight of the secret lay between them, unspoken but heavy, like a stone dropped in still water.

Jenny let out a slow breath. "I don't know what it means. If I slipped through the cracks. If I'm… broken. Or just invisible."

"You're not invisible," Eliza said quietly, her voice firm. "Bell-View isn't just protecting children," she whispered. "They are protecting potential mothers."

"I could have a baby?" Jenny asked in disbelief.

"I'm not sure, but what I do know, is that all young ladies need to know how to take care of themselves and their own desires. Leaving poor girls like Tricia to *figure it out* hasn't worked for the past 5000 years; it's disgusting," Eliza spat out.

Eliza burned with quiet resolve, the kind that pulsed low and hot beneath the skin, not unlike coals in a hearth—controlled, but capable of igniting. She wondered if this was how Audrey felt all the time.

As she approached the veranda, the scent of lavender and lemon tea mingled with the dry spice of desert air. Her eyes settled on her grandmother, seated beneath the shade of the awning, her posture impeccable, her gaze fixed on the distant red ridgelines. Aunt Eunice sat beside her, fanning herself lightly with an ornate folding fan.

"Grandmother," Eliza said, her voice composed, soft but unwavering.

At the sound, Eunice rose delicately, folding the fan with a quiet snap. "It appears I left my reading glasses in my room," she murmured, tone polite, a practiced exit wrapped in gentle propriety. "If you'll excuse me." Her heels clicked softly on the stone as she disappeared through the open French doors.

Eliza lowered herself onto the cushioned bench across from Sophie, smoothing her skirt with practiced fingers, her every movement careful and poised. She could feel the heat of the stone beneath them radiating through the soles of her sandals, grounding her.

"I've been observing the girls," she began, her hands folding neatly in her lap, "and I believe they are lacking in certain areas of their education."

Sophie lifted a silver brow, her interest piqued. A warm breeze stirred the strands of her white hair as she took a slow sip of her tea, the china clinking softly as she returned the cup to its saucer. "Oh? They're well-trained—in languages, dancing, painting, estate management…"

Eliza inclined her head slightly. "They are. But there's something deeper."

Sophie's eyes sharpened, but her face remained calm. "And what do you propose?"

"I'd like to begin a Goddess yoga class," Eliza said, her words deliberate, the syllables tasting of incense and intention. "Something quiet, personal. A space where they can connect to their bodies, to breath, to intuition. To the divine feminine."

The silence stretched—not awkward, but expectant. A desert wren called out in the distance, its cry sharp and lonely against the canyon wind.

Sophie watched her, then set her teacup down with great care. "Goddess yoga," she repeated, the words rolling in her mouth like a foreign fruit. "And what exactly will you teach?"

Eliza met her gaze without flinching. "I'll teach them how to listen. To feel. To remember who they are beneath the performance. I'll teach them how to connect to their inner Goddess."

For a moment, nothing passed between them but the wind and the scent of desert sage wafting in from the garden path. Then Sophie's lips curved, slowly. A knowing smile. A memory kindled.

Their eyes held, and something old, something sacred flickered between them—unspoken but understood.

The divine feminine, after all, had always been passed hand to hand. Quietly. Fiercely. Secretly.

The evening air was thick with the scent of juniper and warm stone, the lingering heat from the day settling into the pergola's polished wood beneath their resting arms. Ice clinked softly against glass as vodka sodas sat untouched for a moment, each man caught in the pull of conversation.

Rick leaned back, taking a slow sip, his laughter rich with amusement as his gaze followed the six young women threading their way toward the small canyon, yoga mats and blankets tucked under their arms, wraps swaying with their steps.

"What is that all about?" John muttered, his glass catching the light as he gestured toward them.

Rick chuckled, shaking his head.

"Eliza started some goddess yoga cult," he said, taking another sip, the bite of vodka crisp on his tongue.

Robert's eyes flickered with intrigue. "I thought you were tight with Eliza," he observed, his tone easy, but measured.

Rick swirled his drink, watching the ice shift.

"Eliza is amazing," he admitted, a hint of admiration woven into his voice. "She's just so different—always thinking, always reading. When we climb together, it's like she's reading the rock for its story."

Dave, ever the strategist, leaned forward slightly, the movement subtle but deliberate.

"I expected her to be rough, coming from a factory, but she is genteel." Rick shook his head slowly, eyes still on the canyon's edge. "There's little difference between Jenny and the other country cousins going to finishing school," he added.

John exhaled, tilting his glass in thought.

"Just when I think I have Eliza figured out, she does something different, like this yoga class," Rick concluded.

Dave let the moment stretch, watching the women disappear into the canyon's embrace, the last flutter of fabric catching the wind before vanishing into the rocks.

"She is unique," he mused.

He had taken a courtesan and unleashed her on the courts, and now, he pondered, what was she teaching, what was she shaping, and why?

As dusk painted the western sky in hues of fiery orange, soft lavender, and deep rose, each lady found her own comfortable space on the canyon floor. The air, no longer scorching, held a gentle warmth that slowly yielded to the cool kiss of the approaching night. The high canyon walls, now softened by the fading light, embraced them like protective arms.

Eliza sat in the center, the deepening shadows casting long, dancing shapes around them. The scent of sunbaked earth still lingered, now mixed with the cooler, slightly sharper aroma of desert blooms releasing their fragrance as the heat subsided. A gentle breeze whispered through the canyon, carrying the faint, soothing rustle of dry grasses.

"Men are taught that their pleasure is natural," Eliza began, her voice a low, intimate tone that carried easily in the still evening air. Above, the first stars began to prick the darkening canvas of the sky, their faint light beginning to glimmer.

"Ladies are rarely taught about their own bodies, their desires, how to satisfy their own needs," she continued, her gaze meeting each of the young women's eyes, now wide and luminous in the fading light.

"There is an old book, *Pussy: A Reclamation* written by Regena Thomashauer. It teaches women to live an empowered life by regaining control over their center of life, pleasure, and power: the pussy," she said the word with a quiet strength, the sound echoing softly against the ancient rock, as if the very canyon held its breath.

"I want to share how you can reclaim your own agency, by learning about your own bodies," she told them, her voice imbued with a serene confidence.

"Now, lay down on your yoga mats"—the smooth, cool surface a welcome contrast to the day's heat—"and cover yourselves with your blankets,"— the woven fabric a comforting layer as the night grew cooler. "Get comfortable. Explore what you want. Discover what makes you feel good."

"Each of you has a Goddess within," she concluded, her words hanging in the twilight, as the moon, a pearlescent disc, began its ascent, a silent sister watching from the heavens alongside the emerging stars, gathering in their dance.

T HE MORNING LIGHT FILTERED softly through the grand windows, casting a warm glow over the breakfast tables as murmurs of conversation filled the air.

William rose, his expression holding a quiet certainty as he cleared his throat, drawing the attention of those gathered.

"Charlotte and I are expecting," he announced, his voice carrying with a steady pride, a quiet joy that rippled through the room.

A beat of silence—then cheers, congratulations, laughter, the celebratory mood settling in like the golden morning light.

Charlotte smiled, her hand resting lightly against her stomach, her gaze sweeping across the gathered family, a moment of acknowledgment, of quiet anticipation for what was to come.

As the resort stay neared its close, the celebration took on a sense of transition, of something ending and something beginning.

As Dave filled his champagne flute, Eliza approached from the side—quiet, composed. He handed her his glass without a word and refilled another for himself.

"A word with you in the garden, dear Uncle David," she said lightly, revealing nothing.

He followed, intrigued, to the same alcove where he'd sat with Sophie just days earlier.

Eliza sipped her champagne.

Dave admired her command of silence—an often-underestimated skill. She let it stretch, just long enough.

"A toast to a growing and fertile family," she said at last, raising her glass.

He clinked hers, eyes sharp, taking a measured sip.

Then came the real message.

"Tricia is being given three choices of where she would like to go after the ball."

The weight of it landed between them. Soft tone, firm intent.

"I expect your support and your influence—regardless of which she chooses."

Another sip. Her gaze held steady. Not a threat, not a request—just fact.

Dave, amused and genuinely curious, asked, "Can I know the three options?"

Eliza did not hesitate. "No. It has been decided by the women."

She didn't blink. "I expect you to ensure that the men follow suit."

Dave smiled, lifted his glass again. Mystified. Impressed.

For the first time in forever, the game had shifted, and Eliza had placed herself firmly on the board.

For the first time all summer, Tricia felt a connection to the other women in the salon. Something had shifted. She thought back to her walk with Catherine—now she'd asked herself, *Did I ever want to marry a man more than twice my age?* Ick. Would Jacque be forced into something like that?

But today, when the eyes in the room turned to her, she felt something new. Not judgment. Not scrutiny. Kindness. Compassion.

Her mother had ensured the staff were absent. This conversation was for family—Barkley-Rochester women only.

"We would like to give you options for your future after the ball," Caroline said.

"Options?" Tricia repeated, cautiously.

"Yes." Her mother paused. "Women in this world have little power, as you've unfortunately learned the hard way—and that's partially my fault," Caroline admitted.

"When we return to DC, you'll visit three nearby places. St. Gabriel of Our Lady of Sorrows—the boarding school where Abi and Bea already study. The Order of Clara Mercy—I know the Abbess personally. Or... Bell-View Farms, where Eliza and Jenny worked in the factory."

Caroline's words were careful, deliberate. Each option delivered with a quiet certainty.

But it was the final one that stopped Tricia cold.

"A factory?" The question escaped her lips, a mixture of disbelief and dawning curiosity. The notion felt utterly alien, a gritty contrast to the manicured world she knew. The other options—the quiet discipline of the boarding school, the serene servitude of the Order—had been predictable, expected paths for a girl like her.

But the factory? The word conjured images of clanging machinery, a starkly different world. It was something... different. Something unexpected.

⋛ ✳ ⋚

Leaving the resort was bittersweet—the sandstone cliffs now held their secrets, the hush of desert wind a memory folded into summer's end. That golden, secluded world had given space for recalibration, quiet alignments, private revelations.

John Barkley, steadfast and unsmiling, drank his scotch, brooding. He had already spoken with Captain Rob and First Mate Omar—no detail left unverified, no variable unobserved.

The return to the Barkley estate at Cape Cod unfolded with orchestral precision. The boys, as always, were split, maintaining the delicate balance that secured the line's strength and succession.

The modern airship—a leviathan bearing its precious cargo. Inside, the pregnant women reclined in engineered comfort, the soft hum of life beneath their fingertips, the gravity of their condition measured but accepted. Within their bodies—daughters, futures, continuity itself—carried high above the earth, an elegant risk wrapped in silk and protocol.

Drones hovered, silent and exacting, their lenses recording every step, every measured smile. For propaganda, for memory—an archive of legacy in motion. This was not spectacle for spectacle's sake. This was continuity made visible.

Below, the estate loomed—old stone, newer steel, and light-filtering glass—anchored by tradition, softened by renewal. As always, the compound waited. And so, the family returned.

⇒ ✳ ⇐

The gentle murmur of conversation threaded through the breakfast room.

John, Robert, and Dave leaned over their numbers, quiet but focused. Eunice, Sophie, and Caroline refined plans, ensuring every detail of the upcoming tours for Trisha's next step were in place.

Eliza, Jacque, Tricia, Abi, Bea, and Jenny surrounded Bobby with easy laughter, familiar warmth—a space where he could sit, listen, be heard. Bobby settled in, his hands firmly wrapped around his cup, his expression determined—but the quiet weight of missing his cousins lingered in his eyes.

Tricia watched the boy's expression, seeing echoes of her own loneliness reflected in his quiet struggle.

"You know, a week can feel like forever," she murmured, offering him a small smile.

Bobby sighed, swirling his drink in slow circles. "Yeah."

Tricia reached for a plate of pastries, nudging them toward him. "And yet, before you know it, it'll be time for the ball."

"Are you really moving away after the ball?" he asked her.

"Yes," she confirmed.

"And Jacque will get married after the ball?"

"I should hope so," she laughed. "We are spending enough money on it."

"So, I will be alone," he said. The words hung in the air. A truth spoken from his innocent insight.

⇒ ✳ ⇐

The hum of monitors filled the quiet room, flickering softly like distant stars aligning. Eliza sat still, her fingers resting on the keys—waiting. There was power in restraint, in knowing that purpose didn't always require presence.

She thought of Tricia, Abi, Bea, and Jenny—each at the edge of becoming, needing space to find their own fire. So, she withheld her shadow. The strongest guidance, knowing the strongest guidance, is sometimes a gentle absence.

Her task was monumental; she would travel first to South America. Highland passes, deep archives, vineyards veined with old secrets—the land had stories to tell, and she intended to listen. Her itinerary would take her to the Costa Rica, Bribri, and Cabécar people; in Panama, to the Guna people; from Colombia to Venezuela, the Wayuu people; and to Ecuador, the Waorani people and the Jivaroan people extending from Ecuador to Peru. Each descendants of mothers.

Her messages went out in whispers—through backchannels, private networks, a nudge to one archivist in Mendoza, a note to an eco-data steward in Chile, a quiet ping to a vineyard liaison with ties to the underground libraries. To Brazil and Bolivia the Bororo people.

She was haunted by the lives she had not lived and knew this was her destiny. Like threads drawn to a spindle, the universe began to send soft suggestions. She wove each thread into her plans.

The hovercraft hummed steadily toward St. Gabriel of Our Lady of Sorrows, its towering silhouette framed against the morning sky.

Tricia sat between Abi and Bea, the quiet weight of decisions pressing against her thoughts.

Then, Abi spoke, her voice steady, deliberate.

"If you want us to come with you to The Order of Clara Mercy or Bell-View Farms, we will."

Bea nodded, her gaze unwavering, silent confirmation of the promise made.

Tricia inhaled slowly, absorbing the offer, the unexpected solidarity.

The choices no longer felt like isolation—they carried companionship, understanding, the possibility of stepping forward together instead of alone.

The hovercraft whispered to a gentle landing on the manicured lawn of St. Gabriel of Our Lady of Sorrows. Headmistress Janet, a woman with a crisp smile and a tweed suit that rustled softly with her movements, greeted them at the entrance. Her handshake was firm and brief, her voice carrying a polished warmth as she insisted on taking them on the official tour.

Caroline, her heels clicking softly on the linoleum floors, walked ahead with the Headmistress, as she pointed out the merits of the school. Tricia trailed behind with Abi, Bea, and Jenny, the air thick with the scent of floor polish and a hint of old textbooks.

The sterile polish of the tour softened as they stepped into a classroom. Sunlight streamed through tall, arched windows, illuminating rows of sturdy wooden desks, some with textbooks open, others with terminals. The front of the room contained state-of-the-art screens for videos and presentations.

Next, they entered the library. Sunlight spilled through large, leaded glass windows, casting intricate patterns on the rows of towering bookshelves. The air was still and quiet, filled with the comforting aroma of aged paper and leather-bound volumes. Deep, plush armchairs invited quiet contemplation in sunlit corners. Terminals were discrete, designed to blend in to the décor of the library.

The tour continued to the dormitories, where the carefully cultivated image of the school gave way to a more intimate reality. Tricia's potential suite, designed for prospective students, from the right families, was spacious, the plush Persian rugs muffling sound, the air scented with fresh linen. Sunlight flooded the room through wide windows, offering views of the manicured gardens. It felt familiar, almost indulgent, a seamless continuation of the comfort and expectation she was accustomed to.

Then came Abi and Bea's room. The contrast hit Tricia like a cool breeze. Smaller, more efficient, stripped of any unnecessary luxury. Two loft beds were stacked neatly over cramped desks, the space feeling intimate yet functional. A single bright but narrow window struggled to stretch its light into the room, highlighting the bare necessities.

The contrast tightened in her chest, a knot of discomfort forming in her stomach. But it wasn't until the Headmistress casually mentioned the community showers that Tricia's curiosity sharpened into a need to see for herself.

"They all share one?" she asked, her voice carrying a clear edge of disbelief, the sound echoing slightly in the tiled hallway.

Abi and Bea exchanged knowing glances, a flicker of amusement playing across their lips. "Of course, Tricia. It's normal here."

Tricia straightened slightly, a decision solidifying within her. "I have to see it for myself." The communal showers were starkly utilitarian, the scent of soap and disinfectant strong in the air, the echoing sound of water droplets amplifying the lack of privacy.

Tricia was quiet on the return walk to the hovercraft, the crunch of gravel beneath her shoes, the only sound for a moment. She looked at Abi, Bea, and Jenny, the afternoon sun casting long shadows ahead of them. "You must think I am terrible," she told them, her voice low and sincere. "So focused on myself and never considering anyone else."

"We all make mistakes, Tricia," Abi said gently, her eyes, the color of warm honey, reflecting the same quiet forgiveness she extended to her father. The gentle breeze rustled the leaves in the nearby trees, a soft sigh in the afternoon air.

The fitting room light was designed to show the flaws, to ensure there were no imperfections, each movement casting soft shadows across fabric that whispered with elegance.

Sophie and Eunice sat at a small table, sipping tea as the young ladies stood for their fittings.

Eliza stood before the mirror, her fingertips brushing the lace with a reverence only beauty could demand.

"It feels like liquid moonlight," she murmured, the scent of subtle florals clinging to the fine threads, an unspoken promise woven into the gown's embrace.

Jacque turned slowly, the weight of her gown shifting like fresh-fallen snow, the gold embroidery catching in the light with breathtaking brilliance. "Do you think it's too much?" she whispered, doubt threading her voice.

Eliza's smile held certainty, the contrast of ivory, cream, and bronze pooling like gilded twilight at her ankles. "Never," she assured, the layered skirt grounding her in a way few things did.

Madame Evangeline circled, her hands moving with the precision of an artist shaping something beyond fabric—something eternal.

"The drape is perfect, Mademoiselle," she murmured, smoothing a delicate crease in Jacque's train. "And the gold thread… it sings in the light."

Jacqueline's ball gown was an ethereal masterpiece, a symphony of snow-white silk that draped like flowing water, shimmering beneath the golden chandelier light. The waist, adorned with intricate gold embroidery, threading its way across the bodice like ivy climbing an ancient wall, each tiny detail shimmering as if kissed by sunlight.

Jacque's gaze flickered downward, her voice softer. "It's so… bare."

The seamstress paused, meeting her eyes with something gentle, yet resolute.

"It is a statement, Mademoiselle. Audacious. You will command attention."

Her nimble fingers adjusted the fit of Eliza's gown, pulling the fabric taut with careful expertise.

"The ivory, cream, and bronze, Madame Elizabeth, they speak of knowledge and strength. The design is… timeless."

Eliza's gown, in contrast, carried a weight of wisdom, blending ivory, cream, and bronze into a vision of regal authority. The waist was structured more deliberately, the embroidery heavier, woven in delicate metallic threads that seemed to speak of strength rather than embellishment. Her sleeves, capped and tailored, lent an air of timeless command, while the bodice, fitted with painstaking precision, framed the deep neckline with an intricate display of gilded lace.

Eliza nodded, feeling the cool weight of the inner lining, a second skin against her own. "It feels powerful."

Jacque lifted the hem of her skirt, testing the volume, the lightness. "The layers beneath create such volume."

Madame Evangeline tilted her head slightly, eyes filled with quiet pride.

"Indeed. A foundation of dreams. But the décolletage… it is a bold declaration, Mademoiselle Jacqueline. Unapologetic."

She stood back, surveying the two women before her, satisfaction settling into the air. "You will have no peers. Perfect."

Together, Jacqueline and Eliza stood in gowns that were both declarations and invitations—one a vision of untouched purity, the other a study in seasoned grace.

Sophie and Eunice watched as their granddaughters let their inner goddess shine to the world in confections of gold and bronze.

≋ ✷ ≋

The hovercraft whispered to a landing on the brick path leading to the Order of Clara Mercy Convent, its descent so gentle it barely disturbed the hush that blanketed the landscape. The Convent, a small oasis in the DC landscape.

Before them rose the colonial brick walls of the convent, weathered with time, moss clinging to the base like a living memory. It stood with the quiet authority of a place untouched by the speed of the outside world, steeped in centuries of prayer and stillness.

The Abbess emerged through the heavy wooden doors—tall, graceful, her eyes ringed with lines that spoke of years spent in reflection, not regret. Her habit moved with the lightest whisper as she stepped forward, arms open in welcome.

"Caroline," she said, nodding warmly, to the First Lady. Then, to Tricia, "And you must be Tricia. We are glad to have you."

Her voice was low, resonant, the kind of sound that seemed to still the heart rather than stir it.

They moved slowly through the convent's corridors—cool and dim, lit only by slivers of light from narrow stained-glass windows. Ruby and amber hues spilled across the flagstone floors, casting fractured halos on the walls, the saints in the alcoves watching silently from their niches, faces carved in perpetual compassion.

"This wing houses the girls who come for a time of discernment and reflection," the Abbess said, her voice echoing gently down the hall. She paused at a doorway and gestured inward.

The room was spare but not severe—four simple bunks, each tucked with folded blankets and a single flower placed carefully at the foot. A small writing desk sat near the window, overlooking a garden of herbs and quiet statues.

Tricia stepped in, her gaze brushing across the beds, imagining the silence of shared sleep, the whisper of prayers before lights-out. She thought again of St. Gabriel's—of the narrow showers and lofted beds— and felt a new kind of kinship stir. Here, there was less of a structure and more of a sanctuary.

"The lavatories are communal, just down the corridor," the Abbess added. Tricia simply nodded this time.

They continued toward the chapel, when they entered, the air changed—denser, sacred. Sunlight fell in long beams from a high arched window behind the altar, cutting through the dim and bathing the nave in gold. LED candles flickered at the altar's edge, their scent mingling with lilies placed beneath a statue of the Virgin Mary.

The hush of the convent settled around them, pressing gently against the air, as if even the earth beneath their feet had learned the art of stillness.

Tricia sat stiffly at first, the weight of centuries-old prayer and whispered stories wrapping around her, brushing against something unspoken in her thoughts.

"Hope and healing for women," she said, her tone calm but unshakably firm. "We are here to walk with you on your journey—to offer a safe, non-judgmental, welcoming place to encounter the mercy of the Lord Jesus. A place of sisterhood. A place to study. A place for the lost to be found."

The words did not rush Tricia—they seeped. Into her skin. Into the edges of her certainty.

"A place for the lost to be found."

The words did not demand—they simply waited.

For the first time since the summer began, she felt something shift—not in certainty, but in recognition.

She didn't need to speak, or defend, or resist. She only needed to listen.

The phrase echoed again in her mind—*a place for the lost to be found.*

She hadn't realized how much of herself she'd lost. But something here—something quiet and ancient—seemed to recognize her anyway.

⁂

The quiet hum of the console reflected in Dave's gaze as he read, calculated, and acted, each report another brick laid into this structure.

The inquiries into potential facilities he could repurpose for cryobirthing —subtle, careful—sent ripples into corners few had considered. A quiet expansion, built for maximum profit and potential.

The lifeguard's father. A steady erosion, carefully bleeding his financial ground dry, a game played with patience rather than aggression.

Then, the report on Bartholomew Jackson—bribes, blackmail, the ugly hand of unearned influence trying to tilt the game.

Dave disdained those who cheated—not because the game itself wasn't ruthless, but because rules mattered, even in a world built on bending them.

And finally, the airship industry—his mind tracing the smooth journey of the last flight, its understated luxury. A niche market, but one worth investing in.

The pieces moved. And Dave ensured they moved in his favor.

Georgette and Marty Washington greeted the hovercraft, their expressions tight. 307/Eliza had sent Georgette a message. Keep everything safe for now, but trust that I have a plan.

The light at Bell-View Farms was different—no chandeliers or diffused glow, just sun through corrugated steel slats and flickering fluorescents that buzzed faintly overhead. It was an unfiltered brightness, catching on sweat-dampened brows, glinting off conveyor belts and steel tools. Nothing here was softened. Everything showed its wear.

Tricia, still in her traveling jacket, stepped into the factory floor. The air smelled of oil, warm grain, and the faintest trace of citrus soap. The soundscape was constant—machines humming, boots on concrete, voices clipped but purposeful.

Jenny led the way, she walked to tables where women were cutting fabric and ribbons and tying them over the tops of jars.

"There's a rhythm to it," Jenny said, pausing by one of the inspection stations. "You learn when to talk and when to move. Efficiency becomes instinct."

Tricia ran her hand along the edge of a packing table. It was cold and dented—scarred from use. She noticed the lockers in the corner, the communal break bench, the water dispenser with hand-labeled cups.

"And you did this every day?" she asked.

Jenny chuckled. "Every day, Eight hours a day, five days a week. You sleep different after real labor."

Tricia watched a girl not much older than her lift a sack nearly her own weight onto a dolly. No ceremony. Just strength.

Jenny continued. "What we built here feeds people. Builds real futures. Nobody applauds it—but it lasts."

Foreman Two passed by, giving the group a polite nod before correcting a misaligned seal with swift, practiced hands.

"Can I see the dorms," Tricia said quietly.

Dorm Matron Two gave Jenny a huge hug. "You are a sight for sore eyes, 305," she said. "I have to admit we watch you and 307 up on the big screen all the time now," she pointed to an old screen in the breakfast area where they ate.

"It is so amazing," 305 replied. "307 really was a long lost heiress all along!"

"We haven't changed your room code," Matron Two told her, "Go ahead and show your friends around."

Entering her room was harder than 305 expected, Bell-View was the only home she had ever known. "This," her voice broke, "was my room since I was sixteen."

Bea didn't hesitate; she pulled Jenny into a crushing hug.

Abi joined, "Don't cry Jenny, we are here for you."

Trica hesitated before joining. Then something shifted, she felt connected, part of a sisterhood she had been denying.

"Look at the size of my room," Jenny said breaking away from the hug with a smile and twirled, regaining her normal sunny disposition. "Every room has its own tiny kitchenette and bathroom."

"You cook?" Tricia asked incredulously. "Way better than 307," she laughed. "She could barely make a grilled cheese sandwich or soup without burning it."

"What do you do when you aren't on shift?" Bea asked looking out the window.

"Anything we want," Jenny responded. "Lots of people go downtown on the weekend, Eliza spent all of her time reading at the library or at the river. She used to save all her money to travel and now she actually is," Jenny realized.

"You can go down to the city unescorted?" Tricia asked. Was this really a choice or a trap? What if she did choose Bell-View.

The young ladies watched Jenny give Matron Two a long hug. "It would be nice to have you join us," she said with sincerity.

When they reached the farmhouse Caroline was having tea with Georgette, as she told her version of the day when Sophie, William, and Edward had come to pick up Eliza, or 307 as she called her.

Caroline had been hesitant to include Eliza's suggestion as Bell-View Farms as a potential choice for Tricia, but sitting her with Georgette, she felt she finally understood.

As they left for the hovercraft, she could see Georgette's tension lighten slightly. What secrets did Bell-View Farms Hold?

The smooth hum of the vehicle, whether airship or hovercraft, vibrated gently beneath Tricia, a low thrum that accompanied her thoughts like a steady heartbeat. The world outside blurred into streaks of color – the fading greens of the landscape giving way to the approaching cityscape, the sky perhaps painted in the soft hues of late afternoon or the deep indigo of evening. The expensive leather of the seat felt cool against her back as she leaned against it, the gentle swaying motion lulling yet also focusing her thoughts.

"I see that now," she murmured, the words almost a whisper against the background noise of the journey. A weight seemed to lift from her chest, not suddenly, but gradually, like the dissipating tension in her shoulders. The memory of the disparity of St. Gabriel's, the hushed reverence of the Convent of Clara Mercy, and the pastoral view of Bell-View Farms flickered through her mind. Each location held a distinct feeling, a tangible presence in her memory.

The realization settled within her, warm and grounding, that the choice wouldn't be forced. Not now. Not anymore. The cool air conditioning of the vehicle brushed against her skin, a stark contrast to the desert heat she had grown accustomed to over the summer, a reminder of the different worlds she was navigating.

It was an opportunity, she realized, the word resonating with a newfound lightness. An opportunity to finally breathe, to step away from the expectations that had always clung to her like a heavy cloak, to become her own person within the walls of any of these three facilities. A sense of quiet power, the unfamiliar thrill of her own agency, began to bloom in her chest, a fragile but promising flower.

The deep ruby swirl of Malbec wine caught the soft light from the window as Madame Mary Margaret and Sister Hope sat in quiet communion, the evening still, as if pausing before the next change.

Sister Hope recounted the visit as the Abbess had conveyed it—the poised elegance of the First Lady, the quiet weight in her daughter's eyes, and the three paths laid before her.

"St. Gabriel of Our Lady of Sorrows —structured, precise, a place of discipline and legacy."

"The Convent of Clara Mercy—hushed, contemplative, steeped in quiet healing."

"Bell-View Farms—earth, labor, resilience, something wholly different."

Madame tilted her glass, watching the rich liquid shift in the candle's glow, absorbing the depth of each option.

A breeze curled through the open window, carrying the scent of the changing season, the soft rustle of leaves against brick.

"Summer fades," Madame murmured, her voice thoughtful, "and choices come with the autumn."

"What do you think it will change if she comes to the Convent?" Sister Hope asked.

"Both everything and nothing," she replied, sipping her wine.

THE GRAND STEPS OF the White House framed the family in quiet elegance, the soft afternoon light casting a warm glow over the carefully arranged scene.

John and Eunice stood at the helm, the steady presence of the first family captured in every poised detail.

Robert and Caroline flanked them, Patricia and Bobby standing beside them—a moment of tradition, lineage, continuity.

William rested a hand lightly on Charlotte's shoulder, her small baby bump just visible beneath the folds of her gown, while Patrick and Paul stood with practiced ease.

Edward, beside Catherine, her swollen belly unmistakable, the weight of expectation and legacy carried between them, Carson and Casey at their side.

Dave, ever composed, stood with Great Aunt Sophie, the quiet authority of experience settled into the space they occupied.

And in the center, radiant in contrast, stood Elizabeth and Jacqueline—ivory, cream, and bronze, met with white and gold, a moment held in stillness, in significance, in recognition of all that had led to this day.

Abigail, Beatrix, and Jennifer stood quietly by the photographer, taking in the splendor of the moment.

≈ ✳ ≈

Robert, Caroline, Jacqueline, and Elizabeth stood in the grand receiving line, welcoming their guests.

Jacqueline inhaled, feeling the subtle pull of the fabric at her shoulders, the intricate gold embroidery catching the fading sunlight, shimmering like quiet fire. A gown meant for power, for presence—but was she ready for that?

She glanced at Eliza beside her, poised, steady. The blend of ivory, cream, and bronze spoke of experience, of wisdom already lived. Jacqueline's own white and gold felt untouched, pristine, yet undeniably bold—a statement of arrival, of beginning.

She had spent what felt like hours standing for fittings, layers upon layers shaping her into the perfect image of a debutante. The neckline had shocked her at first—so daring, so deliberate—but Madame Evangeline had been right. This was unapologetic.

Now, beneath the sky and the watchful gaze of history, she wondered if the gown reflected not just the moment, but the woman she was becoming. The whispers of expectations still echoed—the ball, the future, the choices that followed—but for now, Jacqueline let herself settle into the reality of it.

She was no longer standing in a fitting room, contemplating the plunge of her gown or the sweep of her skirt. She was here, in the open air, in the heart of power, in the place where her life would soon shift.

≈ ✳ ≈

The ballroom shimmered with gilded candlelight, the air thick with laughter and murmured greetings, as the youngest members of the family took in the first hour with wide-eyed wonder.

John and Eunice kept a watchful but gentle presence, ensuring Bobby felt anchored in a sea of movement.

Sophie had promised Dave that Patricia had changed, but Dave, ever pragmatic, held his reservations close.

Rick moved through the room with quiet confidence, the champagne flutes cool in his grip as he offered one to Tricia, a gesture of familiarity, of something that had once been effortless between them.

William and Catherine noted it, their son's kindness flickering between them like an unspoken acknowledgment.

Dave, perhaps for the first time that evening, let his posture ease—just slightly.

Abi, Bea, and Jenny gravitated toward Tricia and Rick, their fascination with the grandeur of the evening making their champagne glasses seem heavier in their hands, the weight of the moment settling into them.

Paul, Bobby, Carson, and Casey had one mission before their inevitable escort to the nannies—devouring every hors d'oeuvre and dessert within reach, their laughter spilling across the room like mischievous sparks in the golden glow of the chandeliers.

"I dare you to eat eel," Bobby told Paul.

"Only if you eat that snail," Paul countered.

Then, as the hour waned, the shift came.

Tricia, Abi, Bea, and Jenny were quietly ushered into the hovercraft, the smooth hum of its descent toward Barkley Manor on Dupont Circle signaling the transition.

Once there, behind the mansion's doors, Dave's housekeeper would ensure they remained under careful lock and key, the night taking on a different sort of hush beyond the gleam and splendor of the ball. Just to be safe, if any of the four left the manor, he had set an alert.

Patrick—Rick, now standing in his tuxedo, not the child Dave once knew—approached with a quiet determination, as the young ladies departed. "Sir," he swallowed, his voice carrying an edge of formality, a choice meant to mark this moment as significant.

Dave arched a brow, intrigued. "That's very formal," he remarked, taking in the measure of the young man before him, a far cry from the child whose first steps he had once watched with amusement.

The ballroom's glow shimmered around them, but in this moment, it was just the two of them, an exchange that felt weightier than the brocade curtains and conversation swirling nearby.

"Yes," Rick continued, holding his stance. "I was hoping that we could discuss an internship."

Dave hesitated just slightly, not because he wasn't sure, but because he was impressed.

He activated his wrist console with practiced ease, entering the details. "Next Monday, 9:00 at Barkley Manor."

No further words were needed. Rick had stepped forward in more ways than one.

The ballroom tittered with elegant anticipation, the murmured conversations shifting to hushed excitement as Robert, Caroline, Jacqueline, and Eliza moved toward the orchestra.

The musicians paused, their instruments resting in brief silence, waiting for the formal introduction that would mark the evening's significance.

Robert's wrist console connected to the speaker system, his voice carrying across the hall with measured confidence.

"Ladies and gentlemen, I would like to formally introduce you to the two very special young ladies for whose ball you are attending—Jacqueline Lee Barkley and Elizabeth Angela Barkley Rochester."

The applause rolled through the room, a wave of approval, of recognition, of expectation.

Jacqueline felt the weight of the moment settle upon her shoulders as Robert took her hand, guiding her forward, steady and sure.

From the sideline, William stepped with quiet precision, his posture effortless as he reached for Eliza, the rhythm of tradition moving seamlessly between them.

The orchestra returned to life, the first notes of *Isn't She Lovely* spilling into the space like liquid gold, wrapping the moment in warmth, sentiment, and celebration.

As Jacqueline moved in her father's hold, her steps delicate but assured, the world tilted ever so slightly. Her golden train swept behind her like the tail of a comet, luminous and bold. This wasn't merely a coming-out—it was a coronation in its own right.

Eliza's motion was more fluid than floating—every pivot an act of choice, every glance a message. Her bronze caught fire in the low light, not as an ornament, but a signal. She did not hide in her moment; she owned it. William, ever the stalwart, followed her lead even as he appeared to guide it— the weight of legacy woven into the sweep of their arms, the certainty of their steps

The other debutantes, fresh-faced and swathed in softer pastels, entered the floor like stars in orbit—some hesitant, all radiant. Behind them, their assigned escorts stood firm. Each movement was a line written in the living scripture of family, legacy, and power.

And in the shadows, watching with hands wrapped around delicate flutes of champagne, men watched with appraising eyes, calculating the worth. Dave smiled and grabbed another drink from the tray of a passing server.

The ballroom shimmered with movement, debutantes stepping gracefully into the dance, layers of silk sweeping across polished floors.

Senator Bartholomew Jackson watched, his expression unreadable, his thoughts winding through family, obligation, and the ever-turning wheel of legacy.

Edgar stood beside him, withdrawn, distant, consumed by grief over some dead whore, a ghost that refused to fade.

Bart barely concealed his irritation. The boy should be here, in the present, looking toward the future.

If Edgar wasn't willing to seek a wife, then perhaps Bart himself would make a new move.

The Barkley-Rochester family exuded wealth, power, fertility—the careful curation of lineage visible in every generation standing before him, the world to see. This was the power he desired.

The dance floor filled, young women stepping into carefully orchestrated moments with their escorts, the future shaping itself in quiet exchanges, deliberate steps, measured glances.

Bart observed, calculating. Replacing Edgar was not out of the question. The fun part was always conceiving the child anyway. He smiled as a young blonde twirled past.

The dance floor shimmered beneath the glow of chandeliers, and Eliza's wrist monitor pulsed with requests—a steady stream of names, titles, and expectations.

Jacque embraced the momentum, letting the night carry her effortlessly from one partner to the next, the measured decisions of Robert and Caroline ensuring that each choice was calculated, every step a potential match.

Sophie smiled sitting on the sidelines with Eunice. William offered a few suggestions to Eliza which she ignored.

Eliza, played a different game. She wielded her selections deliberately, developing a dance card that was daring; raising eyebrows, sparking whispers, and setting the evening into a quiet ripple of intrigue.

Where Jacqueline moved like tradition incarnate, Eliza moved like disruption cloaked in a dazzling display of ivory, cream, and bronze. Delectable and Dangerous.

Each dance was more than just a step—it was a signal. The Sultan bowed with ceremonial elegance, his retinue watching closely from the edge. The coffee baron lingered, murmuring in Spanish about innovation and cross-hemisphere partnerships. The Australian vintner kissed her hand, whispering a promise of soil, sun, and legacy. The Indian Bollywood Mogul, his wealth and influence couldn't be denied.

The Chinese technologist surprised even Eliza with his reserved charm and unspoken intellect, their conversation gliding over renewable grids, predictive analytics, and cultural inheritance with ease. The Swedish prince asked nothing of her; but laughed aloud, when she started speaking to him in Swedish. And the Namibian Prime Minister, perhaps the most unexpected partner of all, spoke softly about land, stewardship, and quiet revolutions.

The ballroom had never held this combination of energies—royalty, enterprise, strategy, and charm—each tethered to one woman's hand.

And as Eliza stood at the top of the steps later, looking down at the glittering expanse of the ballroom, her wrist monitor quiet for the first time all evening, she understood exactly what she had done.

She hadn't simply danced.

She had positioned herself as a power broker.

And in doing so, she had redefined what the ball could mean.

⚛

The dance floor below vibrated with quiet tension, speculation rippling like static through silk as Eliza felt a surge of power.

She let herself unfocus—sensing, scanning—the quiver in the room revealing itself. There: a lotus bloom of influence, unfurling. It pulsed, subtle but certain, leading her along the edge of the crowd, past the orbiting couples – to an alcove, to dear Uncle Dave.

The men around him were sharp-eyed, calculating. Titans of industry, politics, wealth—their nods could shift markets, their silence could bury truths. Some whispered that Dave was wary of the new heiress. Others murmured that he was grooming her for something greater.

Dave looked up as she approached—a flicker of surprise, a measured pause. Or calculation. "Have you come to find me for that promised dance?" His voice was smooth, almost amused. But his eyes were steady. Watching. Measuring. Testing.

Eliza tilted her chin ever so slightly, a quiet assertion that this moment was hers as much as his.

"Yes," she said. Nothing more. Then, she turned toward the ballroom.

Her steps were confident; she had been wearing heels and gowns as an armor for almost a decade—leading before he even moved to follow. The orchestra hushed.

Dave murmured to the conductor—a low request, precise. Not just a song, but a signal. A coded message woven into melody.

The crowd leaned in as the first notes swelled.

Dave stepped forward, extending his hand. There was no hesitation. No question.

Elizabeth Angela Barkley Rochester. His niece. His design. His construct.

And now, his public affirmation.

The music unfolded, every note calculated. Many knowing the old lyrics, a few whispered under their breaths.

I will be your father figure. Dave looked steadily in Eliza's eyes.

Put your tiny hand in mine. Eliza and Dave touched raised hands as the dance brought them together.

I will be your preacher, teacher. Dave twirled Eliza out and pulled her back in to him.

I will be the one who loves you 'Til the end of time – The last notes hung in the air.

The dance floor parted in anticipation.

The message was veiled. But not subtle.

Was this power? Protection? Possession?

Eliza was prepared for the scrutiny, really, there was little difference between ladies in a ballroom or a brothel.

The crowd watched—some intrigued, some disturbed. They were cousins, distant enough. In old money circles and many cultures around the world, that line blurred easily.

Had he declared devotion—as an uncle, a cousin, something more?

But one thing was undeniable: Eliza had been accepted. She belonged to the Barkley-Rochester dynasty now. And with that came all the power and wealth it entailed.

But beneath the speculation was a deeper, clearer truth:

Eliza had been claimed. She belonged now.

To the dynasty.

To the legacy.

To the game.

Eliza held her head high, a swirl of ivory, cream, and bronze as she left the dance floors to join her Grandmother Sophie, Great Aunt Eunice, Aunt Caroline, and Cousin Jacqueline, making an unspoken declaration of her own on where she stood.

Dave nodded in their direction, a spark in his eye, as he left the dance floor to rejoin the men in the alcove. Finally, something interesting.

The question remained who was stronger: the architect or the weaver? The challenge had only just begun.

Madame Mary Margaret lifted her glass, the blood-red liquid catching the glow from the open window as she turned to Sister Hope, the weight of unspoken thoughts resting between them.

At her desk, the Abbess typed with measured precision, each keystroke a whisper into the ether, a message sent but unread—yet charged with purpose, as a gentle breeze brushed her cheek.

Headmistress Janet released her long hair from its confining bun. She breathed the fresh air from the window and sipped a glass of merlot.

Outside, Georgette rocked gently on the porch swing, the rhythm of her movements mirroring the slow rise and fall of the cat's breath against her lap.

And by the fire, the wisewoman stared into the embers, her gaze deep, unfocused—seeing beyond, searching for meaning in the shifting flames, tracing the outline of the inevitable.

The air carried the scent of change, woven with the quiet pulse, unseen yet unmistakable. Touching each with a gentle kiss.

EPILOGUE

 **ADAME MARY MARGARET COMPLETED** her final check of the reception area after reviewing reports from the Widow's Peak. A maid approached, offering a package.

"This just arrived from a courier," the maid said, presenting it with both hands.

Intrigued but cautious, Madame accepted the package and carried it to her private study. A late-night delivery wasn't entirely unusual. Occasionally, a man—emboldened by alcohol and lust—would send a token to a girl: a Tiffany necklace, a Cartier bracelet, a diamond-encrusted Rolex. Technically forbidden gestures, but not unheard of. Dave's recent threat of investigating illicit activity would have certainly uncovered this—because Madame had quietly allowed it.

These gifts served a purpose. They could be sold later, offering a woman leaving the system a taste of small luxury. In rare cases, they even funded a quiet retirement.

But this wasn't jewelry.

Madame unfolded the envelope and paused.

Polaroid photos.

Eliza at the ball. Madame inhaled deeply.

The first photo showed Eliza standing in the center with the First Family; the next captured her in the receiving line. But the final photo made Madame Mary Margaret do a double take.

Eliza, mid-laughter.

Her eyes bright, her ballgown a masterpiece of ivory, cream, and bronze. Not posed. Not polished. Just... radiant. The kind of beauty that wasn't constructed—it simply *was*.

Madame's fingers lingered on the glossy surface for just a moment. A flicker of softness crossed her expression, gone almost as quickly as it appeared.

Not Cartier.

Not diamonds.

Something far more precious: a memory.

The day Eliza had first arrived—so much potential, unspoken and limitless.

Madame locked the photos in a drawer. Tomorrow, she would show them to her inner circle, she would also include Virginia and Audrey, they deserved it.

Tonight, she would sleep well, knowing—however briefly—that Eliza was, in some way, happy.

Senator Jackson was in a foul mood on the way back from the ball. The lost heiress had done more than capture public fascination—she had rekindled a long-lukewarm alliance between the Barkley and Rochester families, making them stronger than ever. That alone was cause for concern. He had investigators pulling at the seams of her story, but so far, everything held. That was unacceptable.

Across from him, Edgar sat silent, brooding over a dead girl—useless. A brothel tart that was supposed to make a man out of him, not geld him. Jackson eyed him with disgust, exhaling sharply before switching the hover craft to manual mode.

He drove too fast.

The anger simmering beneath his skin had nowhere to go but into the machine, his grip tightening on the controls, his pulse steady but his judgment fraying. He clipped a pylon.

The hover craft lurched—spun, twisted—gyroscopes failing against velocity.

The force ejected Edgar, his form vanishing into the night to safety, as the hover craft careened toward the Potomac's edge.

Jackson didn't have time to react.

The hovercraft plunged into the dark waters, the cold swallowing metal and man alike. Silence followed. Then—only the river remained.

⇒ ✳ ⇐

Dave sat in his study at Blakely Mansion, watching. Orchestrating.

On one screen, his courier delivered the package to the Hall of Mary Ann. A silent gesture. A promise kept. On another, Senator Jackson's hovercraft slipped into manual mode. Dave smiled. A mistake—one that easily allowed Dave to piggyback on the system controls.

Manual mode was a liability. Hovercrafts required absolute precision; even a hair's breadth could unravel stability. A tilt too sharp, a correction too slow—and the system would spiral. And when it failed? Pilot error. Case closed. No autopsy or intervention. Dave smiled coldly.

Dave's fingers danced across the console. A small adjustment. Barely a nudge.

The craft clipped a pylon. There it is. A misstep. A sudden lurch. Gyroscopes shrieked against inertia. Dave leaned in. The hovercraft twisted violently—spinning. Losing control.

In a fraction of a second, Dave made a decision: the emergency eject system fired. Edgar. The boy shot into the night sky-flung like a dying star, swallowed in the night, but safe. Then—impact. The craft plunged into the Potomac, lights winking out as the river consumed it. The black water swallowing metal and man alike, ripples spreading, smoothing the surface as if nothing had ever been there.

Dave exhaled, slow and measured. Ripples spread across the screen. Neat. Clean. Final.

"Bye, Bye, Bart," Dave whispered.

He leaned back, processing the silence. The courier. The boy. The careful removal of Senator Jackson.

His mind wandered—uninvited—to his mother, to Aunt Sophie. And to Eliza.

That package had been a last-minute choice. A small mercy. The decision to save the boy, gnawed at him. Was he getting soft?

He stared at the glassy screens. He was the architect. But something else… lingered. Power, yes—but shaped by what?

Was he remaking Eliza? Or was Eliza remaking him?

READERS' CHOICE

GENTLE READER, THANK YOU for coming on this journey through mysteries and marvels, good times and bad. In every timeline there are choices—moments that shift and shape our lives.

Patricia—Tricia Barkley, is at the cusp of making such a decision. This choice is weighty and should not be made alone. Ah, the crossroads—a choice that will shape her future, each path offering its own trials, revelations, and transformations.

- ☐ St. Gabriel of Our Lady of Sorrows presents structure, tradition, and familiarity. Abi and Bea's presence would offer comfort, but would it provide growth, or merely security? We know so little, what secrets does this school hold?

- The Order of Clara Mercy whispers of reflection, quiet strength, and healing. The Abbess speaks of purpose, sanctuary, but Tricia must ask—would she find herself, or simply become part of something greater? Could she be swept into the larger machinations of the sisterhood?

- Bell-View Farms, a place of labor, grit, and self-reliance, stands as the unexpected option. The factory is unforgiving, but honest. Would she walk away stronger, more self-sufficient, or merely hardened? How would this impact Bell-Views bright secret.

And then—the question of companions.

Should she take Abi, Bea, Jenny—all three? If Abi, Bea, and Jenny do not accompany Tricia, where do they go?

- Abigail/Abi with her capacity for forgiveness, and overcoming the untold trails of being raised by an addict could be incredibly nurturing, offering understanding and a gentle influence.

- Beatrix/Bea's steady and unwavering nature might provide a grounding force and practical support. Her sarcasm and strength.

- Jennifer/305/Jenny's optimism and persistent efforts to bring joy could offer a much-needed lightness and joy.

Each would bring a different kind of support, a different kind of perspective. But Tricia must consider—would she be shaped by them, or would she allow the path itself to shape her?

This is not merely a choice of location—it is a choice of self-definition. So, gentle reader, what wisdom will you offer? Which path will challenge her, nurture her, transform her?

ABOUT THE AUTHOR

FOR THOSE WONDERING WHO Ash A. Milton is...it is Amy(A) Sue(S) Hamilton, revised into my new pen name. Why a pen name? Since my previous publications are academic and business focused, I don't want to confuse my readers. *The Project Manager* and *The Consummate Communicator* are both under Amy S. Hamilton. I generally use A.S. Hamilton for my academic writing. So, I had to get creative with this new pen name.

Ash A. Milton moved from Arlington, Virginia to Gary, Indiana in April 2025.

LEARN MORE AT

facebook.com/profile.php?id=61577699210680

instagram.com/ashamilton.universe

youtube.com/@AshAMiltonUniverse

ashamiltonuniverse.com

9 781946 730367